Silent Night

She used a side entrance to the employee parking lot next to the alley, unlocked the van, and placed the box of carefully wrapped puppets on the passenger seat. Closing the door, she heard something behind her.

The hairs on the nape of her neck prickled a warning.

She spun around, her back against the van she had just locked. A shape had separated from the blackness of the alley; the figure looked like a street person, but in the shadows she could not see clearly. She knew it was a man.

The moment stretched between them.

Then the man started forward, his shoulders hunched like a quarterback on the defensive.

He was coming right at her . . .

Dead Silence

"A nerve-tingling foray into the chilling recesses of a sadistic sociopathic mind, *DEAD SILENCE* establishes Donna Anders as one of the masters of the kind of suspense that goes many steps beyond stark terror."

—Ann Rule, author of . . . *And Never Let Her Go*

Books by Donna Anders

The Flower Man
Another Life
Dead Silence

Published by Pocket Books

DEAD SILENCE

Donna Anders

POCKET STAR BOOKS
New York   London   Toronto   Sydney   Singapore

An *Original* Publication of POCKET BOOKS

 A Pocket Star Book published by
POCKET BOOKS, a division of Simon & Schuster Inc.
1230 Avenue of the Americas, New York, NY 10020

ISBN: 0-671-03881-8

First Pocket Books printing September 2000

10 9 8 7 6 5 4 3 2 1

POCKET STAR BOOKS and colophon are registered trademarks of Simon & Schuster Inc.

Printed in the U.S.A.

For my three wonderful young women:
Ruth Aeschliman, Lisa Pearce and Tina Abeel,
with love and gratitude

Acknowledgments

I am forever appreciative of my family, my friends and the various professional people who gave so generously of their time, expert advice, encouragement and support while I was writing this book—especially my friend Ann Rule and my agents, Mary Alice Kier and Anna Cottle. Special thanks to some great guys in my life: Greg Aeschliman and Bryan Pearce. And to Kirsten Aeschliman, Peter Aeschliman, Brad Aeschliman, Taryn Pearce and Ashlyn Pearce, five young people who make me proud. And as always, a profound thank you to my daughters, Lisa Pearce, Tina Abeel and Ruth Aeschliman, who are always there for me no matter what.

And once again, sincere thanks to my very talented editor, Amy Pierpont, at Pocket Books.

DEAD
SILENCE

Chapter One

THE SLIGHT MOVEMENT BEHIND LIZA MACDONOUGH WAS reflected on the window, momentarily catching in the prisms of raindrops splattering the glass. She whirled around, facing the door across the room. She could swear she had heard it close with a soft click.

But no one had come into her office. *She was alone.*

Heebie-jeebies, Liza told herself. She'd had them a lot lately. And today she was suffering from sleep deprivation as well. That was it. Her vision was affected by insomnia, seeing motion where there was none. Not a good sign, considering her state of mind over the past year.

She tucked an unruly strand of hair behind her ears. Even her thick mane of natural waves was not cooperating these days, and as she turned back to the window her older sister Jean's childhood admonishment popped into her head. "Stop poking at your hair, Liza. It looks as wild as Medusa's."

Liza smiled, wryly. Messing with her curls had been her nervous reaction to stress when she was ten and Jean was twelve, and now, twenty-one years later she had resumed the bad practice. Damnable habits die hard, she decided.

The thought was sobering. Her position as an in-house counselor for International Air had recently brought back her own childhood insecurities and fears. Liza understood all too well the anguish of her clients who were coping with the aerospace company's downsizing and the loss of their jobs. Once her family had faced a similar predicament, with tragic results.

She stared out over the glistening Seattle cityscape south of her, scarcely noting the street lights that were flickering on to brighten the approach of another long winter night. Her thoughts lingered on the words of her last client, a divorcée with a young child to support, a woman without family.

"You don't know what it's like to go begging for a job! Damn it all to hell, I can't even afford a babysitter so I can look for one!"

I've never known the desperation of being totally alone, Liza reminded herself. Even during the tough years after her dad's death, when she was still in grade school, she'd had Jean and their mother. Although her own childhood seemed bleak to outsiders, full of secondhand clothes, cheap casseroles and her mom toiling at a minimum-wage job, the three of them had quickly developed a sense of humor about the insecurities of poverty.

"Hey, Babes," her mom would say. "The bank needs their mortgage payment—we have to tighten our belts."

She would prance across the room, her tired face animated by her deadpan of the banker, her altered voice exaggerating a pompous male tone, " 'Your house is your one asset—security for your daughters.' "

Liza and Jean would giggle, for the moment overlooking what "tightening the belt" meant, getting into their mother's playacting as she pivoted, smoothed her hair and went on in a sotto voce.

"'Your girls are pretty, talented and will become responsible adults because the three of you worked together to keep the family home.'"

It was many years later that Liza realized how wise her mother's psychology had been—her playacting therapy. She had kept open communications with her daughters without dumping the real burdens onto them.

Unknowingly, she and Jean had followed their mother's example—lemonade out of lemons, as the cliché went. Jean's eye for style and talent with a sewing needle, encouraged by straight A's in her junior high-school home economics class, had motivated her to alter their Valu Village dresses into presentable garments. The remnants were recycled into clothing for their puppets.

Ah, the beloved puppets. Her and Jean's way to do their own playacting.

Absently, Liza smoothed her suit skirt over her hips, and the window glass before her reflected her image, backlighted by the desk lamp. Tall and slim, she looked the part of a sophisticated professional—except for her untidy auburn hair that the light had burnished with a red sheen. She shook her head. Can't fool a mirror, she told herself. I'm really a blue-jeans kind of woman, even when I hide out in designer suits.

There was a knock on the door. Again she faced her office: her desk that was piled high with case files; the plaid cushions on the chairs in front of it that were vacant now of her desperate clients; and the ocean prints that hung on the off-white walls. Once she had been so proud of the promotion that had included her own ten-by-twelve-foot office. She had even been given the privilege of sharing a secretary with her boss, Al Stark. Now she wondered if she really wanted to be an in-house counselor. Helping terminated employees find new positions had turned into a nightmare.

"Come in."

The door opened and Al stepped inside. "Hey. What are you doing? Working overtime?"

Liza shook her head. "My last client only left a few minutes ago." She shrugged. "I'm just digesting the complaints."

"About the company?"

"Yeah. You must be hearing the rumors, too."

He hesitated, his blue eyes peering at her from behind the thick lenses of his glasses. Abruptly, he glanced away to drop several file folders on her desk. "You realize that there are always negative rumors when there are layoffs, don't you Liza?"

"Of course." She bristled. They'd had this conversation before. "But the current situation seems different. There are just too many people saying–"

"That the company is being unfair–that something is fishy." His sharp words cut her off. "I thought you were a professional." His tone hardened. "But frankly, Liza, lately I'm beginning to wonder. You're letting these people get to you."

"That's not true." She flushed. "But when everyone is saying the same thing I find *as a professional* that I have to take it seriously."

"Just what is it they're saying now?"

She ignored his sarcasm. "That they're confused, that they'd been overworked, doing the job of two people at the time of being terminated. They say it has to be discrimination because the work is there."

"Hey Liza," he said, sharply. "Remember? The company is downsizing. Jobs are going away."

"But what if these people are right? What if something is out of sync? Isn't that part of my job description to make sure that—"

"See," he interrupted again. "That's what I mean." He hitched up his trousers, pulling them over the roll of fat that circled his waist. His balding head gleamed in the lamplight and sweat glistened above his thin upper lip. "I think you're losing your objectivity." He hesitated. "I've made allowances for your fragile feelings, uh, your sense of loss that you're unknowingly transferring onto your clients." He sucked in a labored breath. "But it's been a year since—"

"Since what, Al?" Her voice shook with sudden anger. How dare he use a personal tragedy against her. Whatever was going on at International Air had nothing to do with her husband's disappearance.

He held her gaze.

"What?" she prompted. "Say it."

He shook his head, unwilling to finish his sentence.

Silence dropped between them. Liza took a deep breath. Stay calm, she told herself. Remember Al is as frazzled as you are because of the layoffs.

"I have no intention of taking on the problems of the world," she said finally, ignoring his outburst about Martin. How could he know that her fear for her husband had turned into a feeling of abandonment. "I just want to do a good job for my clients."

"Good." He moved to the door. "We both know all this talk about a company conspiracy is absurd."

"I agree, to a point. It does sound crazy."

"Yeah." He hesitated before stepping into the hall. "People get a little nuts when they lose their jobs. Remember Liza, you have a good position here, especially for someone your age. Don't jeopardize it."

Liza stared at the door closing behind him. Was that a warning? A threat? She grabbed her raincoat off the hat-rack and put it on, then scooped several files into her briefcase. She looked around for Nate Garret's file, which was high priority, then remembered she had taken it home last night. She hoped to work on his evaluation tonight, if she could ever get out of her office. At the last moment, she grabbed the tablet with the session notes from her appointments.

Her handbag strap over her shoulder, she flipped off the light, closed up her office and headed toward the parking lot behind the building. A half-hour workout at the gym might help her sleep later. Just what she needed most right now.

Windblown rain slashed across the blacktop, and as Liza ran toward her Miata convertible, her raincoat flew open to flap like a windsock behind her. She hugged her briefcase against her chest while fumbling to fit the car key into the door lock. By the time she climbed behind the wheel her hair was dripping water onto her face and shoulders.

The office complex of International Air was located next to the computer lab, a huge building restricted to authorized personnel. The main plant was many miles north of the city where the airplanes were assembled and tested. Slowly, Liza drove toward the street beyond the gate, avoiding the lab where Martin had worked.

She sighed. Martin had hated having a regular job; it had been his dream to be a rock star, to be recognized as a singer and guitar player. At thirty-five he had still hoped that his rock trio would land a record contract. Poor Martin. His talent had never matched his ambition, his passion for music. He had always been the Salieri to the more gifted Mozarts of rock.

Liza turned south toward the city center, trying to suppress her old guilt. Maybe she could have been more supportive, not pushed Martin to get a *real* job after they had been married four years. But she had been worried that the rejection of his music was depressing him and hoped that the structure of work might balance his growing sense of inadequacy. She had loved him so much, had only wanted him to be happy, to see his angular face come to life from other accomplishments besides music.

She parked on Olive Street in downtown Seattle, grabbed her gym bag, then hesitated. Was her briefcase and tablet safer in the car or in the exercise club? Car break-ins were common in the area, but then so was thievery in the club. Liza decided that the car trunk was best, and after securing them, hurried into the highrise where she climbed the stairs to the second-floor facility. Once in her sweats she looked for Alice Emery from Personnel at work, her exercise partner and spot person when she lifted weights. After Kristi, the young girl at the front desk, told her that Alice had come and gone, Liza decided to skip the weights. My fault, she thought. She'd missed Alice because of working late.

As she ran the treadmill for fifteen minutes and then rode the stationary bicycle for another twenty, Liza's thoughts lingered on the reason she had been late: a distraught client whose job had been terminated. Martin's gentle admonishment of the past surfaced in her mind, complete with a mental vision of his handsome face. He had been concerned that she was becoming too involved with her clients' problems.

"You can only do so much, sweetheart," he had said, pulling her into his arms. "I know you identify with these people because of your own childhood tragedy, because your father committed suicide and left your family destitute after he was fired." He had feathered her face with kisses, softening his reproach. "Your sensitivity for others is one of the reasons I love you, but I don't want you to lose your professional objectivity."

She had been touched by his words, by his realization of what motivated her choice of career. They had been so close. But after he had taken the job at IA, he had become preoccupied and spent his free time flying the old Cessna airplane he co-owned with two of his musician friends. It was as though he was trying to escape reality, trying to cope with a death—the death of his musical career. And she felt responsible.

No, she instructed herself. Don't go into the whys, the maybes and the what-ifs. It's not your fault that Martin vanished off the face of the earth. He loved you; he would not have hurt you nor left you without saying good-bye. He did not commit suicide, as his friends suggested. He could not do that to you, knowing it would be the ultimate cruelty. Martin was a sensitive man, a dreamer, but never cruel.

Then what did happen to him? The thought lingered as she completed her exercise, got dressed and headed for the front entrance.

"Hey, Mrs. MacDonough," Kristi called after her.

Liza turned back into the club. "Yes?"

"I called to you twice and you didn't hear me." She smiled, defusing any censure in her tone. "I almost forgot. A man was looking for you a little while ago and I directed him upstairs. Did he find you?"

"You mean, tonight?"

"Uh-huh."

Liza shook her head. "There were only a few people in the exercise room, and I didn't know any of them."

Kristi's round face looked puzzled. "I was reading and

didn't pay much attention, but I saw him leave and assumed—"

"What did he look like?" Liza asked, suddenly anxious.

The girl leaned forward, and her long straight hair fell over her face in a swath of black. "I'm not sure." She was momentarily thoughtful. "Fairly tall I think, brownish hair, dark eyes like yours, just average I guess."

"Did he give you his name?"

"Nope." She wrinkled her forehead. "I don't usually talk much to the old guys."

"Old guys?"

"Yeah," she said. "Men over thirty."

Liza smiled, trying to remember how it felt to be eighteen or nineteen. She raised her hand in farewell and strode back through the door. Mistaken identity, she thought. The man didn't fit Martin's description, her first thought when Kristi said someone was looking for her.

Get over this, Liza, she told herself. But as she walked along the sidewalk to her car she knew it wasn't possible. Not until she found out what had happened to Martin.

The rain had stopped and above her the clouds were breaking up, pushed by a high-flying current of wind. The night air smelled fresh and invigorating and she breathed deeply, remembering how she and Martin had loved driving with the convertible top down, winter or summer, so long as it wasn't raining. She hesitated after throwing her duffel bag into the trunk and retrieving her briefcase. Why not, she thought. Simple pleasures shouldn't stop just because Martin was gone.

With several quick motions Liza lowered the ragtop. It was only a short drive up First Hill to her condo, not far enough to experience windchill from the westerly breeze blowing inland off Elliott Bay. For those few minutes, with her hair flying and the cold air stinging her cheeks, she felt as young and carefree as Kristi. She could almost picture Martin in the seat next to her.

The ride was too brief, hardly enough time to clear her head. But she was anxious to get upstairs and free Bella from the kitchen where she had left her this morning. Her white Persian cat was recovering from an infection and still prone to losing her bladder control.

She drove into the security garage under her condominium, waited in the load zone for the gate to close behind her, then swung into her parking stall. For a moment she hesitated, her eyes darting over the quiet area of parked cars. Shortly after Martin's disappearance the building had experienced its first break-in—her apartment. She forced the thought away. She didn't need to scare herself by remembering.

Quickly, she put up the convertible's top and secured it, then with her purse and briefcase in hand, hurried toward the elevator lobby. In seconds she was moving up through the building to the twelfth floor, suddenly exhausted from her long day at work.

Once in her apartment Liza dropped her things in the entry hall before stepping out of her shoes. Then she crossed the white living-room carpet to the floor-to-ceiling windows that faced west over the city and Elliott Bay. Below her the lights of Seattle twinkled like stars in a summer sky, sending a warm glow into the room. The overall effect was calming.

Without turning on a lamp, she padded into the kitchen and poured herself a glass of Chardonnay, her relaxation ritual after a hard day. Moving back to the windows, she sat down in an overstuffed chair and took a sip of wine. Bella rubbed against her ankles, meowing for food.

Bella.

She'd momentarily forgotten the cat who had been shut into the kitchen.

But the kitchen doors had been open.

Liza froze in the chair, her body on full alert. Her glance darted to all the dark places in the apartment—the dining room, the hall that led to her bedroom, office and bathroom.

Bella had been left in the kitchen. She distinctly remembered closing the pocket door to the dining room and the opposite one to the entry hall. How had Bella gotten out?

Who opened the doors?

Chapter Two

SOMEONE HAD BEEN IN HER APARTMENT.

Oh God! Not again.

Instantly, Liza's heart was beating so fast that she was almost hyperventilating. She took deep breaths. Then slowly, quietly, she put down her wine glass and stood up. Should she walk through the apartment, check out the hiding places? Or just get the hell out of there?

Stay calm, she instructed herself. It didn't look like the earlier break-in when the potted plants had been dumped, the sofa cushions cut open and the drapes ripped free of their lining. Besides, how could anyone be in her place? No one had forced the door lock and no one had a key—except the manager. And Joe was scrupulously honest about not trespassing unless it was an emergency: a water leak, an alarm going off, owners locking themselves out.

Bella continued to rub herself against Liza, unconcerned, her round yellow eyes focused on Liza's face. But then cats are not watchdogs, she reminded herself.

Someone could be hiding. Turn on the lights. Act normal.
Make your way to the door.

She picked up Bella, a white fluffball who snuggled into
her chest, purring loudly. On tiptoes, Liza crossed the living room to the glass door that opened onto the covered
deck. The lever was in the locked position and the long
wooden dowel was still in the slider track. No one had
entered through the outside deck.

But who could anyway? A cat burglar who had scaled
twelve floors up the back of a concrete and steel building?

She moved into the dining room, glancing momentarily
out through the garden window to the Space Needle in
the distance, and the pinpoints of light on Queen Anne
Hill behind it. The room was as she had left it: her mom's
antique crystal chandelier hanging above the table, the
china closet filled with half of the family silver and china,
remnants of the days before her father's death. Her mom
had set the table each Sunday with her precious heirlooms
and had continued the practice until she died several years
ago. Since then Liza could not bear to use them. Her sister
Jean felt the same way about her half.

The pocket door between the dining room and kitchen
was slid neatly into the wall. Shit. Was she losing it?
Didn't she close that door this morning?

She slipped through the kitchen to the hall, flipping on
the recessed ceiling lights as she went. Hesitating in the
entry, she strained her ears, listening. The quiet within her
walls was absolute.

Her breathing slowed as she contemplated the situation.
Could she have only *thought* she closed the pocket doors?
She was forgetting a lot of things lately, like returning
calls, a dentist appointment, a scheduled haircut. Maybe
so. She had been in a hurry this morning.

If someone had lain in wait, wouldn't they have leapt

forward by now? Indeed, why would anyone even want to break into her apartment? She had nothing of value to steal, certainly no jewelry or money lying around. Her antique furniture, bought at auctions, secondhand stores and estate sales was not really valuable. Unlike others in the building, she was not rich. If not for her mother's estate, the house they had held onto throughout all of those hard years, she and Martin could not have afforded an in-city condo. It was ridiculous to think that a thief had targeted her.

All of Liza's self-talk did not calm her apprehension. But it did help her overcome an urge to run out into the twelfth-floor hallway and scream for help. There were four units to each floor, and only hers and one other was occupied during the winter. The remaining two owners spent the rainy months in a warm climate. And the woman who lived next to her had an active social life and might be away for the evening. She had to assume that she was the only person at home. And if so, screaming in the hall outside her front door would not draw attention before an intruder—if there even was one—could muffle her cries.

Stay calm, her inner voice said again. Don't let your imagination run away with itself. *Check out the other rooms.*

Holding Bella close to her chest, Liza gathered her courage. It wasn't like that other time when her place had been vandalized; tonight everything was untouched.

But don't forget, the voice went on, there was no evidence of forced entry then either. *Someone used a key.*

A passkey probably, the police officer had said, but only to the units in the building, not to the main entrance. The vandal most likely slipped in the front door, or the garage entry, with other guests to the building. "Happens all the time in high-end condos without an on-site doorman," he had concluded.

Her blood pumping hard, Liza switched on her hall lights and faced the ten-foot corridor that led to the main bathroom door on the left, her office on the right and her bedroom door straight ahead. Slowly, she started forward, illuminating each room as she passed it.

No one was in her apartment!

Reaction set in. Her knees folded under her and she sat down fast on her dressing table stool. Bella leaped out of her arms, her long hair sweeping the carpet as she pranced down the hall.

A moment later, her nerves under control, Liza followed her to the kitchen, found the cat food and filled Bella's dish. Bella immediately began to snarf it down, her pink tongue working furiously.

"Greedy kitty," Liza murmured. "You'd think I starved you."

Liza retrieved her Chardonnay. She needed a little to slow down her motor. How many other things had she forgotten? Nothing vitally important she hoped. But the thought was disturbing. Maybe she needed one of those antianxiety-antidepression drugs people took these days. Prozac, Zoloft, whatever. She'd wait though before consulting her physician; she needed to see how things went.

She leaned against the counter, sipping her wine while she watched Bella eat. The wall phone behind her rang. She jumped at the sound and the liquid spilled out of the glass onto her fingers. She grabbed the receiver with her free hand.

"Hello."

"Hey, Liza, you finally got home." Dave Farrar's deep voice was soft in her ear. "Working overtime again?"

His calm manner evoked his image in her mind: red-haired, intelligent, caring of employees, and a divorced dad who was a good father to his teenage sons. Recently they had struck up a friendship at work.

"Not very long tonight. But I stopped at the club to get in a little exercise."

"Ah, caught you." He hesitated. "Forgot you'd invited me for supper, didn't you."

She set down her wine. Oh shit! She'd forgotten to check her phone messages. And she *had* forgotten their tentative date. "I thought we left it open because you might have to work."

"Well, sort of." She heard the smile in his voice. "C'mon Brown Eyes, admit it. You've been so busy lately you forgot."

"Of course I didn't," she lied, disconcerted by his nickname for her even as she felt flattered. He had recently started calling her Brown Eyes, in a tone that might as well have said, Sweetheart or Darling, and it bothered her. Not that she wasn't attracted to Dave, she just wasn't ready for a relationship yet. "I was just taking veggies out of the refrigerator for a stir-fry."

"Good thing I caught you then. I do have to work. One of our chronic computer glitches reared its ugly head around quitting time." He paused. "Sorry. I couldn't resist teasing you."

She held back a relieved sigh. The prospect of entertaining did not appeal to her tonight although she did enjoy Dave's company. She wanted nothing more than to kick back and relax, maybe have a second glass of wine.

"I'll give you a rain check," she said.

"Thanks, I'll look forward to it." He cleared his throat. "If it's not too late maybe I'll stop by later, okay?"

She agreed, knowing a glitch in the software being written in the computer lab for International Air's new computerized One Thousand Series jetliner was not going to be a simple fix. Dave, an upper management administrator, was responsible for the lab supervisor and programmers who were racing deadlines for FAA certification. As she hung up Liza could not help smiling. For the first time since Martin's disappearance she was beginning to feel like a desirable woman again. A good sign, she decided.

"Have you ever heard of a plane that flies itself with computer chips instead of pilots?" she asked Bella. "Isn't that the silliest—and scariest—thing you've ever heard?"

Bella swished her tail over the hardwood floor as she glided across the kitchen and disappeared into the hall, headed for a nap on Liza's bed. She followed, anxious to shower and get into a nightgown. She needed to go over Nate Garret's file. Nate's boss feared his top software programmer had burned out. I'll need all of my wits to work on that one, she told herself. One more client succumbing to the frenetic pace of racing deadlines.

Some employees were being worked to death while others were being laid off from lack of work. She shook her head. Something was not right. But what?

The phone rang just as she was adding a chopped chicken breast to her stir-fry. The first glass of wine had relaxed her and she was still considering a second. She picked up the phone, hoping it wasn't Dave down at the front door after all.

"Liza? It's Erik downstairs. I was in the neighborhood. Want to buzz the door for me?"

"Erik?"

"Yup. With a bottle of your favorite Chardonnay."

"I've got a stir-fry going. You hungry?"

"Hey, Babe. Just buzz me up. The line is about to go dead."

"Righto," Liza said, giggling. She pushed the nine button on the keypad, heard the entrance door unlock, then hung up, suddenly glad for his company. Erik Lindstrom was her old friend from graduate school, a fellow psychotherapist, the person who had introduced her to Martin. He was like family; it did not matter that she had scrubbed off all of her makeup and was in her nightgown and robe. His quirky sense of humor was exactly what she needed right now.

Liza met him as he stepped out of the elevator, dwarfing the lobby with his tall presence. His dark brows rose in a question.

"In bed already?" He whistled disapproval. "Told you a long time ago that the corporate world wasn't for you, kiddo. They work you 'til you drop, then replace you without missing a beat."

She hugged him. "Glad to see you, too, Erik." She pecked a kiss onto his cheek and stepped back. "Sorry about my appearance. You know me. I like to get comfortable." She tilted her head. "Besides, you always said I looked better without makeup."

"Yeah, I did, didn't I." His pale blue eyes narrowed to study her face. Wolf eyes, she had thought the first time she met him, so attractive with his black hair and beard. "You still look twenty without all the goop." Strong white teeth flashed in a smile. "I'll be damned if I ever understand why you women wear it—first to seem older, then to look younger."

"Face it, Erik. You just don't understand women."

There was a hesitation.

"Or maybe they don't understand me. Maybe my macho guy image is just a facade."

"Hey, remember me? I understand you from way back," she said, joking. "Besides, you've become set in your lifestyle. What woman could compete with skydiving, mountain climbing and living on a Lake Union house-boat?

"You think so, huh?" His grin lifted the serious moment. "Maybe I like white picket fences, soup simmering on the stove, and kids. Time will tell." He shrugged. "Could be I've even mellowed, already met the woman of my dreams."

She smiled back, avoiding the innuendo in his comments. She knew his own personal baggage motivated his concern for others and his hesitation to commit in a relationship. His early years had been difficult: alcoholic parents, overcoming a wild youth and struggling to work his way through college. After earning their PhDs, they had talked of going into practice together, but she had married Martin instead and gone to work for International Air, opting for security, her own bugaboo.

"So on to practical matters. I really was cooking, not sleeping." She ushered him into her apartment. "You hungry?" she asked again.

"Starved."

She lifted the lid on the pan and the fragrance of her stir-fry filled the kitchen. "How does this look?"

"Yummy." He sniffed the air. "Reminds me of the old days when we steamed vegetables because that was all we could afford."

She laughed. "Yeah, and we'd pool our money to buy them."

"Yup. No one understood our love of vegetables. Remember, they thought we were holdovers from the hippie generation."

"The way you tell the story makes it sound like we were married or something." She pulled two plates out of the cupboard while he uncorked the Chardonnay.

"Or something." He poured wine into the glasses.

She lifted hers in a toast. "To the best friend I've ever had."

"Cheers," he said. "Married couples should take a page from our book. Good friendships last longer than marriages these days."

Liza set place mats on the dining room table, lit candles and then motioned Erik to sit down. As they ate, he updated her about one of his worrisome clients, a man who was depressed over failing health. Erik had paid a house call out in Madison Park after the man's wife had called, pleading with him to see her husband before he did something drastic.

"Sad case," Erik said. "The guy's all but given up hope. I talked to his medical doctor about prescribing something for his depression. Wanted everyone involved to know what was going on."

"So you stopped by here on your way home?"

He nodded. "Found I needed some tender loving care myself. You mind?"

"Course not. You've always been there for me."

There was a silence. Liza knew that they were both thinking about Martin, how distraught she had been in the weeks following his disappearance, and how Erik had seen her through those early days until she was able to cope again.

But was she really coping or only fooling herself? Her life was still in limbo, her personal, financial and legal status all on hold. The police had not closed their investigation yet, even though they had questioned everyone who ever knew Martin: musicians, his partners in owning the old Cessna airplane, fellow workers, family and friends. She often wondered if they suspected Martin was still alive, that he hadn't really fallen off the ship where he'd been playing with his trio. Because she needed answers,

Liza had hired Steve Wendall, a private investigator, to look into Martin's disappearance.

"Has this Wendall guy come up with anything yet?"

Erik's question was intuitive. But then he had always tuned into her thoughts. She shook her head. "I know he's talked to people who were on the Skydiver Club Christmas cruise that night. He said everyone enjoyed Martin's trio, were having a great time until Martin vanished. It was assumed that he'd fallen overboard."

"I kick myself for not going." Erik glanced out the window behind her. "I chose the houseboat party that night over being with my skydiver buddies, knowing I'd probably drink too much and shouldn't drive."

She nodded. "And I had that terrible virus with a hundred-and-two-degree-fever." Her fork stilled on the plate. "The police said Martin had been drinking heavily that night."

"I know. I heard that, too."

"Can I ask you something Erik, something I've not asked you before?"

He put down his napkin. "Shoot."

Her gaze had been direct. Now she lowered her eyes. "Do you believe that Martin jumped off the boat? Committed suicide?"

She sensed that he restrained himself from getting up and coming around the table to hold her. Instead he leaned back, placing both hands on his lap. "No, not for a moment. The Martin I've known since we were kids would never have killed himself."

"Then what—"

"I don't know, Liza." He paused, thoughtful. "I knew that he hated working in the computer lab at International Air, even though he had an aptitude for programming and a fascination with online technology. But music was his first love and he was worried about getting too old to land a recording contract." He took a deep breath. "And I know that your marriage had some rocky patches because of that job." Another pause. "Martin still believed in his own future and would never have committed suicide."

"You don't think he felt trapped by his job, me . . . everything?"

"The truth?"

She managed a nod.

"Yes, he felt trapped. But he would have worked his way past those feelings in time. Martin still had some growing up to do."

She stared at her plate, stirring the vegetables aimlessly. She wondered if Erik knew that Martin had still used drugs on occasion. Both of them had in high school, but Erik straightened out by the time he went to college. He was right. Martin had never matured into a responsible adult in some ways.

"Do you think he just . . . left? Because he couldn't stand the responsibilities of being married any longer?"

"No." The word sounded sharp. "Whatever happened, Liza, it wasn't your fault. I've told you that before."

She had to ask, even though his honest answer might not be what she wanted to hear. He had been Martin's best friend, which was the reason she had not put him on the spot before.

"Was there another woman?"

"Never!" His denial was emphatic. "Whatever faults Martin had, he did not cheat on you."

Before she could reply, a knock sounded on the door, startling them both. Liza bolted out of her chair, remembering her earlier apprehension about someone being in her place. Erik pushed away from the table and stood up.

"You expecting company?"

She shook her head. "No one rang from the door downstairs. Must be a neighbor in the building."

He followed her to the hall, watched as she checked the peephole and then opened the door to Dave Farrar whose smile froze as his gaze shifted behind Liza to Erik.

There was a silence.

"Dave," Liza said, breaking it. "I'm surprised you made it. I thought you'd be working on the glitch all night."

Stop babbling, she told herself. You sound guilty as hell and you haven't done a thing wrong. And you look even guiltier in your nightgown and robe. Good thing Erik is dressed, she thought inanely, suppressing a giggle.

"A simple fix, for a change." He spread his hands. "Sorry if I interrupted your, uh, visit, but your neighbor recognized me and let me in downstairs."

"You didn't interrupt anything." She laughed, nervously. "This is my night for friends dropping in."

She could see by Dave's expression that he was wondering if Erik was someone special. And Erik looked as though he had a few questions as well. They were a study in contrasts, although both were equally attractive men.

Liza made formal introductions, surprised that they hadn't met before since they knew of each other through mutual friends. "Dave is head of operations at the computer lab," she told Erik before turning to Dave. "And Erik is a psychotherapist in private practice, an old friend of Martin's. And mine," she added.

The men shook hands.

"Aren't you the guy who teaches a first-jump course at Sampson's Parachute Center?" Dave asked, squinting as though suddenly remembering the information.

"Uh-huh." Erik leaned against the doorway. "How'd you know that?"

"Someone in the lab was talking about you, described

you and said you'd been Martin's friend. The thing that rang a bell was the therapist part, because it seemed so incongruous to your spare-time activities."

"And you also know what those are?" Erik's tone was deceptively low.

"Skydiving and mountain climbing is what I heard." Dave's words were equally controlled.

"And you don't approve?" Erik softened his question with a smile.

"Just not my style." Dave shrugged. "Guess I'm too busy to take on sports that require a huge commitment of time."

"So you're saying you're a workaholic?"

Dave's face darkened. "I work a lot, yes. But I also have a real life, one I don't intend to jeopardize with dangerous hobbies."

"Come in, Dave," Liza said, interrupting their verbal sparring. Their mutual antagonism was obvious.

She hustled Dave inside and offered him a drink. He declined, as did Erik who said he had to get home and write up his notes. Within minutes both men were back at the door, much to Liza's relief. One thing she could not stand were men with a burr on their butts. Neither liked the other and they were not shy about letting their feelings show. Disgusting display of male superiority, of staking out their territory.

The thought stopped her cold. Why would she think that? Both men were only friends, although recently she had asked herself if she could fall in love with Dave if she were emotionally free. She didn't know. And Erik? He was just Erik, the brother she had always wanted.

Egos and testosterone, she thought after they were gone. On some levels men remained little boys, always ready to fight when they felt threatened.

She sighed. Time for bed. She couldn't cope with the male psyche after an emotionally draining day. She hoped tomorrow would be better. Nate Garret's evaluation could wait until morning.

Once in bed she tried not to dwell on how easy it had been for Dave to get into the building. Heebie-jeebies. She had them for the second time that day. She was just glad that she had added a chain lock to her two other locks on the door after her place had been vandalized a year ago.

She was being a scaredycat. Sleep should cure that. The world would seem safer in the daylight.

Chapter Three

THE NEXT MORNING LIZA WAS UP A HALF HOUR EARLIER than usual to work on Nate Garret's evaluation before leaving for work. Time was short. It was already Friday and Hawk Bohlman, a supervisor under Dave, needed her report by Monday. Hawk, a lifer with the company, would be in her face if she were late.

Where in hell is it? she asked herself, frustrated.

She shuffled through the files on her desk, wondering how she could ever find anything in the clutter of notes and papers. Her little home office, complete with computer, printer, copier and fax, was only large enough for her equipment, bookshelves and a chair. Often she worked evenings and weekends to keep up with her caseload. A forty-hour-week just did not cut it. But she wasn't complaining about having too much work. It kept her from dwelling on her own problems.

Deep breaths, Liza instructed herself. You didn't lose the file. It's here somewhere.

But it wasn't.

And where was the tablet with her notes on Nate's counseling sessions? She plunked down on the chair, suddenly remembering. It was in the trunk of the car. She had forgotten to bring the tablet up last night.

Annoyed with herself, Liza searched the dining room, living room, kitchen and bedroom, even the bathrooms. Nate's file was nowhere in sight. But then she had not expected to find it; unlike her office, all the other rooms were immaculate.

Hawk Bohlman's face surfaced in her mind, a sixtyish man with a permanent scowl. Liza had tangled with him before about his abusive treatment of staff, and she did not relish another conflict. Losing Nate's file was a daunting thought.

You haven't lost it, she reminded herself. It's still at work. It has to be. *You only thought you brought it home on Wednesday night.*

Liza took her coffee to the bathroom, sipping it as she put on her makeup and fixed her hair. It was still early when she headed down to the garage. About to unlock the car door, she realized it was not locked.

She stiffened. How could she have forgotten that, too? Had she been so distracted by putting up the convertible top that she didn't follow her usual ritual of securing her car?

Glancing inside, her eyes were drawn to the tablet on the passenger seat. She stared, disbelieving. It hadn't been there last night or she would have taken it upstairs. She *knew* that she'd forgotten it in the trunk when she came out of the gym and retrieved her briefcase. *She would bet her life on that.*

"God Almighty," she said aloud. "Tell me I'm not losing it."

But she knew the symptoms of overload: forgetfulness,

being accident prone, irritability, sleeplessness. She had them all. As she drove out of the garage, Liza was worried. And a little scared.

"I can't believe it!"

Nate Garret's file was the first thing Liza saw when she stepped into her office. She frowned, puzzled. She would not have missed it right in the center of her desk. Something weird was going on. She was not crazy.

Had someone been in her apartment and stolen Nate's file? It was the only explanation, as farfetched as it seemed. But why would anyone bother?

And how had they gotten in? It didn't make any sense.

She hung her coat, but her eyes were glued to the folder with Nate's name on it. Sitting down, she pulled it in front of her, anxious to see if anything was missing. She'd had her secretary type up her notes, except for those from Nate's last appointment that were on the tablet. All of the information she had collected for her report seemed to be there, including the demeanor of the slight, nervous man.

Could Nate have been so concerned about what she would include in her report that he had snooped, maybe removed his file, intending to return it before she noticed it was missing? She knew he was fearful of losing his job.

Hawk's concern was burnout because Nate's genius was so valuable to the software programs for the new 1000 Series jets. But Liza realized that Hawk would fire Nate if he believed the project—and his own career—was in jeopardy.

Nate must be in a worse emotional state than she believed if he had broken into her car and condo just to read his file. No, he couldn't have, she told herself, her theorizing swinging the other way. There was no evidence of a break-in. If someone had been in her place, they had used a key. And Nate did not have one.

The door opened, and she jumped. Easily startled, another symptom of stress, she reminded herself.

Dave stepped into her office, pausing just inside the room. "Hey, what you doing here so early?" He grinned. "First you start working overtime, now you're coming in early. Heavy caseload, huh?"

She nodded, smiling. Dave's calm manner was such a contrast to Martin's high-strung, artistic personality. He had a knack for making his workers relax, coaxing them with praise to a higher productivity level. Hawk should take lessons from Dave, she thought, and wondered if Dave realized the frenetic pace Hawk forced upon his programmers.

He sobered. "Don't push too hard, Liza. We don't want you burning out." He *had* noticed her nervous reaction to his appearance in her office doorway.

"Is that the pot calling the kettle black?"

"Touché." He hesitated. "I want to apologize for barging in last night. Didn't mean to break up your visit with, uh, Erik."

"You didn't." Her chair scraped the floor as she stood up. "Erik dropped in unexpectedly."

"He an old friend?" He sounded casual, too casual? She knew he more than liked her. Was she ready for that?

She stopped her fingers from poking at her hair. "Erik and Martin, my husband, were friends since childhood." She glanced away. "Erik helped me cope after Martin disappeared."

"So you met Erik because of Martin?"

"No, the opposite. Erik introduced me to Martin."

"Oh." Surprise registered momentarily. She realized Dave was now assuming that she had dated Erik first, was maybe dating him again.

"Erik and I met in college, earned our PhDs together and even discussed going into practice together." There was a pause. "We're close friends, that's all."

His expression brightened. "Of course your personal life is none of my business." His tone indicated he would like to change that status. He smoothed his red hair away from his forehead and switched subjects. "You haven't forgotten my dinner party tomorrow night?"

"Course not. I'm looking forward to it." She laughed. "I get it. You're reminding me because you think I forgot last night."

"An overworked counselor forget? Naw. I'd never think that." He controlled a grin. "Seven then. And I'd love it if you came early to help the chef."

"You're having the dinner catered then?" She could not resist teasing him. "Just kidding," she added. "I've heard through the grapevine that you're a gourmet cook." She giggled. "I'll try to come early—to watch. I'm a klutz when it comes to preparing fancy meals. My specialty is stir-fry."

"I noticed last night. It smelled delicious. Sorry I had to miss it."

"I'll fix it again some night, so long as I'm not too intimidated by your culinary skills."

"A deal then." He stepped through the doorway, then popped his head back around the corner. "See you tomorrow night."

She was still smiling after the door had closed. She liked Dave. He seemed to bring out the best in her. Even her sense of humor had resurfaced because of him. A good sign.

Liza closed Nate's file and placed it in the desk drawer with her handbag. I will not forget the damn thing again, she told herself. Nor would she let it out of her immediate vicinity until she had handed the evaluation to Hawk.

*   *   *

The morning passed quickly with a series of clients. By noon Liza felt drained; three men needed job placement but did not want to move out of state. The lone woman had already secured a position with Boeing, the Seattle-based company that commanded a huge percentage of the aerospace industry. All four had expressed anger and frustration over their termination, stressing their belief that it was discrimination, that their complaints were not being heard because something weird was going on behind the scenes.

Too many similar complaints, Liza thought. She had called and spoken to her friend Alice Emery, who was the personnel director. Alice had invited her to lunch in the cafeteria to discuss her concerns.

Liza took her handbag from the drawer, then locked the desk. Paranoid or not, she was not about to take chances with Nate's file again. She was on her way to the door when the phone rang. Damn! That was the problem; she could never get out of her office for lunch. Most days she nibbled a sandwich while she kept on working.

"Liza MacDonough," she said into the receiver.

"Liza, it's Jean." Her sister's soft contralto voice came over the wire. Sexy was the word the boys in high school used to call it.

"Jean?" She was surprised. Her sister rarely called her at work unless there was something important that could not wait until Liza got home. "What's up?"

"I hadn't heard from you in a couple of days and I wanted to make sure you remembered the puppet show tonight."

"Huh?"

"You know, at Hilltop Medical Center." There was a pause. "You did forget."

Liza leaned against her desk. Oh God. She *had* forgotten. Not completely as she must have about Nate's file. The days had crept up on her; she'd thought that the performance of the Puget Puppeteers was next week.

"Of course I didn't," she said, fibbing. "I was going to check in with you this afternoon about the time." Overload, she thought, again. Now she was becoming a liar on top of everything else. She needed to take herself in hand before her forgetfulness got worse.

"Good. For a second there I thought you had." There was a pause. Liza could almost see Jean's classic features sobered in thought, considering. "Are you okay, Lizzy?"

"Fine." Liza went to full mental alert. Her sister had not called her Lizzy for years. Had she seemed so distracted that Jean was worried about her? "I've been busy with my caseload because of the layoffs and haven't had a chance to call, that's all. You know I wouldn't stand you up, Jean."

"I know." Another pause. "Think you could make it by six-thirty to help with the final setup?"

"I'll make it a priority to be there."

Jean's sigh came over the line. "Thanks for filling in, Liza. I really was left in the lurch when my trainee got sick."

"You're welcome, Sis. See you."

Liza replaced the receiver on its cradle, then stood staring down at it, remembering all the backyard productions she and Jean had put on for the neighborhood kids. Those days represented the birth of Puget Puppeteers, Jean's career now.

The twists and turns of life, she thought. So unexpected at times. She anchored her hair behind each ear, then turned back to the door. On with the business at hand, she told herself. No time for maudlin reflections of the past.

Alice waved from across the crowded cafeteria and Liza threaded her way through the tables to the far wall. "I bought you a club sandwich and coffee," Alice said, indicating the food on the table. "I hit the place during a lull and figured I'd better order for both of us before another mad rush."

"Thanks." Liza smiled and sat down. "You know me too well. I hate standing in lines."

"Doesn't everyone?" Alice's blue eyes twinkled in her plump face. "Unless . . ." She raised her plucked brows and looked beyond Liza, "Unless the person standing in front of you is a sexy hunk."

Liza followed her gaze to the two men who had just walked into the cafeteria. One was Nate Garret; she did not know the taller man, although he was vaguely familiar. "Nate Garret?"

"God no!" Alice fluffed her bangs and smoothed her pageboy. "Cooper Delmonte. He's one of Hawk Bohlman's programmers in the computer lab."

Another person who worked under Dave, Liza thought, studying the tall, muscular man whose strong features and attractiveness was a contrast to Nate's nervous demeanor. Well into her mid thirties, Alice despaired over ever finding a man. She was always looking.

"Is Cooper single?"

"Course not. Aren't all the good ones married?"

Alice shot a wide smile in the direction of the men, revealing perfect teeth. Her best feature, Liza thought. That and her outgoing personality. But she would never land a husband by seeming too available. Liza did not dare make suggestions; Alice was too sensitive about the subject.

Nate and Cooper took a table behind a partition and Alice's attention returned to Liza. "So, what are these concerns you wanted to discuss?"

Briefly, Liza filled her in: her clients' accusations that the company was laying off personnel when the workload was accelerating, that they believed the reason for termination had to be discrimination. "They think something secretive is happening, something that is being covered up by the company." Alice heard her through before answering.

"Liza, I know for certain that International Air's hiring and firing procedures are fair." Alice put down the sandwich she had been eating. "If nothing else they can't afford not to be. Otherwise the company would be subject to legal ramifications. Our executives are very aware that an honest image impacts everything from community goodwill to FAA certifications."

Alice's demeanor had altered, reminding Liza why she had the position of personnel director. Alice was a professional in every sense of the word when it came to her career.

"I agree with you, Alice. To my knowledge the company has always maintained a great policy for employees." Liza shook her head. But something just doesn't seem right and I don't know exactly why."

"You know that unrest always happens during layoffs." Alice sipped her coffee. "It only takes one troublemaker to get the ball rolling."

"I know, but—"

"You're feeling sorry for them, identifying with their desperation?"

"Maybe. But I don't think that's the reason for my concern."

"Think about it, Liza." She hesitated. "Mind if I play the devil's advocate for the moment?"

"Go ahead. I value your input."

"Just between you and me, okay?"

Liza inclined her head.

"Your family went through this once when you were an impressionable child, with tragic results."

Liza almost wished she had not shared that information with Alice.

"And only a year ago your husband vanished, leaving you with nothing but unanswered questions," Alice said, gently.

There was a silence.

Alice looked uncomfortable. "I don't mean to bring up painful memories. But since I'm probably your closest friend other than Jean, I realize that you've gone through more losses than all of your clients put together." A pause. "It's normal for you to overreact just a little in these circumstances."

"Are you saying that I'm losing it?"

"Hell no! Only that you might need a little down time yourself." Another hesitation. "Look, how about I give you a complete list of the employees terminated so far in this layoff. Checking them out yourself will put this whole issue to rest. You'll see that the complaints are based on unfounded rumors."

"I'd appreciate that."

"Done." Alice gave her famous smile. "But I warn you, it'll take some time and effort."

"I know, but as you've just pointed out, knowing the facts will be worth it. I'll be able to stop the gossip and help my clients move on." Liza stood. It was almost time for her next appointment. "Thanks Alice. I do appreciate your concern."

They walked out together, then separated with plans to work out together at the gym the following week. Liza was thoughtful. Was Alice, like Al and others lately, suggesting that she had lost her objectivity? We'll see, she thought. She hoped not.

But what if she was right, and her clients *were* being truthful. Liza pushed the thought aside. She would climb that mountain later, once she knew the facts.

Chapter Four

LIZA ALMOST SWUNG THE MIATA INTO THE SUBTERRANEAN parking area across the street from Hilltop Medical Center, but as a twinge of apprehension hit her, she had second thoughts. Later, the underground garage would be deserted . . . and spooky. Her imagination was already on overtime and she did not need to exacerbate it. She found a space on the street down the block from the front entrance, suddenly remembering that the meters were free after six.

Once inside the hospital, Liza headed for the children's wing. With each step along the long halls she felt her spirit lift. She loved to be a part of the puppet show, to know that the children who suffered from such serious illnesses as cancer were temporarily transported into a magical world of make-believe where dreams came true. Both she and Jean understood that children needed to keep their hope alive; sometimes that was all they had.

"Hey, am I glad you got here Liza," Jean said, greeting her.

Liza glanced at her watch. "I'm right on time."

She stepped into a waiting room that had been transformed into a theater. Undersized chairs had been placed in rows before the portable stage Jean was assembling, leaving room at each end for wheelchairs.

"I know," Jean said, and jumped off the stepstool where she had been adjusting a system of light bars. Her dark pageboy swung forward, momentarily obscuring her delicate features. "But I'm running late. Got stuck in rush hour traffic."

"No problem. We still have plenty of time."

Jean grinned. "Like old times, huh?"

Liza nodded, remembering. Then as now, Jean was intense about the puppets, the artistic one. Back then she had created the stories, improvised their own dolls into puppets, sewed material remnants into costumes, and turned tables and blankets into a stage with curtains. A primitive beginning to the professional performances Jean produced now. Puget Puppeteers was Jean's work and her productions made her a good living, even though she regularly donated her shows to charitable groups involving children.

"Yeah, we were always rushing, making last-minute changes in the hope that we'd impress the neighborhood kids."

"Well, it worked. They flocked to our backyard, despite their more privileged lives." The old pain flashed in Jean's large brown eyes.

"Whoa. I don't think any of them noticed we were poor."

"Of course they did." Jean paused. "Even though we kept up a good front, entertained them with our puppet shows and—"

"Our extravaganzas you mean," Liza said, interrupting, trying to lighten the moment.

A smile lit Jean's face. "Yup, they sure were. And you really got into it, a real Sarah Bernhardt when the script called for it." She sobered. "But seriously, kids can be cruel, and they were on occasion."

"They were always pretty nice to me."

Jean tilted her head, switching her attention to the footlights. "I ran interference. They knew that if they ever teased you about your clothes—or anything—they had to answer to me. And that meant they'd be banned from our shows." She laughed. "A little muscle went a long way. Besides, I had Mom coaching me on how to handle the problem."

"Which was to shelter me?"

"Uh-huh, sorta. You had such a hard time getting over Dad's death that Mom and I agreed you didn't need to cope with thoughtless name-calling, too."

Liza tried to swallow the sudden lump in her throat, watching Jean move from the lighting to the props. She had not known. Needing time, she began to unpack the puppets that had been lovingly wrapped in tissue paper— her sister's babies. As she laid the stuffed-bodied, porcelain-headed dolls on a table behind the stage, separating the hand, arm and rod puppets from the string marionettes, she realized that she had somehow missed the depth of Jean's suffering. *Because I was two years younger and self-absorbed in my own misery?* she wondered.

"I was an adult before I understood how much Mom sacrificed for us," Liza said finally. "But I never really thought about the cost to you." *Now I understand why you and Bill have never had kids,* she told her silently. *It was safer to have puppet babies.* "I apologize, Jean."

"For what?" Jean's hands stilled on the props that would slide or clip onto the stage.

Liza spread her hands. "For being a selfish kid, I guess. For not realizing that my big sister was padding my way."

"Goodness! Where did all this come from?"

There was a pause.

How could she say that their childhood may have damaged Jean, her take-charge, dependable sister, far more than anyone had ever recognized. Although the physical resemblance between them was obvious, Jean was smaller, had manageable hair and was rarely verbal about her own feelings—just the opposite of Liza.

"You know, working with the puppets always brings back memories," Liza said, softly.

"Good ones, I hope. Because we sure had fun creating them and our corny stories." Jean glanced up, meeting Liza's eyes. "Just remember, big sisters always take care of little sisters. I love you, it's as simple as that."

"Love you, too." Liza concentrated on the puppets and their props. For all that they'd had a loving mother and the puppets—who had acted out the ups and downs of their troubled childhood—she suspected that Jean might not have resolved some of her own old insecurities.

"That's about it," Jean said, finally. "Everything's ready to go."

"Great! So on with the show."

Liza grinned, their conversation forgotten for the time being. *Moon Spinner*, the story of a poor girl and her sick little brother who meet a magic fairy one moonlit night, was about to begin. She would not allow sad thoughts; she and Martin had helped stuff and sew many of the puppets and had helped brainstorm new scripts. Jean created every aspect of her productions, but occasionally needed Liza to help meet deadlines or substitute as a puppeteer.

For the next hour she was lost in the fantasy of Jean's

story, as was the young audience who laughed and cheered when the puppets' impossible dreams came true.

"Aren't you Liza MacDonough?"

Liza turned from packing the puppets into a box to face a slight, blond woman who had come up behind her. "Yes, I am."

The woman smiled, tremulously. She held out her hand. "I've seen you at the airfield with Martin." She hesitated. "I'm Abbey Delmonte, Cooper's wife."

For a second Liza was disconcerted, then remembered that Cooper Delmonte was the man in the cafeteria with Nate. No wonder he had seemed familiar. Martin had once introduced her to him, a private pilot with his own small plane. But she had no memory of meeting Abbey, a pale woman whose drab attire matched her plain features. That Abbey had referred to Martin in the present tense was jarring.

"And I'm Brandon," the child next to Abbey said in a high soprano voice. "Do you think the Moon Spinner would visit me—like in the story?"

His round hazel eyes were too big for his gaunt face. Liza remembered seeing him in the audience and thinking that he was a very sick little boy. She smiled down at him and wondered if he was one of the cancer patients.

"Anything is possible, Brandon." Liza refrained from hugging him. "If you believe."

"Would you like me to show you how the puppets come to life?" Jean asked him, overhearing.

Brandon nodded shyly.

"C'mon over here then, and I'll let you use a hand puppet." She smiled reassuringly. "It's easy, and you'd be surprised what the puppets tell you."

"Is that okay, Mom?" He looked up at his mother.

"Go ahead, Brandon. I'll be right here."

Brandon moved away to watch Jean whose own hand puppet was already talking to him. His mother kept a watchful eye. "I haven't seen Brandon so animated in a long time, not since his treatment began." She paused. "I wanted to thank you and your sister for your wonderful show. I can't tell you how much it means to me to see my son laughing and happy." She glanced down. "Even if it doesn't last."

"I'm so sorry," Liza said, softly.

"Me, too." She wiped a hand over her forehead, as though to smooth her stress lines. "Somehow it doesn't seem fair for a five-year-old to have a brain tumor."

Oh God, Liza thought, glancing at the little boy chattering happily with Jean. She licked her lips, uncertain about how to respond. She could see Abbey's fear in her blue eyes as she went on, explaining the events of the past few months: Brandon's symptoms, the diagnosis of a tumor that resulted from a defect during fetal growth, and x-ray therapy preceding his upcoming surgery.

"I feel so guilty." Her lips trembled. "I just know I must have done something wrong during my pregnancy to have caused Brandon's tumor."

"I'm sure it's not your fault, Abbey." Liza put down a puppet and gave her a hug. She could not imagine her suffering. But for all that she sympathized, she felt awkward about how quickly their brief conversation had gone to the possible death of a little boy. It's the environment of the children's ward, she thought. Some of the kids in the audience would die here.

"That's what the doctor says." She stepped back, raising a hand, almost in supplication. "I'm so sorry for unloading on you. I'm terribly worried, and it just came pouring out." Her voice lowered. "Brandon is my life."

"Please, don't apologize." Liza patted her arm. "Remember Brandon is in good hands. Isn't it possible that he'll recover?"

She nodded. "But there are so many risks, so many unknowns and . . ." Her words drifted into a silence.

"And?" Liza prompted gently.

Abbey looked down. "For all that I hate the thought of my baby going through this operation, I know he must. But if we lose our medical insurance I have no idea how we'll pay thousands and thousands of dollars—and hospitals don't offer credit."

"Why would you lose it?"

"Because of the layoffs at International Air."

There was a silence.

Cooper Delmonte, a man who owned his own plane, could not be in danger of losing his insurance, even if his job was terminated and he had to pay the premiums himself, Liza thought. He had to make a good salary or have family money. Liza did wonder why she had never seen him at work before today, though the company employed hundreds of people and she had not even met most of them.

"IA *is* downsizing its workforce in several areas of the company," she said finally, wondering what had prompted Abbey's concern. "Please don't worry. I'm sure your husband's position is secure."

"Cooper says that once the software is perfected and the FAA gives certification for the One Thousand Series jet, some of the programmers will be laid off." A pause. "I know Cooper is worried about our insurance, too."

"What is the date of Brandon's operation?"

"It depends on how long his preoperative treatment takes."

Liza shook her head slowly. "I don't think you should worry about insurance right now, Abbey. Just concentrate on taking care of your son." She wanted to say everything would be all right but she didn't dare. Abbey's fears could be valid. The desperate clients she counseled daily could attest to that.

At that moment Brandon came back, jabbering about being a puppeteer when he grew up. Liza expelled a long breath. Ending the conversation was a relief. They said their good-byes and Abbey took her son's hand, heading for the door, where they paused.

"Thanks for listening," Abbey said, her gaze meeting Liza's. "And please tell Martin hello." Then they disappeared into the hall.

Liza stared after them. Abbey obviously did not know about Martin. The lump was back in her throat. And she was exhausted. Hurry, she told herself. Get the stuff packed so you can go home. You need sleep, my girl. Sweet oblivion.

Liza slept in the next morning, not awakening until the phone rang after eight. It was an apologetic Dave canceling his invitation for dinner that night.

"Jeez," he said. "That damn software glitch didn't go away. In fact it's caused a chain reaction. His annoyance came over the line. "I guess I can't depend on a free Saturday night until the project is complete."

"Don't worry about it," she said, trying not to sound sleepy. "I've got a heavy workload, too, and I'll use the time to catch up."

"Thanks for understanding."

The connection was broken and Liza began her day, relieved that she could work uninterrupted on the files she had brought home. By bedtime she was happily tired; Nate's evaluation was ready for Hawk Bohlman on Monday morning.

After another good night's sleep Liza awoke refreshed on Sunday. She was almost ready to leave for the Mission Church where she was the pianist for the morning service when the phone rang. Thinking it was Dave, she ran to grab the receiver before her answering machine picked up the call.

"Hello." She put down her handbag and leather gloves.

"Mrs. MacDonough?"

"Speaking." The rapid-fire voice in her ear was vaguely familiar.

"Nate Garret, Mrs. MacDonough. I'm sorry to call you at home but I need to talk to you."

There was a silence while she shifted gears. Why was Nate calling her at home? How had he gotten her number?

"Uh, go ahead, Nate. I have a few minutes."

"No, not on the phone." He hesitated. "Can I meet you somewhere?"

"I can be in my office by eight tomorrow morning and we could—"

He cut her off. "No, not there. Somewhere today, before you give my evaluation to Hawk."

Another silence.

"Surely this can wait until tomorrow. I promise I won't give the evaluation to Hawk until I talk to you first. Okay?"

"Please, I'll meet you anywhere you say." She could hear his agitation—his fear?

"It can't wait?"

"Mrs. MacDonough this is life and . . ." A pause. "This is very important. Please?"

She hesitated, considering. There were no company rules that said she couldn't meet him outside of her office. "All right then."

Liza gave him the directions to the Mission Church,

and he agreed to meet her at ten, an hour before the service.

"Thank you," he said. "I'll be there."

She hung up, puzzled. What had Nate started to say. Life and . . . *death*?

She glanced at her watch. She would know in approximately forty-five minutes.

Chapter Five

THE WEATHERMAN HAD SAID IT MIGHT SNOW, AND AS LIZA walked the several blocks from the parking lot to Mission Church on First Avenue, she shivered. Damn cold, she told herself. I hope the weatherman is wrong. Although she loved snow, she dreaded being stuck on First Hill until the streets were bare again. There was no way to stop a car on the steep inclines that stretched upward from Elliott Bay, either going up on the ice, or down.

The mission, a nondescript clapboard building, was located near Pioneer Square, a historic section of downtown Seattle and an area that attracted street people. It was funded by donations and local church groups, its primary objective to help the poor and the dispossessed.

Years ago, right after her father's death, the mission's outreach program had made it possible for Liza's family to have Christmas. Both she and Jean had been given a doll, her mother a turkey and food essentials for their holiday dinner. Neither she nor Jean had ever forgotten the mission's kindness: she had been one of the pianists for Sunday morning service since her college days and Jean had modeled her puppet, Moon Spinner, after her doll.

Liza passed several homeless people huddled together in a doorway, a half-filled bottle of Thunderbird wine next to them. How sad, she thought, knowing that some of the transients preferred the street over a bed at the mission because they didn't want "to be preached to."

She walked into the sanctuary, expecting to see Nate waiting for her. Glancing at her watch, Liza realized it was still almost an hour until the morning service. But as the minutes melted away, she was at first puzzled, then annoyed. By the time the service began she realized Nate had stood her up. She would speak to him about it tomorrow morning at work. How unprofessional, she thought. Especially after he had called her at home.

After the final hymn had been sung and the people were leaving, Liza closed the music books and stood up to leave.

"Good job, as usual." Pastor Larsen had come up behind her. "Can't tell you how many times I bless your mother for teaching you to play the piano."

"Thanks," Liza said, smiling. He was a slight man in his sixties who had served the mission for years. Both she and Jean were extremely fond of him. "I was fortunate that my mother took the time to teach me, and that we'd inherited the family piano from my grandparents a few years before my dad died."

He nodded and they discussed next week's music selections before she said good-bye and made her way up the aisle to the front entrance. The sound of approaching sirens was suddenly deafening as she stepped outside.

She hesitated, her eyes on the crowd clustered around a person who lay in the street, many of the people having just left the mission. Several police cars were already on the scene as a Medic One emergency vehicle rounded a corner and came to a screeching stop. She moved closer, listening to the murmur of shocked remarks.

"It was like he jumped in front of the car," someone said.

"Yeah, he seemed to fly off the sidewalk, and the car was going too fast to stop," another person added.

"God Almighty! He has to be *terribly* hurt," a man next to Liza said.

Within a few minutes the medics had examined the man and lifted him carefully onto a gurney.

The crowd went silent, watching.

The injured man lay absolutely still. Then, slowly, he turned his head, his eyes scanning the crowd until they locked with Liza's gaze.

It was Nate!

He tried to speak. Liza pushed to the front of the crowd. "Let me through!" she commanded, shocked. "I know this man!"

A uniformed police officer grabbed Liza's arm, preventing her from going to Nate. "But I know him," she said, protesting.

"Are you a relative?" he asked.

"No, but—"

"Then I have to ask you to stay back. This man needs to get to the hospital."

Liza's gaze stayed locked onto Nate who again tried to speak. The effort was too much for him and his eyes closed as the medics placed him in the ambulance. In seconds it was screaming its way up the hills toward the ER at Harborview Hospital. As the sound faded, the police officer questioned her. She gave her name, then Nate's and how she knew him, omitting the evaluation she had just written about him. She would only reveal confidential information if it became necessary.

"He was late to meet me," she added, shaken. "Maybe he was hurrying and didn't see the car."

"Possibly." The officer glanced up from writing his report. "What was the purpose of your meeting?"

"Uh, company business."

"Company business? On a Sunday morning?"

There was a silence.

She controlled an urge to fidget. "Nate has an important meeting tomorrow and he wanted my advice." Not a lie, she told herself.

"Okay, thanks for coming forward," the officer said, closing his report book. "We have your phone number, Mrs. MacDonough."

She nodded. Free to go, she hurried back to her car and was soon headed up the hill, following the route of the ambulance. Let Nate be okay, she chanted, knowing he had a wife and kids.

But Liza was troubled. The officer had been right. What had been so important that Nate would insist on meeting her at church? And why had he been late? What had he tried to tell her?

Again, she parked her car, then hurried to the emergency entrance. The lady behind the information desk said she would check on the status of Nate, then directed her to the waiting area.

A half hour passed. As she was about to check again, the police officer from the accident scene appeared in the doorway.

"Mrs. MacDonough?"

She stood. Before she could ask he shook his head.

"He . . . he's gone?" Her voice broke.

"They couldn't revive him once he lost consciousness." A pause. "His family is being notified." Again he shook his head, his handsome features tightening. "Accidents like this are tragic."

"It was an accident then?"

He nodded. "Looks like it."

Numbly, Liza thanked him, then left the hospital to drive home. Poor Nate. His job worries were over. And now she would never know what he had been going to tell her.

Guilt overwhelmed her and tears welled in her eyes. How could she have underestimated his panic? Had he been so distracted that he had blindly stepped in front of a car? Now he was dead. Partly my fault, she told herself. I should have spotted it. And I didn't.

"Interfering bitch!" he muttered between clenched teeth. "Mother-fucking cunt!"

He was parked down the street from the emergency entrance and almost a block from the Miata. He had followed her up the hills, watched her lock her car and hurry into the hospital. He forced deep breaths. Don't lose it, he instructed himself. Too much is at stake. It's going to be okay. Nate couldn't have survived.

But he was still alive when the medics arrived.

He pulled a flask from inside his jacket, glanced around to make sure no one observed him, and then he took a healthy swallow of Scotch. As he slipped the flask back inside his pocket his eyes were on the two scraggily looking boys skateboarding on the sidewalk, jumping curbs and weaving their way around people without falling. Must live around here, he thought. Bad area for kids. They'd probably graduate into drugs soon.

He snorted an ironic laugh. What was a bad area for kids? The slums? With the family he had, it could as easily be a middle-class neighborhood, like the one he'd grown up in.

It started to rain, the icy drops splattering against the windshield like sleet. The windows began to steam up. He started the engine, turned the defrost on high and cracked the window, allowing the cold breeze inside. It hit his sweaty forehead like an electric shock.

The boys were oblivious to the rain and continued their competition. He noticed the younger one wore a jacket that was too small. Instantly his mind flashed to his own childhood, to another coat.

"Why won't you wear your new coat?" his mother had said.

"It's not a new coat!" he had retorted. "It's a hand-me-down!"

"You're wearing it!"

His crying and pleading had fallen on deaf ears. He had worn it to school, but only once. He had thrown it in a dumpster, watched from a classroom window as the garbage truck hauled it away, then gone to the principal's office and reported it stolen. His parents had looked doubtful and made him wear his old jacket, the one that fit him just like the kid's on the skateboard. He hadn't cared. The old jacket was the only new coat he'd ever had, until the day when he was able to buy his own. The coat had been a small victory over the dumb bastards who'd always made him wear his older brother's castoffs. They'd never cared that the other kids ridiculed his clothes.

A van honked at the boys, bringing his thoughts back to why he was there. He turned on the wipers so he could see the entrance better. He blew out a long breath. There she was. He had almost missed her.

She ran to her car, wiping at her eyes. Raindrops? Tears? Did that mean Nate was dead?

He did not follow when she left. He knew where she lived. He waited until she was out of sight, then strode into the hospital waiting room and used a pay phone. The emergency room nurse was evasive when he asked about Nate, claiming to be a concerned witness to the accident. But he knew.

Back in his car again he took another swig from the flask. Now all he had to do was make sure that Liza MacDonough did not have incriminating evidence. Piece of cake, he told himself. She was easy.

*   *   *

"I don't know if I'm up for this," Liza said as Dave stopped his Mercedes in front of Nate Garret's Woodinville house.

He turned, his arm sliding along the seat behind her. "Liza," he said, softly. "Nate's death wasn't your fault. No one knew his stress level was so acute."

"But it's my job to know that." She hesitated. "I failed to pick up on the signals. I saw that he was anxious and concerned about his job, but I put it down to overwork and wanting to please Hawk."

"Don't take this on."

Liza expelled a long breath, then faced him. "I'm okay, really." She grabbed the door handle. "Let's get this over with."

Without another word, he climbed out from under the wheel and was on her side of the car before she had stepped onto the driveway. In silence they walked to the front door and rang the bell. As they waited Liza took in the surroundings: the new two-story house, manicured lawn, upscale neighborhood. Expensive, she thought, and realized that the Garrets were probably living beyond their means—from paycheck to paycheck.

Maggie, Nate's wife, opened the door, surprising Liza. She had expected one of the relatives who had invited Nate's colleagues from International Air to the Garret home after the funeral service an hour earlier.

"Hello, Dave," Maggie said, smiling weakly. Her eyes, red-rimmed from crying, shifted to Liza. "I'm Maggie, Mrs. MacDonough. We haven't met but of course I've heard about you." She glanced down. "Through Nate."

"I'm so sorry, Mrs. Garret." Liza's voice broke. She wanted to say more but the words wouldn't come. Instead she embraced Maggie as she and Dave stepped into the entry hall.

"Thank you for coming," Maggie said, swallowing hard. "My boys and I appreciate it."

After taking their coats, Maggie led them into the living room that was crowded with people, many of whom Liza recognized from International Air. A long table in the connecting dining room was filled with food, although most of the guests were not eating. She noticed three boys sitting with an older couple in the corner of the room. Nate's sons, Liza decided, and probably the grandparents.

Dave followed her glance. "They range in age from seven to fourteen." He hesitated. "Sad, huh."

She nodded, wondering how Maggie and her boys would cope. Maggie was a trim blond whose black silk suit, manicured nails and tastefully decorated surroundings denoted a lifestyle she might not be able to maintain without Nate's salary. Dave had already told her that Maggie did not have a career and that the boys had always attended a private school. Liza hoped that Nate's life insurance through International Air would be enough to sustain his family.

"I'm going to grab a cup of coffee," Dave said. "Can I bring you one?"

"Thanks, I'd love one—to fortify myself," she replied, only half joking. Funerals always brought back memories of her father's death.

"Right back."

As Dave moved toward the food table he was stopped several times by people he knew. Across the room Alice Emery waved, then threaded her way through the crowd toward Liza, flashing brief smiles to people she knew. Her outfit, a well-cut black dress and matching suede pumps, attracted many admiring glances from men and women, and Liza suppressed a smile. Wherever Alice went she always tried to look her best.

"I haven't gotten that list down to you yet," she said, approaching Liza. She raised penciled brows. "Too much going on." She indicated Nate's funeral. "Tomorrow okay?"

"Of course. Tuesday is fine." She paused, glancing at the crowd. "Neither of us could miss Nate's funeral."

Alice smoothed her bangs. "Sudden death is always such a shock."

"Isn't it," a deep male voice said behind Liza. She turned to see Cooper and Abbey Delmonte. Abbey, dressed in a navy blue suit and wearing makeup, looked far more attractive than Liza remembered. "It's going to be damn hard to work in the computer lab without Nate," he added.

As Cooper reminisced about the years he had known Nate, Abbey was silent, deferring to her husband. Liza exchanged smiles with her but there was no chance to talk without interrupting Cooper. Around forty with the charismatic personality of a film star, Cooper was a man who knew how attractive he was to women. And if Abbey's manner was any indication of their relationship, he was the master of their house, the decision maker. But don't forget little Brandon, she reminded herself. Worry could be the reason Abbey seemed subdued.

Then Abbey was engaged in conversation by a woman who asked after Brandon. Unwilling to interrupt, Liza turned her attention back to Cooper who was still talking.

"Yeah, I don't know what Abbey would do if something happened to me." Cooper's brown eyes, almost as dark as his carefully combed hair, shifted from Alice to Liza. "She doesn't have a career either, unlike both of you."

"I'm sure she'd manage," Liza replied, annoyed that he would be condescending about his wife who was worried sick about their child. "Women are more resilient than you might think."

Liza was saved from further conversation when Dave returned with her coffee. The moment passed. Good thing, she told herself. The Delmonte family dynamics were none of her business.

A short time later Liza finished her coffee and saw that Dave's cup was also empty. "My turn to get refills," she said.

"No thanks," Dave said. "But you can take my cup."

Liza headed for the coffee urn in the dining room, then decided she'd had enough, and went on into the kitchen where she found Maggie leaning over the sink, crying. She tried to back out of the room but Maggie saw her.

"Please forgive my intruding," Liza began. "I was going to put the cups in the sink."

"Don't go," Maggie said, straightening. "I just lost it for a few seconds." She hesitated. "I'm trying not to do that in front of my boys."

"I understand." Liza put the cups down on the counter. "You're entitled to tears, Maggie. You've just lost your husband."

Maggie sniffled, trying to maintain her control, dabbing at her eyes with a dish towel. "I . . . I loved him so much. I can't believe he's really gone, that he won't be walking in the door any minute now."

"I know." Liza said, gently. "It'll take time to get past that feeling." She remembered all too well. It was how she'd felt for months after her father's death. And still felt about Martin's disappearance.

Maggie twisted the towel nervously. "It's my fault he's dead." Her voice broke. "If only I'd encouraged him to pursue his dream." More tears. "But I was afraid."

"Afraid?" Liza's tone sharpened. "Of what?"

"Of losing all this." Maggie waved her hand, indicating the house. "We needed Nate's income to keep our lifestyle, our boys in private school." She drew in a ragged breath. "Nate wanted to start his own software business, and I thought he should wait until we were more financially secure."

"You mustn't feel guilty. You couldn't have known that Nate would . . . have an accident."

"I pressured Nate, so he felt like he couldn't afford to quit his job at International Air." Maggie slumped into a chair. "He was so talented, Liza." She glanced up. "Do you mind if I call you Liza?"

Liza shook her head. "I'd like you to."

"I feel like I know you, even though we've just met," Maggie went on shakily. "I can see why Nate was so fond of you. He said you'd be fair about the evaluation."

"You knew about that?"

She nodded. "Nate was exhausted and distracted. But God help me, I can't understand how he could have stepped in front of a car."

"None of us can, Maggie." Liza was pricked by her own guilt. She may have missed his signals of being on the ragged edge.

There was a silence.

"Did you know how musically talented he was?" Maggie asked finally. "In his spare time he composed music on his electronic keyboard, then his computer transposed the notes to hardcopy, printouts of sheet music."

"No, I didn't know."

There was a sound in the doorway. Liza glanced up, her eyes meeting Dave's.

"I'm sorry to interrupt," he began, looking awkward about having projected himself into their conversation. "I was just checking on you, Liza." He smiled briefly. "I'll be in the other room."

"I'll be with you in a minute," she replied.

He nodded, then disappeared from the doorway.

Maggie stood up. "I appreciate your being here." She paused. "And for all you were trying to do for Nate."

"I wish I could have done more," Liza said, truthfully. "And Maggie, please call me if you need anything." She fished a business card out of her purse and quickly scribbled her home phone number on it as well.

Her bottom lip trembling, Maggie managed to keep back more tears. "I will. And thanks."

Liza rejoined Dave and a short time later they headed back into the city. All the way down the freeway and across the Route 520 bridge into Seattle they hardly talked. Liza could not shake the feeling that something was wrong. Nate's death *had* been ruled accidental.

But was it?

Chapter Six

THE NEXT MORNING THE PHONE RANG AS LIZA WAS ABOUT to leave, startling her. The strap of her handbag slipped off her shoulder, jolting the briefcase out of her hand. It clattered onto the hardwood floor but she managed to hang on to her keys. "Damn!" She ran to pick up the receiver in the kitchen before the caller gave up, almost tripping over Bella.

"Hello." Her words sounded breathless.

"Is this Liza?"

"Yes it is." A pause. "Steve Wendall?"

"Very good. You recognized my voice."

She pressed the receiver against her ear. Her private investigator had never before called her at seven in the morning. In fact she had hardly talked to him since he took her case several weeks ago. She braced herself. He must have discovered something about Martin's disappearance.

"Barely," she said finally. "What have you found out?"

There was a hesitation.

"First things first. I've used all of my retainer and I'll need more money to continue my investigation."

"But what have you found out so far?" Her tone was sharper. Surely he didn't think that she would just hand over more money without a progress report.

"I'm not sure yet." Another pause. "Just enough to intrigue me. That's why I need more money, so I can pursue some leads."

Liza switched the phone to her other ear. Steve Wendall had been referred to her by a jewelry artist who lived in the building, a woman who leased one of the funky shops at Pike Place Market on Seattle's waterfront. "He may march to his own drummer, but he knows his business," the artist had told her.

So she had called him, been impressed by his intelligent and informed suggestions, and made an appointment with him for the following Saturday afternoon. But when he had ridden up to the coffee shop on a ten-speeder, leg muscles rippling under faded jeans, she'd had instant reservations. Lean, long-haired and bearded, he had looked like an aging hippie. But again, as they talked—she over coffee, he over purified water from his own bottle—his obvious expertise had dispelled her misgivings.

"This will be helpful," he'd said when she handed him an information sheet on Martin: his friends, coworkers, interests and vital statistics. The fact that he didn't have a real office had deterred her at first, but his rates were within her budget. So she'd hired him.

"What kind of leads," she said finally, shifting mental gears back to their phone conversation.

"Hey, Liza, I don't know if you wanna hear this. It might be upsetting."

"Of course I do. Why do you think I hired you? To find out the truth, whatever it is."

But do I really want to know? she wondered, staring out through the dining room window at the distant Space Needle. It was a no-win situation. Either Martin was dead . . . or he had abandoned her. Steve Wendall's tone told her that his information would be upsetting.

"Okay," he said. "Here goes." He drew in a sharp breath. "I think Martin might not be dead. I've—"

His words shot over the wire with the intensity of an electric shock. "How? What?" she asked frantically.

"Whoa. Give me a chance to explain." A pause. "I warned you that this isn't what you wanted to hear."

"That's not true!" she retorted. "I don't want my husband to be dead, even if knowing the truth about what happened to him is not flattering to me."

Another silence.

"Do you want me to continue?"

She nodded, then realized he couldn't see the gesture. "Yes. Please, go on."

He sighed. "You realize that nothing is a fact at this point, just suspicion based upon what I've dug up."

She pressed the receiver into her ear. "Yes."

"All right then. Martin might have been involved in something illegal, gotten in over his head, and run because he was damned scared. His many spur-of-the-moment-flights at odd times of day and night appear, at least on the surface, suspicious."

"Suspicious? But that's crazy."

"Maybe. But then why was your husband so secretive about his flight plans when anyone asked him?"

"Because he didn't know them himself. That was part of his love of flying, being able to take off and head wherever a whim took him. He hated being pinned down to any kind of red tape."

"Yeah, so I heard."

"Look Steve, this information doesn't prove anything."

There was a pause.

"Of course you could be right, if that's all there is to it."

"You don't sound convinced."

"Sorry, but I'm not. There's been gossip, speculation that he and a couple of other pilots might have been into some smuggling."

"Smuggling?

"That's what I heard, but I'm not prepared to give details yet until I'm able to substantiate a few things."

"But you said Martin might be alive. You must know something definite." She paced the kitchen, pulling the long phone cord behind her. "You can't just leave me hanging if you know something."

"I won't leave you in limbo for long," he said, sounding mildly insulted. "It's my standard practice to update the direction of my investigation, especially since more funds are needed to continue." He spoke faster. "But like I said, I have some leads to follow before I get to the facts." His sigh came over the line. "When I have those facts you'll be the first to know."

"Okay, then get them."

"Agreed, so long as you can pay the freight." Another hesitation. "You willing to put up five thousand bucks?"

"You'll give me an accounting of the expenses?" She had to ask. Much as she would pay twice that for the truth, she didn't want him stringing her along down a dead-end street.

"Goes without saying."

She made arrangements to mail him a check, not allowing herself to worry about her dwindling bank account. She had to know what had happened—no matter how costly or painful—so she could get on with her life. After they hung up she stared at the phone. Martin might be alive? Then what would have compelled him to take such drastic action as disappearing, to not even have confided in her? Fear for his life?—or hers?

Steve Wendall's call stayed with her all the way to work. A hundred questions surfaced in her thoughts, dozens of what-ifs. It was only later, while listening to a client's problems, that she was able to forget it for a while.

It was her day for disturbing calls. Liza picked up the phone after lunch to hear Maggie Garret's voice.

"I'm so sorry to call you at work," she said. "But I recalled something Nate said recently." A pause. "It was troublesome and . . . and I felt I needed to tell someone."

"I'm glad you called, Maggie." She sat up straighter in her chair. "I have ten minutes before I see my next client."

"Thanks," Maggie said, and Liza could hear her relief. "I know I'm probably being silly."

"Nonsense, of course you're not. When we lose a loved one we need to process all of our feelings," Liza said, knowing she sounded like a psychologist which of course she was.

You're very kind, Liza. I guess that's why I knew I could call you."

Liza wanted to say, "Just empathizing. I've been where you are Maggie." But she held her tongue. Maggie didn't need to hear another sad story right now.

"So, what do you remember?" she asked instead.

Maggie cleared her throat, and Liza could tell she was trying not to cry. "Nate said that he was upset about something in the computer lab."

"Did he say what upset him?" Liza prompted, gently.

"No, he didn't. It was just the *way* he said it that concerned me, and the fact that worry over it kept him up at night."

"Maybe he was just troubled about one of the software glitches. I know some of the problems have been difficult to solve."

"I asked him that. He said no, but he wouldn't explain further, only that he'd find his own way out of the mess."

"He called it *a mess?*"

"Uh-huh."

Was his accident his way out? The thought came unbidden. Was he a suicide after all? She couldn't possibly say anything like that to his widow. Then, as though Maggie sensed her questions, she continued.

"He didn't commit suicide, Liza." Her voice wobbled. "I knew Nate better than anyone else. He loved me and the boys. We were his world. He would never have deliberately stepped in front of a car, no matter what."

Probably true. Liza combed through her hair with her fingers. But she also identified with denial. She, too, could not accept that Martin may have committed suicide. Nor could she really accept that he had deceived her and was still alive. A stalemate.

Someone knocked on the half-open door to Liza's office. She motioned Alice's assistant into the room. "Maggie, can you hold on a minute," she said. "Someone just stepped into my office and I need to speak to them. I'll be right back."

She agreed and Liza put Maggie on hold to take the employee layoff list that the young woman was handing her. After thanking her, Liza told her she would call Alice later. "And tell Alice thanks," she called after the woman who had turned to go. After the door closed Liza picked up the receiver.

"Sorry about that." She set the printout aside to go over after she had completed her day's appointments. As she and Maggie talked, Liza's mind kept switching to Alice's list, wondering if she might actually find factual discrepancies that could indicate something was amiss. They hung up after Maggie promised to call again with any future concerns.

She looked forward to quitting time. The day had started out unsettling and had not gotten any better. A quiet evening with Bella, a long soak in the tub and a glass of wine sounded good. She needed to relax.

Liza walked along the deck of the harbor cruise ship, scarcely feeling the chill of the winter night. Music wafted outward from the main saloon where Martin's jazz trio was playing Dizzy Gillespie and Louis Armstrong sets, his favorites.

She hummed along, wondering if she should join the party. But she hesitated, her body not willing to obey its mental command. For the moment she was content to gaze at the sky that was salted with billions of stars, and the full moon that rose above the distant islands to shimmer molten paths across Elliott Bay. Paths to magic places, places where dreams came true—*where loved ones didn't die.* Although her green velvet holiday gown was low cut and sleeveless, Liza was oblivious to the cold. Strange, she thought. I'm usually the first person to need a coat.

A waiter appeared from a doorway, a glass of wine on his tray. She would have grabbed it, but he moved too quickly and disappeared around the stern of the ship. For a moment longer she lingered, then moved toward the music. It was time to join the party.

She pushed open the door to the saloon—to instant silence. Her eyes widened, her heart pumped furiously in her chest. The room was empty.

"Man overboard!" someone shouted from the deck.

Liza started running toward the voice, an urgency giving

wings to her feet. Then the spike heel of her pump caught in the hem of her gown and she sprawled onto the deck. Hands helped her up and she was running again.

"Over here!" another person hollered, this time closer. Beyond her view she heard many voices blending into one cry for help. Liza kept going, rounding the stern to—an empty deck. She froze, leaning on the rail to keep herself upright. A movement in the water caught her eye.

Something broke the surface. Suddenly a man's face was illuminated in the moonlight. *Martin's face!*

She leaned over the rail, stretching out her hands. "Grab hold!" she shouted. "I can pull you out!"

Opaque eyes stared back and bloodless lips moved. Liza could not hear the words above the waves breaking against the ship, and the din of voices somewhere behind her. She leaned farther over the rail. Martin's arms lifted, water dripping off his shirt sleeves, but he could not reach her.

Behind her someone grabbed her around the waist so she could stretch even more. Then the hands released her and she was falling into the inky turbulence of the bay. The icy water took her breath as it closed over her head. Frantically she struggled for a handhold. Martin had disappeared, sucked even deeper by the quicksand of currents.

Liza couldn't breathe and her eardrums felt ready to burst. She surfaced once, but went down again. Just before her eyes closed, a braided cord attached to a ring of keys slithered past her like a prehistoric sea urchin. In her head she heard the voices again, closer and closer—coming to make sure that she—

Abruptly, Liza was breathing again, gulping air. She bolted out of the bed, sending Bella sailing off the quilt. For long seconds she was disoriented. It was the cat's yowl that jarred her back to reality. She stood shaking in her quiet bedroom, her nightgown damp with sweat.

It was a dream, she told herself. Only a bad dream.

She walked on rubbery legs to the kitchen for a glass of water, then changed her mind and poured the Chardonnay she had skipped earlier. Self-medicating now, old girl? Because you're strung out by a nightmare?

She tossed her nightgown aside, climbed back into bed naked and sat propped against the pillows to sip her wine. But she could not get settled. Bella watched from the chair next to her, wary of chancing the quilt again.

But Liza could not erase Martin's lifeless face from her mind. Dear God, she prayed. What was he trying to say? What did it mean?

Chapter Seven

"DAMN IT ALL TO HELL!" LIZA SAID, FRUSTRATED AGAIN. "Where is that friggin' printout?"

Her nerves were stretched to the breaking point, her eyes felt scratchy from lack of sleep and her mind was on overload. How could she have misplaced the list of terminated employees? She had made a point to leave it on her desk where she *could not* misplace it.

The overnight cleaning people—that's it, she thought. They threw it away. It was the only explanation. But they've never touched anything on my desk before, she argued with herself. Then what happened to it? Did someone steal it? Dumb thought. Who would even want a list of fired people except her, who'd requested it to look for problems? Her mind went blank. There was no real explanation for the missing document, unless she wasn't remembering accurately where she had *really* put it.

I'm a basket case, she thought, slumping onto her desk chair. Taking deep breaths, she forced herself to be calm.

Please God, of all the things I've forgotten lately, let me forget last night's horrible dream.

The nightmare had been replaying in her mind all morning, a terrifying scenario of Martin's death. Don't think about it, she instructed herself. Get to work.

She laughed, wryly. Here she was, a psychologist, telling herself to stuff her fears. She hoped she did not end up on a colleague's couch. Whatever. It was good advice; she would go to Alice's office, plead dumb and ask for another printout.

She glanced at her watch. A half hour until her first client. She'd go now. Almost to the door she remembered Sam Paparich, a terminated client who was desperate for a new job. The sole supporter of his family, he had needed help in creating a résumé, so she had rewritten it for him. She had it ready but needed to go over it with him. Quickly, Liza called him and they made an appointment for Sunday afternoon, the only day they both had free.

She hung up, remembering the many times that Martin had worried about her working on weekends. "You've got to leave your work at the office, honey," he had told her, holding her close as he feathered her face with kisses. "I'm concerned that you might be projecting your own childhood insecurities onto the people who lose their positions at International Air."

Liza strode back to the door, pulled it open, and almost collided with Dave who had been about to open it. "Hey, Brown Eyes," he said, smiling, his glance admiring as he took in the fact that she was dressed in red. "Where you off to in such a hurry?"

She grinned, disarmed. "A needless errand because of my own stupidity."

"How so?" His green eyes narrowed, interested.

"Oh–" She shrugged. "I lost something and I need to get a replacement."

"So, I don't get it. Why does that make you stupid?" He raised his red-thick brows, waiting.

"I'll explain later," she said, evading.

"Fair enough." He hesitated. "Over lunch?"

"Um, I don't know about lunch," she began. "I may have appointments."

"Why don't you check your schedule?" He walked her back to the desk. "I have a little over an hour. If it coincides with your timetable, I'll take you to Cutters."

"Cutters Bayhouse north of the Market?"

"The very place." He smiled wider, revealing slightly crooked teeth. "All of us Yuppies love Cutters. And it's only a few minutes away, barring traffic." He hesitated. "Having lunch at a window table overlooking the bay is a sure way to slow down the old motor."

There was a pause.

"You think I need to slow down?"

"Wouldn't hurt." He inclined his head toward her appointment book. "Go ahead and see what you've got."

Liza glanced at her schedule. "I have an hour and a half between one and two-thirty, but I should use that time to catch up on my client files."

"Nonsense. You need the break–to fill your well again– brain food for coping with afternoon counseling sessions." His expression softened. "All work and no play equals . . . burnout. And we can't have that, can we?"

She shook her head, and a strand of unruly hair fell over her forehead. "But isn't that a little late for your lunch?"

He moved closer, and before she could step back, smoothed her hair off her face. Abruptly, his eyes lowered to hers, holding her gaze. "It's a perfect time." His voice was softer. "I'm flexible today. For once there are no program glitches, no minor crisis to deal with, no frustrated employees."

She glanced away from his admiring eyes, uncertain about her own feelings. They moved back to the door.

"So, is it a date?"

"It's a date." Liza smiled and contrived a lighter tone. "Lunch at Cutters."

"I'll meet you at my office around one, earlier if you can make it." He dropped an arm around her shoulders, squeezing slightly to punctuate his words. "We'll have a relaxing lunch. Gives me the chance to make up for all the dinners I've postponed lately."

"No need to do that—"

He interrupted. "Course there is. Can't have my favorite girl getting mad at me."

"I didn't—"

"We'll discuss it later, okay Brown Eyes?"

She nodded.

"By the way, red is your color, highlights the auburn tones of your hair." He gave a salute, not waiting for her reply, and disappeared into the hall.

She went back to her desk, remembering that she needed to activate her voice mail while she was gone. God, I am forgetful, she told herself. Dave may be right. A peaceful lunch to break up a hectic day is exactly what I need.

"Good Lord, Liza. You've lost the printout—already? After you were so anxious to check for employment problems?"

Alice sounded distracted, as though something was bothering her other than Liza's lost printout. Dressed in a scoop-necked, green clinging sweater over a black leather skirt rather than her usual business suit, she even looked different today. Liza wondered if she had a date after work and hoped that was the case. Alice, who had recently been working to improve her appearance with exercise and counting calories, looked great.

"Like I said, I left it on my desk, and I think the cleaning people threw it away accidentally." She hesitated, her gaze shifting to the wall of windows and the gray rainy day beyond them. "I'm sorry if this causes a problem."

"Not really, Liza." She smiled, briefly. "But I don't think I have another hard copy."

Liza stood aside as Alice came around her desk to open a filing cabinet. As Alice fingered through folders, Liza caught a reflection of herself on the window, and realized that she was dressed differently today as well. She'd never worn her red velvet suit and matching suede pumps to work before, always considering the outfit inappropriate for her position as a counselor.

Liza turned away from the glass. She knew why she had chosen the red suit. It had been Martin's favorite and she had worn it in defiance of her dream. She had needed the bright color to lift her spirits.

"Just as I thought." Alice closed the file drawer and faced her. "No copy." Her penciled brows shot up, disappearing under her bangs. "I'll have my assistant print out another one and send it down to you." She hesitated. "It may take a day or two. Is that okay?"

Liza nodded. "I appreciate it, Alice."

Alice spread her hands. "I know this is important to you, Liza, even though I feel it's an exercise in futility."

There was a brief silence.

"You may be right. We'll see."

"Yeah, we will." Alice strode back to her desk. "And at least you'll resolve this issue once and for all."

It was obvious that Alice thought her fishing exhibition would come to a dead end. Liza ignored the possibility that Alice was patronizing her, because Alice had not heard the stories of the terminated employees. She *had*, and she meant to investigate, even if it went against the consensus of everyone else around her. Her professional integrity wouldn't allow her to do less.

Liza was the first to break the silence.

"How about us meeting at the gym after work. Get rid of all our stress with a sauna and some exercise?"

Alice shook her head. "Can't tonight."

"How come?"

Alice's expression relaxed for the first time since Liza had stepped into her office. "I have a date."

"That's great," Liza said, smiling. "Do I know—"

Alice licked her lips and went on quickly, as though she didn't want Liza to ask his name. "He's a sexy hunk, let me tell you. I can't quite believe it, but I turn him on."

"Um, well you should believe it, Alice. You're a very attractive woman with a lot to offer a man." She hesitated. "He's the lucky one."

"Thanks." Alice drew in her breath. "Maybe we can get together some night next week at the gym." She smiled, smugly. "I'll fill you in on all the details."

"I'll look forward to it." Liza cocked her head. "I know you're dying to be a wife and mother, and I hope you've found the prince—your one and only." Her words were sincere, belying the silliness of the comment.

"The prince? I don't know yet." She lowered her eyes. "He may not be marriage material." A pause. "But he's damn sexy and I'll settle for that, for now. We'll see what happens."

He's married, was Liza's first thought. But maybe not, she argued mentally. Maybe he was just a gun-shy male who did not want to be trapped by the wrong woman. She hoped it was the latter. Alice deserved a good man.

"Anyway," Alice went on. "In time I'm hoping to change the status quo."

Again Liza resisted asking questions. It was obvious that Alice did not want to discuss details. She turned back to the door. "I'll look forward to receiving another printout."

"I'll get it to you as soon as possible." Alice held up a hand in good-bye. "Talk to you then."

Liza nodded, then closed the door behind her and headed downstairs to her own office. A glance at her watch told her to hurry. It was almost time for her first client of the day.

"Hey, you're a few minutes early," Dave said, looking up from notes he had been dictating to his secretary. His spacious office was on the top floor of the building with a sweeping view of Puget Sound. It was opulent compared to her small utilitarian office.

Liza grinned, already feeling much better than this morning. "Anticipation, my friend. Lunch at Cutters is irresistible. Besides, you said I should come earlier if possible."

"So I did." Dave stood up. "Early gives us plenty of time. Our reservation is for a few minutes after one."

His secretary, an older woman with a pleasant manner, left the room and Dave grabbed his jacket from the back of his chair. Then he led Liza out of his office to the hallway, glancing at his watch as the door closed behind them.

"Would you mind if we made a quick detour past the computer lab? I need to speak to Hawk." He raised his eyebrows in a question. "It will only take a couple of minutes."

"Of course I don't mind." She shrugged her shoulders. "We're still on company time, aren't we?"

He dropped an arm around her shoulders. "By the way, as I said earlier today, you look great. That a new outfit?"

There was a silence.

"Uh, no it's over a year old actually."

"I've never seen it before."

She laughed, nervously. "Probably because I've never worn it to work."

"Why is that?" She felt his eyes on her. "You look gorgeous. More beautiful than a Paris model."

Liza flushed. She'd gotten out of the habit of hearing personal compliments from an admiring man now that Martin was gone.

"Thank you Dave." She hesitated, then decided to be frank. "This was Martin's favorite suit." After all, she was still married, in legal limbo, and although she'd made that clear to Dave the first time he'd asked her for dinner, he had become more aggressive about expressing his feelings lately. She didn't want to mislead him. She liked him too much for that, valued his friendship and opinions, even if he didn't always agree with her decisions, like when she'd hired Steve Wendall, a private investigator.

"Martin had good taste," he said. His tone sounded stilted. Instantly she realized her comment about Martin had been thoughtless.

Their talk paused when they stepped into an elevator with several other people. Seconds later the door slid open on the first floor, Dave took her elbow, and they started along the covered walkway to the computer lab in the next building. The guard at the door recognized Dave and waved them through security. At the lab entrance he paused, turning to her.

"I sense you're not yourself today, Brown Eyes. Anything I can help you with?"

She looked down. His soft words were disconcerting.

She was not used to sympathy. The people closest to her, aside from Jean, always seemed to expect that she would rise to the occasion *because she must*—even if that meant coping with the disappearance of her husband.

She shook her head finally. "Thanks for asking, Dave but I'm okay, really." She paused, knowing that she could not leave her earlier comment about her red suit hanging between them.

He waited for her to continue.

"I just had a disturbing day yesterday, starting with a call from Steve Wendall about Martin, and then Maggie Garret called with concerns about Nate and . . ." Liza spread her hands. "The upshot of it all is that I had a bad dream about Martin's death last night and wasn't able to get back to sleep. Maggie's loss combined with the report from my PI must have triggered the nightmare." She frowned, remembering. "It left me feeling fatigued this morning so I chose to wear red, hoping the color would energize me."

Again he put an arm around her shoulders. For long seconds he was silent while she struggled to stay composed. For heaven sake, she instructed herself. Don't burst into tears. As sensitive as Dave was she did not want to embarrass him. It was unprofessional if nothing else; she was the counselor, not him.

"Maggie needed a shoulder to cry on?" he asked, casually.

Liza shrugged, grateful that he had been tactful enough to change the subject from Martin. "Sort of. I'd given her my card and told her to call me if she needed to talk about Nate." She didn't feel up to going into the details of her conversation with Maggie.

Another hesitation.

"And Wendall?" Dave's tone sounded flat, disapproving? "I hope he had good information since you're paying him for it."

"He needed more money to continue his investigation." Her voice lowered. "Seems he has several good leads he wants to check out." She met Dave's eyes. "He thinks Martin could still be alive."

Dave digested her words. "I see," he said finally. "Did this Wendall give details as to why he thought that?"

She shook her head. "He didn't want to explain further until after he had substantiated his leads. In case he was wrong."

"Liza, can I say something here, as your friend?"

"Of course."

He took a few seconds to formulate his thoughts. A couple walked past, their footsteps echoing on the tiled floor; a door closed down the hall; and beyond the exterior wall a truck downshifted into a load zone.

"You've been on an emotional roller coaster this past year since Martin . . . disappeared," he began slowly, his expression troubled. "You have no proof of his death and no evidence that he's still alive. Isn't that true?"

She toed the floor with the point of her red pump. "Yes, it is."

"And because of that you're in limbo . . . and vulnerable."

"What do you mean?" Her foot stilled.

He drew in his breath sharply. "Only that there are people out there who prey on the suffering of others." A pause. "How do we know this Wendall isn't one of them?"

"Are you suggesting that I'm being scammed?"

"I'm only saying that Wendall should have given you solid information before asking for more money." The frown lines between his brows deepened. "He very well could be a con artist."

"I don't think that's true. The woman in my building who recommended him knows other people who were satisfied with his services. It's possible his professional integrity won't let him speculate without facts."

Liza could not believe she was defending her PI, a man she'd had qualms about herself. But he had sounded sincere on the phone. And even if he were a con man she had no choice but to continue if there was a remote possibility of finding out what had happened to Martin. Her future depended on knowing the truth.

"Okay," Dave said. "Then how about letting me talk to him, just so he knows that there's someone looking out for you."

"You mean, a man because I'm a defenseless woman?"

"Hey, don't get upset," Dave said, holding up both hands in a gesture of surrender. "I'm not being macho here, only concerned."

"I appreciate that, Dave." Liza managed a normal tone. His offer had not annoyed her; his assumption that she was being duped had. *Because that was your first reaction to meeting Steve Wendall*, she reminded herself. Dave only wanted to help.

"Think about it." He smiled, lightening the tension between them. "The offer stands."

"I will," she replied, her tone grateful. "And thanks, Dave. Maybe I'll take you up on the offer later. For now, I'm going to see what Wendall comes up with. He claims he'll have something to report very soon."

Dave nodded, then pushed open the door and they went into the computer lab. "Hawk's office is in the back," he told her. "Mind waiting right here? I shouldn't be gone long."

"Don't mind at all." Her gaze was already darting around the huge windowless room where people sat in front of computers, apparently writing software programs for the new One Thousand Series jet. She glanced at him, an involuntary smile tugging her lips. "I've never been in here before—I'm totally awestruck."

"Yeah. That's a typical reaction. Most folks don't realize how big an undertaking this is." He hesitated. "Probably because no one without security clearance is allowed in here and therefore never sees the layout."

She laughed. "I get it," she said, teasing. "I promise I won't venture further. I'll wait right here."

"Good." There was a smile in his voice. He left her to weave his way toward the far side of the lab, greeting people as he went. She sat down on a chair that backed up to a partition and tried to relax.

The whispery hum of the computers was hypnotic; Liza leaned back against the portable wall and closed her eyes. Lack of sleep caught up with her and she was almost dozing when she became aware of two male voices discussing Internet networks and forums.

"The CB Adult Band is on United Online," one man said, his voice lifting above the low tones of their conversation. "Watch the person with the tag, Snakeoil"—there was a murmur of words Liza could not catch—" . . . and Bojangles."

Liza closed her eyes again. Computer nerds, she thought. They work all day on a computer, then go home and get online for entertainment.

The next fragment of conversation brought her upright on the chair, straining to hear more, ". . . told me the lay-off numbers don't jibe."

"Yeah . . . something weird is happening around here and—"

There was silence.

Liza strained to hear more. Standing, she moved to the

end of the short wall, peering around it, hoping to see who had been talking. No one was there. Beyond the immediate area, the room was filled with busy people, mostly men. There was no way to identify who had been talking only seconds earlier.

"Ready to go?"

Dave's question startled her. She hadn't seen him come up behind her. "Uh, sure."

His brows shot up. "You all right?"

She nodded. "I guess so."

He cocked his head, waiting.

"I just overheard a disturbing conversation."

"Who?"

"I don't know. They were on the other side of the partition and gone before I could see them."

"What did they say that was so disturbing?"

She hesitated. "I don't know. Let me think about it and I'll tell you over lunch." Where I won't be overheard, she added silently. What did it mean? That something weird *was* going on?

He nodded, then took Liza's arm and led her from the lab, down the hall and out to his Mercedes that was parked in a reserved space just beyond the security entrance. She wondered why they had not left the building through the private door that Dave used to access the lab from the parking lot. She guessed it was locked, alarmed and off limits to her.

A short time later they had parked in the underground level below Cutters, taken the garage elevator into the restaurant and were seated at a window table. The waitress took their orders of Crab Louie, then Dave requested a glass of Chardonnay for both of them.

"Dave, I can't drink in the middle of the day," she said as the waitress left their table. "I'll go to sleep."

He reached across the table to cover her hand. "If you do, I'll take you home and put you to bed."

"But—"

"No buts."

The wine was served, and after they had sipped it, Dave was the first to speak. "So, what happened in the lab, Liza?"

She explained what she had heard. "I couldn't help but overhear them. At first I thought they were talking about computer games, but when I heard them talk about something weird going on with the layoffs, I realized that meant International Air."

He inclined his head, waiting for her to continue.

"What I overheard is similar to what my clients have been saying."

"Which is?" He sipped wine, his eyes intent on her face.

"That something is wrong, that there is no reason for the layoffs when there is more work than they can handle."

"Just which of your clients have said this? What is their proof that contradicts company statistics and projections?"

There was a hesitation.

"What kind of proof do you suggest?" she asked softly, belying her feelings on the subject.

"Documentation." Dave's tone sharpened. "Names are needed in order to investigate these claims and the people behind them."

"I can't give out names without client permission, you know that. But it's all a matter of record. Someone in authority needs to get to the bottom of the accusations by employees, figure out if there's something to the rumors."

"*Some* employees," he said, correcting her. "Certainly not a very big percentage."

She took a sip of wine, to give her thinking time. She no longer felt like relaxing.

"You must realize that gossip can sabotage the One Thousand Series jet project." Dave shifted position on his chair, obviously disturbed. "Not to mention careers, mine included if we don't meet deadlines."

She glanced out the window to Elliott Bay. A Bainbridge Island ferryboat was approaching the terminal; a container ship was headed up the Sound toward the Strait of Juan de Fuca; and another weather squall was racing across the water, its heavy clouds threatening more rain.

"We need to start with the names of the troublemakers," he added.

"I can't violate client confidentiality, Dave. I could be sued and my career would be over." She drew in a breath. "The company would be the first to fire me."

He glanced down, swirling the wine in his glass, and she couldn't read his eyes. But she felt his annoyance.

"I'm sorry, Dave. I'd share information with you if I could. And I do intend to look into the allegations, make sure they aren't rumors stemming from anger." She did not add that no one in the company believed her any more than he did.

Abruptly he looked up, and smiled. "I know that, Liza. No one is more caring and honest than you."

He motioned to the waitress, indicating that they needed to be served because of their time constraints. The young woman nodded and a few minutes later served their salads.

Their remaining time together was spent in small talk, and Liza was grateful when they were back in the Mercedes, headed to International Air. Once they were parked and about to separate Dave's hands came down on her shoulders, delaying her departure.

"I'm sorry for being a bastard about the employee gossip," he said. "But I just worry about anything that might jeopardize the One Thousand Series project." His gaze intensified. "Am I forgiven?"

She smiled, seeing sincerity reflected on his face. "Nothing to forgive."

"I'll call you," he said. And then he was gone.

Liza went back to her office. Dave was a nice man. Yet she could not shake the feeling that something more than job dedication was motivating him.

Silly, she told herself. Don't let your paranoia contaminate your perceptions. Dave was one of the best friends she had at International Air.

Chapter Eight

THE BALANCE OF THE WEEK PASSED SO FAST THAT LIZA spent Saturday catching up on client files at home. She was glad that Dave had to work, that Erik was teaching first-jump classes at Sampson's Parachute Center, and that Jean was booked for puppet shows. Liza welcomed a change of pace on Sunday and was on her way out of the Mission Church after the service when Pastor Larsen stopped her with his usual praise.

"Your music selections were inspirational today," he said, smiling, the expression lighting up his thin, tired face. "I noticed more than one parishioner wiping his eyes."

"Thank you." Liza grinned as she buttoned her raincoat. "But I'm sure it was your sermon more than the hymns." She glanced up the aisle to the front doors that were now closed against the blustery winter day. The last of their bedraggled congregation had gone; the sanctuary was empty.

He placed a gentle hand on her arm. "I appreciate how

much time you donate to the Mission, Liza." He hesitated. "If it weren't for caring people such as yourself, these poor souls would never find a way off the streets. That's why it's so important to help."

She nodded. But everyone in the city knew it was because of his efforts that so many homeless people were being given a new start. A slight man with lots of energy, the pastor had an unshakable belief that he could make a difference. Knowing that most of the transients who came for his sermon were only taking refuge from the weather, welcoming a warm dry place to sit for an hour or so, did not deter him for a moment.

"How's Jean doing?" he asked, changing the subject. "Haven't seen her for a while."

"Busier all the time." She grinned. "You know Jean. She can't say no if she thinks her puppet shows will make a difference to kids."

There was a silence.

"Both of you girls are like that." His expression softened, remembering.

Girls, she thought, suppressing a smile. He was in his sixties and still remembered her and Jean as little girls who had lost their father, and more recently, their mother. He had conducted her funeral service.

"I wanted to schedule a puppet show here sometime in the spring for some of the homeless kids," he said, then paused. "Think Jean would be up for that?"

"Give her a call." Liza turned back toward the door. "The sooner the better. She's awfully busy these days, but I know she'd love to do it if the two of you can agree on a date."

"I'll call her tomorrow, first thing." He reached in his jacket pocket and pulled out an envelope. "Almost forgot." He handed it to Liza. "I found this in the sermon bible. I have no idea how long it's been there, or who put it there." He paused. "You didn't, did you?"

She shook her head.

"I didn't open it since it was sealed and had your name on the outside." He shrugged. "Probably just someone requesting a hymn for Sunday service."

Liza turned it over in her hand, not recognizing the handwriting. As she broke the seal, he went on, switching the conversation to the very person who weighed on her mind, Nate Garret.

"I wanted to tell you how sorry I was about that fellow who was hit by the car. I hadn't realized you knew him, Liza."

Her hand stilled on the folded sheet of paper she had just pulled from the envelope. "He was one of my clients from work. I had an appointment to meet him here, at the mission." She hesitated. "But he was in the accident before we were able to meet."

"Was he in trouble?"

She nodded. "Only because he was having some emotional problems caused by job stress I think."

"I see." His blue eyes were suddenly probing. "But he was disturbed enough to request seeing you on a Sunday? And you were concerned enough to agree?"

There was a silence.

"I guess that's about it." Being perceptive is one of your gifts, Pastor Larsen, she told him silently. You always see the underlying issue. "After I'd evaluated him I realized that he might not have told me everything." She fingered the folded paper in her hand. "I should have picked up on how upset he was."

"And you think you know what it was that he didn't tell you?"

"I'm not sure. I'll probably never know now."

"You mustn't blame yourself, child," he said, kindly. "The good Lord never expected us to be perfect."

"Thank you." Liza smiled, grateful for his encouraging words. She needed them right now. Hoisting her handbag strap over her shoulder, she stuck her umbrella under her arm in order to free her other hand and then unfolded the sheet of paper.

"I'll say good-bye now as I'm needed in the kitchen," Pastor Larsen said, grinning. "Sunday dinner will be served in an hour."

He gave her arm a fond squeeze, then moved toward the door that connected the sanctuary with the dining room and dormitory. She watched him go, reminded of how fortunate she and Jean were to have him in their lives. A widower and childless, his compassion for others knew no boundaries. He was about to put on one of his other hats—food server for the hungry people of Seattle.

She glanced down at the paper in her hand, expecting a note and a signature. She stared, puzzled. There was no writing at all, only roughly drawn sheet music, complete with staff and notes.

Slowly she walked back to the piano, her thoughts spinning. She had immediately thought of Nate when Pastor Larsen gave her the envelope, that maybe he had sent her a message after all. Now she was confused.

Dropping her purse and umbrella onto the floor, Liza sat down on the piano stool, propped the paper in front of her, and picked out the notes with one finger. She had placed the envelope next to the page and it kept slipping down onto her fingers. Frustrated, she closed it into one of the hymn books that were stacked on the piano. Again she played the notes. And again the discordant sounds made no sense. It was musical gibberish.

Finally Liza stood up. The envelope could not have

been left by Nate who was a brilliant musician according to his wife. But just in case, she decided to check with Maggie. She refolded the paper and put it into her handbag, then grabbed her umbrella and headed for the door a second time.

Better hurry. Liza glanced at her watch. Or you'll be late for your appointment with Sam Paparich.

Before stepping onto the sidewalk Liza hesitated, pulling on her leather gloves. The rain was a steady drizzle and she quickly opened her umbrella, then lifted her coat hood over her hair. Still she was reluctant to move away from the mission entry and into the wind that gusted along the street, skimming water out of puddles to spray everything in its path.

There were no people visible on First Avenue, although cars with steamed-up windows moved in a steady stream of traffic. "Now or never," Liza muttered, and dashed into the maelstrom.

From the corner of her eye she saw another person step from a doorway several buildings away and turn in her direction. She glanced back, noticing it was a man hunched under a black umbrella that obscured his face. She grimaced a smile. It was certainly a day for protection against drowning.

Her feet were soaked before she had gone half a block, and she still had another two to go. This morning she had not found a parking spot close to the Mission Church because of an event at SAFECO Field south of Pioneer Square. Walking that far to the mission sometimes made her uneasy; it wasn't a safe part of town for a lone woman on the street.

But it's midday on Sunday, she reminded herself. Not late at night.

She crossed First Avenue and headed up a side street, slowing her pace. What the hell, she thought. Why run when I'm already wet. An extra minute or two in the rain will not make any difference to the condition of my clothes.

Once away from the traffic, Liza became aware of another sound. She glanced over her shoulder and was surprised to see that the man was still behind her. A coincidence? Surely he wasn't following her.

Liza shivered, suddenly feeling the chill of the damp, cold day. A gust of wind caught the inside of her umbrella, almost blowing it inside out. Quickly, she adjusted it against the wind, allowing the metal supports to right themselves.

She glanced again. The man was closer.

She walked faster. The footsteps kept pace behind her. Her fear was mounting and she began to run. Her umbrella caught at the wind, impeding her flight. Another look behind her jolted her with pure terror.

He was running, too.

Without a second thought, she threw her umbrella into the gutter, then bolted forward, her eyes on her Miata parked on the next block.

For God's sake, why was he running after her? But she did not have time for speculation. She had to make the safety of the car before he caught up. And then what? Her mind boggled. She would not think of that now.

The Miata was her only option; she was off the beaten track of restaurants and tourist shops. There were no open stores in sight. Oblivious to the puddles, Liza plowed right through them, splashing her hose and the hem of her coat with mud.

Liza had her key out before she even reached her car. With one motion she inserted it and yanked the handle at the same time. Another couple of seconds and she was inside, her handbag flung on the passenger seat and the doors locked. But she wasn't safe yet. She had a ragtop. And ragtops could be cut with a knife.

She started the engine, let out the clutch and sped into the street. Her gaze darted over other parked vehicles, into doorways and along the sidewalks.

The man had vanished.

Steering up the hills, she began to shiver, her body trembling uncontrollably. Liza peeled off her gloves and tossed them aside, turned the heat on high, then groped in her handbag for her cell phone. By the time she drove onto the freeway headed north toward Greenwood Avenue, she had also found Sam Paparich's number. She needed to tell him she would be a little late.

But she waited a few minutes until she stopped shaking. Until she was sure that she had not been followed.

Chapter Nine

LIZA DROVE SLOWLY ALONG THE STREET OF THE GREENWOOD neighborhood, checking addresses, looking for Sam Paparich's house. When she spotted it, a modest 1930s clapboard cottage that had been built on the back third of the lot, she found there were no available parking spots. She sighed. Just her luck today.

She circled the block a second time, looking for a space on the street that might have become available. She sighed again, hating the clutter of cars, trailers and utility vehicles that gave the area a run-down appearance despite the steep real estate prices. She'd detest living here without a garage, never knowing how far from her own house she would have to leave her car.

It had stopped raining as Liza backed into a small space between a pickup truck and a jeep. Lucky for me that I drive a sports car and not a sedan, she told herself, or I could be a mile from Sam's house, not a block away.

But as she switched off the engine, Liza felt apprehensive. She was still shaken by what had happened after she left the Mission Church. At least the man had not been able to follow once she had reached the safety of her car.

Still she hesitated.

Glancing around, Liza saw nothing unusual. Several blocks away she heard traffic moving on a main thoroughfare. Two houses down the street a black dog sniffed the front grass, then trotted down the sidewalk to the next lot. Closer at hand, a cat sat on a porch, watching. A normal afternoon in the suburbs, Liza thought.

Get going, she instructed herself. Or you'll paralyze yourself with your own fears.

She grabbed her briefcase from the space under the back window, and with her handbag hanging from her shoulder, got out of the Miata and locked it. Another glance told her no one was in sight, so she stepped over the curb, picked a path across the weed-strewn parking strip and made it to the sidewalk. As she headed for Sam's house she realized the mud had dried on her panty hose and coat, but her sodden shoes squished with each step. The thought of a hot bath was appealing.

She was smiling when Sam opened the door and invited her into a tiny living room. Liza took off her low-heeled pumps, explaining that she had been caught in a downpour. One look at the immaculate carpeting told Liza that she did not want to muddy it with her shoes.

"Mrs. MacDonough, that wasn't necessary," Mary Paparich said, after introductions by her husband. "We're just so grateful that you're helping us."

"My pleasure," Liza said, sitting down on the worn sofa and opening her briefcase. She handed the revised résumé to Sam for review.

As he read over it, Liza took in her surroundings. Sam and Mary were a middle-aged couple, obviously influenced by the seventies if their Birkenstocks and denims were any indication. According to Sam, they had decided early in their marriage that Mary would be a stay-at-home mom and they would manage on his income. Their two sons, both college students who lived at home, worked part time to help pay tuition. The lifestyle of the family depended on Sam's income.

"This is great," Sam said, looking up. "I can't tell you how much I appreciate your help on this. Although I'm good at my job, I'm not handy at writing, especially résumés."

"And I'm not much help to Sam," Mary added. "I have zero experience in putting together a résumé."

"Fortunately, it is my expertise," Liza said, smiling, pleased by their gratitude. Their home was immaculate. It sounded as though their boys had been brought up in a loving home, and something wonderful was baking in the kitchen. Her stomach lurched, reminding her that she had only had coffee for breakfast.

"Your credentials are impeccable, Sam," she went on. "I haven't padded your résumé, just included some of the things you didn't mention, and reworded a few of your sentences." She paused. "Just remember what I told you. You must dazzle potential employers with your fancy footwork. That means putting yourself in the best possible light, even bragging a little, because you know that you will live up to your words, and much more."

Mary beamed. "I really like you, Mrs. MacDonough. You're saying all the things I always tell Sam—that he's an asset to any company. My grandfather used to say that you should never hide your light under a bushelbasket. He said that sometimes we have to speak up, even if it sounds like bragging."

Liza smiled again. Sam and Mary did not have much in the way of financial assets; their investment in family was their asset. She just hoped that Sam would land another job soon or life as they knew it could come crashing down on them.

The contradictions of life, Liza thought, her mind shifting to the affluent lifestyle Nate Garret had given his family. One man dies, the other man loses his job, and the end result is the same: a family in financial crisis.

Liza went over final touches on the résumé with Sam, then had coffee and freshly baked cookies at Mary's insistence. Liza asked them to stay in touch and left between rainsqualls. As she headed back to her car she felt uplifted. Being with people like Sam and Mary made her realize that life was good, despite the pitfalls.

The rain was sudden, unexpected and heavy. Liza sprinted the last half-block. As she veered off the sidewalk to the Miata, she stopped dead in her tracks. Her heart was suddenly beating furiously in her chest.

"Oh, my God!" she cried, hardly able to believe her eyes.

The trunk of her car was wide open. Her canvas athletic bag that held her workout clothes and water bottle had been flung in the street. Her sweatpants pulsated in the river of rain streaming along the gutter, her top was alongside, plastered against the pavement.

Someone had broken into her car!

The back of her neck prickled. She spun around to see . . . no one. For long seconds she stood there, the rain pelting her face, feeling vulnerable: she was a target for anyone who was hidden from sight who could be observing her every movement.

Of their own volition her legs moved, then her hands; she found herself tossing everything back into the trunk whether it was soaking wet or not. She slammed down the lid, then ran for the driver's door, not surprised when it

opened without the key. She gave a cursory glance inside.
There was no one in either of the two bucket seats, so she
slid behind the wheel and started the engine. For the second time that day she pressed the gas pedal to the floor
and headed for the freeway, her body prickling with the
sensation that whoever had broken into her car was watching her frantic escape.

Someone who witnessed her terror.

It was only when she reached I-5 and was driving south
toward the city that she began to think rationally again.
She should have run back to Sam's house, called the
police, reported the break-in of her car and *that someone
was after her.*

Crazy, she told herself. Why would anyone be after her?
Both of today's incidents might only be coincidence.

But as she headed home she wondered. Somewhere she
had read about the statistics of chance. There was a point
when too many coincidences were no longer random
events.

Twenty minutes later Liza drove into her security
garage, then waited until the automatic door had closed
behind her before parking in her reserved stall. Another
resident drove in as she got out of the Miata, but continued to a lower level and was out of sight a moment later.
She grabbed her briefcase and purse, then hesitated before
pushing down the lock on the door. Apprehension crept
up on her.

Someone could be watching her now.

Her glance flickered over the parked vehicles. She recognized all of them as belonging to people who lived in the
building. There was nothing anywhere that indicated anything out of the ordinary. Liza exhaled a long breath. She
was safe.

She slammed the car door and it locked automatically. With keys in hand, she hurried toward the elevator lobby. Then a sound, no more than a vague scraping on the concrete somewhere in the vast underground cavern, brought her up short, uncertain.

Another sound, this time a shuffling noise. Like the sound a person would make if they accidentally scraped against the side of a metal surface like a car?

For a second longer she hesitated.

Should she go back to the Miata or continue on to the elevator? The sound had come from behind her—*beyond her parking stall.* Had someone been waiting for her return, then stayed hidden as the second vehicle came into the garage?

That question gave wings to her feet, and she bolted toward the lobby door, pushed it open and pressed the elevator button. Amazingly, it was on the garage level and opened immediately. Breathless, she leapt inside and jabbed at the button for the twelfth floor.

As the elevator doors closed she heard the lobby door opening. Or was it just now shutting behind her?

When the elevator reached her floor she had the key ready to plunge into the lock. In seconds she was safely ensconced in her apartment, Bella purring at her feet, the bolt and chain locks firmly in place.

Shaking uncontrollably, Liza slid down the wall of the entry hall to sit in silence, her ears straining for any sound. What was she waiting for? A phantom to come out of the shadows and materialize before her very eyes?

She doubted it. But she was still unable to move.

Liza had her hot soaking bath before it got dark after all. By evening, as the lights of Seattle twinkled on at her feet, she felt calmer.

The bogeyman didn't get you, she chided herself. Even if your day felt like you'd been cast into a suspense movie.

She had immediately called Jean, Erik and Dave after she'd regained her perspective, needing some feedback on what had happened. None of them were home. Later, after consideration, she had called the police about her car break-in, even though she knew there was probably nothing they could do but take a report. She'd included the incident in Pioneer Square and that she'd even thought someone might have been in the garage.

Now, as she leaned back in her overstuffed chair, feeling safe so far above the energy of the city, she could hear the words of the cop in her head.

"A woman walking alone in that part of the city is a prime target."

"You say there was no damage to your car? Maybe you forgot to lock the doors. Sounds like kids to me."

"Underground garages echo sounds, and you didn't see anyone. After the other incidents, it's possible that your imagination was running wild."

Restless, Liza stood up, unconvinced that the incidents were unrelated. But why would anyone be after her? It did not make any more sense than the sheet music someone had left for her at the mission.

Maggie, she thought. She was going to call Maggie to see if the sheet music might have been Nate's. Without turning on a light she grabbed her portable phone and took it back to the chair. It rang in her hand.

Startled, she stared at it for a moment before answering. "Hello?"

"That you, Liza?"

"It sure is, Pastor Larsen." She recognized his voice. Surprised to hear from him, she went on, "Don't you have a prayer group at this time?"

"It's about to begin," he said. "But I wanted to make sure that you were okay first."

There was a silence.

"Um, what do you mean?" He rarely called her at home and never on a Sunday, his busiest day of the week.

"Freddie, a man in the prayer group, just told me he had seen a man chasing you after you left the mission today." His tone was concerned.

"Who is Freddie? I didn't see anyone on the street but the man chasing me."

"He's an elderly man who can hardly walk. He has a room overlooking the street and happened to see what was happening." He paused. "He says the guy didn't catch up with you before you reached your car."

"That's true." She drew in a long breath, then let it out slowly. "Did Freddie recognize the man?"

"Never saw him before." The pastor's sigh came over the wire. "Listen, Liza, I have to go now but I wanted to make sure that you were okay. I can't have my piano player in jeopardy," he added with a note of humor.

She had almost blurted out the other incidents, but they could wait. Pastor Larsen had enough on his plate already without worrying about her. She assured him she was just fine, thanked him for calling and hung up with a promise that they would talk about the incident later.

She stared into the gathering darkness of the night, her mind on Freddie. The homeless people all knew one another. New people on the street did not go unnoticed. Did that mean that her pursuer had not been one of them? Again her mind shifted to the sheet of musical notes. She picked up the phone and called Maggie.

"Yes," Maggie confirmed, after Liza had asked after her and the boys and shifted the conversation around to Nate's music compositions. "Nate wrote beautiful songs but nothing like the piece you've described." A hesitation. "Why do you ask?"

"Just curious," Liza said, evasively. "As you know, you've all been on my mind lately."

"I appreciate your concern, Liza."

Liza could hear the tears in her voice. She listened patiently while Maggie gave a progress report on how she was coping. After promising to call soon, Liza hung up.

She went to bed early, drained by the events of the day. But she could not shake her apprehension. What if her scary incidents today were connected? What if someone was after something? And what if that something was the sheet music?

The thought brought her straight up in bed. Where was that paper? Still in her purse? She threw back the quilt and padded across the carpet to the bureau where she had left her handbag. Pulling the folded sheet free, she took it back to bed with her. The glow of light from the city came through the windows and she was able to see well enough to study the notes. They still made no sense, and as she began to doze off, she realized that she should put the paper in a safe place.

Too tired to get up again, she pressed it into her old childhood pajama doll that always sat on her bed. A safe place, she told herself. Hadn't it once held all of her childhood secrets in the pocket of its belly?

She was smiling when she fell asleep.

Chapter Ten

SURPRISINGLY, LIZA SLEPT SOUNDLY AND AWOKE EARLY THE next morning feeling upbeat. She would not allow yesterday's incidents to cloud her day. It was quite possible that it was all coincidence, she told herself as she ground coffee beans. Except for the envelope with the sheet of strange music.

No! She would not think about that now, she wouldn't start the morning with questions and doubts, fear and paranoia.

She sprinkled dry food into Bella's dish, then went to make her bed while the coffee dripped. Back in the kitchen a few minutes later, she sniffed the aroma of Starbucks' house blend that permeated the air. Almost smells better than it tastes, she thought, pouring the dark brew into a pink mug. She grinned at a random thought. Her mother had always chosen pink for her and blue for Jean, and after her mom was gone she had continued the practice with small things, like her favorite mug.

Leaving the cup on the counter, she went to retrieve her newspaper from the hall outside her front door. Reading the *Post Intelligencer* with her first cup of coffee was her morning ritual.

She flipped back the chain, and then her hand hesitated on the bolt. It was *unlocked!*

Impossible, she thought, alarmed. She always checked the locks before she went to bed. She remembered doing it last night *because she was so scared.*

She jumped back against the wall. Fear took her breath. She stared wide-eyed at her door. Was someone out there waiting for her to open it? Her legs bent under her and she grabbed for her hall table, steadying herself. She resisted an urge to scream for help.

It may not do any good. Would anyone even hear her?

Liza sucked in deep breaths, willing herself to stay calm. In seconds reason began to reassert itself. The peephole. Look out the peephole.

She crept back to her door on tiptoes and pressed an eye to the tiny glass. No one was in the floor's hallway. Still, she hesitated. Someone could be hiding behind the stairwell door or standing just beyond her range of vision.

Ridiculous. Get a grip, she commanded herself. This was a high-security condominium. No one but the home-owners and the manager had keys to the building and the code for the garage gate. There had never been a case of vandalism, except for hers right after Martin vanished. She sank back against the wall. And now her door was unlocked again.

But maybe she had been so upset last night that she only thought she had turned the lever for the dead bolt. She *was* on overload; from her years in practice, she knew that people who were stressed-out forgot the very things they always did by rote.

"Dear God," she whispered. "Please let me know the difference between fact and fiction."

Her words spoken aloud brought her back to her senses. Although she was still apprehensive, she was also annoyed with herself. This was her home, her building, her life; she was not about to allow intangible fears to alter her reality. With resolve, Liza went to the door, yanked it open and retrieved her newspaper. It was only when the door was closed again that she let out the breath she had been holding.

There was no one outside her door.

She chained and locked the door, then took her coffee and newspaper to the dining room and sat down at the table. But she found it hard to concentrate and barely skimmed through the pages, ending up with her horoscope for the day: *"This will be a disturbing time. Make sure you watch your back."*

"That's it!" she said, disgusted, tossing the paper aside. "Even my horoscope is negative."

Not that she had ever believed horoscopes. Nevertheless, it was just one more thought she did not need. Either she was going nuts or someone—someone she could not see—was always just behind her. She needed to know which one it was.

She poured more coffee and took it with her into her bedroom; after she showered, she began to dress for work. All the while she told herself that she could not run scared, that she must take action because action cured fear, as her mother always used to say.

Action means talking to the building manager, she decided as she applied eye shadow. It means making sure that no outsider has a key to the building, she added, powdering maniacally over her blush. Most of all it means reminding him that security is very important to city dwellers in high-rise condominiums and, if there has been a breach, the homeowners needed to know about it.

With her new resolve worn like a shield over her navy suit and white blouse, she finished dressing; she then grabbed her coat, purse and briefcase, said good-bye to Bella and marched out the door. But as Liza waited for the elevator her uneasiness returned. She glanced around the quiet hallway, her eyes resting on the door to the stairwell. It was a relief when she was whizzing down through the building to the lobby and the manager's office.

The door was closed and locked. Without hesitation, she crossed the mail area that separated the office from the manager's unit and knocked on his door. For long seconds she thought no one was there and then realized it was only a little past seven in the morning. Joe Felton and his wife Naomi were probably still in bed.

Oh well, Liza thought. They were on-site managers and this was a serious problem that she needed to address in person.

The door opened and Joe, a fortyish, tall, bony man in his pajama bottoms blinked sleepily at her.

"Mrs. MacDonough. Is something wrong?"

"Sorry to bother you this early," she said, softening her words with an apologetic smile. "But I needed to talk to you before I left for work."

"Early is fine." His voice was croaky from sleep. "How can I help you?"

"I've had a couple of incidents in the building that were a bit scary." She decided not to elaborate. He didn't need to know that she was uncertain about them herself, that she had wondered if she were imagining things.

"What happened?" His tone was more alert now.

"I think there was an intruder in the parking garage last night," she said. "And someone may have unlocked my door during the night." She paused, sensing his doubts. Her words sounded silly even to her ears. "It was unlocked this morning and I know I locked it before going to bed."

"Does anyone aside from you have a key?"

She shook her head, feeling more and more like a hysterical female.

His blue eyes narrowed. "Did anyone come into your apartment?"

"They couldn't. I have a chain lock as well."

There was a silence. Joe's wife Naomi appeared behind him, pulling at the cord on her worn fleece robe. She was a foot shorter than her husband and at least ten years older. She inclined her permed head at Liza. "Morning," she said.

"We've never had intruder problems in the building before," Joe went on. "Except for the vandal in your unit a year ago." He paused, his gaze intent. "And there was no forced entry then, was there."

It was not a question. Was he implying that everything was a figment of her imagination, that she might have staged the destruction herself? Maybe because of her state of mind?

Whoa, she instructed herself. He had not said any of those things. You're becoming far too sensitive, Liza MacDonough. *Paranoid* came to mind . . . again.

"The police decided that someone had a passkey."

He nodded. "I remember."

"Look," Liza said. "I realize this sounds far-fetched." She spread her hands. "But sometimes a person knows things, things that can't be substantiated. This is one of those times."

"What happened in the garage?" Joe asked, going right back to her earlier statement. "Were you accosted? Was there an intruder?"

Oh God, Liza thought. This is going badly. She was

coming across as a frightened old lady. They already had a couple of those in the building.

"Um, no, nothing like that." She paused, knowing how this all sounded to the Feltons. Crazy. "I heard someone," she said finally.

"You didn't see anyone?"

"No, but I know someone was there."

"How?" Naomi asked. "Did they say something?"

There was a hesitation.

"I know I can't prove anything, okay?" Liza didn't care that she sounded exasperated. "What I really need to know is if anyone other than residents have keys to the building or the code to the garage gate."

"No one I know of," Joe said at once. "But I can't guarantee that because homeowners could give a key or the garage code to service people."

Another silence.

"But as you know, our front door and garage entrances are on camera; I'll run the tape to make sure there were no intruders."

She stepped back. "Thanks, Joe. I'd appreciate that."

"Glad to do it. If we have anything underhanded going on in the building, I need to know about it."

She said her good-bye, and after they shut their door, she strode back to the elevator and continued down to the parking garage. There were other people driving out of the building as she hurried to her car. Everything was normal. She breathed a sigh of relief as the gate closed behind her and she headed toward her office.

She would not think about coming home again after dark.

That afternoon there was a knock on her office door. Then it was pushed open by a tall man with curly black hair. "Liza MacDonough?" he asked.

"I'm Liza," she said, putting down her pen and closing the file she had been updating after her last client. "How can I help you?"

His dark eyes were probing, She didn't recognize him as an employee, and he was not a client; she had no other appointments scheduled for the day.

"Owen Barnes," he said. He stepped in front of her desk, reached into an inside pocket of his jacket and pulled out his badge case, which he opened for her to see. "Homicide detective with the Seattle police department." He spoke at a fast-forward speed.

Her eyes went from his badge to his ruggedly handsome face. "A homicide detective?"

"Yeah." He withdrew his ID and put it back into his pocket. "Just wanted to ask you a few questions about a client of yours, a Nate Garret."

"Homicide?" she repeated. Her mind boggled. "Then Nate's death wasn't an accident?"

"I didn't say that." His even tone gave nothing away, nor did his expression. "I'm just following up on something one of the witnesses at the scene said, making sure that we have all of the facts before we close the case." He paused. "Just routine."

"I thought it was already ruled an accident."

"That was the preliminary cause of death." He glanced at the chair in front of her desk. "Mind if I sit down?"

"Oh, of course not. Please do."

"Thanks."

As he lowered himself into the chair, stretched out his legs and removed a pad and pen from his pocket, Liza realized what sounded different about his voice. He had an East Coast accent—New York? New Jersey?

"So," he began. "I understand that you'd seen Mr. Garret, professionally of course."

"Yes, but how did you know that?"

He smiled for the first time, relaxing the stern cast of his features, and she realized that he was in his mid-to-late thirties, younger than she had first thought. "I could say sources, but in this case it was nothing so mysterious." He crossed one ankle over the other. "His wife told me."

Liza glanced away. Owen Barnes spoke softly, yet there was a ring of intensity to his rapid speech pattern, a leashed energy. He seemed low keyed, but she sensed that his body was on full alert. She would not want to be the criminal who crossed him.

"What did this witness say?" Liza asked, masking her interest behind a professional tone.

"A man," he said, clarifying. "The guy thought Nate's sudden leap into traffic seemed involuntary."

"What are you saying, that someone pushed him?" She sucked in a breath. "Did this man see who might have done that?"

He shook his head. "There were a half-dozen or more people waiting to cross, and most of them appeared to be homeless men on the way to the Mission Church. This guy only saw Garret bolt into traffic, not why he did."

"Surely those other men were asked about what happened."

"Unfortunately, there were no other witnesses who came forward." There was a note of disgust in his tone. "That's often the case with transients. They don't want any contact with the police, afraid we'll run a make on them."

"A make?"

"Uh-huh. An identity check through our computers."

Liza remembered Pastor Larsen talking about that issue. Many people who found themselves on the street were running from something and did not want to give their real name, or worse yet, be fingerprinted.

Liza looked him straight in the eye. "So how can I help your investigation, Detective Barnes?"

He did not hesitate. "I want to know how you evaluated Nate's emotional state before he died."

A silence.

"The rights of a person change after they die," he said quietly, anticipating her reluctance to go against patient confidentiality issues.

"I know," she said finally. Another pause. "I just don't want to say anything that would hurt his family."

"Understood. Nor do I. I just want to clear the case so the family can get on with things, like insurance issues."

She nodded, then pulled her fingers from her hair. God, she was doing it again. Her nervous habit. "Nate was probably at burnout," she said finally. "The deadlines in the computer lab were horrendous, and I felt the long hours and pressure were getting to him. He needed a little time off."

"And was that possible?"

She blew out her breath. "His boss—" She broke off. "Is this confidential, Detective Barnes?"

He nodded. "Promise."

Liza hesitated, then went on, cautiously. "His boss, Hawk Bohlman, pushes his people pretty hard."

She decided that the detective did not need to know the full extent of Hawk's treatment of his programmers. She opened her mouth to tell him about the odd sheet of musical notes, of being followed, the break-in of her car and her unlocked door, but quickly closed it without speaking. It sounded too crazy, even to her.

"Do you think he was suicidal?"

"Absolutely not!" She leaned forward over her desk. "Nate loved his family. He was talented in many areas of his life. He would never be a suicide."

The detective almost grinned at her passionate response, but she watched him control himself.

"And you don't know of anyone who would want to do him bodily harm?"

"What would make you ask that, Detective Barnes?" she asked, coolly.

He spread his hands. "Just checking out all possibilities of his death."

She tilted her chin. "And they are?"

"Accident, suicide, homicide."

Their eyes locked.

"I hope you aren't serious."

"I'm always serious, Mrs. MacDonough."

A long silence went by.

"It had to be an accident." She dared him to defy her, clarify why he was questioning her.

"Why?"

"Because Nate Garret had too much to live for, that's why." Her words seemed to echo off the walls.

He held up his hands in supplication. "Hey. I'm only a homicide detective trying to fill out a report." A dimple flashed briefly on each side of his mouth. "Okay?"

She shrugged, noncommittal.

He put his pad and pen back in his pocket, then stood up. "I guess that's about it. No more questions."

"That's good," she said, tartly, reacting to a condescending tone in his voice. "Because I don't know anything more than I've told you."

He hesitated. "Then that's it, as I said."

She stood, pushing her chair behind her, contriving a firm demeanor. "I can't substantiate anything that would indicate a suicide."

"Or a homicide?"

"Of course not. That's unthinkable."

There was a flicker of something in his eyes, but it was gone before she could identify it. Her face warmed. He had seen through her professional veneer—her feelings of guilt concerning Nate.

He strode to the door, then turned to face her. "By the way, Liza, uh, Mrs. MacDonough. If I ever crash and burn I'll look you up." He grinned wider than before, revealing a perfect set of white teeth. "No man could have a more supportive . . ." he hesitated for emphasis, "mental health counselor."

"Employment placement counselor," she corrected him.

His dark brows shot up, he saluted her, and then he was gone.

She stared at the door for long seconds, their conversation replaying in her head. Why had a *homicide* detective come to her office? Did they suspect that Nate had been murdered? That his death might be connected to International Air?

An incredible thought, she told herself. And yet, something was going on behind the scenes. But what? And why would it be so important that someone had to die?

Chapter Eleven

LIZA WAITED AS ALICE'S SECRETARY TRANSFERRED HER CALL. After Detective Owen Barnes was gone, she had tried to make sense of his visit. Maybe it was as he had said, routine. Or maybe it was something more. His questions had reminded her that she still had not gotten the replacement printout of terminated employees.

"Hi Liza." Alice's voice sounded in her ear. "I know why you're calling. The printout, right?"

"Well, two reasons actually." The last thing Liza wanted to do was apply pressure. Alice's work schedule was already more than one person could handle, unless that person was Alice. "But yes, I would like the printout."

"Sorry, I didn't get right to it but . . ." Her words trailed off.

"But, what?"

"A little problem."

"With giving me that list?"

"Uh-huh. Sort of."

"What do you mean?"

There was a silence.

"Come on Alice, what happened? I didn't know there was a rule against an interoffice exchange of information unless there were confidentiality issues, and I don't think there are in this instance."

Another hesitation.

"You know that I had a date with a new man."

"Yes, I did. What does that have to do with this?"

"Only that the person I'm seeing doesn't think I should be giving out printouts from my department."

"My God, Alice. Why are *you* giving out that information to another person in the first place?"

She hesitated again.

"You're right, Liza. I shouldn't have, but in light of his position in the company, and your missing personnel file I—"

"What?" Liza interrupted. "What do you mean, *my missing personnel file?*"

"It's gone. We can't find it."

"How can that be?"

"That's what I'd like to know." Alice drew in a long breath, sounding distracted. "All I do know is that a clerk tried to file a recent performance review, and the hardcopy folder was not there. Although all pertinent information is computerized, the backup documentation for active employees is stored in individual files in our cabinets."

This time Liza was silent, taken aback.

"Could it have been misplaced because of a computer glitch."

"Of course not. Hard files and computer files are two separate things." Alice's sigh came over the line. "I have a person working on it, but it's not top priority. We're assuming it's been placed in the wrong cabinet and we'll locate it soon."

"And what if you don't?"

"We will." A pause. "But if we don't, the onus is on me, not you, Liza. Everyone knows you work here and can reestablish your credentials, including your security clearance. It's your signature on the hard copy documents that we'll need again if we can't find the file."

"Shit," Liza said. "I hope you locate it. I don't want to fill out all those forms again." She switched the phone to her other ear, changing the subject back to the previous one. "So, who is this person who doesn't think I should have a printout?"

Alice's breathing came over the wire. "Look, Liza, I like him a lot, but it's too early in the relationship to confide details." A pause. "I'll send another printout this afternoon, okay? In the meantime I'm checking out the reasons behind his opinion on your printout. I'm going to talk with Hawk and some other people over in the computer lab."

"About what?"

"I have to dash," Alice said, cutting her off. "But expect the list within the hour."

The dial tone sounded in Liza's ear. She hadn't even gotten to her second reason for calling: when they could get together at the gym.

She replaced the receiver into its cradle. Why did she feel even worse now than after the detective left with all her questions unanswered?

For God's sake, what's going on, she asked herself.

She had no answers.

"Maybe this is the wrong thing to do," Liza muttered, crossing the covered walkway to the building that housed the computer lab. "But-you-have-to-do-it," she added aloud, each word in step with her footfall. She had to start somewhere to find out what—if anything—was going on behind the scenes at International Air.

The guard stopped her at the entrance. She requested to see Hawk, the guard called Hawk and she was allowed into the computer lab. She stood waiting right inside the door, watching as Hawk approached, weaving his way through the rows of computers.

He inclined his balding head toward her and it caught the reflection of the recessed lighting in the ceiling. His narrowed eyes beneath thick salt and pepper brows held her gaze as he strode up to her.

"So, what can I do for you, Mrs. MacDonough?" His tone was businesslike, noncommittal.

She managed a smile. "As you know, I'm the counselor for—"

"I know your credentials, Mrs. MacDonough."

He sounded impatient. She controlled her annoyance. She would not be intimidated by his attitude. "Good," she said, curtly. "Then we can get right down to business."

He nodded, waiting.

No sugarcoating, Liza instructed herself. Be direct with this man. "I would like a rundown on why some of your current employees have been let go, when all the indicators point to there being more work than people already on staff here can handle."

"Looks are deceiving, Mrs. MacDonough. Most of the company layoffs have been in other departments."

"I realize that, she said. "I'm just asking about your department."

"There are the main programmers here and there are the backup people." He hesitated, obviously annoyed. "If you'd done your homework you'd realize we haven't let one programmer go, only lower echelon workers whose skills—or should I say their lack of skills—do not transfer into other jobs when their current position terminates."

"Are you saying the terminated people were only temporary employees?"

"Yes, they were in a way." He hesitated. "In the best-case scenario people with limited abilities last a few years with the company if there is a need for them. If not . . ." He shrugged. "They are let go." His gaze was probing. "Of course, many of these people did not choose to continue their education in order to step up into better positions."

She glanced beyond Hawk, to the computer station that had once been Nate's, as pointed out by Dave on her first visit to the lab. Another man sat there now; as she watched, he glanced in her direction.

"An example of someone who did pursue more education," Hawk said, following her glance. "That's John Ellis. He used to be on the lowest income level here, but he took advanced computer training, discovered he had an aptitude for programming and landed Nate's job." He paused. "The company looks favorably on job-focused ambition."

"I see."

His impatient sigh indicated he needed to go. "Anything else?"

Liza did not hesitate, looking him straight in the eyes. "I would like to see the employee work evaluations for the recently terminated employees in your lab."

He breathed in a shocked breath. "That's not company policy."

"Is it against company policy?" she asked, countering.

There was a hesitation.

"You know Cooper Delmonte?" he said finally.

She nodded. "I've met Cooper."

"Good. One of Cooper's jobs as number-two person in

this lab is to see to employee work evaluations." He could not hide his impatience. "You need to talk to Cooper, not me."

He motioned to someone at the other end of the huge room. Liza saw that it was Cooper as he started toward her. By the time he reached them he was smiling broadly.

"Hi Liza," he said, coming to a stop in front of them. He opened his hands in a gesture of "what-can-I-do-for-you?"

"Hi, Cooper," she said. "Hawk says you're the person I need to talk to."

"How so?" His smile broadened, but he seemed to brace himself for whatever it was that she wanted of him.

"Mrs. MacDonough would like copies of our work evaluations on certain employees," Hawk said, impatiently. Do you have time to take care of this? I sure as hell don't."

"Sure," Cooper said, disregarding Hawk's impolite remark. He directed Liza to his alcove at one side of the room. Hawk said his brief good-bye, then headed for his own office. She watched him close his door against the low hum of the computers—and her questions. She suddenly realized that Hawk had not attended Nate's funeral. She wondered why.

"Whew," Liza said, stepping into Cooper's work space. "I don't think that man likes me."

"Don't worry about it." Cooper motioned her to a chair near his desk. "Hawk takes his job too seriously."

She combed her fingers though her hair, removing the stray ends from where they had fallen forward over her face. "Don't we all."

"Yup, that's true." He paused, grinning. "So, what can I do for you?"

Briefly she explained what she needed, omitting her

own reservations about something being amiss with why the company might be terminating people.

"That's an easy request." He fingered through his Rolodex and then wrote down a name and number on a pad. "Sylvia Kempton, the division manager under your friend Alice, is the person to talk to." He tore the page off the pad and handed it to her. "She received all of our performance reviews, and they'll either be in current or terminated files." He hesitated. "The only problem might have to do with the confidentiality issue. But you can talk to Sylvia. She's the expert on that, not me."

"I appreciate this, Cooper."

"You're quite welcome." He walked her back to the door. "I understand your need to know facts; I come up against that responsibility all the time in my position." He paused. "I don't envy you your job, Liza."

She left him at the guard's station and headed back to her office in the next building. She appreciated Cooper's cooperation. He didn't let the concern over his little boy's health interfere with his job, but she bet he was worried sick about little Brandon.

The closer she got to her office the more she began to worry again. How could her personnel file be missing? Because someone needed to know all about her? Someone who didn't like her probing into the layoff policies of International Air? But what good would the information in her file do anyone, she wondered. Her life was an open book, to use the old cliché.

Her phone began to ring as she stepped into her office. She ran to pick up the receiver.

"Liza MacDonough."

"It's me," Jean's soft voice said in her ear. "Where have you been? I've been trying to reach you for almost an hour, and your secretary was clueless."

"Intercompany errands."

"I thought secretaries and assistants did that in big companies like International Air."

"Hardly. That only happens in the movies." Liza sat on the corner of the desk, amused by Jean's concept of the corporate world. Her sister had stated long ago that she could never be one of the penguins who wore black suits and white blouses or shirts to an office. Liza could never convince her that the dress code had been relaxed a long time ago.

"I can tell you're grinning, Liza. Did I say something funny?"

"I was just remembering your perception of a big company office, that's all," she said evadingly. "You're not a conformist."

"Neither are you, even though you do choose to work for that huge company."

"What's up?" Liza changed the subject back to Jean's reason for calling her. She noticed that the layoff printout had been placed on her desk while she was gone. A note from Alice was attached to the top sheet.

"I'm hoping you can substitute for me at the hospital puppet show on Saturday night," Jean's voice continued in her ear.

"How come? You and Bill have a hot date or something?"

A sigh. "Nothing so romantic. I double-booked without realizing my mistake until it was too late. Now I'd hate to have to cancel one of the hospitals. By now the kids are really looking forward to the event."

"Oh." Liza thought fast. Dave had mentioned dinner sometime on the weekend, if he didn't have to work. Since he had not brought up the subject again, she figured it was safe to help Jean.

"Bill will help me, and my current apprentice—you've met Sarah—will assist you. If you can do it," she added, hopefully.

"I think I can," Liza said, slowly, still thinking. Saturday was the logical night for a date with Dave, but there was still Friday night.

"Please, please, please!" Jean pleaded, reminding her of how Jean used to beg her to do something when they were kids.

"What the hell," she said, grinning at her sister's dramatics, the very thing Jean maintained was Liza's forte. Jean was her sister and Dave was only her friend, and she knew that he'd understand that family obligations were important. "You can count on me, Jean. I'll do it."

"Great. We'll talk later about the shows, okay?"

After a few more minutes they hung up, and Liza grabbed the printout and Alice's attached note. Alice had suggested they meet at the gym the first of next week.

Liza turned to the termination list, but her mind was still on Alice. The two of them used to work out at least twice a week. She wondered again what was bothering her friend. The secretive new guy in her life? Liza grinned at a sudden thought. Maybe Alice was getting her exercise in bed these days.

She put the printout in her briefcase to take home. Still uncertain of exactly what she was looking for, aside from determining if there was company manipulation involved, Liza decided she was too nervous about the whole matter to concentrate on it at work. Besides, she had downloaded a copy of her client files on her computer at home. She could crosscheck them with the list, although a quick glance at the names told her that most of the people on Alice's printout were not employees she had seen in a professional capacity.

A short time later, as she left the office for the day, the phone rang and she ran back to take the call.

"Good, I caught you." Erik's chuckle came over the line. "I figured you'd still be there. You're becoming a workaholic, Liza."

"I was just leaving."

"Hey, I won't keep you. Just need you to do me a very big favor."

She braced herself. "Sorry, I'm not up for skydiving, mountain climbing or a bungee jump."

He laughed. "Don't I know it. You don't know what you're missing."

"Like missing my life?" she asked, dryly.

"Seriously," he said. "What are you up to tonight? You wouldn't happen to be free, would you?"

"Is this an offer of a date?"

"Yeah, you could say that. I need someone to run my slide projector for my class."

"I thought you had a remote clicker."

"I do, but I don't have three hands. I'm also demonstrating the physical moves along with the slide show."

"Well, I'd planned to work at home."

"Uh-huh. Like I said, all work and no play makes Liza . . . tired."

"You consider it playing to operate a slide projector?"

"Yup, because of the other huge job perk that goes with it."

"What's that?"

"You get to spend time with me."

She burst out laughing.

"Okay, but only if you give me a little time at home first, so I can go over some work I need to do."

"Please," he said sotto voce. "Don't sound too enthused. I know how wild you are about my first-jump classes."

"Yeah. We both know I'm *dying* to take your class."

"I won't hold my breath."

They hung up with his promise to pick her up before seven, giving her almost an hour to review the list. She was smiling as she headed toward her car, happy to see a break in the rain. Erik was incorrigible when it came to the sports that terrified most people.

"Hey Brown Eyes! Where you going in such a hurry?" Dave fell into step with her.

"Where else?" She grinned up at him. "Home."

"Have time to stop for a drink?"

"How about a rain check." She had reached the Miata and opened the door. "I have some work to do before the weekend." She hated fibbing, but there was no point in causing friction. Dave's animosity toward Erik was obvious.

"Jeez, I understand that." He hesitated. "Maybe this weekend will work out." He grinned. "For a change."

"Sounds like a plan, work permitting." She didn't mention the puppet show on Saturday night either. If he was really able to shake free of obligations, then she could negotiate for Friday. The last thing she wanted him to think was that she was making excuses, putting him off.

He held the door as she climbed in. "Hawk told me you were over in the lab earlier."

"Uh-huh." She dropped her briefcase and purse onto the passenger seat. "I needed to check out some personnel issues with him." She gave a laugh. "Turns out I needed to talk to Cooper instead."

A gust of wind whipped through his red hair, and he patted it back into place. "It's always the personnel problems that are the biggest challenge in running a company. Inefficient people create headaches."

"That's for sure." She shook her head. "Like misplacing my personnel file."

"What?"

"Mine is missing." She glanced at the cumulus clouds building on the twilight horizon. "And crazy as it sounds, I can't help wondering if its being gone is connected to my prying."

His expression didn't change, but she felt him tense. "What do you mean?"

"I told you about what I'm hearing from my clients." She shrugged. "Maybe there's some truth to the rumors. Maybe someone thought they could get something on me from my file, use the information against me if needed."

"For God's sake, Liza. That does sound crazy." A hesitation. "Is there something in your file that can't see the light of day?"

"Of course not!" She started the engine. "But why is it gone?"

Slowly, he shook his head. "It's not gone. It's misplaced."

"By one of those inefficient employees?"

He laughed. "You got it."

She raised her brows. "Time will tell." Then she closed the door, unwound the window and said good-bye. He was still standing there when she drove out of the parking lot.

Chapter Twelve

"I'M A BLOCK AWAY." ERIK WAS CALLING FROM HIS CELL phone. "You ready to go, sweetheart?"

"I was just waiting to hear your sexy voice," Liza said, reverting to their easy way of kidding each other. "Meet you out front in one minute."

She hung up the phone, slipped into a down jacket, grabbed her gloves and handbag and headed for the lobby. She popped out of the front entrance door onto the inlaid stone floor of the building's portico just as Erik drove his Jeep Cherokee into the load zone. He had the passenger door open by the time she reached it.

"Hey, way to go," he said, his pale blue eyes appraising her. "Can't remember the last time I saw you in Levi jeans."

"You just don't see me all the time, that's why," she told him, settling onto the leather seat and buckling up.

There was a silence.

"Too true. Not like the old days."

Liza glanced, meeting his eyes. She knew he alluded to

their college days, which had been an ongoing struggle for both of them. Being able to laugh at pinching pennies, dressing in worn jeans and sharing cheap meals had enabled them to keep a sense of humor. And to keep on. She smiled, remembering.

"Thank God!"

He cocked a brow. "I wouldn't say that. There are worse things than being poor."

"Like what?"

"Circumstances beyond our control, problems that have a direct bearing on the quality of our lives—like no longer having the wind at our back."

There was a silence.

"Like my life now?" Liza asked.

He looked away to concentrate on his driving. What had she seen: disapproval, sadness?

He reached to pat her knotted hands on her lap. "Your life will get better, kiddo." He glanced at her. "Has to."

"Maybe it won't." Her voice wobbled.

"It will." He downshifted onto the northbound on-ramp of I-5. Once he had manipulated the Cherokee into the car pool lane, he shot her another quick look. "I promise, sweetheart."

Somehow, maybe because she needed to, Liza believed him.

"Hey, what brings you to Erik's class? Don't tell me you want to be a jumper?"

Liza turned at the sound of the familiar voice.

"The last thing I'd ever do—willingly—is jump out of an airplane, Cooper," she replied, surprised to see Cooper Delmonte. Beyond him the dozen or so students who had come into the classroom at Sampson's Parachute Center—a building on the grounds of a small airport north of

Seattle in Snohomish County—talked in hushed tones. Erik's class would begin in five minutes.

He grinned. "So what are you doing here then?" He glanced at Erik who was writing the safety steps of parachute jumping onto a blackboard.

"Just helping out my friend—uh, my and Martin's friend." Good Lord, she thought. Dave might hear from Cooper that she was with Erik, after she'd turned down drinks with him on the pretext of having to work.

"How so?"

"Erik and I were college friends."

"A boyfriend?"

"Nope, although I think Erik is a very good catch." She laughed. "If any woman could ever catch Erik."

"So?"

"So—what are you asking?" she countered.

He shrugged. "Nothing really. Just idle curiosity." He paused. "I was surprised that you knew Erik and wondered how." He hesitated. "I expect that it's just a coincidence that you are here—and so am I."

"Yeah, it sure is."

There was a silence.

"So your husband also knew Erik?"

She smiled at him for the first time, remembering. "I met Martin through Erik, and it was love at first sight."

"Wonderful state to be in." Although he grinned, his expression seemed fixed.

She had a sudden thought. "You sound as if you don't believe in love at first sight?"

"Of course I do. Doesn't everyone?" He grinned. "But I also believe that many people think they're in love and they're really only in lust."

"That sounds cynical, Cooper."

He waved his hands in a gesture of surrender. "I'm only

saying that men are interested in some women because of lust, others because of love."

"And women look at it from a different perspective."

"Women are more sensitive in matters of love."

She shook her head, clucking her tongue. "My thoughts exactly." She hesitated. "Unfortunately."

He considered her words. "I would think both are the case with you, Liza."

"Both?"

Slowly, he took off his leather jacket and draped it over a chair in the front row of folding chairs. "Uh-huh," he said, meeting her eyes again. "A man could easily fall in love—and lust—with you."

She blinked quickly. Surely Cooper was not flirting with her. She stared at him for long seconds. His expression was unreadable, and she decided to change the subject back to his original question.

"Erik needed a third hand tonight for his presentation."

He shifted his weight from one foot to the other, waiting for her to continue.

She shrugged. "That's why I'm here, to help Erik." She paused. "You didn't say why you're here."

"Easy question. I'm the pilot for these guys." He waved a hand. "When they're ready for that first jump, that is."

"Oh." Liza tried to hide her surprise.

He anticipated the question she didn't ask. "Extra money," he said, abruptly serious. "Abbey and I are pretty strapped right now with Brandon's medical expenses." He gave a sad laugh. "Insurance doesn't pay for everything."

"I'm sorry," she said. "About little Brandon. He's a sweet child."

He nodded. "We have hope that he'll be better after the surgery."

"When is that scheduled?" She had assumed Brandon would have had his operation by now.

"He caught a virus and the surgery had to be postponed." He hesitated. "We expect the docs will give the go-ahead in the next week or ten days."

"I hope he makes a full recovery," Liza said, feeling sympathy for him and his little family. She moved away to put down her purse and gloves on a chair at the side of the room, then placed her jacket on top of them. Turning, she saw that Cooper had followed her.

"I heard that you were selling Martin's share in the Cessna to his two partners. Is that a firm deal?"

She nodded. "Unless Martin comes back." She hesitated, feeling uncomfortable. She didn't like discussing the deal; it made her feel like crying to think that Martin might never pilot his plane again.

"Then it isn't sold?"

She took a deep breath. Don't be so sensitive, she instructed herself. He's only asking a question.

"I retained an option to buy it back if—" She broke off, unable to finish her thought.

He patted her arm gently. "Sorry, I didn't mean to pry." His tone echoed his words. "I wanted to buy Martin's share but hesitated to make an offer under the circumstances. My own fault for not asking sooner."

Liza stepped back, fastening an unruly curl behind her ear. How could Cooper afford to even consider buying an airplane? she wondered. She would never have sold it but for the fact that it was too costly to keep without Martin's income. Life, she thought. There was no predicting its unexpected changes.

"Hey, Cooper." Erik turned from the blackboard, finally taking notice of their conversation. "I didn't know you knew Liza."

"Well." Cooper grinned. "I hadn't realized that you two knew each other either."

"Liza and I go way back."

"That's what I'm told," Cooper said, his gaze shifting between Liza and Erik.

Erik put down the chalk, moving to the easel that held three-by-five-foot-demos. He thumbed through the cards to check proper sequence. "Of course I knew you worked in the lab with Martin. Since Liza works at International Air I should have figured you'd know her."

"Everyone works for International Air except you, man."

"True," Erik said, grinning. "I'm a rebel."

"Without a cause?" Cooper asked, joking. "How about a beer after class." His invitation included Liza.

"Sure," Erik said. "So long as that's okay with Liza."

Cooper's gaze shifted to her.

"Okay, if it's a quick one." Liza glanced away, too aware of Cooper's steady regard. "Can't forget that a workday comes early."

Erik strode to the podium, smiling a welcome to the group of would-be skydivers. He indicated that it was time to begin the class.

Cooper took a seat near the front and Liza moved to the side of the screen, her finger on the remote clicker, waiting for the signal from Erik to begin the slides.

She felt eyes on her but when she glanced at Cooper he was looking straight ahead. Liza was glad when the lights were lowered and she faded into the shadows. She looked forward to the class being over.

"You think you'll need me on the weekend?" Cooper sipped his beer, his question directed to Erik.

"Yeah, I think a couple of the guys are ready." Erik, paused, considering. "I'll give you a call by Wednesday, okay?"

Cooper nodded. "I'll figure on it then."

Liza put down her wine glass. She was ready to go. A half-hour at the airport tavern was long enough. Her eyelids were beginning to droop. She needed to get home and into bed.

"Hey, Liza," Erik said, teasing. "Are you daydreaming?"

"Huh?" She came back to the conversation with a jolt. Both men stared at her, grinning.

"Cooper and I were just talking about Martin's plane, and I asked you what's the latest from your private investigator."

"I'm behind the times here." Cooper scratched his chin, his brown eyes interested. "What's this about a PI?"

"I hired a man to investigate Martin's disappearance," she began, and paused, giving Erik a meaningful look. What in hell are you doing? she asked him silently. You know that I don't share details of my personal life with someone I hardly know.

"Liza's in limbo, personally and financially, until something is resolved one way or another," Erik said, jumping into the sudden silence.

"Tough situation." Cooper shook his head, his eyes on Liza. "It's really a puzzle."

"Yeah, it is." Liza glanced away, uncomfortable with where the conversation had gone. She switched topics to Cooper's son. "I'm doing another puppet show on Saturday night at the hospital, and I'd like to invite Brandon to attend," she said, smiling. "He really seemed to enjoy the last performance at the hospital."

Cooper grinned back. "He hasn't stopped talking about the show yet, or your sister. He thinks she has some magic up her sleeve—or something." Cooper's expression softened. His love for his son was obvious, and Liza found herself liking him better. "I'll tell Abbey. I'm sure they'll want to go—if Brandon can."

She nodded, pleased. "All the kids love Jean's shows. The puppets have been a family thing for years. Even Martin helped stuff the puppets for the production I'm doing on Saturday." Her words trailed off. She didn't want to open up the subject of Martin again.

Realizing his earlier blunder, Erik pushed back his empty glass and stood up. "Time for the sandman."

Within a few minutes good-byes had been said and she and Erik were back in the jeep headed home.

"Sorry, Liza."

She glanced at him. Light from the dash cast shadows on Erik's face, and she could tell that he was concerned.

"About what?" She grinned. "Asking me to listen to all that macho stuff about cheating death?"

"No, you know, my slip of the tongue about Wendall." He accelerated around a slower car. "I assumed everyone knew about the guy since he is out there asking questions."

There was a silence.

"You're right. Everyone probably does know. I think I'm just supersensitive about Martin."

He reached and gave her knee a squeeze. "Then I'm forgiven?"

"Only if you grant me three wishes. Winning the lotto, my own South Sea island, and no more boring talk about flying without wings."

For a second he was quiet. Then he burst out laughing. "You got 'em, kiddo. At least the last one."

She laughed, too. But she knew that everyone would soon hear about her private investigator. Now that Cooper knew, he would probably tell others.

C'mon, girl, grow a thicker skin, she instructed herself. What did it matter? No harm done.

Chapter Thirteen

"WE HAVE TO STOP MEETING LIKE THIS, BROWN EYES."

Liza turned from locking her car door, smiling. "Are you suggesting something . . . clandestine?"

"Only if you're agreeable."

The wind off Elliott Bay whipped her coat around the top of her boots, and she put a hand down to stop her skirt from flying up her legs. "Should have known," she said, shaking her head. "The only other person at International Air who puts in more hours than I do is—she spread an arm in a gesture of a Jay Leno introduction—Mr. Dave."

"Too true," he said, crossing the few feet from his car to hers. "Very few people start work—he glanced at his watch—two hours before anyone else, before it's even daylight."

They started walking across the well-lit parking lot toward the office building. "I'm not so noble," Liza said. "I have some files to update before my regular day begins."

There was a silence.

"Because you went to your friend Erik's first-jump class last night?"

"How did you know that?"

"Just talked to Cooper, not five minutes ago on my cell phone."

"And—" She was pricked with sudden annoyance.

"And nothing." He grabbed the door to the building and opened it. "I just realized why you weren't free for drinks last night."

Liza started through the doorway, her response abruptly cool. "Erik needed help to run his slide projector. He was in a bind, and since he's helped me so many times in the past I couldn't refuse." After she spoke, Liza realized her words sounded like an excuse. "I'm always there for my friends when they need me," she added firmly.

"One of your endearing qualities, Liza." He had held on to the door to keep it from closing too fast, and his arm kept her from moving forward. He smiled down at her. "Sorry if mentioning it offended you but—" He let the door go. "I'm jealous of the time you spend with another guy."

His words were candid, his expression was serious, and she appreciated his honesty, which seemed genuine. She might be overreacting to his comments.

"And I'm sorry if I seem grouchy," she said. "I didn't sleep very well last night."

"Insomnia? Not chronic I hope."

"Nope." She quickened her steps toward the hall that led to her office. "Only a passing phase."

"Good."

They hesitated when they reached the place where they would separate to go in opposite directions.

"I'll call you about getting together on the weekend."

She nodded, disconcerted by the intimate tone to his voice.

Without warning, he grabbed her upper arms, pulled her closer and kissed her. "To seal our date," he said, a smile lighting his face momentarily.

Taken aback, Liza only nodded again. Then he was gone, striding off toward the walkway to the computer lab before she could think of an intelligent response—or explain about the puppet show on Saturday night.

But she liked the feel of his lips on hers; perhaps it was finally time to move on with her life.

By noon Liza felt as though she had already put in a full day and was glad she had brought her lunch and a thermos of coffee. She sat back in her chair, breathed deeply and then unwrapped her sandwich. One nice thing had happened this morning; Sam Paparich had called with news of a job. He had thanked her many times during their conversation.

"I got the job, Mrs. MacDonough, thanks to you. If you hadn't rewritten my résumé, and quizzed me on how to answer interview questions, I know I wouldn't have gotten it."

She had assured him that it was his credentials that counted, but she knew that his résumé and the interview had been critical. His call had cheered her up. Helping people is what life is all about, she had reminded herself after hanging up.

Having finishing her lunch Liza sat sipping her coffee, thinking. She'd called Dave earlier to tell him about the puppet show and was told that he was out of the office for the day. She wondered if Alice had ever found her missing personnel file, and decided to call her.

Alice picked up on the first ring, surprising Liza. She had expected an assistant during the lunch hour.

"Hey, you skipping lunch these days?" Liza asked, joking. "No diet—or man—is worth not eating."

"Yeah, that's for sure."

There was a hesitation.

"Actually, Liza, I was just contemplating whether or not I should call you. I think I need to talk with you."

"You haven't found my personnel file," Liza said, second guessing her.

"We did find it." A pause. "That is, we didn't actually look for it because it turned up in its rightful place in the files."

Another pause.

"How can that be, if it was gone?"

"That's just it." Alice's tone sounded a note too shrill. "Maybe it was there all the time and we just missed it."

"But you don't think so."

"I don't know." Alice expelled a long breath. "I don't know what to think—about several things."

"What do you mean?" Liza switched the receiver to her other ear. "Alice are you upset about something?"

A silence.

"I guess I am." Her voice was lower.

"Can you talk about it?"

"I think I have to." Alice hesitated. "I've uncovered a problem, Liza."

"What?" Liza pressed the receiver into her ear. She had never before heard such uncertainty in Alice's voice. "I'll come up to your office. I'm free for another twenty minutes."

"No. No, please don't do that." Alice lowered her voice. "Let's meet at the gym, in the sauna where we can talk in private." Another hesitation. "Say six-thirty?"

"I'll be there, Alice." Liza pushed back her chair and stood up. "But I could also come up to your office right now—"

"No," Alice said again, interrupting. "I'll see you at six-thirty in the sauna."

The dial tone sounded in Liza's ear.

For the rest of the afternoon Alice's words surfaced in Liza's mind. Her friend was more than concerned; she sounded fearful. She was glad when her work was completed for the day and she was free to close her office.

She needed to know what was scaring her friend.

By the time Liza finally made it out to her car she was running late. Two last minute phone calls, both from stressed clients, took almost half an hour. It was already going on seven when she turned off Olive Street into the parking lot, locked her car and jaywalked across the street to the entrance of the athletic club's gym.

Kristi, the regular girl behind the desk, glanced up. "Alice said to tell you she'd be in the dressing room."

Liza nodded, and paused. "She been here long?"

"Uh-huh." She glanced at her watch. "Almost an hour, but she exercised first."

"I hope so." Liza grinned. "Alice can't stand the sauna for more than ten or fifteen minutes."

"That's all you'll get to have tonight, ten or fifteen minutes," Kristi said. "Unless you want to skip your massages that are scheduled at seven."

Liza started toward the stairs. "I'm late so I'd better get up there now."

Liza went into the empty dressing room and quickly took off her clothes. Apparently Alice was already in the sauna booth. Hurrying, she banded her hair into a ponytail, placed her clothing in a locker, and wrapped herself in one of the club's big towels. She headed for the sauna, her water bottle in hand, her rubber thongs flapping against her heels.

She smiled, remembering the first time she and Alice

had dared the sauna rooms, knowing they had to be naked in front of other people. They'd talked about doing it for weeks as they exercised, had even bought identical water bottles and thongs before actually making the decision.

The exercise room on the floor above Liza sounded crowded, and she could hear rock music coming from an aerobic class, but the shower and sauna area was almost deserted. Only one of the sauna rooms was in use and Liza assumed Alice occupied it, although she wondered why Alice had not waited for her. Probably because you're late, dummy, she told herself. Alice must have doubted that you were even going to make it.

Liza opened the door, made sure it was Alice on the bench, then stepped inside and closed it. The heat hit her like a physical blow and she had an urge to skip the whole thing. "Hey, don't you think it's a little too steamy?" she asked her friend.

No answer.

"Don't tell me you've dozed off," Liza said, feeling a twinge of apprehension. "No wonder you're sleepy. It's too hot."

Again no response.

Alice sat draped in her towel at the end of the bench, leaning against the corner wall. Her eyes were closed and tentacles of steam swirled around her, like snakes who had been charmed out of their lairs.

Liza crossed to her, picked up the water bottle that lay on its side at her feet, and held it out to her friend. "Wake up, Alice. Let's get our rubdown. You've been in here long enough."

Once more, no response.

Alarmed, Liza grabbed her shoulder. Before she could rouse her, Alice slumped forward and slipped off the bench to the floor.

Horrified, Liza flung both water bottles aside, yanked the door open, and the steam billowed out with her screams for help.

"Up here!" she hollered. "Someone help me!"

Then she tried to pull Alice from the sauna room. By the time Kristi and others were there to help, Liza's limbs shook from the exertion of trying to lift Alice. She gulped back hysteria. "We've got to start CPR." Her voice shook with fear. "Help me get her flat."

"Did she have a heart attack?" someone asked.

"Nine-one-one's been called," Kristi said, sounding as scared as Liza. "They're on the way."

A woman in sweats and a headband stepped forward. "I'm a nurse." She knelt beside Alice, her eyes meeting Liza's momentarily. "Let me do this."

"We've got to wake her up." Liza fought panic. "She must have passed out."

The woman nudged Liza away, but her voice was gentle. "You need to get dressed."

Liza hadn't realized the towel had slipped away from her body.

Alice was pronounced dead at the scene.

"She may have fainted and died from heatstroke," a paramedic said, noncommittal. "Could even have been her heart. We can't say at this point."

"What we do know is that she was in there too long without water, and it was too hot." He pointed to Alice's water bottle. It was almost full under its screwed on cap.

Liza watched as they placed Alice on a gurney, shrouded her body, and wheeled her away. There was no siren as the emergency vehicle pulled away from the curb and headed toward the hospital morgue.

Oh, dear God! Liza thought, her eyes blurring. How can

this be? Alice was in good health; she'd never mentioned a health problem. She swallowed back a sob, trying to control herself. If only I had been on time Alice would not have gotten overheated—and died.

"Mrs. MacDonough?" The male voice was vaguely familiar.

She turned to face Detective Barnes. Surprised, her first thought was that she was glad to be dressed, her thongs and water bottle zipped back into her athletic bag. Somehow her clothing felt like a weak defense against her feelings of loss and guilt.

"Why are you here, Detective Barnes?" she asked, shakily. "Aren't you a homicide detective?"

He stepped into the reception area of the club where she was sitting, trying to compose herself before attempting to drive. He'd obviously just come from the sauna; he must have arrived while she was dressing. She had already given her statement to the first police officer who had arrived with the paramedics.

"Yeah, that's my professional title."

"Then why are you here?" She swallowed hard, trying to maintain her composure. "This isn't a homicide."

He inclined his head. "How do you know that?"

She shook her head, fighting more tears. "I only know that Alice went into the sauna without me because I was late." She hesitated. "She stayed too long, waiting for me."

He nodded. "Why were you late?"

"Phone calls from clients."

"Emergencies?" His voice was low, interested.

"A client call always involves a problem."

"So that made you late. How late?"

She glanced down. "Twenty minutes."

There was a silence.

"Tell me what happened."

She went through the chronology for a second time, starting with her brief comments to Kristi, to entering the sauna and finding Alice sitting on the bench with her eyes closed. She drew in a ragged breath. "Then I called for help, and you know the rest."

He had been jotting notes as she spoke and now he looked up. "I guess that's all," he said finally, and put his notebook into his pocket. "I'll walk you out to your car." A hesitation. "Are you okay to drive?"

"I think so," she said, sounding unsteady.

He led her out of the reception area, then hesitated. "I need to check one more thing first. Be right back."

He headed back toward the sauna, and she followed. When he paused in the doorway Liza almost bumped into him, but she hardly noticed. Her eyes were on the place where she had discovered Alice; yellow plastic tape roped off the area and two policemen stood guard, making sure that the scene remained secure, that no one contaminated it with their presence. Several other plainclothesmen were inspecting the sauna room and the space around the door. Alice's water bottle had been closed into a large plastic bag.

"What's going on?" Liza managed to say, surprised that Alice's death was causing this type of activity.

He glanced at her, as noncommittal as the medic had been. "Routine. Homicide always checks out sudden-death scenes, to make sure that the person died from natural causes." A hesitation. "Even the water in your friend's bottle will be analyzed, although there doesn't seem to be any indication of foul play here."

She licked her lips, unconvinced.

"Were you thinking there might be something wrong? Mrs. MacDonough?"

She shook her head. "I don't know what to think. I only know that Alice is dead, and I can't believe that's possible." Liza's gaze darted between Detective Barnes and the men working the death scene, watching as he spoke to one of the officers. Then he took her arm and led her back to the front entrance.

"My car is in the lot across the street," she said.

"I know. I'll see you over there."

How had he known that? she wondered as they crossed the pavement, shiny from the recent rain. At the Miata, she paused to open the door and throw her things onto the passenger seat. Then she turned back to the detective.

"What do you really think, Detective Barnes?"

A gust of wind lifted his curly hair and a slight smile touched his lips. "I think you should go home and try to sleep," he said. "I'll call you tomorrow." He hesitated. "I'll know more then, after the medical examiner has finished."

"Will there be an autopsy?"

He shrugged. "That's up to the medical examiner."

He held the door for her and she had no option but to get into her car. In seconds she was out on Olive headed toward Boren Avenue where she would turn up the hills to her condo on Spring Street. She had only gone a block when she noticed the Seattle Police cruiser turn into traffic behind her. It followed her all the way to her condo, but kept going straight when she swung into her driveway. As the automatic garage door lifted she was plagued with questions, one uppermost in her thoughts.

What in the hell was happening? First Nate, now Alice.

It worked. He had done it again. The thought was intoxicating.

He watched from a doorway down the street. The sirens had attracted a crowd on the sidewalk, but the police had pushed them back, creating a barrier between the Women's Health Club and the spectators.

Perfect, he thought, stepping deeper into the doorway, feeling the chill of a north wind. No one would notice him among all the other scurrying people in the downtown area. He was safe.

A police car had arrived almost immediately behind Medic One, followed in a couple of minutes by other officers.

"You dumb fuckers," he had muttered aloud. "You'll never figure this one out."

The wind strengthened as the minutes passed and he turned up his collar. His fingers began to tingle from the cold, but he relished the sensation. They were all so goddamned ignorant. He could afford a little discomfort in exchange for the jolt of power their stupidity gave him.

His earlier worry was forgotten. His concern about how he would kill her was a distant memory. All he had ever needed to do was keep his wits and think it through. In the end it had been easy—and so perfect. She would die in a place reserved for women only.

When he saw the covered body being lifted into the hearse, he knew for certain it was over. She was dead, no longer a threat to him. Still he lingered, savoring his power over all of them. He waited until he saw the man escort Liza MacDonough across the street to her car, hesitating for a few minutes while they talked, and then watched Liza drive away.

She drove past his hiding place, looking straight ahead. But in the light from the street, he caught a brief glimpse of moisture on her cheeks.

A bonus.

About to step out of the doorway he saw the police car swing in behind the Miata. Damn! he thought, and waited until both vehicles were out of sight.

Next time, he told himself. For the moment, nothing could take away his sense of ultimate power. He could wait to deal with Liza MacDonough.

But not for long.

Chapter Fourteen

BY ROTE, LIZA PEELED OFF HER CLOTHING, TOOK A SHOWER and slipped into a nightgown. Then she sat in the dark, the haunting music of Kenny G. turned low, Bella asleep on her lap, and stared at the lights of the city. Out on Elliott Bay a glittering superferry, like an enchanted ship from a fairy tale, glided over the water toward a distant island in Puget Sound.

Tears streamed down her cheeks unchecked. Alice was dead. Flamboyant, outgoing Alice, whose biggest hope in the world was to find a man and get married, was gone forever. That was no fairy tale.

The phone rang, startling her. Bella jumped from her lap and Liza hurried to the kitchen and grabbed the receiver from the wall-mounted telephone.

"Hello?" Her voice wobbled.

"I'm downstairs," Dave said. "I heard what happened. Buzz me in."

"I . . . I'm not up for company and—"

"Just buzz," he interrupted, his voice concerned. "I'm coming up."

She opened her front door to him several minutes later. He hesitated for several seconds, his green eyes filled with concern, his red hair in disarray, as though he had been raking his fingers through it. Without a word he pulled her into his arms, holding her while her tears soaked into his sport jacket. For God's sake, take control, she told herself. You're not a little kid. But her efforts to calm herself did no good. She simply could not stop crying.

"How did you know . . . about Alice?" Liza asked when she could finally speak.

"Shhh. I'll explain in a moment."

He led her to the sofa and they sat down, his arm still around her shoulders. With Dave comforting her, the darkness seemed to enfold Liza with a sense of peace. Only the reflected lights of the city and the tranquil music intruded into the room.

"Better now?" he whispered a short time later.

She nodded.

"Good." He kissed her forehead, much as a father would soothe a child.

A long silence went by.

"Hawk told me about Alice," he said finally.

She straightened, lifting her head from his shoulder. "But how would Hawk know? It only happened a couple of hours ago."

"One of the men in the lab told him. The guy's wife is the best friend of Alice's roommate. A police officer went to Alice's apartment with the sad news. The roommate was upset, called the friend who called her husband at the lab."

"The roommate knew I was there, too?"

"Yeah, the cop mentioned that you were there." A pause. "Even if he hadn't, I probably would have assumed you might have been because you and Alice often worked out together."

More tears welled in her eyes. "I don't know what happened. How could she die like that?"

There was a hesitation.

"Were you with her when she died?"

Liza shook her head. With halting sentences she told him what she knew, how she had found Alice. "There was no sign of anything wrong—except she was dead."

"I'm so sorry, Brown Eyes. It was an awful thing to go through."

"If only I hadn't been late." Her words lost their volume. "I feel so guilty."

He pulled her back into the curve of his arm. "This isn't your fault. No one can predict death."

"Thank you, Dave," she said, softly. "You're a good friend."

Another silence.

"Do you think you'll be able to sleep?"

"I don't know. My whole body feels wired, like a current is running through my veins."

"You have any whiskey around here?"

She shook her head. "Only a bottle of wine in the refrigerator."

Again he kissed her head, then gently extricated his arm and stood up. "Be right back."

She heard him get the wine, then the glasses. While he uncorked the bottle she understood why everyone at International Air liked him so much. He was a genuinely caring man.

Dave came back with the wine and they sat in silence sipping it and listening to the music. When she emptied her glass he refilled it.

"I'll get drunk," she said, protesting.

"Good. We'll get drunk together."

"Aren't you forgetting that you have to drive?"

She sensed his grin. "Guess I forgot to tell you. I'm staying here tonight."

"But—"

"No buts." A pause. "Don't worry. I'll behave. Tonight is a mission of mercy, not a seduction, okay?"

She relaxed even more, and by the time he helped her into bed, she was too tipsy to protest. True to his word, he did not take advantage of the situation, and as she drifted toward sleep, Liza felt safer than she had in a long time. And that was the last thing she remembered before morning.

Dave left even before she was out of bed, having been beeped on his beeper. He had made sure she was all right, advised her to take a sick day and told her the coffee was dripping in the kitchen. Then he blew her a kiss and was gone.

Liza went to work anyway; staying home meant dwelling on what had happened. Besides, if she canceled appointments she would never catch up.

During her lunch break Liza faced up to what she had been thinking all morning: she needed to talk to Alice's office staff, explain what had happened. Alice had treated her employees like family, especially when they were having hard times, professionally or personally. Also, she wanted to ask a few questions about her own personnel file that had gone missing and then mysteriously returned. And whatever recent concerns Alice had been worried about, in particular the problem she had wanted to discuss with Liza in private. Although Alice would not have confided to her employees, one of them may have noticed if something was amiss.

Swallowing back her own feelings, Liza headed up to Alice's office. With each step she fought back tears. You must *do* this—you must *face* this—she told herself. Alice is not coming back.

She stepped into the Human Resources Department and hesitated. On the other side of the large room of individual work stations was Alice's office. She moved toward the reception desk and Pat, Alice's secretary, looked up as she approached. Without a word, the petite, middle-aged woman got to her feet and embraced her.

"How could this happen, Liza?" she asked, stepping back and blinking hard.

Liza shook her head, fighting her own tears. "She was already gone when I got there, Pat." She hesitated. "One of the medics thought she may have been in the sauna too long."

Briefly, Liza told her what she knew, that she had come to work despite her grief because she believed that was what Alice would have wanted her to do.

Pat nodded. "Same here. If all of Alice's friends stayed home they'd have to shut down half the company."

They discussed the good times they'd had with Alice and then Liza broached the second reason she was there.

"I understand my personnel file was missing."

"It was misplaced," Pat said. "Or else it was simply stuck against another file and we missed it." She shrugged. "That happens sometimes because there are so many of them. Sylvia—you know Sylvia Kempton?"

"She's the division manager under Alice."

"Uh-huh. Well Sylvia said the whole filing system of hard copies needs to be reorganized." She hesitated. "Maybe that will happen now since Sylvia is the logical choice to fill Alice's position." More tears welled in Pat's brown eyes. "Poor Alice. Dying like that when she'd finally found Mr. Right."

"Alice told you about the new man in her life?"

Pat grabbed a Kleenex and dabbed at her eyes. "Only that she'd fallen for this wonderful guy. She didn't tell me his name, and I never saw him. I think he was so important to her that she worried about jinxing their relationship if she talked about it too soon."

"So you don't know anything about him?"

"Nothing." She paused. "But the last couple of days Alice seemed preoccupied, maybe even upset. I wanted to ask her what was wrong but didn't dare. I was afraid they might have broken up."

There was a silence.

"And no one else in the office knew about him either? Not even Sylvia Kempton?"

"I don't think so. I was Alice's main confidante. You could ask Sylvia but she's been out sick all week."

"I know," Liza said. "I've tried to make an appointment with her, about another matter."

Pat's eyes were suddenly direct. "Is it important to know who he was? Alice's death was from natural causes, wasn't it?"

Liza was momentarily disconcerted by the question. "I have no reason to believe otherwise, Pat. I just thought someone should tell him, in case he didn't know."

She expelled a long breath. "You're right. But I guess there's nothing we can do about it since we don't know who he is."

Several minutes later Liza left Pat with a promise to call her if she had any new information. But disturbing thoughts spun in her head as she descended the stairs to the lower floor. *Her file had been missing.* Alice had been a perfectionist about her work and something had happened that upset her, something she would only discuss in private. Had it been Alice's intention to talk about the new man in her life? Liza wondered. Or was the problem about the missing file? Or was it about the employee termination printout?

Now she would probably never know.

Liza left the office right after her last client. Although appointments had kept her mind occupied, her free time had been spent explaining Alice's death to coworkers and her boss, Al Stark. She felt drained by the time she turned her car up the hills toward home, avoiding Olive Street. Right now she could not imagine ever working out at that exercise gym again.

Erik called shortly after she got home, offering to come over after she told him what had happened the night before. Liza assured him that she was adjusting and only needed sleep. When Dave called with a similar suggestion she told him the same thing. But when she awoke dreaming about Martin in the water again, she had second thoughts. By morning she felt as fatigued as she had the night before.

Once back in her office the day melted away from a busy schedule. It was late afternoon before she was able to call Detective Barnes, wondering why she hadn't heard from him in the two days since Alice's death. Surprisingly, he picked up the phone himself.

"Detective Barnes," he said, his New York accent resonating in his words.

"This is Liza MacDonough." She hesitated, uncertain. "I was wondering if the medical examiner had come to any conclusions yet about Alice Emery—if there was an autopsy."

"Ah, Mrs. MacDonough," he said. "How are you doing?"

"Better, but still incredulous. I can't believe Alice died like that."

"Like what?"

She switched the receiver to her other ear. Odd question. "Like she did, in the sauna."

"Yeah, well it seems it was natural causes." A pause. "She'd been on a diet, was probably already dehydrated and shouldn't have been taking a sauna. Plain and simple. Her heart stopped."

"But, she was healthy."

"All the more shocking." His sigh came over the wire. "Her medical records show a heart murmur, probably hadn't given her a problem until the other night."

"I didn't know about that."

"And the medical examiner found traces of a diet suppressant in her blood."

"Diet pills?"

"That's right." A hesitation. "By the way, the water in her bottle tested pure." He gave an ironic laugh. "As pure as any water is these days."

The receiver felt hot against her ear and she realized she'd been pressing it into her head. "That's it?"

"For us it is. The death was ruled accidental and her death certificate signed. It will probably be listed in The *Seattle Times* obituaries today. The body was released for cremation just a few hours ago."

"Cremation?"

"That's what I was told. As instructed by her family."

Liza thanked him and hung up, wondering why she had the impression that Detective Barnes was not as convinced about the postmortem outcome as he said. Nevertheless, it was over. Her living, breathing friend of a few days ago was being reduced to ashes. She swallowed hard, striving to control another urge to cry.

No! she told herself. Stop being a drama queen. It's life—people die. Remember Alice as she was. That is what she would want you to do.

She did not realize her hand still rested on the receiver until the phone rang under it. She yanked it up, thinking it was Barnes calling back.

"Yes?"

"It's Pat from upstairs."

"Oh, Pat. How can I help you?"

"I only have a minute to talk," she began. "My grandson's birthday party." A pause. "But I remembered a nickname that Alice once called this man in her life."

"What was it?" Liza's words shot out of her mouth like a burst of rifle fire.

"Snake something. I only remember Snake."

It was an anticlimax. "That's it?"

"Yes, I'm sorry I don't know more." Another pause. "I know it's not his real name. I wanted to tell you just in case it meant something to you."

"I appreciate that." Liza thanked her and the dial tone buzzed in her ear. She stared at the phone, repeating *Snake* over and over in her mind, wondering why it jogged something in her memory.

Then she remembered where she had heard the name before. Snakeoil—the overheard conversation in the computer lab. She threw on her coat, grabbed her things and almost ran out to her car. Two minutes later she was headed home, impatient to get to her computer. She felt excited and apprehensive at the same time.

Hell, admit it, she told herself. You don't know what you're feeling these days.

Liza sat before her computer, typing commands to access United Online, her entry to the Web. Once there, she searched for a CB forum, and wondered if it had anything to do with CB radios that truckers used. The men she'd overheard talking in the computer lab had definitely called it that. She felt a surge of adrenaline when the screen came alive with an actual listing of chat forums.

For long seconds she hesitated. Then she clicked her mouse to scroll the series of topics, looking for anything with CB in it. Which meant what exactly? she asked herself. And what did it have to do with computer programmers?

She laughed when she found the CB forum; *Cyber Bullshit* had nothing to do with truckers.

She went into several threads, and they were totally unrelated to anything about computer-lab nerds. She continued to surf the forum.

Her hand stilled on the mouse, her eyes glued to the thread line that read: Computer music.

She clicked on it because it was so irrelevant to the content of the forum, and her mind flashed to the sheet music left for her at the Mission Church.

There were only three posts. It was not a thread that was of interest to many people.

Liza brought the first post up on her screen. She straightened on her chair, suddenly feeling the hair raise on the back of her neck. She resisted the impulse to look over her shoulder, knowing her entry door was double-locked.

No one can see you on your own computer, she reminded herself. But her apprehension remained. What if she was on someone's buddy list, and they realized she was reading their posts?

No one would recognize her tag because it didn't include her real name. On her home computer she was Moonspin after Moon Spinner, Jean's puppet.

"We must retrieve Bojangles's latest piece," was the first post from Snakeoil.

Those were the names from the conversation in the lab.

"How and when?" Comet responded.

"Do whatever it takes, and soon." Skydiver wrote in the third post, dated three days earlier—*before Alice's death.* "Just remember, we're all in this together."

In what? Liza asked herself. A conspiracy that involved International Air? Something Alice had discovered, perhaps the problem she wanted to discuss with her in the sauna?

She continued to scroll topics and found nothing else that was written by Skydiver, Comet or Bojangles.

She logged off.

And then sat looking at the blank screen. What did it mean? Maybe nothing. Maybe it was all coincidence. Maybe Bojangles, Comet and Snakeoil all lived across the earth from Seattle. Maybe she was jumping to conclusions, making crazy assumptions because she had been primed by her clients' accusations about the company and feeling guilty about Alice's death.

And maybe she wasn't.

What if Snakeoil worked at IA? Then Comet did as well. What if Bojangles was Nate? And the *latest piece* was the sheet of musical notes that had been left for her at the Mission Church?

But why would they exchange messages on an open forum?

The answer was instant. Because E-mail can be traced and conversations can be overheard, as she knew very well.

Liza felt the crawly sensation on the back of her neck again. Was Snakeoil the same Snake that Pat had told her about—Alice's new man?

Oh God! Liza thought. What did it all mean?

Chapter Fifteen

LIZA WAS READY FOR WORK EARLY THE NEXT MORNING, BUT she had a third cup of coffee, waiting for a decent hour to telephone Maggie Garret. She needed to know if Nate belonged to United Online. At seven-thirty she made the call.

"Oh Liza," Maggie said. "It's ESP. I've been thinking of calling you today."

Liza tensed. Had Maggie heard about Alice's death?

"You once offered your professional help if I ever needed it," she went on, and Liza realized that Maggie didn't know about what had happened to Alice. Liza decided not to tell her; Maggie didn't need to hear about another sudden death of an IA employee. "Does your offer still stand?" Maggie asked.

"Yes, of course it does, Maggie." Liza walked into the dining room from the kitchen, stretching out the coiled cord. "What can I do for you?"

"I'm having some problems with the boys." Her sigh came over the wires. "Especially Josh, my fourteen-year-old."

"What kind of problems?"

"It's like he doesn't care about school, or his friends, or any of the sports he was involved in." A pause. "I know he was devastated by his dad's death, and hasn't had time to adjust yet but . . ." Her voice trailed off.

Liza waited, giving Maggie time to compose herself. She could hear that Maggie was close to tears.

"I'm worried about how he's handling his grief, afraid that it'll become a way of life if I don't do something to stop him."

"That's very wise of you." Maggie was not blinded by her own grief; her first concern was for the welfare of her boys. Sad, Liza thought. She and Nate had sacrificed everything for a big income and then become trapped by a lifestyle that was beyond their means—with tragic results.

"And Pete, he's eleven, is acting like nothing happened, that his father isn't dead."

"And your youngest? How is he doing?"

"Seems to be adjusting the best of the three. But he's had several bedwetting accidents, and he's seven."

There was a silence.

"Maggie, would you be receptive to family counseling?"

A long breath came over the line. "A short time ago, when I believed our family was perfect, I might not have been, but things have changed. I need help in coping with this. I want my boys to be happy again. They're my whole life now." She gulped. "Liza, I'd appreciate it very much if you'd take us on as a family?"

"Family counseling isn't my expertise, Maggie." Liza plucked dead leaves from the herb plants that she grew in the garden window of the dining room, considering options. "But I have an old friend, an excellent therapist who specializes in family counseling. I highly recommend him." She moved back to the kitchen. "I can give you his name if you'd like."

"I'd appreciate that, but I'd hoped you could help us right away."

"I think Erik has emergency appointments built into his schedule." She gave Maggie Erik's name and phone number and instructed her to mention she'd referred them. "He'll give you a session even if he has to adjust his own time to do that, Maggie. He's a very caring man who understands what happens to a family when a loved one dies."

"I'll call him right away." A silence. "I'm sorry, Liza. I jumped right into my own problems, but you called for a reason."

"I did." Liza switched the phone to her other ear as she turned back toward the dining room. Then, realizing that she was pacing, she sat down on a kitchen stool. "I wanted to ask you if Nate belonged to United Online."

"He did," Maggie said. "I saw the charges on our Visa bill."

"Do you know anything about the forums he frequented?"

"I'm sorry, but I don't. I've never had much interest in the computer beyond word processing."

"Lots of people don't," Liza said, glancing at the clock. She needed to get going.

"Why do you ask?" Maggie cleared her throat. "You don't think Nate was involved in one of those cyber-sex forums, do you?"

"Oh God no! Sorry if I misled you, Maggie. I was just wondering if there were online people we needed to notify," she said, improvising. "It occurred to me that he might have friends on the net, like some of the other programmers do."

"He never mentioned it."

"Then I won't worry about it."

There was a brief silence.

"Well, I've got to dash, but I'm so glad that you're contacting Erik," Liza said, changing the subject again. "I think he can help you and your boys cope with what's happened."

"Thanks, Liza. I can't tell you how much your input means to me. I'll let you know how it goes."

"You're welcome, Maggie, and I look forward to hearing from you." A pause as Liza had another idea. "Actually, I do have a suggestion for something you and the boys could do as a family. Did you know that my sister owns Puget Puppeteers?"

"Yes, I heard about her wonderful shows from Abbey Delmonte."

"All the kids love Jean's productions," Liza said. "The reason I mention this is that I'm filling in for her at Hilltop Medical Center tomorrow night. The show is for pediatric patients. I'd love it if you came and brought the boys." She hesitated, smiling. "The puppets always have a message that is uplifting to kids." She drew in a breath. "And this story is about two little girls who also went through the death of their father. It's really very good, Maggie. My sister wrote the script that was based on what happened to us when our father died."

"Oh, I'm sorry. I didn't know."

"I'll tell you about it some day."

"What time does it start?"

"Seven P.M.," Liza replied.

"We'll be there. And thanks again, Liza." The phone went dead as Maggie disconnected.

Slowly, Liza replaced the receiver into its cradle. Then she grabbed her things and headed for the elevator that would take her to the garage level. Her conversation with Maggie had not given her very much new information. But she had learned that Nate was on United Online. *Maybe he was Bojangles.*

The minute she stepped into her office building Liza realized that there was a sense of excitement in the air: people in the hall were animated and vocal. "What's going on?" she asked one of the workers.

"The One Thousand Series jet is having its first testing aloft today," he told her. "Everyone has his fingers crossed."

She stopped in her tracks. She had known that today was D-day—and forgotten. Dave must be on pins and needles. A lot was riding on how well the software actually functioned in controlling the working parts of their new prototype.

Liza thanked the fellow, then sprang forward and hurried to her office. She needed to call Dave. He must be wondering why she hadn't been more supportive about such an important day. If the innovative software really performed as he hoped, it would streamline flying and reduce the possibility of pilot error. Success would mean a huge career boost for Dave. Oh God! She had been out in the ozone because of her own problems.

She called him the moment she stepped into her office. He picked up the phone after the first ring.

"I wanted you to know that I'm rooting for a perfect flight," she said without identifying herself.

"Thanks, Liza. I knew you were in my corner." She heard the anxiety in his voice. "It's a big event in my life." He gave a laugh. "I think I could say my career is riding on how well things go in the next few days."

"Surely not your career?"

"Well, at least my future with the company." He paused.

"But it helps to know you're on my side. I figured you hadn't forgotten my big day."

"But I should have—"

He interrupted. "I know you've been under your own stress, Brown Eyes." A hesitation. "Since we already have a tentative date for this weekend, what do you say we celebrate if this flight goes well. Say tomorrow night?"

A silence dropped between them.

"Dave," she began, wondering why he hadn't mentioned celebrating before, when they'd talked about a dinner date. If he had she probably wouldn't have agreed to the puppet show. "I can't tomorrow night. But I'll be out there rooting for success." His silence was so long that Liza jumped into the void with her excuse. "I promised Jean I'd fill in for a puppet show on Saturday night."

"Isn't that a lot to ask of you after . . . Alice?"

"I'd already agreed to do the show before that happened." She hesitated, feeling awful about disappointing him. "And since we didn't have a firm date for Saturday night I figured we could—"

"But you need downtime, Liza," he said, interrupting again. "You can't just keep going . . . like nothing happened. You need to give yourself some time to get over your friend's death."

She picked up a pen and doodled on her desk pad, trying not to feel guilty, remembering how caring he'd been to her when Alice died. He was a good friend and she hated knowing that she'd let him down.

"I know that, Dave," she said finally. "And I want to celebrate with you. Can we figure out a time? Maybe after the puppet show?"

"Okay then," he said, agreeing. "If possible, we can at least have a toast after your show. Where is it?"

"Hilltop Medical Center, the children's wing."

Another silence.

"We'll connect later then," he said, a trifle too cheerful. "After I know how the tests go."

As they were about to hang up, Liza blurted, "Good luck, Dave."

"Thanks, Brown Eyes. I hope we won't need it. Talk to you later."

Liza sat staring at the phone after they'd hung up. She felt unsettled, knowing how disappointed he was on top of his stress over the One Thousand Series jet. She would make it up to him. The last thing she wanted to do was jeopardize their friendship.

Liza woke up antsy on Saturday morning. Unable to concentrate on her own work for most of the day, she went to the hospital early to make sure the stage and props would be ready for the seven o'clock performance. Sarah, Jean's trainee, arrived a short time later and the set-up went smoothly.

Oh Martin, she thought, as she unpacked the puppets, remembering that he had helped sew and stuff some of them. Where are you now? What was so terrible that you would disappear without a word? For long seconds she cradled Earth Mother in her arms, the last one Martin had worked on and the star of tonight's production. The beautiful marionette, elaborately gowned in green satin, was Liza's favorite. Jean had created her in the likeness of their mother, complete with similar wisdom and character traits that she had incorporated into the story.

Shortly before curtain time Maggie arrived with all three boys. While Sarah, a young mother with children of her own, gave the boys a brief demonstration of puppetry, Maggie was able to update Liza about what had transpired since their conversation.

"Dr. Lindstrom gave me an emergency appointment when I called him yesterday morning. The boys and I saw him at five last night."

Liza suppressed a smile. *Dr. Lindstrom*. Strange to hear her unconventional friend referred to as *doctor*. "How did it go?"

"Great. All three of my boys were really taken with him." She hesitated. "Especially Josh who was intrigued by all of the framed photos on his office walls."

"Yes, those pictures would fascinate any boy." Liza did smile then. "Although bungee jumping, mountain climbing and jumping out of planes takes the meaning of sports to the limit. In my opinion," she added.

"Mine, too." Maggie grinned back. "But it got Josh thinking about how much he loved his own sports, and that's what matters to me right now." She hesitated. "Dr. Lindstrom was really a positive influence on all of us."

About to take their seats, Maggie turned back to Liza. "Abbey Delmonte asked me to thank you for the invitation, but Brandon has to stay away from possible exposure to another infection. His surgery is scheduled for early next week."

"Will you let me know how it goes?"

Maggie nodded and then sat down with her boys.

The curtain opened and the show began. Liza was immediately caught up in the voices and action of the characters, and the story of two lost orphans who fall into a rushing stream. Terrified, they wash up behind a dangerous waterfall and discover a secret tunnel to Earth Mother's magical kingdom. The black passageway gradually brightened as a white light illuminated the splendor of Earth Mother's domain.

Working the puppets, listening to the Oohs and Ahhs from children in the audience, Liza again marveled at

Jean's talent and creativity. Not only was the story imaginative and unique, it incorporated a message of hope for the sick children. And the way she'd figured out how to use lights and sound for dramatic effect was next to genius.

The curtain fell to applause, whistles and hoots from the kids who had regained new confidence in their own future. Liza felt blessed.

Because Sarah had a babysitter at home with time constraints, Liza told her that she would handle dismantling the stage and repacking. Sarah left right after Maggie and the audience of kids had been taken back to their hospital rooms.

Fred, a man from the hospital maintenance crew, helped her dismantle the stage. Liza left him folding chairs while she took the puppets outside to Jean's van.

She used a side entrance to the employee parking lot next to the alley, unlocked the van and placed the box of carefully wrapped puppets on the passenger seat. Closing the door, she heard something behind her.

The hairs on the back of her neck prickled a warning.

She spun around, her back against the van she had just locked. A shape had separated from the blackness of the alley; the figure looked like a street person, but in the shadows she could not see clearly. She knew by the size and build that it was a man.

The moment stretched between them.

Then the man started forward, his shoulders hunched like a quarterback on the defensive.

He was coming right at her.

Her eyes darted. He was between her and the hospital entrance, out of the glow of light. She ran around the van, the key in her hand to open the driver's door, and heard him behind her.

At that moment several women stepped from the building, chattering, obviously employees getting off work. Liza glanced over her shoulder. The man was gone. He had disappeared back into the shadowy darkness of the alley with its doorways and dumpsters, as though he had only been a figment of her imagination.

Quickly, before the women reached their vehicles, Liza sprinted to the hospital entrance and stepped inside the building. Once safe, reaction set in, and she had to lean against a wall and take in deep, calming breaths. After regaining her equilibrium, she proceeded to the room where she had performed the puppet show. Fred, a thin man who spoke with a lisp, had finished with the stage and was about to leave.

"Need any help to carry the equipment out to your van?" he asked.

"I'd really appreciate that," she said, still shaky. Had he not offered she would have requested a security person. "There was a street person in the parking lot," she said. "He was a little threatening."

"Awful isn't it?" he said, lisping. "First Hill is not very safe after dark."

She shrugged. "I think that depends on what part of the hill. I live north of Madison and it's rare for anyone to be accosted over there."

He glanced up from where he had been getting the equipment ready to carry outside. "I don't doubt that. That's an area of high-priced real estate."

"Pardon me?"

He grinned. "All I'm saying is that lots of rich people live in those condos."

"Not in my building," she said, annoyed by his stereotype. "We're all working people."

He shrugged and picked up his first load of equipment

to take outside. "Personally, I like a house in the suburbs."

Liza nodded, suddenly realizing that Fred was only making conversation; he wasn't being intentionally sarcastic. And she was grateful to have his help. Someone could still be out there in the dark, waiting for her to come back outside—waiting for her to be vulnerable.

In silence they started for the van with their first load together. Liza's uneasiness returned as they left the building and started across the parking lot. The night was quiet. Nothing moved.

Then her gaze switched to the van.

Abruptly, she stopped. Fred bumped into her back, and the side panels from the stage hit her so hard that she fell onto her knees. The box of props in her arms clattered onto the blacktop.

The passenger door was open.

"Oh no!" she cried. Leaping to her feet, she ran to the van. *The box of puppets was gone!*

"Call the police!" she commanded Fred.

He stood, staring, his mouth open.

"Don't just stand there!" she cried. "Someone broke into my sister's van and stole her puppets!"

He seemed paralyzed.

"Go! Now!" she screamed, and her words finally registered. He dropped the staging and ran for the hospital door, glancing over his shoulder as though he thought someone would stop him before he was safe.

Adrenaline gave her a hit of courage. At that moment her anger was beyond fear. "Come out of the shadows, you bastard!" she hollered toward the alley. "I dare you to face me." No answer. "Why would you steal puppets? They're worthless to you. Give them back and I won't press charges."

There was a shift in the darkness, as though someone

had moved in the shadows. A thrill of fear shot through her, but her adrenaline was still high and she stood her ground. Someone had stolen Jean's babies.

Fred and a security guard burst through the door and ran toward her. Then a siren sounded on Boren Avenue. The police were only seconds away. The shadows in the alley no longer moved.

Then the police car screeched to a stop in the parking lot and two officers jumped out. They checked out the area, took down the facts and determined that the thief had used a flat metal device to slip between the window and door panel to trip the lock.

"If the van had been newer that wouldn't have been possible," one officer explained kindly. Late model vehicles have new safety features that stop some break-ins."

Fred and several other staff members loaded the rest of the equipment into the van, as the officers made a more thorough inspection of the parking lot, dumpsters and alley. It was no surprise to Liza that they saw no one and did not find the puppets.

Liza had called Jean from her cell phone, but Jean wasn't home yet. She didn't leave a message on the answering machine; the theft was too traumatic for that. She'd drive to Jean's house, then wait until her sister returned to tell her in person.

She drove slowly toward Madison Park where Jean and Bill lived in a restored vintage 1920s house. Liza kept an eye on the rearview mirror, halfway expecting someone to follow her. No one did.

Two thoughts circled her mind. How could she tell Jean? And the fact that only the Harlequin puppet was left of all the characters Martin had helped stuff. The harlequin was still safe at Jean's house.

"Oh Martin," she said into the quiet of the van, "there's

hardly anything left of our life together . . . except memories. Even the puppets are gone now."

Liza forced back tears. She would not cry. She needed to be strong for Jean.

He had opened the van door, and with leather-gloved hands taken the box of puppets before she was barely back inside the hospital. Quickly, he had placed them in his own car trunk and closed the lid. About to drive away he had hesitated.

"Too good an opportunity to miss," he had told himself and gone back to the alley, waiting in the dark for her to come outside.

And then she had brought the skinny wimp with her.

His whole body had twitched with the urge to feel his hands on her neck, his fingers squeezing the life from her body, as she stood taunting him, daring him to show himself.

"I'll come out in the open, bitch," he had muttered under his breath.

He had started for her, but the police had arrived just as he'd been about to step from the shadows.

"Our time to meet is coming, don't you worry," he had whispered. "I'll be the last person you ever see."

He had driven away, but only several blocks. Now, as he parked at the back of a bank's parking lot and raised the lid of his car trunk he forgot about Liza MacDonough and thought about recouping what was owed him. Ripping the cover from the puppet box, he removed each cloth body and split it open with a knife, then smashed the head. In each case he found nothing.

He took more time with the girl puppets. "You're going to die," he told each one as he destroyed them.

The last one, a carefully wrapped mother-doll, stared at him with a mocking expression. Hated memories of his unhappy childhood surfaced; uncontrollable anger surged within him.

The knife was suddenly alive in his hand. He stabbed and ripped at the cloth body over and over until there was no stuffing left. The green satin gown was in tatters.

His breath came in short, gulping pants. He took the head in his hands, fingering its porcelain face. The smiling lips suggested kindness. But he was not fooled. Cruel words came out of the mouths of nice people.

"I'm going to smash your pea brain, Mother," he told it, remembering how she had always made him wear hand-me-downs and ridiculed him in front of others for wetting the bed.

He lifted his arm, savoring the moment. Then he crushed the back of its head. Taking deep breaths, he forced his thoughts back to why he had stolen the puppets.

Son of a bitch, he thought. He had found nothing.

He glanced around, making sure that no one had observed what he had done. Then he tossed everything back into the box and closed his car trunk again. In seconds he was headed back toward the hospital. He circled the streets surrounding the huge complex of medical buildings, and decided that the police had concluded their investigation and were gone.

He laughed aloud. "People of Seattle," he muttered. "You're so predictable—and stupid."

He was smarter than all of them, especially the cops whose next thought was probably on their coffee break. And her. He needed to send her a message, one she would understand.

Slowly he drove back into the alley that divided some of the hospital buildings. He brought the car to a stop near the back entrance that she had used earlier. Quickly, he jumped out and placed the box of destroyed puppets next to the door, where someone would find them.

"See what you think of that, Mrs. Hot-Shot Counselor," he said once he was safely back inside his car and a block from the hospital. "See if you'll have time to figure it all out before you die."

He turned on the radio, stepped on the gas and headed for home, suddenly elated. Killing puppet people was almost as satisfying as the real thing. His power was growing stronger and stronger.

No one could stop him now.

Chapter Sixteen

THE NEXT DAY LIZA TURNED OFF MADISON ONTO JEAN'S street, slowed at the driveway and pulled in behind Bill's Lexus. She knew Jean and Bill were at home because she had called from the Mission Church after the Sunday service.

She had not seen Jean last night. After waiting an hour for them to return, she had realized they must have gone out for a late supper. So Liza had locked the van, gotten into her own car, which she had left there earlier, and gone home.

At midnight she had finally talked to Jean, told her what had happened, and promised to fill in the details after church the next day. The theft had kept her awake all night, and she knew that Jean would not have slept either. She had played the piano for the congregation by rote, smiling and trying to seem normal until she was free to go.

Jean opened the door even before she rang the bell. Without a word, she pulled Liza into her arms, hugging her close. Once inside the house, Jean quickly closed the door and locked it. A significant gesture, Liza thought. Jean's babies had been stolen.

"A police officer called a few minutes ago," Jean said. She swallowed hard, struggling with her emotions. "The puppets were found in the hospital parking lot near a back entrance this morning."

"Oh good!" Liza's relief was instant.

Bill, a tall man with a gentle set to his angular features, stepped forward from the doorway and placed an arm around Jean. He raised his hand to greet Liza, but his usual smile was missing.

"They were smashed and ripped up," he told her. "Someone is bringing us the pieces." He pulled Jean closer, understanding her despair. "Although the heads were crushed, the officer said the faces are mostly intact—thank God."

Liza glanced down, suppressing her own need to cry. She busied herself by taking off her coat and putting her things down on a chair. Then she looked up, meeting Jean's eyes.

"We can make new puppets, Jean. Exactly like the damaged ones, using the same faces."

Jean nodded, her eyes brimming with moisture. "It's just that . . . that . . ."

Bill pulled Jean against his chest as her words faltered. Over her dark head his eyes met Liza's. In that moment she saw that Bill knew the depth of Jean's loss.

She nodded so that Bill realized that she understood. He was a good man. Jean was fortunate to have him.

They moved from the hall to the living room, through the dining room and into the kitchen. All of the rooms had been decorated with antiques and collectibles that Jean and Bill had bought at auctions and yard sales, an avocation they shared.

"I feel awful," Jean said, her voice quaking. She poured coffee into mugs for both of them. Bill had gone upstairs to get photographs of the destroyed puppets.

"And I feel like it's all my fault," Liza said.

"But you couldn't have known anyone would break into the van." A pause. "We both know the hospital is located in an area where people have been accosted after dark."

Ironic, Liza thought. Jean was trying to make her feel better. It was typical; Jean had always been the caregiver.

They sat down facing each other across the kitchen table while Liza explained the details of what had happened the night before, including the person who had stepped out of the shadows in a threatening manner.

"I never dreamed that he would break into the van after I'd made sure it was locked," she said. "I wasn't gone long and he had to have been nuts to do it. Anyone could have come out of the building and caught him."

"There are a lot of unpredictable people on the streets." Jean's tone was stronger.

"But why would anyone steal puppets, and then destroy them? It doesn't make any sense."

Jean shook her head, obviously keeping her emotions in check. "I only know I'll recreate my little people. And hope no one ever hurts them again."

Bill joined them, making a point to change the subject by asking Liza about her work. She explained briefly about the layoffs; when she heard they were having Sunday dinner with his parents, she stood to go.

"Please let me know about the puppets after you get them back," she told Jean. "It goes without saying that I'll help in any way I can."

Jean walked her to the front hall, then embraced Liza. "I know Lizzy. I figured you'd help, and I'll probably take you up on the offer." She hesitated and Liza opened the door. "It's not your fault, Liza, you must know that. These things happen and are beyond our control."

Liza nodded. "I know. But I do feel responsible. I should have called Security after seeing the guy step out of the shadows." She hesitated. "He scared me, and I knew his intentions weren't good."

Once Liza was back in her car heading west toward the city, she realized that Jean had stepped into her old role of comforting her little sister again. Oh Jean, I don't want you to do that, she thought. I want you to have a life beyond me and the puppets. I want you to finally be free enough of your old baggage to have a real baby one of these days.

But her thoughts didn't cancel out the fact that Jean was devastated right now. Nor did it take away from her own guilt. Lately it seemed that everywhere she went something terrible happened. First the deaths: Nate's and Alice's. Now the puppets. Who would be next?

The thought scared her.

Her resolve to start calling the people on the layoff list that afternoon went as flat as the discordant notes on the mysterious sheet of music. She just wasn't up to it. She felt like a psychological mess, her nervous system on red alert and her emotional reserves at an all-time low. I'll wait until Monday or Tuesday, she told herself. The project has waited this long, it could wait a little longer.

Early evening she had a call from Dave who was preoccupied with the software testing for the One Thousand Series jet. "So far, so good," he said. "We'll celebrate after the flights are complete."

"And successful," she added, contriving a positive tone to her voice.

"You got that right, Brown Eyes." A hesitation. "Sorry I didn't call you last night after your show. I was tied up here. How'd it go?"

"The kids loved it," she said, and told him about the performance but omitted telling him about the puppets. She'd tell him later, after the testing was over and she could explain in person. He had his own concerns right now.

They hung up a few seconds later. She was getting ready for bed when Erik called. "Hey, why didn't you tell me about the puppets?" he asked, sounding hurt. "Remember me, your friend, the person you call when you get in trouble?"

"How did you know?"

"Maggie Garret. She didn't leave the hospital right away; she'd gone to check on Brandon Delmonte in the children's wing, and heard about it from one of the nurses."

"Maggie called you on the weekend?"

There was a silence.

"Not jealous, are you?"

"For goodness sake, Erik. Of course not. I was just wondering what I'd gotten you into. I didn't think Maggie was the type to bug someone outside of office hours unless it was an emergency."

His grin sounded in his voice. "She's not. I'd given her my home number because she had some serious concerns about how to cope with her oldest boy. A problem came up today so she called." A pause. "I think we got it ironed out. She has great kids. They're going to be okay."

"With a little help from you." She switched the receiver to her other ear so she could poke an arm through her nightgown sleeve. "Thanks for being there, Erik."

"My pleasure," he said, sounding pleased. What happened to the puppets?"

She told him quickly so she would not burst into tears. "Jean was devastated."

Her words drifted into another silence.

"So were you, sweetheart."

She blinked hard, swallowing a sudden lump in her throat. "I guess I was," she said finally. She could never hide her feelings from Erik. "And I feel guilty."

"You mustn't."

"Can't help it. Especially in light of all that's happened over the past year." She paused. "It seems that everyone around me gets shattered by tragedy."

"That's a ridiculous statement and you know it."

"Realistically I know you're right. But emotionally I can't get past that thought."

"I'm coming over."

"No, please don't. I'm okay, really. I'm about to climb into bed," she said, contriving a stronger tone. "I'm just a little down right now, probably because of Alice's death." She had told him about finding Alice dead at the sauna just a few days ago. He must think I'm the grim reaper, she thought. The harbinger of disaster.

"You sure? I could spend the night."

She smiled despite her depressed mood. First Dave had spent the night because of Alice, now Erik wanted to spend the night because of the puppets.

"I'm sure. But thanks, Erik. You're a dear friend."

"If not a sexy friend."

"You're both, as I'm sure your many girlfriends can attest to."

"And you?"

"I'm not a girlfriend, but I agree with the girlfriends."

His sigh came over the wires. "Good enough for now." A pause. "But promise me one thing?"

"Sure."

"You'll call me immediately if anything upsetting happens again?"

"I promise."

"Okay. You have a good sleep."

"I'll try."

"And I'll catch up with you tomorrow."

The dial tone sounded. A few minutes later Liza was snuggled under a down quilt, Bella curled up at the end of the bed. She just knew she would not sleep. But she did.

The next afternoon she postponed several appointments to attend a memorial service for Alice. It seemed unreal: there was no coffin or burial because she had been cremated, and there was no one present who knew Liza except Pat, Alice's secretary. Pat explained that others from work, like Sylvia Kempton, could not get the time off to attend because of project deadlines. That reminded Liza that she needed to talk to Sylvia.

Liza went back to the office to conclude her day's appointments, then went home and crashed. Tomorrow is a new day, she told herself. Now that Sylvia was back from sick leave, Liza meant to ask her about obtaining the job evaluations on some of the terminated employees, especially those who had worked in departments like the computer lab where people were overworked. She wanted to see if the records contradicted her clients.

But Tuesday brought new stresses, both good and bad. Maggie called in the morning to tell her that Brandon Delmonte had undergone his brain surgery, that he was in recovery but that she had not yet heard if the operation was a success. "I'll let you know as soon as I hear," Maggie told her.

Liza hung up, thinking about the oddities of life. A short time ago she had not known Maggie, then after

Nate's death she had wondered if Maggie could cope with widowhood, and now she and Maggie were becoming good friends. Maggie was a woman of strength and character.

A short time later a rumpled looking Dave stepped into her office.

"You've heard?"

She glanced at him from where she was sitting behind her desk, and shook her head. "Heard what?"

"Our test plane suffered a malfunction and crash-landed."

"Oh no!" She jumped up, dropping her pen on the floor. "What happened?"

He shook his head. "We don't know yet. The One Thousand Series jet was flying through severe weather over the Cascade Mountains, a situation a regular plane would not attempt, and there was a problem with the rudder." He hesitated. "Thank God no one was hurt and the plane is all in one piece. It made it back to the airport."

"Why would you have it fly in such conditions?"

By his expression she could tell that he was terribly upset. "We always test our planes in severe conditions; we subject them to the worst possible scenario." He pushed his mussed hair from his forehead. "I'm just hoping that we don't have a serious setback here."

She came around the desk and hugged him. "I hope not, too, Dave. Let's pray it has nothing to do with the software."

"Jeez! That's my fear. Our FAA certification is already in limbo until we know the exact cause."

Liza pulled him closer. "It'll be okay, Dave. Whatever the cause, you can fix it." She stepped back to look into his face. "Isn't that why you have test flights, to discover the bugs before certification?"

As he looked down into her face his expression softened. "You're right, Brown Eyes. This isn't the end of the world. I'll try to remember that."

He pulled her back into his arms and kissed her, long and passionately. Then he stepped back. "I have to be on deck here, but I'll call you the second I'm free."

Liza nodded, taken aback by the meaning of his kiss. After he was gone she tried to put it out of her mind. She was a married woman in limbo because her husband had vanished. She didn't know how she felt about Martin anymore or whether he was alive or dead. One thing she did not need was more uncertainty in her life. But Dave's kiss did point out one thing, she longed to be happy again.

Shortly before quitting time, Liza completed her work and decided to call a few of the people on her list of terminated employees. The first entry had an address but no phone number and directory assistance was unable to give out unlisted numbers. Several other names without phone numbers ended with the same result. Liza decided to talk with them in person since everyone on the list lived within the city.

She glanced at her watch. I have time to go by one of the addresses before dark, she decided a little later as she got into the Miata. The residence was only a few minutes away in the Fremont area of Seattle. Liza headed north from the parking lot rather than south toward home.

She slowed her car to a crawl after crossing the Fremont Bridge, following signs into an industrial area of warehouses and small offices. By the time she reached the address on her list, she was confused by the boarded-up buildings and empty lots. Liza circled the block twice, rechecking the numbers. There was no mistake. No residence existed at the address on her printout. It was an empty lot.

She drove home, her thoughts spinning. It must have been a computer misprint. Tomorrow morning she would check with Sylvia Kempton who was in charge of Records, which meant she would know what was going on. If anything.

"Are you saying that you have a list of terminated employees?" Sylvia asked the next morning after Liza had requested an address verification. About to pull up the information on her computer screen, she hesitated, her hazel eyes fixed on Liza.

"I thought you knew?" Liza wished she had not mentioned that fact with her inquiry about the nonexistent address. "Alice gave it to me, at my request."

"I suppose you know personnel information is confidential and that the company could be held accountable for violating State codes?"

"Yes, I did know that, but I believed that wouldn't apply to me since I am an employee here and have signed the company confidentiality agreement." She tried not to sound annoyed by Sylvia's sharp tone. "Also, my need for the list is in line with my client/counselor duties."

"How so?" Sylvia tilted her head, and her blond pageboy flared away from the curve of her cheek.

"It has to do with the complaints of terminated employees I've been counseling and trying to place in new positions." She hesitated, controlling the note of irritation that had crept into her voice. "Because of confidentiality, I can't divulge their concerns. At least not at this time until I've followed up and decided whether or not these rumors are valid." A pause. "That's what I'm trying to do."

"And your follow-up includes the names and addresses of these people?"

Liza nodded.

There was a long silence. Liza kept her gaze level, determined not to give ground. Sylvia does not need to know details, Liza reminded herself. The more you say the less likely she will be to help you. But it was a puzzle; what was the big deal about the addresses of people who had already been fired? Now was not the time to request personnel evaluations, she decided wryly.

Sylvia was the first to glance away. "Since Alice figured it was okay to give you the list in the first place, I suppose it won't hurt to check out the problem." She faced her computer, her hands on the keys. "So what was the name?"

Liza told her. The name came up on the screen with the address and no phone number. "There is no such place," she added. "It's an empty lot."

"You drove out there?"

"Uh-huh."

"It has to be a typo." She scrolled down a couple of lines. "Payroll checks were sent to a post office box." Sylvia turned on her chair, facing Liza. "Are you sure there wasn't a house on that lot that was recently torn down? You said it was a rundown area that was both industrial and residential."

"I never thought of that." Liza pushed up the sleeves of her white sweater, then bent forward to see the screen better. "Are you suggesting that the employee moved and didn't update his personnel information?"

Sylvia nodded. "It happens all the time, especially when they use a post office box for their correspondence or are having their paychecks directly deposited into a bank account." She shrugged. "We cope with that problem every day. Not just address changes, but insurance claims, wrong Social Security or phone numbers." She tapped a finger against her temple. "Some people are careless, they just don't think about updating their data until they need to. And until then, we have to go by the info in our files." A pause. "I'm sure Alice must have told you about that."

"Of course, Alice did mention those problems." Liza swallowed, glancing toward the office that used to be Alice's. She did not want to ask who was in line for the top position, although she guessed it would be Sylvia as Pat had said. Alice's death was still too raw for her to talk about it with Sylvia. Liza turned to go. "Thanks for your help."

"You're welcome." Sylvia stood, pushed her chair back and came around her desk. "I'm happy that I could put your concerns to rest."

"Just about," Liza said, evasively. "I'll probably drive by several other addresses to satisfy myself that the Fremont mistake was just a random thing."

"Don't you think that's an exercise in futility? After all, none of the people on the list work here anymore."

"Probably. We'll see." Liza hesitated at the door, thanked her again and started toward the stairs. No doubt Sylvia was right. But just in case, of what? she asked herself. She was not sure.

A la Niña winter, Liza thought. Rain and wind. One storm after the next. She turned the wipers on high and peered through the windshield, feeling almost claustrophobic in her small car. The first address on Queen Anne Hill had checked out; at least there was an occupied house on the lot. She was headed to the second location on the northwest slope, figuring it would still be light by the time she got there around four-thirty.

You're not playing hooky from work, she told herself. This is part of your job.

The rain slowed to a light sprinkle as she found the street and turned into a narrow lane that wound down the side of a wooded hill. Houses were set back in the trees, and Liza suspected that the view of Puget Sound was fantastic from some of their windows. When she found the right number on a mailbox she drove into the overgrown driveway.

"Damn!" she said, as branches scraped against the car doors and the windshield.

She stopped, hesitant to scratch the paint job, then wound down the window. The sweet fragrance of wet evergreens filled the car. The house was fifty or so yards farther up the lane, but there were no lights on. Whoever lived there was probably still at work.

Okay, it's a real residence, she told herself. You can go now.

She hesitated, studying the rundown appearance of the place: the porch was sagging, the yard was overgrown, and there was no sign of life. Beyond the house, the woods looked dark and forbidding, even though she could see lights through the trees. The neighbors were home. A comforting thought.

Does anyone really live here? Liza wondered, knowing it would only take a couple of minutes to make sure. That was the reason she had come, to determine that it was not another bogus address. Still she hesitated.

The quiet of the approaching night had settled around her, as though it waited for her to decide. Crazy thought, she told herself. Don't be a silly ninny. It's now or never. It'll be dark in two minutes.

Her hand was on the door lever when she had another idea. She could come back in the morning before work.

You're scared, admit it, she told herself. Your antenna is up, screaming danger.

No! A year ago she would not have thought twice about walking to the porch and back. These days she was scared of everything. She must not allow intangible fears to alter her life.

With resolve, she climbed out of the Miata, half ran to the bottom of the porch steps and stopped, her gaze fastening on the boarded-up windows behind the overgrown shrubs, then moving over the clapboard siding, looking for any sign of life. In those few seconds the night closed in. Her apprehension returned with the sensation of being watched.

She was vulnerable.

There was a sound in the bushes at the far side of the house. A snapping twig? Goose bumps rippled over her flesh. Her legs threatened to buckle under her.

Then she was running, heedless of the wet branches slapping at her face. Behind her she imagined the sounds of someone following, altering the dark air currents that swirled around her. She reached her car, jumped inside, started the engine and backed wildly out of the driveway, heedless of dents or scratches this time.

She was almost to the road and realized that her headlights were off, that she was headed for a ditch. Slamming on the brakes, the tires skidded to a stop. Liza, teeth chattering like castanets, drove forward a few feet, straightened the car on the driveway, then backed into the street.

She pressed down on the gas pedal, glancing at the rearview mirror. She glimpsed red taillights disappearing in the opposite direction. Where had a vehicle come from? She hadn't seen a car on the road.

Not a car with lights.

The wind had come up, bending and twisting the small firs and pines that lined the road. The stillness of a few minutes ago was gone. No one watched from the woods now. An immediate threat to her no longer existed.

For now.

Chapter Seventeen

"HEY, WAIT UP, BROWN EYES." DAVE FELL INTO STEP WITH her several mornings later as she headed across the parking lot to her office building. "Good news. The moratorium on the One Thousand Series jet is over. We've been okayed to continue testing."

"I'm so glad." Liza smiled, noting how much more relaxed he seemed than the last time she had talked to him. "What was the problem?"

"There wasn't any, that is *not* a technical one. The software performed exactly as it should, and everything else did, too."

"Then why the crash landing?"

"Freak weather conditions, including wind shear." They continued into the building. "You know we test in all conditions, and this was a time when no planes were in that area, having been diverted because of weather." He gave a laugh. "Seems we outdid ourselves. No airplane can withstand everything the elements throw at it." He cocked his head. "That's where we come in. We need to use good judgment."

"So you're able to use the same test plane?"

He nodded. "You bet. Using a different one would send up a red flag, like something *was* wrong."

They had gone a few steps past the entrance when Dave was stopped by one of his programmers. Liza waited, listening to their upbeat conversation about the testing. But she wondered. Despite what Dave said, had a software glitch caused a malfunction that impacted maneuverability in severe weather? Or had the freak conditions only pointed up a flaw in the system? She would never know. Whatever it was, Dave and the company would fix the problem and move forward toward FAA certification.

Stop being such a doubting Thomas, she instructed herself. It's none of your damn business. The plane will be perfect when the testing is complete, and Dave is feeling much better about the whole process. Those are the only important issues here.

"Liza." Dave snapped his fingers in front of her face. "Didn't you hear what I said?"

"What?" She'd been lost in her own thoughts. She saw that the other man had continued out the door and Dave was grinning at her. "I guess I zoned out."

"I noticed." He paused. "Late night?"

"Actually, I was in bed early." Liza was not up to explaining that she had not slept well, or why. She still had a hangover from the eerie incident at the abandoned house on Queen Anne Hill several nights ago. And since then she had been unable to contact several other names on the list, and she intended to do a drive-by of those locations when her schedule permitted. It didn't help that there were so few daylight hours, and those she spent at the office. One thing was certain, she would not investigate the sites at dusk.

"Good," Dave said, pleased. "Catch up on your beauty

sleep because when the testing is complete we're going out on the town."

"Promises, promises," she said, teasing.

"Yeah, I know I've broken a few dates." He dropped an arm around her shoulders as they headed down the hall. "And I'll be tied up this weekend. But after that it's party time."

About to separate, Dave hesitated. "Hey, I got sidetracked by all the talk about the testing and forgot to tell you about some other good news. Mick, the guy I was just talking to, told me that little Brandon Delmonte's surgery was a success and his doctor expects a full recovery."

"That's wonderful." She paused. "How did Mick know?"

"Mick works with Cooper. He heard this morning when Cooper came to work."

"Thanks for telling me, Dave. Brandon is a special little boy."

"Yeah, I know." He made a mock grimace. "I should have sent flowers, a toy, something, although I chipped in with the guys from the lab on some computer games."

"I'm sure that's fine."

"Did you send something?"

She nodded. "Jean and I sent two puppets, a little boy and his dog."

"I thought so," he said, his expression softening. With a quick motion, he planted a kiss on her forehead, then strode off toward the walkway to the next building. "I'll give you a call tonight," he called over his shoulder.

Bemused by his action, Liza went into her office and had just hung up her coat when Al Stark arrived. "I'm late for a meeting, but we have to talk," he said, sounding breathless.

She waited, wondering what was on his mind.

"Sylvia Kempton called yesterday about some evaluations I'd sent to her office, and she happened to mention your visit." He sucked in air. "Ran the whole length of the parking lot to get out of a damn monsoon, and I gotta catch my breath."

There was a silence. She should have known. Sylvia was making sure that Liza's boss knew about the printout.

"I thought you had gotten past all the rumors and gossip of a few disgruntled employees, Liza." His breathing had returned to normal. "What's going on? You know employee information is confidential."

An alarm went off in her mind. Play it down, she thought, or he'll demand the printout. Al was another company man who would rather look the other way than take a stand that might jeopardize his position. She needed to convince him that what she was doing was proper procedure.

"Just some old business," she replied calmly. Which is true, she told herself. "I needed some personnel statistics before I could close several files, that's all. Verifying information with Sylvia was a shortcut, and completely within company protocol." Not a lie either, she added mentally.

He stared at her and she could almost see the thoughts spinning in his head as he tried to find another meaning behind her words.

Finally he nodded. "Okay then. I was just making sure that you weren't continuing on with all that silliness about discrimination in the layoffs. I was beginning to worry even more about you."

Her anger was instant. She bit back the words that sprang to her lips. Al did not notice. He was already at the door. With a final salute, he was gone.

That evening Liza sat in a long flannel nightgown at her computer. Outside her window the wind howled up the hills from Elliott Bay, gaining speed in the narrow corridors between buildings, blasting against her windows. Beyond the rain-splattered glass, the city lights seemed as everlasting as a mystical sky of stars in high summer. For long seconds she focused on the spectacle, then turned back to the CB forum that had come up on the screen.

She began to scroll through the current messages; she had been monitoring the forum since the first time she had found the posts between Snakeoil and Comet. There had never been another communication, and she wondered if she had read the wrong meaning into them, her pattern lately.

Almost to the end of the posts her hand stilled on the mouse that would click her to the next message.

"Try tomorrow night." It was from Snakeoil to Comet. There was no response from Comet.

Try what? She had no way to know.

Liza stared at the words that were from one unknown person to another, but for all the world to see. If they had criminal intent why would they expose themselves? Again, just like the last time she had asked herself that question, the answer was instant. Internet forums were vast, random and constantly changing. Participants hid behind tags and it was often impossible for other users to discover their real names. Brilliant, she thought. If that was what was really happening.

She logged off, then stared at the blank screen after turning off her computer. Her mind churned with the events of the past few weeks: client complaints, Nate's death, her own apprehensions about Martin, Alice dying, the destruction of the puppets, the scary feelings of being followed, watched and threatened.

Am I going nuts? she wondered.

The ring of the phone startled her. She grabbed up the receiver. "Hello."

"Liza?" Erik's voice came over the wires.

"Oh . . . Erik, hi."

"For God's sake, what's wrong? I didn't recognize your voice."

There were a few seconds of silence.

"I guess I needed to clear my throat," she said, evading.

"Okay, so what *is* going on? If you don't tell me I'm coming over."

"Erik, I really appreciate your concern but I'm okay. I can't imagine why I sounded *that* different."

"C'mon, Liza, this is your old friend Erik. I know you. Something is wrong."

"I don't know if it is or not, Erik. All I know is that there are a lot of things that aren't right." A pause. "And I don't know exactly what those things are either."

"I'm coming over."

"No, please don't. I'm okay, just confused."

"Explain."

"There's so much I don't know where to begin."

"The beginning is a good place to start."

She switched the phone to her other ear.

I'm okay, really. My confusion is about my clients, the deaths of Nate Garret and Alice, the scary incidents that are happening to me, and the bogus addresses of terminated employees—and of course, Martin's disappearance." A pause. "But I'm trying to sort it all out."

"My God! Why haven't you told me about all of this?"

She blew out a long sigh.

"I didn't want to seem like a flake, a person who couldn't cope. But now there are the online people who are sending computer messages to each other that seem kind of mysterious and I'm even more confused and—"

He interrupted. "For God's sake, Liza, this is a baffling conversation, to say the least. Start at the beginning."

"As I said, I don't know where to begin. It would take two hours at least to outline what's been going on."

"I've got two hours."

"I don't. I need to sleep."

He took a few seconds to digest her words. "Will you be okay until tomorrow night?"

"Yes."

"I'll pick you up at seven. We'll have dinner at a nice quiet restaurant where we can talk—that okay?"

"That would be nice." A hesitation. "And I'll explain then what's been going on."

"Good. I'll look forward to hearing it." Another pause. "Now lock your door and go to bed, Liza. And call me if anything—I mean the smallest concern—comes up. Will you do that?"

"I promise."

After saying good-bye they hung up.

Liza went to bed, feeling more secure than she had for some time. It would be a relief to confide everything, no matter how crazy it sounded. Erik was the one person in the world who would not consider her a nut case. She snuggled under the quilt, looking forward to tomorrow night. She was thinking one minute, drifting off to sleep the next.

"We're going to the Sorrento Hotel?"

"Uh-huh." Erik turned the Cherokee into the half-moon courtyard and stopped at the top of the curve. "I have a reservation at the Hunt Club Restaurant for seven-thirty." He opened the driver-side door and came around to Liza's side as she stepped down. "Keys are in the ignition," he told the attendant.

"Hey, isn't this place a little pricey?" she asked, grinning. She had wondered why he was wearing slacks and a blazer rather than Levis and a leather jacket. At first she had thought it was because he knew that she would still be wearing her work suit and high-heel pumps.

"But small and quiet. And only a couple of blocks from your place."

He took her arm, guiding her past the doorman into the turn-of-the-century hotel lobby, pausing to tell the maître d' about their reservation in the dining room, then continuing into the Fireside Room. A small table was available near the fireplace and they took it.

"How about a glass of wine while we wait?" he asked.

She nodded, pleased by his take-charge manner. It felt good to let him make the decisions.

He ordered two glasses of Chardonnay and after the waitress brought them, Erik raised his in a toast. "To peace, serenity and happiness."

"And to being safe."

He raised his brows in a question but did not ask it. They clinked glasses, then sipped the wine.

The minutes passed quickly until it was time to be seated in the Hunt Club, a sedate, elegant restaurant with a European ambience. They had talked about Maggie Garret's problems with her boys, his first-jump classes and the publicity surrounding the One Thousand Series Jet. He was leaving her concerns for later, until after they had eaten, Liza decided.

Again he took the lead, ordering salads and seafood for both of them and a bottle of French wine. Liza wondered when he had gained his sophistication. She remembered him as her friend and co-sufferer from graduate school, the daredevil who defied death, and the man who marched to his own drummer. For the first time she realized that he had become a cultured man. She could not stop her smile.

"What?" he said, noticing her expression.

She shrugged. "Nothing."

"Yes, something. Tell me."

A chuckle escaped her lips. "Really, nothing."

"I know," he said, leaning his long frame back in the chair so he could stroke his beard. "You're surprised that I can function in polite society. Right?"

She laughed out loud. "Okay, that's kind of what I was thinking. I guess I hadn't really thought about you dating all these years, although I knew about some of your longer relationships." She hesitated. "You probably have a woman in your life right now and I don't even know about her." Then she waved a hand. "Sorry, none of my business."

His pale eyes altered somehow, as though he were amused. "I do," he said. "But she's not available right now."

"Married?"

He shook his head.

"Doesn't realize how much you care about her?" It was like they were back in college, playing their twenty-questions game with each other.

"Yeah, I guess you could say that." He poured more wine into their glasses. "At least she knows where I live, that she can arrive on my doorstep at any time."

"She lives out of town?"

"At the moment, out of *my* town."

The waiter brought their dinners, and for the next half-hour they enjoyed the meal, chatting and laughing about the old days in school. After their plates were taken away, Erik sat back, his eyes suddenly direct.

"So, how about an after-dinner drink by the fireplace?"

She nodded.

He motioned to the waiter for the check, signed a Visa

slip and then stood up. She followed and he took her arm
again, leading her back to the Fireside Room. There were
no seats, and then a couple by the fireplace got up to leave.

"Eureka," Erik said. "Fate intervened. We have a table."

She grinned, feeling a little tipsy from the wine, wondering if she should have another drink.

"Yes, you really can have one more glass of wine," he
said, reading her expression. "Number one, you aren't
driving. Number two, you only live three blocks away.
And number three, you have your good friend Erik to take
care of you."

She grinned. "That's scary. How did you know what I
was thinking?"

He put up flat silencing hands. "Don't ask. Maybe I'll
tell you next year at this time, okay?"

She shrugged. Next year, ten years, they would still be
friends, of that she was certain.

He ordered and their wine was brought to the table a
few minutes later. A piano player had started to play soft
music in their absence, and it muffled the low conversations of other customers. The whole effect was soothing
and reminiscent of an earlier time.

"Now," he said, his narrowed gaze reminding her of
wolf eyes again. "I want to know what's going on."

She gathered her thoughts. "So much that I don't know
where to begin."

"As I said last night, the beginning."

"I've told you a few things."

"Out of context?"

She nodded.

"Then start at *A* and take me through to *Z*. I'm not
averse to hearing something twice."

She started out hesitantly, about her evaluation of Nate,
his stressed-out voice pleading with her to meet him at the

Mission Church, and then his accidental death. She faltered, remembering.

"It's okay, Liza. The guy's death wasn't your fault."

His hand covered hers on the table and she was able to regain her composure. Shit, she thought. A few glasses of wine and a sympathetic listener and she was ready to lose it. She needed to stay together, stick to the facts.

"Please go on, Liza," he said, his tone supportive.

She gulped another sip of wine, knowing it was the last thing she needed if she meant to sound rational. But her gaze was level when she began again. And then her story came out nonstop, from client complaints to Nate's evaluation, to being chased through Pioneer Square, her car broken into, her condo door unlocked, to all of her sensations of being watched and followed. She explained her feelings about the sheet music printout that was left at the Mission Church, that she believed it might have been a coded message from Nate, and someone out there might want it back. She ended with her information about the CB forum and her suspicion that Bojangles had been Nate, and that Snakeoil and Comet felt they were in jeopardy. Of what she did not know.

"And I can't shake the feeling that Nate's and Alice's deaths were not accidental."

"Murder?"

She swirled the wine in her glass. "I have no proof."

"Tell me about the sheet music."

She explained.

"Where is this sheet of music now?"

"I have it."

"Can I see it?"

She hesitated. "Do you think that the person behind all of this is . . . Martin?"

He looked startled. "Jeez, why do you think that?"

She spread her hands, feeling unprepared for the question. "I don't know. I'm asking you."

"No way!" Erik leaned toward her. "Martin had his weaknesses, but he would never be behind the kind of conspiracy that you've just described. He was insecure about his future, but he was never a sociopath. And that's what we might be dealing with here."

She looked away, chastened.

"And that means you're in danger." He hesitated, his expression set in stern lines. "It sounds like someone is after you, Liza, someone who believes you have information that can incriminate him."

"The sheet music?"

He nodded. "You say you have it?"

"At home."

They had finished their wine and he stood up. "Let's go back to your place. I want to see it."

She got to her feet, feeling a little wobbly. "You're welcome to look at it." She took her shoulder bag off the back of the chair where she had dangled it by the strap. "But I don't think you'll be able to make sense of it any more than I could."

He took her arm and directed her out through the front entrance. "We'll see."

The attendant brought the Cherokee, Erik tipped him and they were soon on the street headed for her condominium. He parked out in front, escorted her through the front door security and up in the elevator to her apartment. She had her key ready.

Erik pushed the door open, then held it for Liza to go in first. They were both in the entry before realizing that something was wrong.

"My God!" Liza cried. "It's déjà vu!"

"What?" Erik was right behind her.

"Not again," Liza whispered, horrified. She would have run into the living room but Erik held her back. Someone had ransacked her apartment.

"Shhh," he said in her ear, pulling her back toward the door. "We have to leave—now!"

"Bella! Bella!" she cried, ignoring him, trying to free herself from his hold. Her cat had not been at the door, had not responded to her calls. She needed to know that Bella was safe.

Erik managed to get her back through the doorway and into the hallway as the door closed and locked automatically behind them. "Liza," he said, his tone urgent. "Someone could still be in your condo. We have to get help."

Her legs turned to jello. Erik helped her—half-carrying, half-pulling—into the elevator, and they rode back to the ground floor and the manager's unit. Erik was still pounding on his door when it opened.

"Someone broke into my apartment," Liza cried, her voice faltering. "Whoever it is might still be in there!"

"Call Nine-one-one," Erik ordered the man.

They all stepped into the manager's unit and the door closed behind them. Safe for the moment.

Chapter Eighteen

JOE, THE MANAGER, TOOK ACTION AT ONCE. WHILE HIS wife Naomi called Nine-one-one, he grabbed a baseball bat and ran to the elevator with Liza and Erik. "The intruder is probably gone by now. But you wait here with the wife until the police arrive," he told Liza.

"I'm coming, too," she retorted. "I've got to make sure Bella is okay."

No one would hurt a cat, she reassured herself. They would have to be crazy. Her mind faltered. Crazy like everything that had been happening lately?

Joe hesitated, holding the door. "There's another person in your apartment?"

"Bella is a cat," Erik said. "Liza's baby." He stepped aside for Liza to enter the elevator. "C'mon, let's get up there. No point arguing. Liza isn't about to stay here."

As the elevator went up through the building no one spoke. Liza realized that if someone had still been in her apartment they would be gone now via the stairs or the other elevator.

Why hadn't she thought of the stairs?

Stupid, she thought. The stairs led to an outside entrance that was not locked to anyone exiting the building, only to those trying to enter it. By the time the door opened on her floor, she knew they would not meet the intruder. He was long gone.

But what about Bella?

Liza unlocked her door and Joe stepped into the entry first, his bat raised to defend himself. "Wait here," he instructed firmly.

Joe slipped into the living room, glanced around, then moved cautiously down the hall toward her bedroom, office and the bathrooms. Erik went through the kitchen to the dining room, circling through the living room back to Liza after having made sure the deck door was still locked.

"No one is here now," Joe said, returning to the entry hall. "But some wacko sure as hell was." His expression was tight with anger. "The place is a mess."

Liza stepped around both men into the living room. "Oh my God!"

Her stomach lurched, her flesh went cold and she grabbed the back of the sofa to steady herself. Chair cushions had been tossed on the floor, drawers and doors to all of her cabinets stood open, the contents spilling onto the white carpeting. Someone had gone through all of her things.

"Bella! Bella!" She ran down the hall, looking in each room for her cat. "Here kitty, kitty, kitty," she called, forcing the shrill note from her voice. She saw the devastation of her apartment, but her first concern was to find Bella.

She could hardly get into her bedroom. Everything was ransacked; even her bedding had been pulled from the bed. No sign of Bella. Had the vandal stolen her? The thought hit her like a shower of ice.

"Shit," Erik said behind her. "What in the hell was someone after?"

Mutely, she shook her head. Then she heard something. She tilted her head, listening.

"What was that?" Erik stepped around her and opened the closet door. Again, chaos.

Something moved behind the shoes. He bent closer and Bella shot out of the closet to run under the bed. Liza got down on her hands and knees to coax her out. Bella meowed, but would not budge from the far corner. Her cat was terrified but appeared unhurt.

"You're safe now, sweetie," Liza said, softly. "No one's going to hurt you. You come out when you want to."

Liza stood up, taking in the full ramification of the mess. Her jewelry-chest drawers were pulled out but a glance told her that nothing was missing. Another quick walk through the apartment verified that none of her valuables had been stolen. The bottle of coins she had been saving was still in her office, as were her computer, printer, fax and other equipment. Her television sets and music system had not been touched, nor had her silver service.

Two policemen arrived at the door with Naomi. "What happened here?" the younger, smaller officer asked.

"Someone broke into my place." Liza's voice quavered. Don't cry, she ordered herself. Bella is fine and the mess can be cleaned up. Sensing her distress, Erik placed an arm loosely around her waist. She cleared her throat and tried again, "They trashed everything."

The second officer, a tall, graying man with a ruddy complexion and built like an aging linebacker, examined the door locks while his partner walked through the rooms, jotting down notes in a tablet. "No sign of forced entry," he said. "Was the door unlocked?"

Liza shook her head. "It locks automatically when it

closes." She paused. "And then I use my key to also set the bolt."

Joe nodded. "That's a safety feature on all of the doors." He hesitated. "Our security is pretty tight."

"Is there another entrance to your unit?" The officer took off his cap and secured it under his arm.

"Just the deck." Liza controlled an impulse to fidget under his steady dark gaze. "But the slider was still locked, and besides, this is the twelfth floor. Someone would have had to scale up the building."

The officer smiled for the first time. "You live in the city and haven't heard of cat burglars?" He sobered. "Anyone else have a key to your condo?"

She shook her head. "I only have one set."

He took out his notebook and jotted something down. "Anything missing?"

"I haven't checked everything yet, but my valuables all seem to be here."

Again, he scribbled something down.

The younger officer returned. "The apartment is secure. Just a scared kitty under the bed." He shook his head. "But someone sure did a job on this place. Tore everything apart, as though the person was looking for something or had a grudge against you." His gaze was direct. "You have any enemies? Anyone who wants to get back at you for something?"

"I don't know of anyone who would do this to me. As far as I know I don't have any enemies."

"Liza, you have had some incidents lately," Erik said, gently. "Maybe you should tell the officer about them."

She glanced down, her thoughts spinning, wondering if she should mention them. She checked them off in her mind. There was nothing she could prove, nothing that even seemed credible, like the strange sheet music. Except

Nate's and Alice's deaths, and they had been ruled accidental, not homicides. Wouldn't she sound like a hysterical woman with an overactive imagination? She decided to test the water.

"I was chased by a man in Pioneer Square several weeks ago, and my car was broken into while it was parked on a street in the Greenwood area."

"Did you report these incidents?" the older officer asked, looking up from where he had jotted down her words.

"Yes, but there's nothing they could do."

"Anything stolen in your car break-in?"

She shook her head. "My gym clothes were thrown out in the gutter, that's all." She realized she was knotting her hands together and tried to relax. "It scared me, though."

His eyes narrowed. "Someone might have been looking for something." He plopped his cap onto his head. "Some areas of Greenwood have lots of break-ins, and of course any woman walking alone in Pioneer Square is a target."

"What do you mean someone might have been looking for something?" Erik asked.

The officer shrugged. "Money, drugs, car parts like CD players that could be sold for drugs. Happens all the time." He shifted his gaze back to Liza. "I suggest you report any other incidents like that in the future."

His radio came alive in his jacket pocket. He pulled it out, listened momentarily, then turned the volume down. "I guess that's it for now," he told Liza. "We'll file a report and call you later with the case number, okay?"

She nodded, suddenly overwhelmed.

The younger officer strode after his partner, then paused by the door. "We'll check out the building before we go, and the security cameras. Who knows, this person may find himself on candid camera, and then we can nail him." He hesitated. "That's about our only hope. Break-ins often fall between the cracks for lack of evidence."

"I know," Liza said faintly.

"And I suggest you change your locks because someone either has a copy of your key or a passkey," he added.

Erik's arm tightened protectively. She was unable to speak. One other person did have a key—Martin. He had always carried his keys on a braided cord hooked to his belt. But Martin and his keys were probably deep in the waters of Puget Sound.

Or were they?

"Passkeys won't work in our system, only a master key like mine," Joe said, answering the officer and diverting Liza's thoughts. "I'll check with our management company to see if anyone else has one."

"Good idea," the younger policeman said.

Joe took Naomi's arm and together they followed the officers into the hallway. "I'll show them around the building," he told Liza. "And I'll look in on you later. Make sure your chain and bolts are in place."

"One more thing," the younger officer said, turning back. "We don't know what's going on here but this person has access to the building. I'd suggest you be on your guard. And call us if anything more happens."

They were concerned about her safety.

She swallowed back the urge to cry as she watched the larger policeman open the door to the garbage-chute closet, step inside and close it. He came right out but he had made his point. He fit. It was a place to hide. She sniffled hard. She would never again step into that closet without wondering if someone was hiding in that tiny space.

Erik closed the door behind them and locked it. She stood in her hall, the tears she had restrained finally rolling down her cheeks. Silently, he led her to the sofa and sat her down. And then he held her until she stopped crying.

"I'm sorry," she managed finally. "I'm devastated by all of this . . ." She waved a hand, indicating her torn-up apartment. "I keep asking myself why? Why me?"

"I don't know, Liza. But whoever it was waited until you were gone. They had to be looking for something because nothing was stolen." A pause. "Unless it was the weird sheet of music. I assume you had it on your piano."

She straightened. "My God! I thought about it in terms of telling the police about Nate and Alice, but I never even thought about it being gone." She jumped up. "Someone was trying to get it, I just know it."

"Yeah, I wondered why you hadn't mentioned it and decided not to. I figured you didn't want to get into an ambiguous area of company conspiracies, accidental deaths that seem suspicious and all the other random incidents."

"Because it sounds crazy. Too many people already believe I'm acting stressed out, obsessing about my clients' complaints."

"So you *do* believe all of this has to do with International Air."

She blew out her breath. "I don't know what to believe. I don't even know if that odd music was from Nate." She hesitated. "Maybe one of the parishioners left it—as a joke. Maybe I'm reaching to connect everything together." She gulped a ragged breath. "Maybe I am losing it, Erik, and I just don't realize it."

"Hey, just a fucking minute. Let's have some perspective here."

She almost smiled. He had reverted to his favorite adjective from college days. He was not as calm as he had seemed.

"This mess we're looking at isn't a figment of your imagination." His words came faster. "Unless you, me, the cops, Joe and Naomi are all suffering from folie à mob—we all had the same fantasy."

"Maybe this is just another random event."

"C'mon, get real. There's nothing random about this. Someone came into a high-security condominium and went directly to your unit."

He was right. She could not deny it. Someone had singled her out, ransacked her living space, and taken nothing. Unless . . . she was reminded of the musical printout.

"That sheet music wasn't on the piano." She started down the hall. "It's in my bedroom."

He followed as she stepped over debris to the pile of rumpled bedding. Sorting through it, she found the pajama doll at the bottom with her pillows. "I've had this doll since I was a child," she said, her hand groping inside the pocket that once held her little-girl nightgown. She pulled out the sheet, then stared at it in disbelief. The vandal must not have known about bed dolls that stored pajamas and gowns. It gave her a small pleasure to think that she might have thwarted the person who had trashed her home. She handed the musical score to Erik.

He looked at it for long seconds, turned the page over and then back. He frowned, his dark eyes puzzled. "This doesn't mean anything to me."

Liza led him back into the living room where she righted the piano bench and sat down. "This is how it sounds." She played the discordant notes.

There was a silence.

"Bizarre."

"I know." Her hands were still on the keys. "That's why I said it could be a prank, a joke."

Another silence.

"I don't know. My gut instinct says this is important."
He shook his head. "I can't tell you why."

"I know," she said softly. "That's exactly what I think."
He stepped back.

She stood up. "So we're back to square one."

"I don't know that I ever left square one."

Liza took the paper with the mysterious notes and
pushed it into her handbag. A safer place until she knew
what was going on. She was just glad that the burglar had
not realized that the doll on her bed had a secret pocket.

"Okay, here's the deal," Erik said. "You can't stay here
tonight so I'm taking you to my houseboat."

"I can't leave."

"Why not?"

She turned away, uncertain of her own feelings.
"There's Bella who's still too traumatized to come out
from under the bed." She hesitated, then faced him. "And
I'll be damned if I'm being scared out of my own home.
Someone may have violated my space, but I'm not about
to fall down and play dead." As she spoke her anger gathered force. "Just let the creep try to get in while I'm here."

Erik grabbed her by the shoulders. "Just what would
you do if someone did, for God's sake?"

She blinked quickly. "No one can get past my door
before I could call Joe or Nine-one-one."

"You won't leave?"

"No, I'm staying."

"Then I'll spend the night here."

"Didn't you say you had to be at the airfield at daylight
for your first-jump class?"

He nodded.

"You'd have to go home first for your gear, which means
you wouldn't get much sleep, and it would still be dark
when you left here anyway." She grabbed his arm. "I

appreciate your concern more than you know." She swallowed, but her resolve to face her fears gathered strength. Didn't a thrown rider get back on his horse or risk never riding again? "Thanks so much for being such a good friend, Erik, but I'm safer in this condo than anywhere else." She paused. "As long as I'm in here with all my auxiliary locks in place. Besides, whoever broke in must be satisfied that I don't have what they were looking for."

He was silent, digesting her words.

"Besides, I have to stay here sooner or later. This is where I live, my personal space where I hang my clothes and store my beauty aids." Her attempt at humor did not alter his expression.

"I can't change your mind?"

"No. Actually, I'm going to leave everything as is, coax Bella from under the bed and just go to sleep." She managed a laugh. "After I've locked myself in."

Erik took a little more convincing, but after Joe had phoned from downstairs to check on her, he agreed. "You have Joe's number next to your bed?"

"I will have it, believe me."

"I don't feel right leaving you."

"It's okay. I'm fine, really. The creep isn't coming back tonight."

After a little more convincing, Erik finally left. Liza kept busy after he had gone, remaking the bed, brushing her teeth, enticing Bella out with a special cat treat. She left a living room lamp on, then changed her mind, flung back her quilt and got up to turn it off. The city lights reflecting through the windows would take the blackness out of the rooms without artificial illumination. Safer that way, she told herself, but the thought stopped her in midstride, just before she stepped into the brightness of the living room.

Why is it safer? she asked herself. Because an intruder

can't see you as easily? Because someone out there might be watching you through binoculars?

The breath caught in her lungs. She jumped back, her legs crumpled like one of Jean's puppets and she folded onto the carpet, suddenly feeling like a bug under a microscope.

Breathe deeply, she instructed herself, as she had done many times recently. You're acting like a baby. No one can see you from the street twelve floors below.

But what about from the hundreds of windows in other buildings.

Stop it! This is your home, you know every inch of the floor, each piece of furniture, all the knickknacks, pictures and plants. Let the vandal beware. She wasn't afraid of a damnable coward who crept out of the night to destroy another person's property.

But she was.

She pulled herself up slowly. A gust of wind hit the windows, vibrating them. It was the North Wind from a fairy tale her father had once read to her and Jean, she thought, grasping for a reality within a fantasy. Those were the golden days before he died. In her mind's eye she saw again the round head of an evil North Wind in the picture book, his cheeks puffed with malice, poised to strike.

Enough already, she instructed herself, drawing in another deep breath. Then, without even glancing at the windows, she went directly to the lamp and switched it off. Then she made another loop through the rooms, rechecking the front door locks. Like a wraith, she slipped through the darkness to her bed, climbed in and pulled the quilt up to her chin. Something safe about blankets, she thought, inanely.

The ringing phone beside her brought her straight up to a sitting position. She grabbed it. Somehow even its sound felt like a threat. Face it, she told herself. You may have fooled Erik but you're scared stiff.

"Hello?"

"Liza?" Dave's voice came over the wire. "Did I wake you up?"

"No, I wasn't asleep yet." Her voice lacked volume. She glanced at the illuminated face of the clock. Eleven. Why was he calling so late?

"I left several messages earlier, wanted to take you out for a spur-of-the-moment bite. Then I decided you'd gone out for the evening. Just got back myself and figured you'd still be up." She'd forgotten to check messages. "How about dinner tomorrow night?"

She took a shuddering breath. "I can't, Dave."

"Hey, Brown Eyes. You sound strange. Is anything wrong?"

There was a long silence.

"Everything's wrong."

"What? Are you okay?" he asked, sharply.

She nodded, then realized he could not see her through the phone. "I'm in one piece."

"What in the hell happened? I can tell that you're upset."

"Someone broke into my apartment while I was out having dinner with Erik, and . . ." Her words trailed off.

"And?"

"They trashed it."

"For God's sake, call the police."

"They've already been here and gone."

"Put Erik on the phone."

"He's gone, too."

A pause.

"I'm on my way."

"No, really I'm—"

Her protest was too late. The dial tone was already sounding in her ear.

Chapter Nineteen

"YOU NEED A GOOD NIGHT'S SLEEP BEFORE TACKLING THIS mess," Dave had said after taking one look. "That means my house." His tone did not allow refusal.

Not that she'd wanted to. Once the silence had settled over her apartment after Dave hung up, her fear had intensified. She'd found herself straining her ears to identify any sound, then getting up to check the door locks. She felt violated . . . and vulnerable. She knew she would never relax enough to sleep.

"Besides," he'd added. "I'm not sure it's safe for you to stay here alone tonight."

It was a relief to have the decision taken out of her hands after all. Because Dave had early Saturday appointments the next day, they took separate cars; she followed him in the Miata out to Magnolia Bluff where he lived. Dave had spoken to the manager who was relieved that Liza would not be staying alone until after the locks were changed the next day. And Bella had seemed perfectly content to be left sleeping on Liza's bed, her traumatic experience apparently forgotten.

It was after midnight when he drove into his three-car garage and indicated that she pull in next to him. The automatic garage door closed as she got out of her car, grabbed her overnight bag and purse, and followed him into the house. She stood in the kitchen, suddenly feeling awkward in the raincoat that she had flung on over her long flannel nightgown.

Forget the false modesty, she told herself. Dave was the one who had suggested that she not take the time to get dressed. Not wanting to linger in her apartment one moment longer, she'd grabbed her things and left. They had not had time to talk yet, but she intended to fill him in.

"Relax, Liza," he said, looking rumpled and upset himself. "Everything's going to be okay. Nothing was stolen and by Monday you'll have the whole mess cleaned up." He paused. "In fact, I think you should hire someone to clean it up for you."

She shook her head. "Another person wouldn't know where things went." She caught herself clasping and unclasping her hands and jammed them into her coat pockets. "Besides, I'll feel better doing the work myself."

There was a silence. Then he closed the space between them and pulled her into his arms, holding her against his chest. "Poor Liza," he crooned. "My brave little Brown Eyes." He stroked her hair as he spoke. "I hope they catch the bastard."

She swallowed hard, sensitive to his compassion. She willed herself not to cry again. "Me, too," she said, shakily.

Dave stepped back, holding her at arm's length to peer into her face. "Hey, you're worn out. Let's get you settled."

He picked up her bag and led her into the bedroom

wing and ushered her into a guest room. She had never been beyond the living area, and the huge deck with the panoramic view of Puget Sound far below it. An elegant house, she thought. Did he choose the furnishings or did he have an interior designer? One thing was for sure; it was high-end—and expensive.

"There's a bathroom through that door." He pointed it out. "When you're settled in I'll have a nightcap ready for you in the living room." He smiled. "It'll help you sleep."

"Thank you, Dave," she said.

"No one is more welcome. You make yourself at home." She nodded and he left her.

Liza glanced around, feeling a little out of place in the exquisitely appointed room: cherry mahogany furniture, pale blue carpeting with draperies and bedspread in deeper tones—and genuine Tiffany lamps. There was not a speck of dust on anything. He has a housekeeper, she decided as she took off her raincoat and hung it in the closet, then washed her hands and brushed her hair. A forest green satin robe hung from a hook on the back of the bathroom door. For female guests? she wondered—and took it down, considering whether or not to put it on. Either that or just the nightgown. She decided to wear it. Her smile was involuntary. Satin over good old homespun flannel.

Stepping into the living room, she hesitated. Lovely, was the word that came to mind. He had turned on the gas fire in the fireplace, lit three small glass oil lamps on the coffee table in front of the sofa, and placed two half-filled brandy glasses next to them. Soft music from a built-in sound system was a soothing backdrop to the peaceful setting. Beyond the wall of floor-to-ceiling windows, the sky was clearing and a full moon peeked from behind fragments of high-flying clouds. He glanced up, saw her, and patted the cushion next to where he sat.

He picked up the glasses and handed her one after she was settled. "Happiness, for us both," he said, holding his glass up in a toast.

"And good friends."

"The best of friends, always."

They sipped the liquor, his eyes never leaving her face. His expression intensified somehow. "For all that you've gone through tonight, you look beautiful."

She glanced away. Her mother used to say, "when you feel overwhelmed by a compliment, just say thank you."

"Thank you." She swirled the brandy, watching as it caught the reflected firelight. "But anyone would look good in such a gorgeous robe." She wondered how many other women had worn it. A few, she decided. He was a man, not a monk. And he had been divorced for at least five years.

"Not everyone." Dave took another sip. As though sensing she was uncomfortable, he changed the subject to her break-in. "The police have any leads?"

She stared at the flames, trying to keep her composure. "I don't think there's much they can do unless the security cameras turn up something, like a picture of the intruder."

"How in hell did he get in the building in the first place?"

"He either had a key or someone let him in."

There was a hesitation.

"Sounds like this vandal was looking for something."

"Uh-huh. That's my conclusion as well." A pause. "And I had the feeling that the officers thought so, too."

"They say so?"

Liza took a bigger sip, trying to speed up the process of relaxing. "No. But I think they had a strong suspicion that I might be hiding something. It was so obvious that the intruder had keys to the building and to my unit." She stared at the amber liquid in her glass. "Otherwise their questions and comments were pretty ordinary, like what they'd say to any homeowner who'd experienced a break-in."

"And you can't think of anything you own that might have prompted someone to break into your place?"

She considered her answer, then decided to be honest. "There might be one thing."

He placed his glass on the table, his brows arched in a question, waiting.

"The strange sheet of music that was left for me at the Mission Church on the Sunday Nate died," she said. "I think it was from Nate."

"Music?" He leaned closer, his expression puzzled.

She filled him in, that Nate had been terribly stressed and wanted to talk to her before she gave his evaluation to Hawk, that she'd assumed that Nate had stood her up. "Now I wonder if he was scared, if the music had some significance to his situation."

"That's crazy, Liza. You think this discordant music has significance? To what situation?"

"I don't know. Maybe it had to do with his job."

"Impossible. I would have known if that were true. Nothing happens in the lab without my knowing."

"Nothing?"

He took her glass and placed it next to his. Then he held her hands, gently massaging the skin. "Brown Eyes, whatever that music is, Nate didn't write it."

He didn't believe her. No one would. It sounded far-fetched, even to her ears. There was no proof that the sheet of music came from Nate, or that it had any connection to the posts she'd seen on the Internet, she reminded herself. Nothing to substantiate any of the recent incidents, or bear out her suspicions. The weird musical notes could be a parishioner's joke, and the trashing of her condo may not be related to anything. She sighed. Tomorrow was time enough to consider the situation when she did not feel so vulnerable.

"I'm so sorry about what happened." Dave pulled her closer, so that her head rested on his shoulder while he gently stroked her back. "You didn't need this on top of Nate's and Alice's deaths and the theft of your sister's puppets." His hand stilled. "Is it possible that tonight was connected to the puppets, that someone followed you home and waited for a chance to search your place?"

"I don't think so. Why would anyone want puppets?"

"Who knows? There are a lot of crazies out there."

Liza watched the firelight flicker into the shadowy room, feeling close to tears again. What was the matter with her? She had never before felt so violated, so fragile. It was as though her pent-up fears had suddenly overpowered her ability to control them. Her emotional state was an even bigger mess then her apartment.

"You okay?"

She nodded, knowing she should go to bed. But unwilling to reveal how close she was to breaking down, Liza kept her face averted.

"You aren't," he said softly, shifting position so he could tilt her chin.

She closed her eyes, willing herself to regain her dignity, her ability to speak normally.

"Oh, my Liza. Go ahead and cry. Get it out of your system. You're safe here."

"I already did." She gulped. "I don't want to cry again."

And then she did.

He snuggled her closer, crooning words to soothe her. After a while he led her to bed, but instead of the guest room, he continued on to the master suite at the end of the house that bordered Discovery Park. In passing she noted the absolute splendor of his bedroom. Too spent to resist, she allowed him to help her out of the robe and under the covers.

"Don't be nervous, darling," he said softly. "I'm not seducing you." He kissed her, his lips lingering on hers for long seconds. "We'll save that for a happier time. For now you need to sleep."

The brandy was working. Vaguely she heard him securing the house for the night. She was almost asleep when he climbed into bed beside her. Gently he pulled her close. I trust him, she thought. And that was the last thing she remembered for several hours.

Liza came awake slowly, and for a moment was disoriented. Then she remembered. Dave, his house, his bed. She smiled into the dark, listening to his steady breathing. It was almost kinky. Sleeping together and no sex—twice. Like a brother and sister. No, not like that; there was an attraction between them, one she was not ready to deal with yet.

Through the windows she watched the clouds scuttle across a sky washed clean by the recent rain. The moon had risen, casting a silvery glow over Puget Sound and into the room. Wind nipped at the gutters, rattled a downspout, snapped branches against the siding, and hummed through the evergreen woods of Discovery Park next door. Liza tried not to think about the day ahead. Instead, she counted stars as they peeked from behind the clouds that trailed out of the heavens like hanging ivy.

Try tomorrow night.

The post on the forum between Comet and Snakeoil popped into her mind. She would have sat straight up but for Dave sleeping next to her.

Last night *was* "tomorrow night."

* * *

Liza awoke when Dave sat down on the bed next to her, a mug of steaming coffee in his hand. He was impeccably dressed in fawn slacks and an oxford shirt, ready to leave for work.

"Welcome back, Sleeping Beauty."

She propped herself on an elbow and combed back her tangled hair with her fingers. "I overslept?" she asked, grinning.

His green eyes twinkled. "It's almost nine. And I wanted to say good-bye before I have to leave." He handed her the mug. "After we have our coffee."

"Nine! You're usually at work by seven. I can drink it while I dress. I don't want to make you even later."

"Not necessary. You can go back to sleep, or shower, whatever, after I'm gone. Leave when you're ready, the garage door will close automatically behind you."

"Sensor controls?"

"Uh-huh."

Was she comfortable being in his house without him? It seemed too intimate. He was a caring, attractive man, but where was their friendship leading? Relax, she told herself. Dave was not pushing her. She shouldn't read anything into the situation, even though he had made his intentions clear.

"Mmmm," she said. "Coffee tastes delicious."

"Starbucks house blend."

"No wonder I like it."

He had been sipping his coffee while they chatted and now he put his mug on the nightstand. "One thing I do ask of you, Liza."

She waited.

"You have your cell phone with you?"

She nodded.

"Promise to call Joe before you leave here, alert him

that you'll be arriving within a half hour." He paused. "When you reach Boren Avenue, call him again so he can meet you at the garage door and walk you up to your apartment."

"Necessary precautions?"

"Unfortunately, in the short term at least."

"I had planned to do that, Dave." A hesitation. "But I appreciate your concern more than I can say." She glanced out the windows, noticing that it was one of those rare winter days in the Northwest: sunshine, blustery and cold. Maybe the brighter weather would lift her spirits.

"You probably want to postpone dinner tonight, right?"

She nodded and managed a smile. "I'll take a rain check."

"I'll call you later, just in case you're up for pizza at home."

They finished their coffee, she got up, put on the green robe and watched him leave from the doorway between the kitchen and garage. After he was gone she made the bed, showered and put on jeans and a sweater. Then she poured another cup of coffee to sip on while she applied a quick makeup job. She was anxious to get home and start the clean-up of her condo.

As Liza drove away from the house into the brilliant day, she reached for her sunglasses. The road paralleled the high fence along the edge of Discovery Park, and nearing an opening to its parking lot, she slowed her car.

On impulse, she turned in and stopped where she had a view of the long grassy slope that ended at the bluffs above Puget Sound. In the distance the islands, green and mysterious, seemed to lay at the foot of the snowy Olympic Mountain Range. Beyond it all, a long mass of sun-frosted clouds hung like a giant wave about to break, undulating into constantly changing images. There would be rain before noon, but for now it was a startling spectacle.

There were a dozen or more cars parked near her, their drivers either jogging or walking the trails with their dogs. Several elderly women sat together on a bench, enjoying the break in the weather.

Liza got out of the car, and wishing she had a down jacket, put on her raincoat instead. Grabbing her athletic shoes from the trunk, she sat on the seat and put them on. Then she grabbed her keys, locked the Miata, hoisted her handbag over her shoulder, and headed toward an empty bench halfway down the slope.

Fresh air will clear your head, she told herself, pulling on her leather gloves. Although she would have loved to walk the trail along the bluffs, she settled for the several hundred yards to the bench. She had too much work ahead of her to linger for long.

Between cold gusts of wind the sun was warm on her face. Liza watched a flock of seagulls riding the air currents, then a boy trying to fly a kite. She felt herself relaxing and leaned back, allowing her eyes to close. For a moment she would only think good thoughts. She felt safe; the park was full of people.

She came back to reality with a jolt. "My God!" she cried, glancing at her watch. "I dozed off."

She jumped to her feet. A half hour had passed since she had called Joe from Dave's house. He would be wondering what had happened to her.

The sun had gone down behind darkening clouds and a man was now flying the boy's kite. A father showing his son how to do it, she thought, and started back toward her car. The park was almost deserted now, people fleeing before the rain came again.

At first she attached no significance to the man running

up the slope toward her, pulling the kite string behind him. It was the boy's shouting that caused her to pause, glance behind her.

"Hey, Mister! Give me back my kite!"

The man was much closer. As she watched he let go of the string, allowing the kite to soar without restraints, and ran even faster toward her.

But it was his appearance that triggered her terror. He wore an oversized black coat that hung to his ankles, mirrored glasses and a mass of tangled hair—a wig?

For a moment Liza stared, paralyzed as the space dwindled between them.

Then adrenaline hit her brain. She started running, her feet barely touching the ground, her breath coming in ragged gasps. There were only two cars left when she reached the parking lot. In seconds she was locked inside the Miata and headed for the street.

Once she was blocks away from the park, Liza called Joe with trembling fingers. Had the kite-flyer really been after her?

Who was he? She didn't have a clue.

Chapter Twenty

JOE MET LIZA AT THE GARAGE DOOR AND ACCOMPANIED her to the apartment where Bella greeted them in the entry hall. Everything would have seemed normal but for the chaos.

Don't dwell on it, she instructed herself. Just get started.

She made coffee to drink as she cleaned. Joe came back with his tools to change the tumbler in her lock, and when he finished he gave her new keys.

"They conform with the system in the building so my master key should be the only one aside from yours that will open this door." He hesitated. "But remember what the police officer said, Liza. Since we don't know how the intruder managed to have a key that worked, I advise you to be careful. Keep the chain on when you're home."

"I'm having an alarm system installed." Liza had decided just that morning. Once in her apartment she felt safe. But what about coming home? Someone could be waiting for her.

"I should hear on Monday from the police about the

film on the security camera. I'll let you know right away."
He paused. "I have your work number. Want me to call
you there?"

"Please, as soon as you hear."   ·

He nodded and left. She quickly set the door locks.

She listened to upbeat music while she straightened and
cleaned and carefully avoided thinking about Discovery
Park. Or that someone was after her. Maybe she should
buy a gun; the next time someone chased her she would
stand her ground and find out what was going on. And
why.

No good, she argued mentally. If that person meant her
bodily harm and she had to defend herself, could she
really shoot? Liza vacuumed faster. She would end up
being shot by her own gun. She could not even kill a spi-
der—and she *hated* guns.

By the end of the day Liza was exhausted, mentally and
physically. Although she had not completed the clean-up
she had made progress. Trouble was, she found herself
washing everything, bedding down to the mattress, knickknacks, all the towels in the bathrooms, everything and
anything *HE* might have touched. But she wondered how
long it would take to cleanse her mind of having been violated. She suspected a long time.

She pleaded fatigue when Dave called with his earlier
suggestion of coming over with pizza. "I'm relieved Joe
changed the lock," he said. There was a brief silence. "Sure
you don't want company?"

"If I did it would certainly be you," Liza replied, kindly.
Then she reminded him that she had to stay alone sooner
or later, thanked him again for his help, assured him her
condo was secure and said she was going to bed early. A
minute later they hung up.

Liza fell into bed and, surprisingly, slept until the ringing phone awakened her in the morning. She grabbed for the receiver on the nightstand. She had barely said hello when Jean's voice was in her ear.

"Liza, are you awake?"

She glanced at the clock. Seven A.M. "Waking up."

"I figured you'd be up getting ready for church."

"That's not until eleven, Jean."

Something was wrong; Liza could hear it in her sister's voice. She sat up, letting the quilt fall away. "And I'm not playing today. One of Pastor Larsen's newest converts used to be a pianist and he's substituting for me."

"Oh good." Her relieved sigh came over the line. "Then you have time to talk."

"What's wrong?"

"Umm, I don't know if it's anything significant. Maybe it's a coincidence."

"Jean, you're upset. Something's happened." A pause. "What?"

She had not told Jean about her break-in, intending to call her after she was past the urge to cry. Jean, the worrier, did not need another worry. She would insist that Liza move in with her and Bill until they knew what was going on.

But when would that be? Liza asked herself. Until recently the past year had been one long roller coaster ride of ups and downs. Now those uncertainties had escalated into unrelenting, ongoing terror.

"Someone broke into our house last night while we were gone."

"What?" Liza swung her legs from under the sheet and sat up on the edge of the bed.

"I still can't believe it," Jean said. "This has never happened to us before."

"Was your house wrecked? Was anything stolen?"

"Nothing. Thank God for the burglar alarm. It went off and scared the creep away. The neighbors said the police were there within five minutes."

There was a long silence.

"Liza, are you there?"

"I'm here."

"Are you okay? I'm so sorry to upset you like this but—"

Liza interrupted. "Jean, my condo was broken into on Friday night." She switched the receiver to the other ear. "It wasn't a forced entry. Someone had a key."

The sound of Jean's sucked-in breath came over the wires. "What happened?"

Liza explained what she knew and that she had called the police. "Nothing was stolen, but my place was completely trashed."

"Liza, why didn't you call us? You shouldn't have stayed there alone."

"I spent Friday night at Dave's house. The manager changed the locks yesterday morning and I'm having an alarm system installed tomorrow or Tuesday."

"Oh my God! What's going on?" Jean's voice shook. "This is probably a dumb question, but do you think someone was after more puppets?"

"I asked myself that, too. But it doesn't make any sense. What would anyone gain from stealing puppets?"

"That's what I've been pondering since someone stole them out of the van," Jean said, sadly. "It's almost too much of a coincidence that both of our homes were burglarized shortly thereafter. Aside from us being sisters, what other connection could there be but the puppets?"

"I don't know. Maybe there really is no connection."

What indeed? Liza wondered, as she listened to Jean's concerns. She was not about to scare Jean even more by telling her everything that had happened lately. Aside from Alice and Nate's deaths, Jean didn't know about the other incidents. Jean's creative mind would imagine all sorts of reasons, and she would worry herself sick over Liza's safety.

Besides, Liza reasoned, how could the puppets be linked to Nate's music? If it was his music. Or to the lay-offs at International Air? Or to people dying in accidents? Maybe there was no correlation, and she was imagining a conspiracy that did not exist.

She and Jean talked a few minutes longer; after promising to call immediately if anything else happened, Liza hung up.

But what if there was a conspiracy? Why would it involve her? And now Jean? It was a dangerous puzzle.

Liza ordered an alarm system the next morning, then made arrangements with Joe to be available that afternoon so the technician could see her apartment and give her a price. She was a half-hour late in leaving for work.

Once she reached her office, Liza hung her coat, put her briefcase on her desk, her handbag under it and hurried down the hall to the ladies' room. Back in her office again, she hesitated, her eyes on her desk. Had her briefcase been moved? She glanced around, expecting what? The phantom? Her burglar? A puppet thief?

The paranoids are after you, Liza MacDonough. Get a grip. No one moved your briefcase.

But as she started work she was unsettled. Something *was* going on, someone *was* threatening her with an ominous presence. She needed time to think in peace. She had to be missing something. But what? Maybe she should hire Steve Wendall to investigate her life as well as Martin's. She stared out the window at another gray morning. Her PI had not been high on her priority list lately.

She needed to call him. Deep in thought, she did not hear the door open.

She jumped when Detective Barnes stepped into her office. "Sorry, I didn't mean to startle you."

"I startle easily these days," she said, coming around her desk. "My planets must be in the wrong configuration."

Her attempt at humor fell on deaf ears. Detective Barnes did not crack a smile. Maybe he's as dour as he looks today, she thought. A humorless man in a humorless profession.

The shoulders of his raincoat were soaked and his dark curly hair glistened with raindrops. "Mind if I sit down?" he asked. "I just ran through a downpour from the back lot and I'm bushed. Must be a full four blocks." He spoke with the same rapid-fire delivery she remembered from the last time she talked to him.

"Please do. Can I hang up your coat?"

He shook his head. "I can't stay long. Just wanted to swing by and see what's going on."

She went back to her chair and sat down, wondering what he had on his mind. Maybe new information about Nate or Alice?

"I saw you had an incident at your condominium." He stretched out and crossed his legs at the ankles.

His words surprised her. He was a homicide detective, not a street cop. "Break-ins aren't your department, are they, Detective Barnes?" Their eyes met, hers with a question, his noncommittal. "How did you hear about it?"

"It's all in the computer." A pause. "I understand nothing was stolen."

"That's right. Everything was just thoroughly trashed."

"Uh-huh. And your condo is in a high-security building, right?"

She nodded. "It's thirteen years old and this is only the

second burglary." She did not add that the first one was also her unit a year ago.

"Mind telling me what happened?"

"Do you mind telling me why you want to know?" she asked, her curiosity getting the best of her.

"Not at all." He straightened. "I always follow up on my investigations when new information surfaces."

His answer was too pat, Liza told herself. There was more to his visit than he was saying. But she decided to explain, as crazy and disjointed as it all sounded. What did she have to lose? Maybe it was time to get everything on record, just in case. Of what? she wondered. In case she was next on a phantom's hit list?

She told him about coming home to find her place trashed, that she had changed her locks and ordered an alarm system. She ended with the sheet of music that had been left for her at the Mission Church. "Nate was to meet me there that morning but didn't show up." She paused. "I believe it might have been Nate who left that music."

"There was no name on the envelope?" He had taken a notepad and pen from his pocket to jot down notes as she spoke, and now he looked up.

She shook her head. "Only mine."

"So you think your vandal was after this sheet music?"

"Yes," she said, holding his gaze, refusing to be intimidated by his cool demeanor.

"Did this person get it?"

"No. I'd hidden it and the intruder didn't find it."

"Could you explain why you feel it was Nate's music?"

"It would take quite a while, I'm afraid."

"I've got time. How about you? I know you must be busy."

She glanced at her watch. "I'm okay."

He slipped out of his raincoat and let it drape over the back of his chair. "Go ahead then, shoot."

"Some of this pertains to International Air and has to remain confidential, or I could lose my job."

"Whatever you say will stay between us." A hesitation. "You do realize that Nate no longer has the rights of privacy?"

"Because he's dead?"

"That's right." He wiped his wet hair off his forehead, settled back and waited for her to begin.

Liza started with her sense that something was wrong with the layoff procedures because of her clients' complaints, explained Nate's evaluation and his upset, and that Alice had also intended to confide an upsetting problem. Liza took a ragged breath, averting her gaze to the window. Then, in chronological order, she related all of the incidents that had happened to her, from her car break-in, to being chased twice, to her condo door being unlocked.

She glanced up to see the detective tapping a finger on his knee, his eyes fixed on his notepad. She wondered what he was thinking—that she was a flake, a hysterical woman with an overactive imagination?

There was a long silence as he continued writing. When he looked up she glimpsed a flicker of emotion on his face. Concern or disbelief? The expression was gone before she could decide, replaced by his usual air of professionalism.

"That it?"

"I think so." She found herself twisting a curl around her finger and stopped. Why was it important that he believe her? Because she had begun to doubt her own credibility?

"Tell me about the puppets?"

Her eyes widened. She had forgotten the puppets but apparently he already knew about them. Liza explained. "They were found in the hospital parking lot the next day." She blinked quickly, trying to hold back tears. "Destroyed."

Another flicker of expression on his face. "Puget Puppeteers is your sister's company?"

She nodded, not trusting her voice.

He glanced away, giving her time to compose herself.

"Someone broke into my sister's house on Saturday night," she said, finally. "The burglar alarm scared him off."

"Jeez. You're kidding."

That was something he *hadn't* known, she decided, seeing his surprise. He asked for Jean's full name and address, scribbling it down on his notepad. Then he looked up.

"Could you describe the man in the alley?"

She shook her head. "He was in the shadows but I had the impression that he was a transient."

"How about the guy in Pioneer Square?" His words picked up speed, like a courtroom lawyer peeling away the layers of evidence.

"He was dressed in a long black coat and was under a huge umbrella because it was raining so hard." She hesitated, trying to conjure up the man. "His size was obscured under his clothing and I never saw his face. When he got closer I was running and didn't waste time by looking back."

"And the kite-flyer in Discovery Park?"

"I had a better look at him. He was wearing the oversized coat again, mirrored sunglasses and he had long, tangled, dark hair. I thought it was a wig. When he got close he looked like someone out of a Halloween movie."

"So you think the person in Pioneer Square and the guy

in Discovery Park are one and the same." It was a statement.

Liza dropped her gaze to her knotted hands on the desk. "Yes, I do," she said, firmly.

"Why?"

She chewed at her bottom lip, trying to put her feelings into words. "I don't really know. My perception of them, I guess."

"A woman's intuition?" he asked, smiling briefly.

"I guess so," Liza replied, grinning back. For a fleeting moment the stern set of his features had softened. In other circumstances she would have found him an attractive man.

Another silence went by.

"I understand that your husband disappeared over a year ago," he said, surprising her again with his change of topic. "Do you think he might somehow be connected to—"

"Of course not," she said, interrupting, not about to admit that the thought had crossed her mind. "How did you know about Martin?"

He put up a flat hand in a gesture of surrender. "His case surfaced in the Washington Crime Information Center computer when I did my usual background check concerning your connection to the Nate Garret and Alice Emery accidents."

"You checked me out?" she asked, sharply. "I haven't broken any law and both deaths were ruled accidental."

"Just procedure. You were involved with both of them at the time they died."

"Why would Martin come up? That's my private life." She tried to control her annoyance. "He didn't know Alice or Nate."

"Hey, this is a computerized world these days." He looked apologetic. "And the WACIC is a great tool to help us piece together seemingly hopeless puzzles. Victims, bad guys and complainants alike go into the computer, and incidents related to any one of them come out on the same printout."

"Martin came up because of me?"

"Uh-huh. The case is still open."

There was a brief silence.

"Martin worked in the computer lab," she said, hesitantly. "But he was a lower level employee than Nate and I don't think they'd even met. Martin was into music, not computers. He only worked there for a paycheck."

Detective Barnes studied the toe of his soggy shoe. "I know."

"What else do you know, detective?" She hesitated. "Do the police have any new leads on Martin's whereabouts?"

He spread his hands. "Not that I'm aware of. Sorry."

Another pause.

She pushed back her chair and stood up. "If I've answered all of your questions then I'd better get back to work," she said, realizing that he could not know how tormented she'd been over Martin's disappearance.

"Just one more thing," he said, standing, too. "Could I have a look at Nate's file?"

"I know the dead have no rights, but I can't let you take the file out of my office. Could you look at it here?"

"No problem."

She moved around the desk to the filing cabinet. "There isn't all that much in it—my notes and the evaluation of his mental state. I don't have his personnel information."

He took the folder and sat back down. As he read she tried to do some work. It was no use. He was a disconcerting presence. Finally, he closed the file and got to his feet.

"Typical stuff," he said, frowning. "No mention of what might have been distressing him."

"I presume that's what he was going to tell me."

He put on his raincoat and started for the door. "Oh, I almost forgot." He faced her, the intensity back in his eyes. "I'd like to take a look at that sheet music. Do you have it with you?"

"In my purse. It's been there since Friday night when I stayed over at a friend's house."

He waited.

She grabbed her handbag from under the desk. Standing, she opened it and peered at the contents. She did not see the sheet of music that had lain against the leather side. "It has to be here. I know I didn't take it out."

The detective stepped closer. "Maybe it slipped under your wallet?"

She turned the purse upside down, emptying it onto her desk top. Their eyes met. "It can't be gone!"

"It appears that it is," he said. "Do you ever leave your purse unattended?"

"Never!" She gulped air. "Except this morning before you arrived. I went to the ladies' room down the hall." She plopped onto her chair, remembering her sense of someone having moved her briefcase. She told the detective. "But surely I would have seen them. I was only gone three minutes."

"Not necessarily." He moved back to the door. His hand was on the knob when he turned back. "Listen, Liza—okay if I call you Liza?"

She nodded, for the moment too upset to do anything else.

"Listen," he said again. "Until we know what's going on, be careful. Watch your back." A pause. "And if you should find that music, give me a call. Otherwise I'll be in touch." Then Detective Barnes stepped into the hall and was gone.

She stared at the closed door. The professional homicide cop was concerned for her safety. His warning scared her. Be careful of what? An unhinged client? Someone trying to keep her from knowing what was going on at the company? Martin?

And why had Detective Barnes come by in the first place. There was no homicide case. And if it had nothing to do with either Nate or Alice, then what did his visit mean? His job was to investigate something. Me? she wondered.

The ringing phone sent shock waves through her veins. Pull it together, she instructed herself. You're on company time.

When she picked up the receiver she sounded almost normal. It was Joe, her building manager, with the news that he had heard from the police officer about her break-in. The security camera had not filmed the intruder; someone had knocked it askew so that the lens had pointed at the floor.

It figures, she thought. Whoever was trying to terrify her was succeeding. If she was not such a rational person she could almost believe that she, her condo and her office were haunted.

Maybe so, Liza reminded herself. But not by anything supernatural. Her phantom was a living, breathing human. And she did not intend to be his next victim.

Chapter Twenty-One

LIZA MADE IT THROUGH ALL HER APPOINTMENTS, UPDATED her client files, then sat back, fatigued by the day's events. She had arrived late in the morning and now she contemplated leaving early. What the hell, she told herself. Why not? It was only going on five but it was already dark outside.

She was leaving a message for callers on her voice mail when the phone rang. She picked it up to hear her condo manager's voice.

"Sorry to bother you again at work, Liza," he said. She smiled. One nice thing had grown out of all her trials and tribulations lately; she was now on a first name basis with Joe and Naomi, both of whom had taken a genuine interest in her safety. "I've got a bid from the alarm company and wanted to run it by you," he said.

"That's great. I'll go over it when I get home."

"When you go over it is why I'm calling," he said. "If the company has the okay now, they have time tomorrow to do your job." A pause. "The technician is right here in the office with me. He understands the situation and is willing to put you at the top of their scheduled appointments."

Liza smiled again. She could picture Joe applying pressure, painting a scary scenario. She sobered. *It was a scary scenario.* "What's the bid?"

He told her.

There was a silence while she did mental arithmetic. After sending Steve Wendall a check her savings account was dangerously low. And payday was still a week away. She would have to put the charge on her Visa, pay it off in payments if necessary. She sat down, feeling too weighted down by the financial implications to continue standing. But *you have to protect yourself*, she told herself. *You have no other option.*

"Tell him to go ahead. If he can put the cost on my Visa."

She heard him ask the technician. "That's fine with him; he says everyone uses charge cards for their services."

"Good."

"He'll leave the contract for you to sign, which includes a place for you to fill in your Visa information."

Liza hesitated. "You think this is the best price I can get, Joe?"

"I do Liza. I'll explain why later."

Liza could tell that Joe didn't want to discuss his reasoning in front of the man in his office. "Okay, I'll go by what you say." A pause. "Thanks, Joe. I appreciate your efforts on my behalf."

"Just doing my job," he said, but his tone said he was pleased. "Call me when you leave work and I'll meet you in the garage."

"I won't be right home. I have to stop by my sister's house." Another pause. "I don't want to interrupt your off-time."

"No problem, Liza. I'm here. Whenever you get here, give me that call." A short laugh sounded in her ear. "Naomi would have my hide if I didn't follow through on this. She's very supportive of women in, uh, untenable situations."

"Thanks again, Joe." She didn't ask him to elaborate. It was enough to know that Naomi was on her side. "I'll call you when I get close to home."

Slowly, Liza replaced the receiver into its cradle. Over the course of the day since Detective Barnes had left, the puppets had surfaced in her mind many times. How were they meaningful in what was going on around her? Her mind had spun in circles and she had come up with nothing, except that she wanted to protect the last puppet Martin had helped create. Harlequin, a minor character in several of Jean's productions, did not have a role in the current shows. And the only safe place for him seemed to be her condo now that she had added safety precautions.

Grabbing her things, Liza hurried out to her car. Climbing under the wheel she wondered why she had not heard from Dave since Saturday night. Hopefully, she had not hurt his feelings by turning down his offer of pizza. It was unlike him not to have called.

It took longer than expected to get through the city traffic to Madison Street, and she almost decided to forget going to her sister's house.

No, she told herself. You might regret it later if something happened to the Harlequin puppet.

While Liza waited at a red light she called Jean on her cell phone, explained that she was stopping by and was about to disconnect when Jean's anxious question came out of the receiver.

"Is everything all right?"

The question was becoming a family cliché. "It's fine,

Jean. Nothing more has happened." A pause. "I'll explain
when I get there."

"Are you still at work?"

"I'm on Madison headed east across First Hill. I should
be there in ten minutes."

"See you then."

A short time later Jean was waiting in the open doorway
as Liza got out of the car and darted through the drizzle to
the front porch. A glance told her that Jean and Bill had
made some changes, too. A floodlight had been installed
on the outside corner of the garage and small garden
lamps had been placed among the shrubbery to illuminate
the dark places in the yard. All the regular exterior lights
were also lit.

"Bill installed them," Jean said, noticing Liza's
appraisal. "They have light sensors so they'll come on
automatically at dusk."

It was incredible that they had to install alarms, more
lights and extra locks, Liza thought, hugging Jean close,
relieved that she seemed okay. If they could only figure
out what was going on.

They went into the house and straight to the kitchen
where Liza put her purse down and draped her coat over a
chair. Without asking, Jean poured two glasses of
Chardonnay, handed one to Liza and then sat down at the
table across from her. "We need it," she said, sipping.

Liza explained that her alarm system was being installed
the next day, and then her feelings about the Harlequin
puppet. "I guess I have this crazy intuition that if anything
happens to it Martin won't be coming back."

Jean nodded. "I don't need Harlequin right now and of
course you can keep him for a while. I understand how
you feel, Liza. It's the only one left that Martin helped create." A hesitation. "After all of our new safety precautions,

the puppets are safe now whether they are stored at your house or mine."

Liza swallowed some wine, washing down the sudden lump in her throat. Her emotions were on the ragged edge, her feelings scattered. She didn't know if she even wanted Martin back if he'd deserted her. But she did need to know whether he was okay or had fallen off the ship and drowned. Without knowing one way or the other her future seemed so uncertain—and dangerous.

"Are you alright, Lizzy?" Jean asked, softly.

"Just a little jumpy." Liza resisted the urge to confide her conversation with Detective Barnes. All it would do is make Jean more apprehensive about the reason behind his visit. Besides, he hadn't told her anything new. "I'll get over it with a good night's sleep."

They talked, speculating about the break-ins and the theft of the puppets, but there were no answers. Liza finished the wine and then stood up. Jean wrapped the Harlequin puppet in tissue paper, placed it in a shopping bag and handed it to Liza. They walked to the front door in silence.

"You okay to drive?" Jean asked.

"I only had a glass of wine, not enough to affect me. I'm fine."

"Give me a call when you get home," Jean said after they hugged good-bye and Liza had stepped onto the porch.

Liza nodded, then ran back through the rain to her car. She honked and waved as she left the driveway, Harlequin on the seat next to her. As she neared her condominium her nervous system went to full alert. Even the whine of the tires on the wet pavement seemed to hum a warning—be careful, be careful. She grabbed her cell phone to call Joe.

*   *   *

After she locked the door behind Joe, Liza stepped out of her damp shoes, put down the athletic bag she had brought up from the car trunk, and hung her coat in the hall closet. Then she carried the Harlequin puppet into her bedroom. For long seconds she stared at its orange and black satin body, its garish face, the sequins and tassels, remembering.

"You'll be safe on my bed," she told the puppet and set him against the pillows.

Liza undressed, put on a robe and went to the kitchen where she took a container of her homemade vegetable soup from the freezer. She emptied it into a saucepan and turned the stove burner on low to heat it. On the way to run a bath she retrieved her sweats from the athletic bag, dropped them into the washer and turned it on. Time to get back on my exercise regime, she told herself. Time to get back to my life.

She was filling the tub when she remembered her answering machine; she had forgotten to check her phone messages. Hurrying into her office, she pushed the play button and heard Dave's voice, "Hey, Brown Eyes, you left work early. And now you're not home. Damn it!" He laughed. "Don't feel bad, I'll just have a lonely supper without you." A pause. "Just teasing. Catch up with you tomorrow. Bye." Liza was smiling as she went to take her bath.

A short time later she was back in the kitchen to dish up her soup when the phone rang. She grabbed the receiver with one hand and put the pan back on the burner with the other.

"Hello."

"Liza, Steve Wendall."

"Steve." She opened the oven door to pull out a heated roll before it burned. "I've been wondering about you. What's going on?"

"I've stirred up some shit." There was a lot of background noise. She pressed the phone into her ear. "Got some action going."

"What happened?"

He said something but she could not quite make out the words.

"Steve, you're fading out."

"Sorry. Bad connection." His voice sounded a little stronger. "I'm at the parachute center and there's an orchestra of loud sounds, including airplane engines." A pause. "Are you up for a while?"

"Sure. Are you calling back?"

"No, thought I'd come over with the update." Another pause. "I've dug up some information and we need to discuss how to proceed with it. Okay?"

She had been pacing as they talked and the phone cord had twisted around her waist. "Of course. Come over."

"See you within an hour then."

"Wait! Don't hang up, Steve."

"Almost did."

"I know you'll explain when you get here but can't you tell me what this is all about? Is Martin alive?"

More static and noise. His voice was fading again. ". . . and Martin was involved in illegal activities with this guy. Also, I have a witness who saw that same man on the Christmas cruise—" His words came in and out like he was switching off and on. Finally, "This connection is fucked. If you can hear me, Liza, I'm hanging up. Be there as soon as I can."

The dial tone sounded and she hung up, frustrated.

Liza ate part of the soup and then gave up on it. She had lost her appetite. She put her bowl and utensils into the dishwasher, then loaded the wet laundry into the dryer, but she could not get the PI's words out of her head. Was Steve saying that Martin was involved in criminal activities? Martin had often been gone evenings and on weekends, flying or playing with his band somewhere.

For a moment she stood at the window, transfixed by the city lights, remembering Martin. He was the man who'd played the Mission's Santa Claus each year, had helped set up puppet shows for sick kids, had donated musical performances at charity fund raisers. The only illegal thing he'd ever done was smoke marijuana and he had always been honest about it. Martin valued honesty. He cared about people. He would never have been involved in criminal activities; Liza would stake her life on that.

She wandered around her apartment, watering plants, feeding Bella, waiting for Steve Wendall's call from the front entrance. And who was the other man involved in the alleged illegal activities? Someone she knew?

Liza glanced at the clock. An hour and a half had gone by since his call. Where in hell was he?

The bell signaled that her clothes were dry. She folded her sweats and placed them back into her athletic bag. Her water bottle was still inside and she pulled it out, then went to the sink and dumped it. Although almost full, the contents had to be stale; the water smelled like old almonds. About to rinse and refill, her hand stilled on the faucet, her gaze glued to the initial strip on the bottom.

A.E. *It was Alice's bottle.* The identical containers had been switched by accident at the sauna that night. It was her bottle of water that had been analyzed by the crime lab.

It took a minute for the significance to sink in. Then she ran to find her briefcase and Detective Barnes's card with his phone number. His voice mail picked up.

"This is Liza MacDonough," she said, and explained that something important had happened. "Please call me back as soon as possible." She added her work and home numbers and hung up.

Another glance at the clock told her that it was now over two hours since Steve Wendall called. Restless, she sat down at the piano to look over the pieces she planned to play on Sunday.

But her mind was on the stolen sheet of music. The notes, so discordant and odd, seemed to ring in her head. She had always been able to play by ear, recreate a piece once she had heard it, and she had gone over the mysterious composition many times.

With one finger, Liza tapped out the notes from memory. Close, she thought. Could be off a little but not much. All were in B-sharp. As she went over it again, refining and tweaking the sound, she realized there was a recurring pattern: B A D G E. If she had remembered correctly. She went to find a pen and paper, came back and wrote everything down before she forgot.

She turned on the television but could not concentrate. Where was Steve Wendall? He should have called if he had changed his mind about coming over.

By the eleven o'clock news she knew he was not coming. Her annoyance had given way to a vague apprehension and she decided to call him. The ringing at the other end of the line went on and on. No one answered. She finally replaced the receiver in its cradle. A few minutes later she was in bed, fatigued but wide awake.

Count sheep, count backward, anything to fall asleep, she told herself. But all she could think about was that Steve Wendall had stood her up.

And the man before him who had not kept his appointment with her—Nate.

And the last woman—Alice.

Chapter Twenty-Two

THE CESSNA CAME OUT OF THE CLOUDS, LIKE AN INSECT *drawn toward the runway lights. Another small plane waited at the end of the field, its engine revved up in anticipation of takeoff. Noise filled the night around him.*

He stood in the deep shadows at the far end of the parachute center, his presence obscured by the thick shrubbery that grew against the chain-link fence. His car was down the road on a side street behind a convenience store. He could not be seen by anyone at the airport.

They might remember him.

It's shit that I'm even in this position, he told himself. He was above the rabble, the macho punks who believed jumping out of airplanes made them a man. The fuckers. Too stupid to be anything other than a grandstander; he had known many of their types.

His glance darted to the aged Fiat convertible, red and rusting and parked right in front of the entrance—Steve Wendall's car. Her PI. Fury threatened to overwhelm him. She was a bug that needed to be squashed. A fuckin' cunt whose sniffin' nose was longer than Pinocchio's. She had to die.

Soon.

Be patient, he instructed himself, taking deep breaths. Do not let your emotions override good sense. Panic is the one thing you can't afford. Stay calm, be cool. Don't forget your image as a law-abiding citizen, a sensitive man who listens to women and cares about babies.

The words in his head were his mantra. His racing heart slowed. Once more he concentrated on the entrance to the parachute center where there had been too much activity for him to accomplish what he had come to do.

Five minutes passed. No one else came out of the building. It was safe for him to proceed.

Slowly, he moved away from his place in the darkness and out into the light. If anyone suddenly appeared he had several stories ready: he was here to meet someone or he was just leaving himself. In the worst case scenario he could skip the whole thing. Until it was safe.

No one came out of the building. He was in the clear.

Hesitating near the Fiat, he glanced around, his ears strained for the smallest sound. Nothing seemed amiss. No one was in sight. It was safe for him to proceed.

Quickly he stepped next to the passenger side of the Fiat. Although the top was up he knew it was unlocked. He had checked earlier. Another glance told him no one was in sight.

He opened the door. The water bottle lay on the cracked, black leather seat. He reached for it with one hand, pulling a vial from his jacket pocket with the other. In less than ten seconds he had emptied the clear liquid from the tiny glass tube into the plastic container, shaken the bottle and replaced it on the seat.

The perfect crime, just like the last time.

Then he stepped away, his eyes darting everywhere, his senses alert for sounds or movement, slipping ever deeper into the shadows. Once clear of the parking lot he turned and ran back into the safe haven of the night.

Hey, you hippie mother-fucker in your frizzed-out hair and Birkenstocks, see if you can investigate this. He sent his message subliminally. *Eat your vegetarian food and drink your sixty-four ounces of pure water a day. It's good for your health.*

And your death.

Liza was up early the next morning, having spent a restless night, waking up periodically to wonder why neither Steve Wendall nor Detective Barnes had called her back. She checked her answering machine. No messages.

As her coffee dripped she called Steve's number. Again, the ringing went on and on.

Something was wrong, she just knew it.

And what about the detective? She dialed his voice mail and left another message.

By the time Liza was ready to leave for the office she had come to a decision. She had no clients scheduled for today; she would go into her office, pick up her work and do it from home so that she'd be there when Steve Wendall called. Flextime was a job privilege she had not used. Now was the time to get with the new century, she told herself.

Surprisingly, Al agreed. "It will do you good to have a quiet day to write evaluations and update files," he said. "A change of pace helps to guard against burnout." He patted her on the back and sent her on her way.

How nice of Al, she thought, smiling as she ran through the stormy morning to her car. Drenched, she climbed inside, started the engine and headed for First Hill.

"La Niña, will you ever have mercy on us drowning humans?" she asked, her eyes on the gray sky.

As Liza was about to pass a freeway on-ramp she abruptly changed her mind about going straight home. Twisting the wheel, she drove onto I-5 and headed toward

520, which would take her across Lake Washington to the east side. She was too antsy to wait for answers: Steve Wendall not showing up, Detective Barnes not returning her calls, the CB forum on the Internet and all the other unanswered questions. She could start with what she did know: Nate Garret's computer. Maggie would have just seen her boys off to school and should still be home.

A half hour later she drove up to Maggie's Woodinville house, just as the winter sun sent a shaft of light from behind a break in the clouds. A good sign? She needed one.

She rang the bell and waited.

Maggie was surprised to see her. "Come in, come in!" she said. "What an unexpected pleasure."

"I was in the area and thought I'd take a chance that you were home," Liza said. "I had a question about Nate's music system and hoped you'd be able to answer it." A pause. "So long as I'm not imposing on your time. I don't want to disrupt your schedule if you have other plans."

Maggie shook her head. "Cup of coffee?"

"Sure. Sounds good."

They went into the large country kitchen that looked like a picture from *Better Homes and Gardens*. Liza wondered how long Maggie would be able to keep her home.

"My parents stepped in to help me," she said, guessing Liza's concern. "I don't know what I'd do without them." She poured coffee, placed the mugs on the table and they both sat down.

"I'm so glad you have a supportive family."

Maggie nodded. "I've enrolled at Seattle Pacific University starting next quarter so that I can add a teaching certificate to my degree. I always wanted to go back to school but never took the time." She smiled sadly. "My parents have made it possible for me to keep the house and my boys in private school until the end of the year. Once I have a job I'll be able to support us." Tears welled in her eyes. "I'm very fortunate in that respect. I just wish that Nate was here to see me finally fulfill my dream of teaching."

Liza reached to pat her hand as Maggie composed herself. She listened while Maggie told her about how Erik was helping her boys cope, then heard about Maggie's hopes for her family's future. They were on their second cup of coffee before they talked about Nate's computerized music system and the songs he had composed on it.

"Would you like to see them?" Maggie asked.

"If you're up to it," Liza replied, suddenly feeling like an intruder. Although she wanted to see the system, she didn't want to upset Maggie.

"Sure," Maggie said, standing to lead the way to the back of the house. "No one has used it since Nate." She hesitated. "Except Detective Barnes who asked to see Nate's backup files."

"Detective Barnes was here?"

"Uh-huh. I was surprised, too, but he had proper credentials and I didn't see any reason why I shouldn't let him. He said it was just a routine follow-up."

"When was that?"

"A few days ago."

Right after his visit to my office when he found out about the sheet of music, Liza thought. "Did he say what he was looking for?"

"No, he was vague when I asked him that. He just said he was tying up loose ends on the case." She paused. "He also said that the driver who hit Nate had been shattered by the accident and was in counseling."

Liza nodded, understanding "Did he find anything of significance in Nate's backups?"

"Nope, just the music compositions, all the songs I already knew about. Then he thanked me and left. I wondered what in the heck was going on, especially since you'd already asked about Nate's music." She glanced away. "But then I don't know anything about police procedure in this kind of situation."

"Mind if I look at the backup files?"

Maggie shook her head. "Although I'm beginning to wonder what all the mystery is about." Her eyes were suddenly direct. "There's no other reason, is there Liza? Something that might have to do with Nate's death?"

"No mystery," Liza said, avoiding a direct answer. It would be cruel to tell Maggie about all the strange things that had happened, incidents that might not be related to Nate. After all, she had no proof, no real evidence that any of those incidents were even connected to each other. "Someone from the company said that Nate had composed a song for a birthday event, and I offered to check if it was all right with you."

"That sounds like Nate," Maggie said, diverted. "He was always doing nice things for people."

It took a couple of minutes for Liza to determine what Detective Barnes had already discovered: there was no weird musical score in Nate's backups. A few minutes later she had thanked Maggie and was back in her car, headed away from the Garret's beautiful house.

Why had Barnes checked Nate's computer? she asked herself. He was a homicide detective, and Nate's case was closed, ruled accidental.

He did believe it was an accident, didn't he? Liza was beginning to wonder.

Liza drove slowly along the back streets to her building. As she approached the garage entrance a man stepped out of a car parked next to the driveway, waved to her, and then pointed to the front entrance.

Detective Barnes.

She nodded, then continued into the garage, parked and took the elevator to the lobby entrance on the first floor. The detective was waiting beside the resident board right outside the exterior glass door. She opened it and let him inside.

"I was beginning to wonder if you had gotten my message," she said, assuming that was why he was here.

"I called your office this morning. Your secretary said you weren't in today, that you were working from home."

They stepped into the elevator and she punched the twelfth floor. Detective Barnes was a puzzle. Surely he had more important things to do than wait for her. Again she wondered about his motives.

Once in her apartment she saw that the security technician had not yet arrived to install the alarm system. She offered the detective a chair at the dining room table, and as he took off his coat and sat down, she started coffee dripping. Then she took the chair opposite him.

"What is Steve Wendall to you?"

His question took her aback. It was the last thing she expected him to say. "Steve is a private investigator I hired to look into my husband's disappearance."

He nodded, waiting.

She got up to pour coffee for them. "He called last night from Sampson's Parachute Center and was coming over with a report, but he never showed up." She hesitated. "I haven't been able to get a hold of him since. He doesn't answer his phone."

"Did he say what was in his report?"

Her hand stilled on the mug she had just placed in front of him. "Why? What does my private investigator have to do with anything?"

There was a silence.

"Steve Wendall died last night, in a car accident."

Her knees buckled and she sat down hard on her chair, her coffee splashing onto the table. For long seconds she could not respond. "What happened?" she asked, faintly.

"He was on the freeway going south and apparently lost control of his car. Crashed into an overpass abutment at full speed. Didn't have a chance in his old Fiat convertible."

"My God!"

"What time did you talk to him last night?" he asked casually, too casually?

She told him, her words wobbling. "He tried to tell me something but between the airplanes taking off and a bad connection I couldn't hear him." She paused. "He said he would explain when he got here and hung up."

Detective Barnes looked thoughtful. Then he sipped his coffee and Liza wondered if he was taking the time to process what she had said. "So you don't know what he was going to report?"

"Only that he claimed to have information that Martin was involved in illegal activities with another man, and that he had a witness who saw that man on the Christmas cruise the night Martin vanished." She hesitated. "My husband could not have been involved in anything criminal."

He inclined his head, acknowledging her. "Why not?"

Disconcerted, she spread her hands. "I just know. Martin was dedicated to his music, hated his job at International Air, but he was not dishonest."

"Oh yeah, he worked for your company." He had taken his ever-ready notepad from his pocket and was scribbling notes. "Did Wendall have physical evidence, too?"

"What do you mean?"

He shrugged. "Anything tangible he was going to show you? Notes, records, anything like that?"

"I don't know." Her gaze was direct. "You would know that better than I. Was anything found in his car?"

He hesitated again. "I'm afraid there was nothing left."

A hollow feeling spread upward from her stomach. "I don't understand."

"The car caught fire."

"You mean . . . he burned to death?"

He nodded.

"Do you think someone killed him?"

"The Washington State Patrol said it was an accident, that there was no indication of foul play. There is no way of determining if he'd been under the influence of alcohol or drugs—or anything else—now."

"Steve was a health nut. He didn't drink or do drugs."

Detective Barnes kept on scribbling. Then he swallowed the last of his coffee and stood up. "I'm sorry, Liza." He paused. "This has been a hard few weeks for you."

She gulped, trying not to burst into tears. Keep your cool, she told herself. Hysteria will not make things right. "Too many people close to me are dying sudden deaths. Why?"

"Might just be a coincidence."

"It isn't, Detective Barnes. Something is going on and I don't know how to sort through everything to find out what it is."

"If there is something it'll surface."

"When? After more people die? Surely you're above giving false hope, detective," she retorted, her voice still shaking. She knew he had suspicions despite what he said. Or he would not be standing in her dining room.

He considered her questions. "I've cross-checked the deaths through the state's HITU computer repository," he said finally.

"What's that?"

"HITU—Homicide Information Tracking Unit—is basically a clearinghouse of information. It stores the records about missing persons, homicides, rapes, sex offenders and other crimes." He paused. "The system allows us to monitor crimes and make connections between similar cases in different jurisdictions." He put on his raincoat. "There were no matches for the deaths of these people you know, Liza. In other words, no similarities."

Her breath blew out in a long sigh. "So you do suspect murder."

"I didn't say that. It's routine to look at all possibilities."

He was being ambiguous again. You're not fooling me, Barnes, she told him silently. Too much has happened to be accidental and you know it—evidence or not.

He started toward the door just as someone knocked. "You expecting someone?"

She shook her head.

His body posture altered somehow, as though he had gone to full alert. He glanced out the peephole and then opened the door. Joe, and a man with the name of the alarm company stamped on his shirt pocket, stood in the hall.

"I saw your car in the garage, Liza, so I figured I'd better knock before barging in." Joe inclined his head toward the other man. "Brian is here to install the alarm."

"Oh, thank goodness," she said. She did not introduce Detective Barnes, sensing he did not want her to. She walked into the hall with him.

"You're getting your alarm system today?"

She nodded.

"Good." The elevator door opened and he stepped inside. "Be real careful, Liza. I did hear everything you said. I'll stay in close touch." Then the door closed with a soft whoosh.

She was back in her place before she realized that she had forgotten to tell him about Alice's water bottle. Maybe there could be incriminating fingerprints on it, maybe there was enough liquid left to analyze. I'll leave another message, she thought.

And hide the damn thing.

Chapter Twenty-Three

LIZA'S NEW ALARM SYSTEM WAS INSTALLED BY THREE o'clock. During those early afternoon hours the sky had brightened, the clouds had broken up and retreated to the horizon, and a cool winter sun sparkled on the rain-drenched city. An uplifting sign, she told herself. And her condo was virtually burglar proof.

A sound interrupted her thoughts, startling her. She turned down the loud volume on her CD player, silencing the voice of Elton John singing *A Candle in the Wind*, her own small tribute to Steve Wendall. Then realizing what she'd heard, Liza ran from the living room to the kitchen and picked up the phone.

"Hello?"

"Hey, what are you doing tonight?" It was Erik calling and she could tell that he was in good spirits. He did not wait for her reply. "Cause if you're home I'm inviting myself over for a stir-fry. Of course I'll bring the chicken parts and wine. How about it?"

She smiled, remembering the many occasions over the

years when she had heard the same impromptu spiel from
him. Her good friend was on a campaign to cheer her up.

"It's a deal. What time?"

"Is seven too late?"

"Seven is fine, but why so late?"

"I'm out at the parachute center. Since the weather
cleared momentarily we're taking advantage of it so several
students can do their first jump. Fortunately, I was able to
round up a pilot." He paused. "After the flight I have a little paperwork, and then I'll wade out into the rush-hour
traffic and hope it's not a three-hour commute back to the
city."

"You're at the parachute center?" Liza's voice went flat.
For a second she had forgotten Steve Wendall's death. She
had meant to call Erik tonight and tell him. Now she
would explain later, after they had eaten.

"Yeah." A hesitation. "What's wrong, Liza?"

"I'll tell you tonight."

"Tell me now. I've got time."

"I had an alarm system installed today," she began.

"I'm glad you decided to do that." Another pause. "But
that's not what's bothering you. C'mon, what's happened
now?"

She told him.

There was a long silence.

"Son of a bitch," he said, his voice deceptively soft. "I
just talked to the guy yesterday afternoon when he was
here. He was asking about Martin and I told him we'd
been friends for years—that I'd always counted on Martin
in a pinch."

She swallowed hard, unable to respond for a moment.

"I saw him talking to other people here, including some
woman from your company."

"A woman from International Air?"

"Uh-huh." A pause. "Sylvia . . . Kemper. Something like that."

"Sylvia Kempton?"

"Yeah, that's it. Sylvia Kempton."

"What was she doing there?"

"I have no idea. One of the plane mechanics knew who she was and where she worked. That's all I know."

"Has she been there before?"

"Don't know." He turned from the phone and said something to someone. "Liza, I think I'll cancel this flight and—"

"No Erik. Please don't. You may not have another weather opportunity anytime soon. I'm okay, really. We can talk when you get here."

"You sure?"

"Positive."

His sigh sounded in her ear. "All right then. But I know you're upset and I hate to hang up." A pause. "Anything else you need for supper? I don't want you running to the store alone."

"Nothing," she said. "In fact I have the chicken. Just bring the wine. And yourself."

"Remember what I said. Don't go out."

"Promise. See you when you get here."

Their conversation ended and Liza was left wondering about Sylvia Kempton. What was Sylvia doing at the parachute center? Maybe it had nothing to do with anything, a coincidence. Sylvia, or someone she knew, could be a pilot. It was even possible that she jumped out of planes for fun. But the thought that she had been at the parachute center the day Steve Wendall died was disturbing.

It was half-past six and Liza had everything ready to go for supper. She had completed her office work, then checked the CB forum and found no new messages. Now she sat relaxing in the living room, Bella on her lap, her oil lamps flickering on the coffee table, waiting for Erik's arrival. A phone call sent her to the kitchen to grab it.

"It's Erik," he said. "I'm still at the parachute center and I can't make it for supper."

She heard a pitch in his voice that she had never heard before. "What's up, Erik?"

There was a long silence.

"You've got your own problems, Liza. I don't want to add to them."

"Hey, your problems will be a diversion from mine." A pause. "Surely it can't be worse than canceling supper," she said, jokingly, sensing that something was terribly wrong.

"Much worse."

"For God's sake, what?"

"One of my students had an accident."

"And—"

"The parachute didn't open. He was killed."

Liza sat down on the kitchen stool. "How could that happen?"

"That's what I've been agonizing over." He hesitated. "It was my parachute, Liza. I folded it myself."

"Had someone tampered with it?"

She heard him take a ragged breath. "The police came. So far it looks like an accident. A horrible, terrible, fatal accident."

"Why did he use your parachute?" Liza forced herself to relax her hold on the receiver. "Is that procedure?"

"No. We traded chutes in the plane. He'd almost freaked out, was suddenly superstitious about jumping, uncertain about his ability to pack his own chute. I knew it was okay because I always oversee those things, check and double-check all the safety issues."

"It wasn't your fault, Erik."

He drew in another breath. "I should have postponed his jump, but he seemed okay once he had traded chutes with me. The other guys in the plane encouraged him to go for it, that if he didn't he never would."

"So he jumped."

"Uh-huh. I followed a few seconds later. His chute, which I was using, opened normally. My chute didn't and he plunged to his death." His voice shook with emotion. "I don't think I'll ever get over this, Liza."

"I'm so sorry, Erik," she said, knowing her words were inadequate. She was certain the faulty chute had been rigged for him, but she did not voice her suspicion. He was already distraught, probably in shock. She would pursue that line of thought later. "When are you free to leave?"

"I can go now. There's no problem as far as what caused his death. Everyone here, and the police, believe it was an accident." His words came faster, crowding into each other. "Even Cooper reminded me that occasionally a parachute malfunctions."

"Cooper?"

"Yeah. He was the pilot and is as upset as I am. We all know this kind of an accident can happen. Fortunately it's rare."

"Erik, I still want you to come. You have to eat."

"I don't think I can eat."

"But you'll come?"

There was a hesitation.

"I should just go home, Liza. I'm in no shape to see anyone. I'll probably just embarrass myself by breaking down and bawling."

"I'm your friend. You've seen me cry like a baby many times. And you shouldn't be alone." She took a shaky breath. "You could have been the one to die."

"I know." His voice was hardly more than a whisper.

"I'll see you when you get here."

"Okay," he said, finally. "See you."

"And Erik?"

"Yeah?"

"Be careful."

She hung up, and was on her way to turn up the Elton John CD, feeling it was *really* appropriate now, when there was another call. She went to answer it, believing it was Erik having second thoughts about dinner.

"I'm not letting you change your mind," she said, firmly.

"I promise I won't, Brown Eyes, so long as you let me in on what I'm promising."

"Oh, Dave. I thought you were someone else."

"Your friend, Erik?"

"How did you know?"

"Just a guess." A pause. "Everything all right?"

She hesitated, controlling an urge to fall apart, a feeling that had become all too familiar lately. It was time to pull herself together.

"I just heard some bad news," she began. "On top of other terrible news."

There was a silence.

"Start at the beginning, Liza. I'd like to hear what's happened."

Liza told him, from her PI's call about Martin to Detective Barnes's visit concerning Steve Wendall's accident, to the death of the skydiver. Her voice trailed off as she finished.

"I think someone tried to kill Erik," she said. "And probably did kill my private investigator, even though both appear to be accidents."

"Liza, I understand that you're distraught, that this is a

final blow on top of everything else that's happened. But it's crazy thinking. The police would know if these deaths weren't accidents."

"Someone is fooling everyone," she said, her voice stronger. "I just know it. Too much has happened to be coincidence." She hesitated. "I believe that all of the deaths—Nate's, Alice's, my PI's, this rookie skydiver's—are somehow connected to Martin and International Air." She gulped a breath. "I don't even know what Steve Wendall learned about Martin."

"Whoa, Liza. Take it easy. There's no evidence to support your assumptions of murder. Unless you know something that I don't." A pause. "Do you?"

"What do you mean?"

"Well, for starters, do you have information that connects the deaths, facts that the police don't know about?"

"I don't have facts, Dave. Just circumstantial stuff that points to something being terribly wrong. But I think I'm on the right track to find that proof."

"And you think someone at International Air is involved?" His tone, although low, had the ring of a prosecuting attorney. "Why?"

Liza forced herself to calm down, to speak slower, realizing that she sounded hysterical. "There is the common litany of my clients, the fact that both Nate and Alice wanted to tell me something, that Martin also worked for International Air." She hesitated, trying to find a stronger common thread in the whole mess. She could not quite pull it all together; facts seemed to flicker in and out of her mind just beyond her grasp.

There was another silence.

"Hey, Brown Eyes," he said, gently. "You know I'm in your corner, but this is convoluted thinking. I know this has been a hard year, that you've weathered some tough times."

He paused, as though he was trying to be diplomatic, to spare her feelings. "I agree that all of these accidents are a weird series of coincidences, but they are accidents nevertheless, substantiated by police investigations."

Was he patronizing her? she wondered. Because he believed she was losing it? Obsessing on the subject?

"I know all that," she said. "And I know I can't prove any of it, including whether or not Martin is really dead." She felt defeated by their conversation. Now, as before, he did not believe her.

"Martin could not have survived Puget Sound, especially in the winter," he reminded her kindly. "And I'm so sorry. All these doubts have to be terrible for you. But sooner or later you'll come to accept that he's not coming back."

"You may be right, Dave," she said, her voice stilted. He did not understand her feelings on this at all.

"I'm going to hang up now," he said. "I'll be there in fifteen minutes or so."

"No, please don't come over," she said. "Erik will be here, and I'm okay, really." She paused, composing herself. "But thanks for caring, Dave. I do appreciate your worrying about me."

"You sure you don't need company?"

"Yes, I'm sure. Besides . . ." Her voice drifted off.

"Besides, what?"

She had almost said that Detective Barnes might call or come over but caught herself in time. She was not up to another lengthy explanation, a rehash of incidents that Dave already believed were coincidence. "Erik is pretty shook up. It's best if—"

"I get it. He doesn't need an audience right now."

"Thanks for understanding."

"No problem, Brown Eyes."

"And for listening to all my ramblings. I hope you know that I'm really not a nut case."

"Of course you're not. I know exactly who you are, Liza. Don't forget, I have a vested interest in keeping you safe and happy." She could hear the smile in his voice. "You'll call if you need me?"

"I promise."

"Good."

They hung up on a positive note.

But their conversation had left her feeling even more uncertain about everything. She could not stop thinking about Martin, wondering what Steve Wendall would have told her. Had he discovered that Martin was alive but so involved in illegal activities that he had staged his own death? Left her in limbo? Could she have meant so little to him?

She moved to her bedroom and picked up Harlequin, holding his cloth body and porcelain face close to her. Memories swept into her mind: stuffing the puppet bodies, laughing and joking while they worked, she and Jean making late-night snacks while Martin sewed little heads to torsos.

Liza sat down on a bedroom chair, holding the Harlequin, remembering. Her fingers stopped on loose cloth where the head was attached. A glance told her that the stitching was loose. She tried pulling the threads. Abruptly, the head came off in her hands.

She stared in disbelief.

Thousand dollar bills and Styrofoam stuffing fluttered onto her lap and the floor around her feet. The money had been inside the puppet's body.

Martin had been the one to stuff the body; he'd secured the head onto the puppet's torso.

Good God! Had he also hidden money in the other puppets, the ones that had been stolen and destroyed?

What did it mean?

Chapter Twenty-Four

FOR LONG SECONDS LIZA WAS IN A STATE OF SHOCK. THEN, slowly, she gathered the money into a small stack on the palm of her hand—fifty one-thousand-dollar bills. Her mind boggled with the implications. Unless someone else had tampered with Jean's puppets, Martin was the person responsible for the hidden money.

Why would he have done such a thing? If he'd had money he could have quit his job, pulled out all the stops for his musical career. She hesitated. Unless the money had been acquired by illegal means, as Steve Wendall had hinted during their last conversation.

Questions without answers circled in her mind. How could Martin have been involved in something shady without her having known? But in retrospect she recognized that Martin had never discussed his flight destinations, had not adhered to time constraints.

Had he lived a dual life? Had she been duped by a man who had professed to love her? And what would have happened if she had found out? Would he have left her? He knew that she would not go along with breaking the law? Maybe he had only been biding his time, hiding money until he had the means to go for his dream of fame and fortune—without her.

Had Martin been the street person who stole the puppets because he had hidden money in their bodies?

Was he the man in disguise who had been after her?

Liza leaped up. Her nervous system was on overload, verging on a panic attack. Wouldn't a wife recognize her own husband? Even if he had disguised himself?

No, not in this case, she decided. The person in the oversized black coat, wig and sunglasses had completely obscured his identity.

She forced herself to push back feelings of rejection, abandonment and fear. Her imagination was working overtime. She was jumping to conclusions. Martin was not here to defend himself. She could be wrong.

Liza placed Harlequin back on the bed, put the currency next to it, and went into her office to call Jean. She had to make sure that her sister had not lent the puppets to anyone else or left them overnight somewhere before she called Detective Barnes. Jean answered on the second ring.

"It's Liza."

"What's wrong?" Jean's question shot over the line. "I can tell, something has happened."

Liza struggled for a normal tone. It was obvious that Jean was operating in a fight-or-flight mode, expecting the worst.

"Everything is fine," she said, lying. "I was going over all that's happened and had a question about something concerning your puppets."

"What?"

"Did you ever lend them to anyone or maybe leave them at one of your performances for a day or two?"

"Of course not, Liza. You know better than that. My puppets stay with me." A hesitation. "Why are you asking?"

"Nothing important. I was just sitting here looking at Harlequin, thinking about what happened to the others, and speculating about the possibility that someone might have been jealous of you having such a successful company," she said, improvising.

"Liza, you sound funny. Are you sure that everything is okay?"

"Everything is fine, Jean. I'm just feeling nostalgic I guess, remembering the nights when we created Harlequin and Earth Mother and Moon Spinner and all the rest of the little people." Her voice faded. "Those were good times."

"Yeah, the good old days," Jean said, dryly. "Before the thought ever crossed our minds that someone would destroy my dolls and break into our houses."

There was a momentary silence while Liza decided how to broach the subject of Martin without arousing Jean's suspicions. Finally she decided it was best to talk about him openly.

"I know Martin enjoyed those times."

"He seemed to."

"Remember how much of a bind you were in at first? All those shows scheduled and the cast hadn't even been assembled yet." She gave a laugh. "Literally."

Jean laughed, too. "True. Without you and Martin, the curtain would never have gone up on schedule."

There was a hesitation.

"But you had others helping you, too," Liza said, careful not to form her words in a question that could arouse Jean's curiosity.

"No, just you and Martin. Bill was out of town on business, remember? Or he would have helped and I wouldn't have needed anyone else but you."

"Yup, I do recall." A pause. "How is everything else? No other incidents?"

"Nothing. But then the creep would be crazy to break in here now. The lights and alarm would guarantee him being caught in the act."

"Everything is fine here, too."

Liza chatted for a minute longer and then hung up with a promise to check in daily. Immediately, she picked up the phone again and punched in Detective Barnes's number. As expected, his voice mail picked up. She waited until after the beep had sounded and then spoke quickly, spacing her words for effect.

"This is Liza MacDonough, again. Please call me. It's urgent." Then she replaced the receiver into its cradle as reaction set in. Martin *had* been responsible for the hidden money. What else had he done?

The constant waiting for the pieces of this deadly puzzle to come together was getting to Liza. Antsy, she sat down at the piano and tapped out the notes from the mysterious sheet of music. Nate's composition? Bojangles? If Nate had been Bojangles then the key to the mystery had to be in the bizarre series of notes.

She plunked out the piece again, trying to think as Nate had when he wrote it—if Nate wrote it, she corrected herself. There had to be a pattern, a message from one musician to another. But the discordant notes still sounded as abrasive as a fingernail on a blackboard. Bella arched her back, gave a low growl and then headed for the bedroom. Despite her concerns, Liza grinned. Her cat knew bad music when she heard it.

Stumped, she stared at her hands that had stilled on the

keys. If Nate was the Bojangles that Comet and Snakeoil had discussed on the forum, then *the last piece* had to be the one retrieved *from her purse.*

And that added credence to the possibility that the break-ins at her condo and Jean's house coincided with the other post about "trying tomorrow night." If Snakeoil had been Alice's new boyfriend then he may be the person responsible for Alice's death.

Why? Liza asked herself for the umpteenth time. Her glance shifted to the glittering lights of the city as unanswerable questions spun in her head. The shrill of the phone jolted her back to reality, sending her across the room to grab the receiver.

"We're downstairs." Erik said in her ear. "Buzz us up."

She pressed the nine to give him access to the building, wondering what "we" meant. A minute later she heard the elevator, checked the peephole and opened the door, surprised—and relieved—to see Detective Barnes standing next to Erik.

"Please come in," Liza said, stepping aside.

It was a solemn pair she led to the dining room table where they all sat down. Erik declined supper, which she offered to microwave for him. "Thanks anyway, Liza," he said, handing her a bottle of Chardonnay. "No appetite. But I'll have a glass of wine."

"I don't drink wine," the detective said when she started to pour him a glass. "Only beer."

Without comment, Liza went to the refrigerator, pulled out a Heineken, grabbed a glass and placed both in front of him.

"Uh, thanks," he said. "Guess I can have one since I'm off duty."

"You came over on your own time?" Liza sat back down. "Is that usual procedure?"

He wiped a hand over his thick curls, patting them into place. "Didn't your second message say it was urgent?"

She nodded, realizing that he had answered her question with his own. His habit when he did not want to give a direct answer.

"I know about the accident at the parachute center," he went on. "And Erik filled in some of the details on our way up."

She turned to Erik. "How are you doing?"

"Pretty shattered," he said. "The rookie's death hit all of us skydivers pretty hard." He paused to take a sip of wine. "Made me realize it could happen to anyone."

"So what's going on?" The detective directed his question to Liza.

"I'll show you," Liza went to retrieve Alice's water bottle from where she had hidden it in the linen closet, and the thousand dollar bills she had placed in a baggie and stashed under a stack of towels. Before heading back to the table she grabbed the Harlequin puppet from her bed.

"Show and tell," she said, shakily, and placed the items on the table.

Detective Barnes leaned closer, examining without touching them. His eyes were suddenly direct. "Start with the telling," he suggested.

Liza explained about the mixed-up water bottles and how she had been horrified to see Alice's initials on the bottle, *after she had dumped the water.*

"I put it in a plastic bag and hid it." She looked away from his probing gaze. For God's sake, did he think she had switched the bottles on purpose? she wondered, unable to read his expression. "There's still a few drops in the bottom," she added.

He picked up the bag, careful not to cause friction against the bottle. Using the plastic as a barrier between it and his fingers, he unscrewed the cap and smelled the contents. He shook his head. "No odor."

"Oh, you don't smell anything?"

"Should I?"

She shrugged. "I smelled a faint fragrance. Then I realized it kind of reminded me of almonds, of all things."

The detective's hand stilled on the bottle. "You sure?"

"Positive."

"What's the deal?" Erik asked, looking as curious as Liza.

"Cyanide poison has the scent of almonds," Detective Barnes said. "But only one person in twelve has the genetic ability to smell it." He jiggled the bottle and the remaining water swirled. "Should be enough here to test."

Liza had been standing as she explained the smell. Now she sat down on her chair, suddenly needing the support of something other than her legs. "What will you do if there is poison?"

"First things first. I'll have it examined for prints and poison. The results will determine my course of action."

"I hope I didn't accidentally wipe them off." Liza said, shakily. "Or they're gone now because too much time has passed since Alice's death."

The detective took a swig of beer, then set down his glass. "Being wiped off is one thing. But fingerprints won't go away by themselves."

"How so?" Erik asked.

"Prints can last for fifty years. For example, if Liza still had that sheet music and it was that old, the crime lab could pick up fingerprints from it with the Ninhydrin Process."

Liza did not ask him to explain; it was enough to know that modern forensic science had the technology to do such a thing.

There was a silence as the detective picked up the currency.

"Where did the money come from?" Barnes asked, glancing at Harlequin. "Something to do with the puppet?"

Liza nodded again, and told them how she'd found the money. "Fifty one-thousand-dollar bills."

Erik whistled softly. "Are you saying that Martin stuffed that puppet?"

"Uh-huh." She hesitated. "Believe me Erik, I wish I could find another explanation. Jean claims the puppet was never away from her, and I believe her. You know how protective she is about her little people." She stopped herself from knotting her hands. "The only person who could have put the money in Harlequin was Martin." She glanced at the detective. "What does it mean?"

He shook his head. "I don't know yet. But we sure as hell are collecting puzzle pieces. The next step is up to the guys in the crime lab."

"You think the money in this puppet was the motivation for someone to steal the others?"

He drained his glass. "Like I said, we'll wait for the lab reports, and the facts. No point in jumping to conclusions."

"Hard not too," Erik said, obviously upset. "Too many fucking things are happening—like people dying."

Detective Barnes stood up to go. "Look, we'll get to the bottom of all of this. No one wants that more than I do."

"Then you do believe that something terrible is behind these seemingly unrelated events." Liza got up, facing Barnes, who had not refuted her statement. "Is there any way to look into the names behind the tags on United Online? The servers don't give out information."

"It's on my list."

"Because you think something's wrong. Right?" Liza pressed her point, wanting to hear that he really did credit her suspicions.

There was a hesitation.

"Yeah, something is hinky."

"Hinky?" Erik glanced up from his glass. "What does that mean?"

"Cop talk for a gut feeling that the whole scenario is as discordant as the mysterious sheet music."

"Like fucked?" Erik asked.

"Just like that," Barnes said, starting for the hall. "I'll be in touch when I know something."

Erik gave a salute. "Thanks Barnes. I know I'm a little out of it, but I appreciate what you're doing."

The detective hesitated at the door. "I'm hoping the crime lab boys will finally give us something solid."

"Finally?" Liza asked.

"Yeah. The situation has been off kilter from the beginning. But there was never anything to go on, no connecting link, no probable cause, no suspects."

"And there is now?" She was pressing him for answers.

"We'll see, okay?"

He had placed the water bottle, puppet and money into a shopping bag Liza had handed him. Now he took his evidence and continued out to the hallway.

"Watch yourself," he told her before stepping into the elevator. "Things seem to be escalating. Someone might be getting pretty nervous."

"You be careful, Detective Barnes." Liza gave a nervous laugh. "You've got all the evidence."

He nodded. Then he was gone, riding down to the front entrance. She quickly closed her door and locked it, then got the wine bottle and went back to the dining room to fill her and Erik's glasses.

Did Barnes have a suspect? She doubted it. But maybe he would have one soon.

Chapter Twenty-Five

LATER, AFTER ERIK HAD TALKED THROUGH HIS GUILT OVER the skydiver's death and finally calmed down enough to drive home, Liza sat propped against her bed pillows and pondered the layoff printout. She crossed out the people who were her clients, made an *X* next to the terminated employees she did not know, highlighting those names where checks had been sent to a post office box rather than a street address. There were twenty-three in all, and she meant to authenticate all of them.

Suspicious of everyone now, she intended to find out what Nate, Alice, and Steve Wendall had tried to tell her.

Lives could depend on her discovering the truth.

She placed the printout on her nightstand and switched off the lamp. Then she lay in the dark, staring out the window at the city lights, contemplating her next move.

Tomorrow afternoon I'll start my own investigation, she decided. She had comp days coming and taking an afternoon off would give her a good start on the list. Clearing up any doubts about bogus addresses would benefit both her and the company. As Dave always pointed out, bad publicity was not good for International Air or the One Thousand Series jet project. But good or bad, she meant to uncover what was going on.

And that *was* what? she asked herself one last time that night. And then she fell asleep.

Liza strode into Al Stark's office the next morning with a smile on her face, affecting a casual air. "I need the afternoon off," she told him. "I lost a filling and have to see the dentist." She did not dare say what she was really doing. He would probably take her honesty as more evidence that she was on her way to burnout.

"No problem, as long as you can reschedule your clients."

"Only two for the afternoon, and they can both come in tomorrow."

He shrugged, grinning. "Go ahead then. We can't have your counseling talents compromised by a toothache. Your clients might complain."

She thanked him and turned to go, almost bumping into Hawk Bohlman who stood in the open doorway behind her. He inclined his head in greeting. She knew he had listened to her conversation with Al. A creep, she thought. A ruthless man with no scruples.

Liza nodded hello to him, then went into the hall and headed for her office. Once inside, she breathed a sigh of relief, then hung up her coat and prepared for the morning. She placed her handbag with the client printout under her desk next to her feet. She would not let it out of her sight, positive that Sylvia Kempton would not give her another copy. Her first client was not scheduled until ten, her second at eleven, and then she was free to go.

There was a knock on her door.

"Come in," she called.

It opened and Dave poked his head inside. "You under the weather? Heard you have a toothache."

"Boy. News travels fast." She paused. "You can come in, you know. I'm not contagious."

He grinned. "Can't. I'm already almost late to a meeting, but I wanted to check on you first."

She got up and came around the desk. "I'm fine, really."

"Which one?"

"Pardon me?"

"You know, which tooth?"

"Um, a back molar."

She blushed and glanced away, feeling as guilty as a ten-year-old who had been caught cheating on a test. She never had been a good liar.

There was a silence.

"Hey, Brown Eyes, anyone ever tell you that honest people aren't good at fibbing?"

Her gaze flew back to his and she saw the crinkling at the corners of his green eyes. He was restraining a grin.

"I, um, am talking to my dentist, but I'm also doing something else," she said, evading.

Hadn't she read that a good con artist always conceals the lie within truths. Her something else was as true as the dentist was a lie, although she would call her dentist and make an appointment. So what she told Dave was not a total deception. Game playing? she asked herself, and knew that was exactly what she was doing. Dave would disapprove of her plans for the afternoon.

"Dare I ask what?"

She shook her head. "Tell you later."

"That important, huh?"

"Oh no," she said. "Just something that I have to do." Not a lie, she told herself, and suppressed the fact that lying by omission was still a lie.

"Have anything to do with International Air?" His question sounded offhand, too offhand?

A hesitation.

"I thought you were rushing to a meeting. You have to be late by now, Dave." She gave a laugh. "How about if I fill in the details later?"

"Fair enough."

She stepped to the door, ready to close it after him.

"One more thing, Liza."

She waited, holding her gaze level with his.

"I'm putting my dibs on Valentine's Day. Dinner at a very romantic Italian restaurant, violin music and all. What do you say? Will you ink me in on your calendar?"

"Valentine's Day is still a while off," she said with a laugh.

"I know. The very reason I'm asking now—to beat out all my competitors who'll be asking between now and then."

She smiled and placed her hand over his on the edge of the door. "I'll ink it in and look forward to going."

"Great." He looked genuinely pleased. "So will I." He hesitated, "By the way, yellow is a good color on you."

"Thanks." She had worn the cashmere turtleneck sweater because it would be warm, the same reason she had chosen her black wool-gabardine pants suit.

He stepped back. "Call you tonight."

She nodded and was about to close the door when she noticed that someone stood behind Dave in the hall. *Hawk Bohlman.*

He must have heard their conversation, the second one of hers he'd overheard today.

Liza watched them hurry down the hall to the stairs. Obviously they were going to the same meeting. Slowly she shut the door and went back to her desk. But she could not shake her apprehension. She did not trust Hawk Bohlman.

He was a wild card. But was he a murderer?

She had grabbed a deli sandwich to eat on the way and it was one o'clock by the time she pulled up at the first address in the Belltown area of Seattle. It was a four-story building that housed small businesses, but as far as she could tell, no residences.

Maybe there are living quarters in the back, she thought. Or on the upper floors. Sometimes apartments could be found in odd places in the city.

She got out of the Miata and headed for the first business, a video store. Down the sidewalk several people loitered around a bench, chatting and sharing drinks from a bottle in a paper sack. Not the best part of town, Liza thought, and quickened her step.

The door to the video store set off a run of musical notes to alert the clerk, who entered the shop from a back room. As she stepped up to the counter he spoke in heavily accented words, "Can I help you?"

She smiled. "I'm looking for an apartment in this building. Could you direct me to its entrance?"

He blinked so quickly she wondered if he had a nervous tick. Then, as he began explaining the building, talking so rapidly that she scarcely understood him, she realized he was European, although she couldn't identify his country of origin. But she got the gist of what he was trying to say: there was no apartment.

She showed him her printout with the name and address. "Anyone in the building by that name?"

"No person," he said, then smiled, tapping his chest. "Read English better than talk English," he said, his words again spaced out and carefully articulated.

"Thank you," Liza said.

She went back to the door and stepped outside. She believed him, but decided to check out the building herself anyway, just to make sure. One walk around it convinced her that he had been right: there was no apartment.

She got back into her car and headed for the Wallingford district north of the city center, the next address on the printout. Liza switched on the radio to easy-listening music and felt herself relax—a little. She was crossing the Fremont Bridge when she suddenly realized that a black sport utility vehicle had been behind her since she left Belltown. It had maintained a distance; because the windows were tinted, all she could see was that the driver looked like a man. Her fingers tightened on the wheel; fear jolted her upright on the seat.

He was following her.

She went through two green lights, a block apart, watching her mirror as she went straight toward Wallingford rather than left to Ballard. The vehicle followed, barely making the light.

Anger flashed through her. She felt like floor-boarding the gas pedal, see if he would dare to keep up with her. Instead she reduced her speed, and the vehicle closed to within a block. Then it slowed as well, pacing her.

Without warning, she jammed on the brakes and swung to the curb, stopping her car with a jerk.

Let the bastard figure that out, she told herself. At least she might see who was driving when it passed her. The creep would not dare hurt her in broad daylight; there were people walking on the sidewalk and a steady stream of cars.

The vehicle braked, then turned into a driveway, backed out and reversed its route, veering off on the first side street. It happened so fast that she was unable to determine the year or its make. All she knew was that it was black with tinted windows and four doors.

"Damn it!" she cried. "I didn't time that right. He was too close to a corner."

He, she thought. She was not positive. It could have been a she.

You screwed up, she told herself once she was moving forward again. Now the person knows you saw them and will be more careful next time.

The thought put an even bigger pall on her day. By the time she pulled up at the Wallingford address, a house this time, Liza was so apprehensive that she didn't get out of the car for five minutes. Not until she was sure that no one else had parked on the street.

The paranoids may get you yet, she told herself. But the vehicle that had followed her had not been a fantasy; it had been as real as all the other incidents. She was not crazy, unless she had been having psychotic breaks and everyone else involved was suffering from the same disorder.

She locked the Miata behind her, then headed up the wooden steps that led to a sagging porch. A tabby lay on the uneven board floor, scarcely moving as she rang the bell. Thirty seconds passed. She rang it again.

There was a rustling sound on the other side of the door. Suddenly it opened, but only the length of a chain lock.

"Yes?" a shaky female voice asked. "What do you want?"

"My name is Liza MacDonough. I'm an in-house counselor for International Air and I want to talk to you about checks from my company that have been sent to this address."

She pushed her business card through the narrow opening and a wizened hand grabbed it. Stepping back, Liza gave the elderly woman time to examine it.

"What checks?"

"The payroll checks that go to your post office box twice a month," Liza said.

She glanced behind her. No vehicles moved on the street, no people walked on the sidewalk. She looked back to the printout.

"They're made out to a Neil Edwards who lives at 2106. Isn't that this street number?"

"Yes, but there is no one here with that name." Liza heard the clatter of locks being undone. Then the door opened to reveal a tiny, stooped woman who was at least eighty-years-old. "I live here alone, and have for the past twenty years, since my husband died," she added proudly. She had obviously decided that Liza looked trustworthy. "No one with that name has ever lived here."

"Do you have a post office box?"

"Course not. Why would I when my mail comes right to my house?" She indicated the box that was attached to the siding next to her door.

"Have you ever rented a post office box?"

"Are you deaf, young woman?" The small face crinkled into a frown. "I have never had one in my whole life."

"I must have the wrong address," Liza said, managing a smile. "I'm sorry to have bothered you."

There was no mistake, she told herself as she walked back to her car. Most of the addresses on her list were bogus. She would bet her life on that.

Back in her car again, Liza headed for the next address. By dusk she had found seven people who *did* actually work at International Air—and fifteen more who did not. The latter were unaware of the phony name attributed to their address and did not have a post office box.

Then who had cashed the company payroll checks?

All afternoon Liza kept watching her rearview mirror.

There were no other incidents, nothing out of the ordinary. Nevertheless, her apprehension persisted. But unless someone followed her, they could not know where she was going next, she reminded herself. Somehow that knowledge was not comforting. Her phantom always seemed to materialize out of nowhere.

She had one address left. A houseboat on Lake Union, close to where Erik lived. Wait for tomorrow, a little voice said in her head. It's starting to get dark.

Should she or shouldn't she? she wondered. A glance in the mirror told her that no one followed. But then it was rush hour and hard to keep track of all the traffic.

Go for it, she told herself. You need to substantiate every address on your list if you're ever going to get someone at IA to listen to your clients' concerns. Besides, the houseboat address was on her way home.

She swung off Westlake Avenue, heading for Eastlake on the other side of Lake Union. If she called Erik he would give her directions so that she could drive right to the place. Expedite finding the location before dark.

She did not notice the dark van get into the turn lane a block behind her.

Chapter Twenty-Six

FINDING THE ADDRESS WHEN IT WAS ALMOST DARK SEEMED hopeless. Liza drove slowly along the street next to the lake and knew she was in the right vicinity, but in the congestion of houseboat communities and condominiums that lined the east side of Lake Union, she couldn't find the place.

Call Erik, she told herself. He knew the area like the back of his hand. He could direct her to the right cluster of houseboats.

She pulled over in front of a line of mailboxes that leaned against each other for support, the only space available off the narrow, potholed street. Funky, she thought, grabbing her cell phone. Who would ever believe that there was such an area so close to the city center: a bohemian ambience and high-priced houseboats. The owners did not seem to mind that the only parking was on the street, on a first-come, first-served basis.

Erik's answering machine picked up with the message to call his office or his cell phone number. Liza disconnected. He was not home yet, probably on his way. She tried his cell phone first and got him.

"Liza, what's up?" he asked after realizing who was calling.

"I need directions to a houseboat address."

"I thought I was the only person you knew who lived on a houseboat," he said, sounding surprised.

"You are."

"Whew! For a moment there I thought your friend Dave might have bought one." A hesitation. "I wouldn't put it past him since he's so competitive with the competition."

"What competition?"

His sigh came over the airwaves. "I was kidding you." Another pause. "So why are you looking for this place?"

She explained that the address belonged to someone who worked for International Air and let him assume it was a client. She read the street number from the printout. "I'm hopelessly confused."

"Hey, I know exactly where you are. I jog past those mailboxes every morning. You're only a couple of minutes away from my place."

"I know that, Erik," she said. "So I'm hoping you can tell me how to pinpoint this address?"

He gave her directions, and it appeared that she was within a block of the houseboat community she was trying to find. "I'd stop by and make sure you found the place but I can't right now. Call me back if you have a problem, okay?"

"I will—thanks," she said, wondering why he couldn't swing by and show her the address. It would only be a couple of blocks out of his way. She was lowering the phone when she heard his voice again. "Did you say something else?" she asked.

"Yeah. It just occurred to me. What in the hell are you doing out there, Liza? It's getting dark."

"Not quite. And my errand here will only take a couple of minutes."

"Can't it wait until tomorrow, when it's full daylight?"

"Come on, Erik. I'm not a baby."

His sigh came over the wire. "If it can wait until after nine I'll go with you."

"That's too late." A pause. "I'm fine, really."

"Then I can't dissuade you?"

"Don't be silly. I'll talk to you later."

There was a brief silence.

"Be careful then."

She said she would, thanked him and they disconnected. She decided to leave her car where it was and got out, locking the door behind her. The mailman would not need to deliver mail to the boxes until tomorrow.

With her purse and the printout in hand, Liza headed up the street toward the next houseboat community. A sign hung over a gated archway with the words PARADISE LOST.

She grinned. It would be *paradise* to live in a floating house on Lake Union with Capitol Hill to the east, Queen Anne Hill to the west, and the downtown Seattle skyline to the south. And the *lost* part? People like her who couldn't afford the prices attached to such a paradise.

Even Erik could not afford to buy a floating home now. He had bought his houseboat right out of graduate school for less than fifty thousand dollars, a one-story rundown shack that he had remodeled and added onto as he could afford it over the years. Now his trilevel was a showplace, a cozy floating home with lofts, alcoves, bay windows, skylights, a wood-burning Franklin stove and two bathrooms. His small sailboat was moored alongside. Erik would be a great catch for some lucky girl, she told herself, and stepped through the unlocked gate into Paradise Lost.

A glance at the resident board told her she had the right place. But she wasn't surprised that the name next to the houseboat number did not match the name on her list. She would check it out anyway; someone could have sublet their place or the IA employee might only be a roommate of the owner.

It was getting dark fast and automatic lights had come on along the planked walkways of all the houseboat communities on the lake—except at Paradise Lost where many of the exterior bulbs were burned out. As Liza walked onto the uneven walkway that led to the houseboats she saw that the whole place was pretty rundown. Without illumination it was getting harder to read house numbers. She came to an intersection, and hesitated.

Which way do I go? she wondered. Left, right or straight ahead?

The wooden walkways were not the orderly, forward routes over the water as in neighboring communities. Instead they veered off into a maze of dead ends and circles. And from outward appearances, the people who lived at Paradise Lost lacked pride of ownership. For all she knew, these shabby houseboats might be rentals.

Liza moved to the left, toward a light. The numbers went the wrong way and she returned to her starting point, which was about thirty feet from shore. Her second try took her straight ahead and it was not the right direction either. She wished there was someone to ask but most of the houseboats were dark.

The people who lived there hadn't gotten home from work yet, she decided. She started along the walk that led off at an angle, narrowing as it led farther onto the lake. It was almost by accident that she found the right houseboat, its front door only inches from the main passageway where she stood. A yellow glow shone out through a small hexagon window higher up on the weathered siding. Someone was home.

Then she saw the FOR SALE sign tacked on the door. She lifted the knocker, a metal gargoyle head, and tapped it against its backplate.

She waited, hearing the water lap against the timbers beneath her. Out on the lake a motorboat skimmed across the surface, its sound fading as it passed. A few seconds later she felt the wave action under her feet, rocking the boards so hard that she had to brace herself against the houseboat. Gee, she thought. Not a very stable structure.

Liza knocked again, this time louder. Again she waited, and again there was no answer.

A door opened behind her. Unnerved, she spun around to face a blond, forty-something woman on the other side of the walkway. "Can I help you?" the woman asked in a throaty voice, sudden light from the room behind her splashing onto the decking between them.

"Oh, please." Liza smiled, relieved. "I'm looking for Mr. Walker, your neighbor."

"Mr. Walker?" The woman shook her head. "Don't know him. But then I haven't met most of my neighbors since I'm a recent homeowner. A job and the short winter days haven't been conducive to getting acquainted yet." She hesitated. "Where did you say he lived?"

"He lives right here, across from you." Liza indicated the houseboat behind her.

The woman tilted her head. "I may not have met most of the residents, but I know you have the wrong address."

"Are you certain a Mr. Walker doesn't live here?"

"No one lives there, the place hasn't been occupied in the six months I've been here."

"Really? Are you sure?"

The woman nodded. "I've heard that the owner lives in California, and the place has been vacant for over a year. I can't remember his name, but I know it's not Walker."

There was a silence.

"Hmm . . . well thanks for the information," Liza said. "I appreciate it. Saves me a little footwork."

"Glad I could help." The woman started to shut the door. "Be careful on your way out of here. It's getting pretty dark and some of the decking is uneven."

"Thank you. I'll watch myself."

The woman stepped into her house and Liza heard the lock slip into place. She started back the way she had come, taking the woman's advice to be cautious. But her mind was on the fact that she had just substantiated the sixteenth fake address.

When she came to the fork in the walkway, she hesitated, trying to remember which way to go. All of the corridors led between houseboats and seemed to lead shoreward. She knew from experience that some did not.

Abruptly, she realized the boards under her feet were vibrating. Someone else was on the passageway.

She whirled around. No one was in sight.

Taking a chance, Liza veered away from the corridor with the light, remembering it had led her the wrong way a few minutes earlier. Walking faster, the boards shaking now against the strain of hurrying footsteps, she prayed she had chosen the right course through the maze. The route was suicidal without lights. She could fall in the water and drown without ever being noticed.

It was a dead end.

The arm came around her suddenly, yanking her backward against the body of her attacker. A hand over her mouth stifled her scream in her throat. She smelled the rank odor of perspiration.

"You fuckin' cunt!" a hoarse voice whispered behind her, his breath hot against her ear. "It's your turn to die."

She was dragged backward toward the edge of the walkway. Struggling and twisting, Liza tried to free herself. It was no use. The man who restrained her, who was trying to suffocate her, was much bigger and stronger. She suddenly knew she could die if she did not extricate herself.

He meant to throw her into the lake.

Her life on the line, Liza squirmed harder, turning her head from side to side, gulping for air. His arms crushed her breasts, pinned her arms against her sides and cut off her breath. Her scream was a muffled croak behind his hand. In desperation, she bit down on a finger.

He yelped, jerking his hand away. She sucked in a breath, but before she could scream he slapped her face. Her vision exploded into brightly colored dots. Her body sagged. Then his hand was back over her mouth, so tight against her teeth that she could not move her lips.

She felt herself drifting off from the lack of oxygen. She fought a sinking sensation as her vision blurred.

She would die if she passed out.

That thought gave her a burst of energy. She must get away. Thrashing and squirming, Liza tried to break his hold. The sleeve of her raincoat tore away from its stitching and several buttons popped onto the planking. She kicked backward, trying to hit his shinbone with her heel. He winced when she succeeded. She kicked it again.

But she was losing the battle.

Abruptly, she was flung aside to sprawl onto the board walkway. Wood splinters pierced her knees and the palms of her hands as she skidded over the wooden surface.

Stunned, Liza tried to regain her perspective. She was

free of the painful restraints of his arms, but it took a moment before she could respond to that freedom. She felt the vibration of retreating footsteps on the decking beneath her.

She got up on her knees just in time to see him disappear into the dark, veering to avoid the couple who had scared him off. She was on her feet, holding onto a piling to steady herself when the elderly man and woman rushed up to her.

"My dear," the woman said. "What happened?"

"Good God, Charlotte," the gray-haired man said. "This woman is bleeding."

"I'm okay." Liza tried to reassure them. "Just shaken up."

"What happened?" the woman asked, anxiously.

Both were dressed in jeans, baseball caps and windbreakers. In other circumstances Liza would have smiled to see the seventy-something couple decked out like teenagers. Now she could only grimace from the pain. Her slacks, torn at the knees, were soaking up blood from her scraped flesh, her skinned palms throbbed with slivers, and her throat ached from the pressure of hands on her neck. She wondered if she had broken any bones.

"That man attacked you," the woman said.

Liza nodded. "Did you get a look at him?"

"Too dark." The woman looked at her companion. "We have to make someone install new lightbulbs. We can't have people being accosted next to our own front door."

Liza reassured the couple that she did not need medical aid, and they helped her back to the Miata. She thanked them, got in and started the engine. Her body shook, rattling her teeth like dice in a tumbler. She pressed her lips together to stop the alarming clatter, gripped the wheel with both hands and headed home.

She could have been killed. If not for the elderly couple, she would probably be deep in the water of Lake Union right now.

They passed within a couple of feet of him. He shrank deeper into the shadows, making sure that the cluster of overgrown evergreen shrubs obscured his presence. The noisy bitch. She had the luck of the devil. He'd hoped she would have returned to her car alone.

He looked down at his clenched hands; he had fucked up again. She was still alive.

Liza called ahead to have Joe meet her in the condominium's garage. He went upstairs with her and saw her safely into her apartment. She explained that her disheveled appearance was due to a fall. She couldn't bear to get into details, but she did leave a message for Detective Barnes.

After doctoring her hands and knees, she sat in the dark trying to make sense of what had happened. Had her assailant been following her to each place—the person in the black sport vehicle—waiting for his chance? Was he down in the street right now, watching the lights go on and off in her apartment, training night-vision binoculars on her windows?

She had to face it. The paranoids had finally gotten to her. Although her attacker was real, it did not mean that he was always watching her. She felt hollow, spent and terrified. Who was *he*?

The phone rang and she jumped. Liza heard the answering machine pick up but made no move to get it herself. She didn't want to talk to anyone. She didn't know who to trust, except Jean and Detective Barnes. After her message, Dave's voice filled the room.

"Hey, let me know when you get home. I've been curious about how your afternoon went. I'll call back later."

He wanted to know about her day? Maybe he already knew. Maybe he was just playing it cool. She dropped her head into her hands. Crazy, she thought. It was impossible for her to believe that Dave would harm her.

Fifteen minutes later there was a hang-up call, and a while later, another one. The next call was Erik saying he was sorry he hadn't been able to show her the address, that he hoped his directions had helped. He'd scheduled a group of students at his houseboat and had barely had enough time to get home before they arrived, and now the last person had finally left. "Call, or I'm gonna worry."

Liza sat in the quiet of her living room, unable to forget that Erik had known exactly where she was going. And Dave had known her plans for the afternoon—as had Hawk. She fidgeted, wishing that Detective Barnes would call her back.

A sudden thought brought her to her feet. One other person would know the route of her investigation—the person who had stolen the first printout that Alice had given her.

Oh God! How could she have forgotten that?

Chapter Twenty-Seven

BY MORNING LIZA'S FEAR HAD BEEN REPLACED BY ANGER. She could not allow the shadowman to alter every area of her life. If he wanted to kill her, then she had to defend herself. Although she hated the thought of a gun, she would definitely buy a whistle and pepper spray. She vowed he would not get away with terrorizing her. He was the person with something to hide, not her.

She drove out of the garage on her way to work, braking at the street for traffic. About to accelerate, Detective Barnes ran down the sidewalk from the front door, waving at her to stop.

"I called your apartment from the entrance phone. I must have just missed you," he said.

"A woman has to make a living," she said, dryly. "I have to be on the job by eight."

There was a silence. "Are you okay?"

"Of course." She hesitated. "And thanks for calling back last night. Not that I needed to talk to you about anything serious—or anything." Somehow she could not stop the angry words, even though she realized she was transferring all of her anger and fear onto him. "A woman living in the city gets used to someone trying to kill her." She gave a ragged laugh. "Being a homicide detective, I'm sure you hear of such incidents on a daily basis."

It was a breezy morning and the wind whipped his curly hair into a tangled-up mess. But he seemed oblivious to the elements; his expression reflected concern. No, Liza thought, perversely satisfied. He looked alarmed, even fearful.

"What in the hell happened?"

She told him.

"For God's sake, why didn't you tell me that in your message? I would have called you, but it was after eleven when I got home last night and I didn't realize it was an emergency." He sucked in a quick breath. "But why in the fuck—excuse my profanity—didn't you call the police about the attack?" He paused. "I was at a birthday party. My sister's kid."

She glanced away, deflated and ashamed of herself. "Sorry. I didn't mean to lash out at you. You're right. How could you have known what happened."

"I don't like what I'm seeing here, Liza. You're in shock." He hesitated. "An irrational reaction to what happened last night, what's been happening for the last few weeks, might get you killed." Another pause. "You have to keep your cool."

"Are you admitting I'm in danger?" she shot back.

"I'm a homicide detective and—"

"And—you're admitting nothing," she said, interrupting.

"Jeez," he said, frustrated. "Don't put words in my mouth. I know you've got someone after you. I'm just trying to figure out what in the hell's going on."

"Join the club."

"Will you promise me one thing?"

She nodded.

"I know you have a cell phone and I want you to call me the second—not the minute—but the second that anything seems out of sync. Agreed?"

"Agreed," she said finally, her anger collapsing back into fear. "I promise."

He stepped away from her car. "Good." A hesitation. "And remember, Liza. Homicide detectives are just people, too, despite our specialized training." He smiled suddenly. "Give me a break. I'm checking out more things than you might guess—behind the scenes. In the meantime, you have to stay safe. Okay?"

She nodded again, close to tears. "I'm sorry if I seemed ungrateful."

His gaze intensified. "Understandable." He waved a hand. "Just do as I said. Let me know the next time you even think about going out there to investigate by yourself. I promise that you'll have some backup."

"Thanks, Detective Barnes."

"Owen."

"Thanks, Owen."

Another car came out of the garage and honked for her to move forward. "I have to go," she told him.

He got out of the way. "I'll be in touch. And remember, call if anything even *seems* suspicious."

"I will." She rolled up her window and headed out to join the morning rush hour traffic. It would be a long day.

"What is it that you're saying, Dave?"

He came around his desk to take Liza's hands. "Only that you've presented a pretty weird scenario here: an elaborate plan to defraud the company, a cover-up, and deaths that might not be accidental. In fact, it borders on lunacy." He hesitated. "There is no company conspiracy, Liza. And both Nate and Alice's deaths were just tragic coincidences."

"But it could be true."

"It's not likely. No one could get away with what you've suggested."

She withdrew her hands from his. She probably did seem like a nut case, marching into his office with her accusations. Her projection of what might be happening had dropped almost full-blown into her mind on the way to work. What if someone was falsifying payroll records for personal gain?

Although she had suggested her theory, she had not told Dave about the attack last night, nor had she told Erik. As long as Detective Barnes knew about it she had decided to keep her own counsel, at least until she knew who to trust.

"You don't believe a thing I've said, do you?"

"Sweetheart, I believe that you *think* it's true. And maybe there is some truth in what you say. But I'm also compelled to point out that there is probably a logical explanation for all of this address confusion, like a computer glitch."

She blew out a breath, frustrated. "The people with the fake addresses were not legitimate—*not real employees,* Dave." She put more space between them. "But they received real checks from the company, and after a while, they were let go, probably replaced by other bogus workers. In the meantime, *real workers* were terminated, to make room for the fake ones, so someone could collect payroll checks from the bogus employees. It's that simple."

"And I'm telling you, Liza. It's not that simple." He sounded exasperated. "You've implied that all of this has to do with the computer lab—and that's impossible. What in hell do computer programmers have to do with the layoffs of employees from all other areas of the company?"

She was silent. What indeed? But *someone* who worked for International Air *was* involved, and that someone had access to confidential company computer files. Was that someone a person who had taken advantage of Nate's programming genius?

She started again, explaining about her clients' complaints, the printout list Alice had given her—twice—and her own footwork that had proven that sixteen employees were probably bogus.

"Someone is collecting those checks, Dave," she said. "Someone who is also aware of how many fake people can be hired without sending up red flags to the auditors and management." She sighed. "People are being fired to make a place for these fake workers on company records and payroll. Then the remaining employees must do the work of two people, subjecting them to burnout. In the meantime, someone is cashing the checks of those bogus employees."

"Are you saying that someone is stealing from the company?"

"I'm saying that I think someone is accessing company programs, altering records on an ongoing basis, and defrauding the company out of thousands of dollars each month." She sucked in a quick breath. "I think an in-house audit should be conducted on payroll accounts to make sure that every name on the list is a real employee."

"Preposterous! This company employs thousands."

"But checking each person out is possible. Admit it."

"I can't admit to something I don't believe is valid. You're speculating, creating a mystery where there may not be one. Where is your proof? If you go to the company with a wacky suggestion based only on intuition, all you'll gain is a pink slip with your name on it."

"As I said, I can prove that sixteen terminated employees were receiving payroll checks at post office box numbers." She waved a copy of the layoff printout in the air. She was no longer lax about evidence; the original was in her handbag. She intended to give copies to Al, her boss, and to Sylvia Kempton as well, and request an investigation. "And those people do not, and never did, live at the addresses listed in their files."

"Have you checked each individual personnel file of those sixteen people?"

She glanced away. It was her hope that Sylvia would allow her to do that. But she wondered if she could trust Sylvia; Liza couldn't forget that she'd been at the parachute center the night her PI was killed.

"Well no, not yet," Liza replied, slowly. "But my list is the main one and I assume it's up to date. A name and address is the most pertinent information for any employee, and if those are false, then there is nothing left to substantiate that the person really exists. Even Social Security numbers won't jibe with a fake name when they're checked out."

He didn't speak for a long time.

"It just doesn't make sense, Liza." His expression was strained. "The people you're talking about don't even work for International Air now."

"But that's the point," she insisted. "Don't you see? They may never have been real. And I bet that there are other recent hirelings who aren't real either."

"What is it you think I can do?"

"Take a closer look at what the programmers are doing. Report my findings, appoint someone to look into my allegations, make sure no one in the lab is accessing the company personnel files from one of the computers."

"For God's sake, Liza. If I didn't already know you I would think you'd lost your mind. This is insanity."

"I'm not nuts, Dave. And I'm trying not to resent your suggestions that I've lost it. If something is going on here then you, or I, need to inform our superiors."

"You know that accusations without foundation could start a firestorm that could easily get away from us. This type of gossip could even undermine the One Thousand Series project, make the wrong people leery of its innovative concept, and cost us the needed time to meet deadlines for certification."

She stared at him, horrified. Something was wrong at IA. People were dying. And Dave's priority was the project? His career?

Their eyes locked. She was the first to look away, uncertain. Maybe she was wrong. Maybe her information did not have anything to do with the company layoffs or the computer lab or Nate or Alice. And maybe everything that had happened to her was not connected to IA either. It was possible that Dave was right.

She didn't believe her own argument. Proof or not, something *was* going on. She might finally have come up with a vital piece of the puzzle, but it was not enough to make sense out of the whole picture.

"Hey, Brown Eyes. Don't look so upset." He closed the space between them and pulled her close. "I promise I'll investigate your concerns. And if I find anything out of the ordinary I'll report it at once."

She nodded, but she had her doubts. He was too concerned about FAA certification for the new jet.

Dave tilted her chin so that he could see her face. "I keep my promises," he said.

"Will you let me know what you find out?"

"Of course. Can I borrow that printout for a day or so?"

Liza handed him the copy, the one she'd made for him. A minute later she was headed back to her office. She did not intend to wait for him to get back to her before pursuing the matter. Time was of the essence, she told herself. She did not mean to be the killer's next victim.

"Shit, Liza! Are you telling me that you told Dave Farrar to investigate his programmers because of the cockamamie story you just told me?"

She nodded at Al, waiting.

He paced his office, stopping abruptly to point a finger at her. "I thought you had gotten over all that pissing and moaning by disgruntled clients. I've told you over and over that a counselor must not magnify complaints."

"Careful, Al. If you believe I've gone off the deep end then you better be concerned that I don't report you for profanity and harassment on the job."

He opened his mouth, then closed it again. He strode around his desk to the chair and sat down. "You aren't serious," he said finally.

"Of course not." She leaned forward over his desk and placed another copy of her printout down in front of him. "But I am about this, Al. Will you please look into it, just in case I'm not being an alarmist?"

"Seriously, there has to be a logical explanation. What you've proposed could not happen in a company like IA. Nor could it get past the auditors. It's friggin' impossible."

"You could be right, but will you check into it?"

"I'll look into it on one condition."

"Which is?"

"That if I don't find anything amiss you'll promise to take some vacation time."

"Will you get started on this today?"

He nodded.

"Then it's a deal. I'll stop back later to see how you're doing."

This time he shook his head. "You do that."

"I will." She grinned. "And thanks, Al. You might be surprised at what you find."

"I doubt it. But we'll see."

She glanced at her watch as she left his office. One more quick stop, before her next appointment. She had to pursue all possibilities. Maybe someone she talked to would finally take her seriously.

"I can't talk long," Sylvia Kempton said. "I'm due at a department staff meeting in a few minutes."

"I'll be brief." Liza told her about the sixteen bogus addresses and then handed her another copy of the printout Alice had given her. "I've marked the fake ones," she added.

"Sixteen? Last I heard you'd only found one."

"That's true. But now I've taken the time to verify all the names on the list."

"Wasn't that a lot of work, on a hunch?"

Liza nodded. "But worth it. Believe me, Sylvia, this mess is more than a hunch."

Sylvia was silent, and Liza thought she was only pretending to study the list to give herself time to respond. Is she nervous? Liza wondered. Or running scared? It was hard to tell. She wondered if she should ask her about being at the parachute center. No, Liza decided. Now was not the time if she wanted Sylvia's help.

"I'll certainly examine the files in the light of what you have here, Liza," she said slowly. "But I expect that I'll find everything to be completely above board, and a logical explanation for any discrepancies."

"While you're checking could you also mark the various departments of the company where these people worked? And I'd like the names of the people who wrote their job evaluations." Liza managed a smile. "Could you do that for me?"

"Yes, I suppose so, but, um, I'll have to conform to confidentiality rules as outlined in the state regulation codes." She glanced up. "We don't know that the employees on this list aren't real, Liza."

"No we don't. But your examination of their files should tell us everything we need to know."

"I'm sure it will."

"Will you get back to me with your findings?"

"Yes, of course."

"Thanks Sylvia, I appreciate it." A pause. "I am very concerned about all that's going on here. I hope you can make this a priority." She softened her words with another smile.

Again Liza headed back to her office. And again she was unsettled, wondering if Sylvia would really be any help. Could she even be trusted? Sylvia was definitely apprehensive about something. It seemed obvious that someone was influencing her. But who?

A name popped into her mind. Dave? How in the hell could she even think that? Dave was her friend. More than a friend, really. Yet, he was also upset with her investigation. And he was threatened by *anyone* who might jeopardize his One Thousand Series Jet project.

Or his own career.

Chapter Twenty-Eight

THE DOOR TO LIZA'S OFFICE SPRANG OPEN AND ERIK STRODE inside. "What the fuck's going on?" he demanded, angrily. "Why the hell didn't you call me last night? Or at least pick up the phone when I called you?"

Startled, she jumped up. "What are you talking about? Why are you here?"

"Because a certain homicide detective paid me a visit and scared me half to death." He glanced at his watch. "Less than an hour ago."

"But . . . but don't you have appointments and—"

"I canceled them."

Liza came around the desk and he pulled her into his arms, holding her without speaking. She could feel the tension in his body, and she felt terrible. Finally, she stepped back so that she could look him squarely in the face.

"I'm so sorry, Erik. I have no excuse except that I was probably in shock." She hesitated. "I was so shaken up that I didn't know who to trust."

"Not even me?"

She lowered her eyes.

"Because I knew where you were going?" he asked. "I was suspect because of that?"

She nodded, unable to lie to him.

There was a long silence.

"I did not, would not, *could not* ever hurt you. How could you possibly believe that, for even one second?"

"I wasn't thinking straight, Erik. I was so trauma-tized . . ." Liza's words drifted into another silence.

"You must know that I'd do anything for you, that you're my best friend on earth."

She looked up. "Can you forgive me? I do know that. And I know you would never hurt me."

"I'm glad you realize that." His pale blue eyes glinted. "And I sure wouldn't take kindly to anyone else who did."

"Am I forgiven?" she asked softly.

"Only if I am, for putting a bunch of rookie parachute jumpers ahead of you when I knew you shouldn't be out there alone in the dark." He paused. "I'd invited my students to a free class on safety precautions; it was a way to salve my guilt over the skydiver's death."

There was another hesitation before he continued.

"Barnes will tell you that my alibi was legitimate."

"Please, don't explain further." She felt guilty for even doubting Erik. He had never lacked empathy and concern for the suffering of others. He had never demonstrated a psycho-pathic personality. "There's nothing to forgive you for, Erik. It was my decision to rush headlong into a bad situation. I knew better and did it anyway. Detective Barnes doesn't have to verify your credibility with me, you know that."

Erik shook his head, obviously troubled. "You know Liza, his hands are tied. He doesn't really have a case, only a gut instinct. He has no suspects and no probable cause for anything that's happened, from the accidental deaths and the break-ins to the unexplainable incidents. I guess we're lucky that he's even taken an interest."

"I know. But it makes me wonder why—what he thinks is really going on here."

Erik sighed. "Tell you what, we need a break from all this speculation and intrigue. How about having dinner with me, the Leschi Lake Café on Lake Washington? I know how much you love their clam chowder with a splash of sherry."

"As long as I can have a glass of Chardonnay to go with it," she said, attempting a lighter tone.

He nodded, his eyes steady. "Even two or three."

"Good. I might need them."

"When can you get out of here?"

"Another hour."

"I'll see you at your place." He glanced at his watch. "About five-thirty."

"Maybe a little before that."

He acknowledged the time, then dropped a kiss on her cheek, gave a salute, and was gone, the door closing gently behind him.

Liza finished her work, then closed up her files, put on her coat and headed out to her car. She left the parking lot and turned onto the street, surprised when Erik swung his Cherokee in behind her. He honked and waved her on, then followed her all the way to First Hill, parking on the street as she went on into the garage.

"Just wanted to make sure you were safe," he told her a few minutes later as she got into his car.

"But you can't follow me home every night," she said, protesting.

"We'll see. The creep needs to know he went too far this time."

* * *

After a surprisingly relaxed dinner at a window table overlooking Lake Washington, Erik had seen her safely home. "I want you to consider quitting that job," he had said just before leaving her condo. "Maybe going into private practice." He had put up a flat silencing hand when she had opened her mouth to protest. "Just think about it." Then he had stepped into the elevator.

Now, as she lay in the dark watching billows of cumulus clouds gallop across the night sky like flocks of fluffy sheep, she pondered her situation. Would leaving International Air solve her problems? Probably not, because she wasn't the one who'd caused the mayhem in the first place. And she was sure she'd still be a target no matter where she worked.

Because someone believed she was in possession of dangerous information.

As usual there were no answers and only one conclusion: she didn't know what was really going on.

Unsettled, she went to get herself a glass of water, then ran back to the nightstand with it to grab the phone before its shrill ring woke up her cat. Liza glanced at the illuminated clock next to it. Not quite nine. Early yet. It must be Jean.

"Owen Barnes here," his voice said in her ear. "You weren't asleep, were you?"

"In bed but not asleep."

"Guess you're exhausted, huh? A couple of beers makes me sleepy, too, especially after a rough day."

There was a silence.

"How did you know that I had anything to drink?"

"Just guessing. I knew you and your friend Erik went out to grab a bite."

"Erik told you that?"

"Uh-huh," he said, not elaborating. "I was just calling to hear how things went today. Anything else happen?"

She explained that she had taken her conclusions about

the layoffs to Dave, to her boss, and to Sylvia Kempton in personnel. "They all felt I was mistaken. That there was a logical reason for my findings, but they each promised to check out the printout I gave them."

He didn't respond.

"Are you still there?" she asked.

"Yeah, I'm here. Just processing."

"Your conclusion?"

"Confusion."

"What does that mean?"

"Only that it's odd that all three people discount your facts."

"What do you mean?" Liza sat down on the edge of her bed.

"Just that something is really screwed up here. Why would they deny your information? In my book, you presented them with facts."

"Maybe because they're afraid of jeopardizing their jobs."

"Are you suggesting that International Air is behind all of this?"

"No, of course not. I believe all of them have their own concerns, whether it's about their career or something they need to hide."

"Explain that."

"I can't because I am not in a position to prove anything. It's all speculation on my part."

"Speculate. Off the record," he added.

"You won't take this as gospel?"

"It's off the record, remember?"

She blew out a long breath and began. "Dave Farrar is concerned about FAA certification for the new One Thousand Series jet. He feels that negative PR will not only impact the project, but his career status with the company as well. My boss, Al Stark, is indecisive about company issues that are beyond his expertise. He worries about making a wrong decision that might cause problems and put his own position in question."

"And that leaves Sylvia Kempton. Does she also worry about her job?"

"I don't have a good fix on Sylvia."

"Come on, Liza," he prompted. "I've said this is off the record, and I'm not allowed to record telephone conversations without your permission."

"Okay," she said, finally. "The first time I talked to Sylvia about the layoff printout was right after Alice died. I attributed her hesitancy to grief, even though I felt she was evasive. Then Erik told me that he'd seen my PI talking to Sylvia at the parachute center shortly before Steve's accident."

"I know, Erik told me about that."

"When?" Her voice cracked with surprise. She had meant to tell the detective herself, and she always forgot to do it because of the larger, more frightening incidents that had taken precedence in the days since.

"On our way up to your condo the night the skydiver died." He paused. "Go on."

She took a sip of water. "When I talked to her today I felt she was deliberately vague—nervous about my query, even reluctant to take my requests seriously."

"Why didn't you share this information before, Liza?"

"I guess it didn't seem like information."

"Everything is information in a homicide investigation."

"Homicide investigation?"

"I misspoke."

"*Is* this a homicide investigation?" she asked, pressing her question.

"You know that I'm looking into all the coincidences that seem related here," he said, again avoiding a direct answer. "I have no hard evidence, but let's just say I'm tenacious when I believe something isn't what it seems."

"You mean you have a *hinky* feeling about what's been going on." She switched the phone to her other ear. "Isn't that the word you used to describe this situation before?"

"Yeah, I guess I did."

A few seconds later they ended their conversation. "Remember, call me if anything happens that is even a fraction out of the ordinary."

Liza promised and hung up. She sincerely hoped that nothing else happened. But she'd hoped that before.

And it had.

The clouds must really have looked like sheep, because after talking to Detective Barnes, Liza had gone to sleep immediately, secure in knowing he believed her story—and that her alarm was armed.

She awoke with new resolve; she would go to the computer lab and talk to Hawk and maybe John Ellis, the programmer who had been promoted to Nate's position. John Ellis might know if anything had been amiss with Nate's computer. But she would choose a time when Dave was gone; she didn't want to create more conflict between them.

Although she no longer notified Joe each time she left the building, he was waiting for her when she stepped out of the elevator at the garage level. He walked her to the Miata, then watched as she drove away. "Be sure you call when you come back tonight," he had told her sternly. "I gotta answer to Naomi, and she says we're your surrogate parents for now."

Liza had promised, but restrained herself from asking

who had *really* been instructing him. Detective Barnes? Erik? Whoever. It was reassuring that people cared, that she wasn't alone in . . . in what? she asked herself. The situation was still out of focus, but she was getting closer to a clear picture. And someone out there knew it.

Her morning went smoothly; she spoke to Dave shortly before noon and turned down his invitation for dinner that night because she was still unsettled about their last conversation. But she did learn that he would be in meetings all afternoon and away from the computer lab. It was her chance to see Hawk Bohlman. And depending on how that went, maybe John Ellis. She suspected that Hawk might be concealing evidence about the layoffs.

Right after lunch Liza left her office and took the walkway to the next building. The guard looked at her badge and waved her through. She continued into the huge installation that housed the many work stations for the programmers. Each person worked on a small piece of the software, and because of security reasons, were unaware of the total concept that would fly the new One Thousand Series jets and launch International Air into the new millennium of air travel.

Glancing around, Liza did not see either Dave or Hawk. Her gaze went to Nate's former station where John Ellis sat working at his computer. She headed for him, stopping next to his chair. "You're John Ellis, aren't you?" she asked.

He faced her. "Yes, I'm John." His voice was high and thin, and vaguely familiar.

"I'm Liza MacDonough," she said. "A counselor from the Human Resource Department."

He blinked nervously, and his gaze veered away from hers. "Yes, I know."

She raised her brows.

"One of the guys mentioned your name when you were here with Mr. Farrar," he said, still fidgety.

Liza suddenly remembered where she had heard his voice; he was one of the men behind the partition, the conversation she had overheard as she waited for Dave.

"How do you like working for IA?" she asked, contriving a friendly tone, waiting for a chance to address his involvement with the CB forum.

"The work is a challenge. I took Nate Garret's position and he's a hard act to follow."

"Did you know Nate very well?"

"Only as a coworker." He looked away, as though he wanted to end their conversation. "I was only here a few months before Nate died." He hesitated. "Has Hawk Bohlman requested that I have a performance evaluation, Mrs. MacDonough?" His voice faltered. "Is that why you're here?"

"No. Why do you ask?"

"Because you did one on Nate and now I have his job."

"Are you suggesting that there's something about this computer that compromises the programmer?" she asked, softening her question with a smile.

"Of course not."

"No secret programming going on behind Hawk's back?" she asked lightly, masking the seriousness of her question.

He shook his head. The overhead lighting shone through his thinning hair to his scalp. Tiny bubbles of sweat lined his upper lip and brow. He's a nervous wreck, Liza thought.

"If you're here to see Hawk you'll have to come back," John said. "He's gone for the day."

"Where is he?"

"Up north at the assembly plant, checking out some onboard glitches on the One Thousand Series jet."

She digested the information. "As I said, I'm not doing an evaluation on you, John. But I did want to talk to you about the CB forum on United Online. And Bojangles."

He swallowed hard. "Bojangles?" His voice had lost its volume.

"Uh-huh. Nate was Bojangles, wasn't he?"

"Why would you ask me that?" He was evading a direct answer with his own question.

"Are you Snakeoil, John?"

"Oh God, no."

"Then you must be Comet?"

He dropped his gaze, so obviously upset that she almost felt sorry for him. But he had information that she needed and she was not about to let him off the hook.

She waited for him to speak.

"I don't know anything." He sucked in a gulp of air. "I'm doing a good job and that's my only concern. If I lose my position and income I'll lose custody of my kids. And that would be the worst thing that could happen to me."

"What about losing your life, John?"

"Are you threatening me?"

"Of course not. It's just that some odd things are happening around here, like the layoffs and people having fatal accidents. Someone is a very dangerous person." She leaned closer. "Are you sure you don't have anything more to say?"

"Not another word."

He turned away from her and went back to his computer keyboard. But not before she had seen his expression. Her words had terrified him.

She stood behind him for a moment longer, then strode back to the door. Although he had not admitted to anything, Liza knew that she had found Comet, that Nate had been Bojangles. But who in the hell was Snakeoil. Hawk? Cooper? *Dave?* For a crazy moment, she thought of Martin, too. Nobody was who he was supposed to be.

Liza had come to the lab to see Hawk again and to talk to Nate's replacement. Now she felt exhilarated, as though she was gaining ground. She stopped in midstride. It was definitely time to confront Hawk about specifics, like phony workers in the company and who in his lab was responsible for programming them into the personnel records. What safer place was there than the assembly plant with its hundreds of workers.

Okay, Mr. Hawk Bohlman, I'm on my way, she thought, and quickened her step. She could button up her office and be on the road within the hour. Liza suppressed her own sense that she was acting recklessly again. She had no choice. More than ever it was a race against time to find answers before anyone else met with an accident.

Including herself.

Chapter Twenty-Nine

IT WAS MIDAFTERNOON WHEN LIZA DROVE ONTO THE AIR-
plane assembly plant campus of International Air thirty
miles north of Seattle. Adrenaline had canceled out her
fears; she had to find out who was terrorizing her. At least
make another step in that direction.

She parked in a visitor lot and was almost overwhelmed
by the size of the installation. She had only been to the
site once before with Al, and they had driven directly to
an office building. She did not remember the grounds, or
the buildings being so gigantic. She had no idea which was
the one Hawk had gone to in order to check out the
onboard computer glitch, although she assumed he would
be in the hangar where the planes were assembled. She
needed directions and headed for the information center.

A tour of the facility was about to begin and she overheard the guide's short spiel about company history and
the layout of the installation. Damn, she thought, realizing she was a long way from where she needed to be.

As the group boarded a nearby bus for the assembly

plant, Liza slipped into their midst. Going along was the fastest way to get to where she needed to go. Besides, she'd just heard the guide say that anyone who wasn't on the tour would need special clearance to get into the hangar. She doubted Hawk would give her that even if she knew where to page him.

The bus took them to the largest building Liza had ever seen; once inside, the group moved through an underground utilities access tunnel to an elevator. The place was made for giants, she thought, stepping onto a lift big enough to accommodate all of them. As the door clanked open at a balcony above the work area there was instant silence. The full impact of the enormous building was awesome: planes in various stages of assembly looked to be six or seven stories high, cranes that moved along the ceiling carried huge parts as if they were tinker toys, and hundreds of workers seemed like busy ants on anthills. One of the ants could be Hawk.

As the tour moved on, Liza headed back to the elevator, knowing it had been silly to think she could find Hawk. But then she had not realized the magnitude of the facility. She would confront him tomorrow in his office.

No one was waiting for the lift when she stepped onto the oil-stained board floor and pushed the down button that would take her back to the tunnel. The door groaned as it closed, then suddenly began to open again.

A man stepped inside. As the conveyance jerked into motion, descending slowly, he faced her.

Hawk Bohlman.

She cringed backward, her body moving of its own volition. Fifteen feet separated them. She had come to confront him, yet now she felt confronted, and terrified.

"Isn't this a little off your beaten track?" he asked, a smile twisting his lips.

"How did you know I was on this elevator?" Her question sounded illogical, even to her own ears.

"I didn't. Why are you?"

The elevator, on its gradual descent, stopped suddenly with a terrific screech. The sound of metal gears grinding together indicated that the mechanism had stalled between floors.

A glance at the level indicator told her she was in trouble. They were stuck several feet above the tunnel—with no way out.

For long seconds neither spoke.

Hawk started toward her—or toward the elevator pad behind her? She punched blindly at the buttons.

Abruptly the pulleys and winches jerked the conveyance into motion, lowering it again. Hawk hesitated, his eyes on her face.

Then the door started to slide open, creaking and groaning behind Liza. She darted out into the concrete tunnel and turned toward the exit. Several hundred yards behind her two male workers were headed in the same direction. She sucked in air, trying to slow her rapid breathing, relieved to see people within shouting distance.

"Hey, what the hell's wrong with you? Are you a nut case or something?" Hawk called after her, obviously unaware of other people in the tunnel. His harsh laugh followed her down the corridor.

She came to a skidding halt and whirled around, her eyes meeting his glinting stare. "Are you Snakeoil, Hawk? The person who killed Nate because he was on to what you're doing in that lab of yours? Because he was on to the reason that people are being fired to make room for phony employees?"

"My mistake," he shouted back. "You're not a simple nut case. You're a lunatic! Why would I have killed Nate after sending him to you for an evaluation?"

"Why indeed! You tell me!"

He stepped closer. "And why are you saying *killed?* Nate's death was an accident."

"Like Alice's? Like my private investigator's? Like the jumper at the parachute center?" Her heart was beating so fast she could hardly get the words out of her mouth. "I know the truth, Hawk."

"And so do I." He started toward her. "You've lost touch with reality."

"Don't you wish!"

"What the hell are you accusing me of? Messing with the company's hiring and firing practices?" His voice was loud and angry. "You think I'm Jesus Christ?"

"I think you're a man with something to hide." Her words bounced off the concrete walls. "I believe you know more than what you've admitted about the layoffs, the deaths and why someone is after me!"

"You're not only crazy, you're a fuckin' troublemaker. And I'm just the guy to take you down a few notches."

"Is that a threat?"

"It's a promise!"

He was closing the space between them and she backed away. The other men in the tunnel were only fifty or so yards behind him, and she realized he still hadn't seen them. Their presence was all that kept her from running.

"Is there a problem?" one of the workers asked as they approached. Hawk was visibly startled, unable to mask his anger before the men saw it.

"No, nothing's wrong," he replied, gruffly. "Just a little disagreement."

The men glanced at Liza, waiting.

"Mr. Bohlman is right," she said, but her voice shook. "We were having a discussion about the company layoffs and his possible involvement," she added, emboldened by their presence and the name tags on their shirts.

They looked unconvinced. They must have overheard more than she realized. Voices echoed in the tunnel.

"I was just leaving." She glanced between the two men. "May I walk with you to the entrance?"

"Sure," the taller man said. "That's where we're headed."

Liza accompanied them to the steps that led outside. Just before she left the tunnel she glanced behind her. Hawk was gone.

Jogging all the way, it took Liza ten minutes to get back to her car. At least it's not raining, she told herself, unlocking the Miata. Her run through the blustery cool air had restored her confidence, although it had not taken away a crawly sensation of being watched. She wondered where Hawk had gone, if he had taken a shortcut to her parking lot.

Remember the paranoids, she reminded herself, wryly. He could not have known where she had left her car. He was not a mind reader.

But she quickly climbed behind the wheel and was about to pull the door closed when someone grabbed the outside handle and opened it again.

"Gotcha."

Dave's voice did not stop her shocked reaction. Her limbs went limp, the gray day darkened, and for a second she felt as though she would float into its low clouds. Then her heart started beating again and the moment passed.

"Hey, Liza. I didn't scare you, did I?"

She managed a nod. "I thought the lot was empty. Where did you come from?" Her words sounded faint, lacking volume.

"I'd just parked when I saw you." He pointed across the parking area to his Mercedes.

She nodded again, trying to regain her composure.

"You okay?" He squatted in the shelter of the car door next to her seat so that they were on eye level. He took her hand from the steering wheel and kissed it.

She smiled faintly. "I'm fine, just startled, as you can see."

"I'm sorry I frightened you, Brown Eyes. I figured you'd seen me running across the lot to catch you before you got away." He paused. "What brought you up here anyway?"

"Um, an appointment," she said evading.

"Yeah, me too. Over at the hangar."

She glanced away, not up to discussing her real reason for being there. She wondered if Hawk would tell him.

"Guess I'd better get on the road," she said. "I still have a few things to do at the office."

He stood. "Yeah, you'd better if you want to miss some of the rush hour traffic." He closed the door and she rolled down the window.

"Sorry I was such a ninny. I usually don't startle so easily."

"I'm the one who's to blame. Next time I'll shout." The wind caught at his hair, lifting it into tangles as he stepped back. "Get going," he said, grinning. "If I get home early enough I'll give you a jingle tonight."

She smiled acknowledgment, rolled up the window and backed into the lane that led out of the lot. As she turned onto the main road, Liza glanced in the rearview mirror. Dave still stood where she had left him, watching her go. She wondered what he was thinking.

A few minutes later she drove onto the freeway and headed south, realizing that she had not gained anything from her trip to the hangar—except a dangerous enemy.

The afternoon had ended in an anticlimax. There was still no solid evidence, nothing tangible to connect anyone to all the frightening events that had started with the company layoffs. And without a suspect there was no probable cause, and Detective Barnes did not have a case.

If only she still had the original sheet of music. If only she had taken better care of it after Pastor Larsen had handed her the envelope.

The envelope.

She remembered placing it among the hymn books at the mission. Could it still be there? she wondered. If so, it might have the fingerprints Barnes was looking for.

She swung out into the passing lane and accelerated. She would skip the office, go in early in the morning to catch up on her work. Right now, she was going to church.

One way or another, she was determined that Barnes would have a case.

Chapter Thirty

THE STREETS IN PIONEER SQUARE WERE JAMMED WITH vehicles; it was stop-and-go traffic because of an event at SAFECO Field several blocks south of the Mission Church. Liza managed to fit the Miata into a small parking space that had been ignored by drivers with bigger cars.

A chill crept over her as she stepped out of her car into the cold afternoon air and started down the sidewalk to the traffic light. Waiting at the corner, she breathed in the salty fragrance of bay water, the smell triggering memories: picnics on the beach when she and Jean were little girls, a church camp the summer before her dad's death, and later, sailing with Martin and Erik when the wind was up and the chop of the Sound had sent lesser sailors running for shelter.

Martin. Where was he now?

The light changed and Liza crossed the street with the other pedestrians, buttoning her coat as she went, feeling cold to the bone.

At the next corner Liza turned up a side street, away

from the crush of traffic. She slowed her pace as she approached the mission, her gaze darting everywhere, making sure that no one followed her this time or lurked in one of the boarded-up doorways.

The door of the church was unlocked, as was normal during the day, and she went inside. The noise of the city muted as did the ferry signals, train whistles and traffic sounds beyond the four walls where she stood pondering the ominous silence.

What the hell had she been thinking? She had placed herself in another vulnerable position. No one knew that she was here. Alone.

It's suicidal, she told herself. She should have called Pastor Larsen from her cell phone, let him know she was on her way. At least she could have left a message for Barnes? She had promised to call him before going out to investigate.

This was not investigating, she reminded herself. She was not in a spooky place. Pastor Larsen was probably in his office or in another part of the building. She resisted calling the detective now. She would not buy into her own paranoia and become handicapped by irrational fear.

Still she hesitated just inside the sanctuary, her glance moving over the empty pews, down the center aisle to the pulpit, then to the piano at the side of the dais. Behind its bench was a door to the dining room, a door that was now closed.

The church was empty.

Then why were her senses on full alert? Was it only a result of all that had happened over the past few weeks? Or was there something—or someone—hidden nearby, watching.

Ridiculous, she told herself. She needed to mind her senses, not her imagination. Her eyes said she was alone; her ears did not pick up any unusual sounds.

Slowly, she headed for the piano, her gaze darting ahead, checking out the shadowy areas of the room. This is a church, she reminded herself. A safe place.

Reaching the piano, Liza glanced around again. Nothing moved. She sat down on the bench, placing her handbag beside her. Then she went through the stack of music books, her hands trembling. The envelope was there, flattened between the last two hymnals in the pile. Very carefully, conscious of not touching it any more than was necessary, Liza held it gingerly by its edges.

"Way to go!" she said aloud, scarcely believing her luck. She had doubted that an empty envelope would survive substitute pianists and subsequent church services. But as the echo of her words died away, apprehension gripped her again.

Still holding the envelope by its edges, Liza slipped it into an unused compartment of her purse. Remembering what the detective had said, she was aware of not obliterating fingerprints. She stood to go and the legs of the piano bench scraped the board floor.

There was a faint sound, indistinguishable, somewhere in the building. Was someone here with her?

She froze, listening. She had been so excited about the envelope that she had not paid attention to her senses, the very thing she had instructed herself to do. Had she really heard something? she wondered. She didn't know exactly what had alerted her, but something had definitely changed.

Liza faced the empty pews. Nothing seemed different, but she knew it was. It was as though the air patterns had been altered when someone moved through them, sending silent waves into the serenity of the church.

Someone evil.

She stood paralyzed, uncertain. Was it just her imagination again? She didn't think so. But it was possible. These days her brain scarcely knew how to determine the difference between what was and what wasn't a real threat. Liza wondered when she would be a normal person again.

But for now she needed to get out of there. Would anyone hear her if she screamed for help? She didn't know for sure that Pastor Larsen was on the premises.

Grow up, she told herself, still hesitating. There is no reason to scream. Little men are going to take you away if you don't pull yourself together. A normal person does not call for help without a reason.

Liza glanced at the door behind the piano. Should she go out that way? But what if there was no one in the kitchen or dining room either. She'd be trapped. Just march down the aisle to the front entrance, she told herself. It's the quickest way out.

But someone could be hiding in one of the pews and she wouldn't see them until it was too late.

Her mind went back and forth as she tried to gain perspective. No one was there or she would have seen them. And the longer she hesitated, the faster her imagination spun out of control. Stiffen your backbone, she commanded herself. Get some courage.

Liza moved forward, slowly at first, and then unable to control the impulse, she ran. She was about to open the door when a hand came down on her shoulder.

Her knees buckled and she grabbed the knob for support. Her breath was trapped in her throat. She was unable to utter a sound.

"Liza, are you okay?" An arm circled her waist, supporting her. "I'm sorry if I startled you."

"Pastor Larsen." Her voice shook. "I didn't see you come into the church."

He inclined his head toward another side door near the front entrance. "I thought you must have heard me. I'm so sorry," he repeated. "And I'm surprised to see you."

She tried to pull herself together. "I came by to find an envelope I'd left among the hymn books." She managed a laugh. "I'd just found it and was about to leave."

He stared at her, studying her face. "Are you sure that nothing else is bothering you?"

She shook her head, not wanting to explain that she had already been scared out of her wits before he startled her. "Just tired I guess."

"You're on your way home?"

She nodded.

"Where are you parked?"

"Just a block and a half away." She smiled. "Right on the street."

"I'll walk you back to your car."

"I'm fine, really," she said. "That's not necessary."

"Of course it is," he said. "My parishioners would never forgive me if you were accosted on the street again. You must still be a bit shaken."

She nodded again. "I admit, it was a little scary."

"It's settled then. I'm walking you to your car." He held up his hand when she was about to protest. "Please, Liza, let me do this little thing."

She was relieved, knowing that Pastor Larsen would not be dissuaded anyway. He walked her back to the Miata, nodding at or blessing many of the homeless people who lingered in doorways along the sidewalk. Liza wondered if they had been there earlier when she had traversed the route. Probably so, hidden in the shadows—but she'd checked and saw no one. Like the phantom in her life, only these people were benevolent wraiths. She felt safer, surrounded by her pastor's flock.

"Thank you," she told him, before getting into her car. "I appreciate your concern."

He hugged her. "And I appreciate all the many hours you donate to our church." He stepped back, smiling.

She said good-bye, started the engine and then headed down the street. At the first stoplight Liza pulled out her cell phone and called Detective Barnes, surprised when he picked up.

"Barnes here," he said.

"It's Liza MacDonough. I'm just leaving the Mission Church."

"What's up?"

"I found the envelope."

"The envelope?"

"The one that came with the sheet music."

"*That* sheet music?"

"Uh-huh. The mysterious music that I think Nate wrote. The envelope might have fingerprints."

A silence.

"My God. Where is it?"

"In my purse."

"Where are you?"

"Headed up Jackson, stopped at a light. On my way home."

"Okay. I'm leaving Homicide right now. Two minutes behind you. Meet you at your building."

"I'll go on up to my apartment."

"No. Don't do that. Wait outside in the load zone. Keep your motor running and doors locked—and don't get out of your car."

"You make it sound ominous." A pause. "Do you think someone is following me? Or waiting for me at my condo?"

There was a brief hesitation.

"Just taking precautions, okay? See you in five minutes."

Liza ended the call and dropped the phone into her lap. She continued up the hills slowly, stopping for each caution light, giving Barnes a chance to get to her building. Headed up Madison, she turned on Minor Avenue for a short distance and then pulled into the load zone of her condominium.

Seconds later a dark sedan raced around the corner from Madison and pulled up behind her. When the car door opened and Detective Barnes stepped onto the street, she was relieved and rolled down her window.

"Any problems?" he asked coming up to the Miata.

She shook her head. "Only been here a minute."

Liza pulled out the envelope and handed it to him. "I can't believe it was still there. But then no one ever disturbs my stuff on the piano. Our transient worshipers are respectful of another person's belongings." A hesitation. "It's the people I trust who seem to be untrustworthy."

He studied the envelope. "You recognize the handwriting?"

She shook her head. "Maybe it's Nate's, I'm not sure."

He nodded. "I'll check that out. We should have answers pretty quickly."

"I hope so. And thanks for coming, Detective Barnes—and for being on my side."

"Just doing my job." He grinned. "But you're welcome anyway."

She picked up her phone. "I'll call Joe, let him know I'm coming in."

"Good. I'll wait until you get in the building. And I'll be in touch soon."

"Wait," she said as he turned to go back to his car. "Have you heard anything about Alice's water bottle?"

"Still waiting for the report to come back on the bottle and the money," he said. "But I'm putting a rush on the envelope, getting it to the crime lab tonight. It's possible that I could have the fingerprint information by late tomorrow."

He agreed she would be the first to hear, then got into his car, backing up just far enough so that she could maneuver out of her spot. He followed her into the driveway; when Joe appeared as the gate was opening, Barnes backed away. He drove off as the gate closed again behind her.

Liza was relieved to be home safely. Detective Barnes was on her side and that realization was gratifying.

And scarier than ever.

Why had she gone to the church? He hadn't been able to see what she had put in her purse. It was not the sheet music; he had already destroyed that. Whatever it was had interested the detective enough to want it right away.

He pounded the steering wheel. The pain did not ease his anger. He tried to calm himself, but his frustration was suffocating him. He pulled out his flask and gulped Scotch. The alcohol would help.

The rage within him was barely under control. But it had to be. Too much was at stake. His whole future. She had to be stopped.

Now.

Chapter Thirty-One

"WHAT IN THE HELL IS GOING ON, LIZA!" AL DEMANDED, bursting into her office the next morning. "I thought you'd gotten past all that conspiracy bullshit! Especially since the terminated client referrals have slowed down lately."

"You've been talking to Hawk Bohlman." She stood up, bracing herself.

"Hawk just left my office. He's very concerned about your behavior, that you were way out of line going to the lab and upsetting one of his programmers. John Ellis told him about your visit, that you'd questioned him."

Her anger was instant. "My reason for talking to John Ellis was work related. He's the man who took Nate Garret's place and—"

"I know who he is," Al said, interrupting. "My point is that John Ellis is not your client, nor is Hawk, who also told me about your accusations when you went up to the assembly plant yesterday."

"Hawk is the one who was out of line, not me," Liza

retorted. "He can't even have a rational conversation without getting on the defensive."

"That's just it, Liza. Rational from whose point of view? Yours?"

"No Al," she said, deceptively calm. "I'm speaking from an IA counselor's point of view."

"The fact remains," he said, dismissing her argument. "You have no business going over to the computer lab or to the assembly plant and asking questions that allude to this uh, intrigue crap that you've fixated on. For God's sake, Liza. This whole issue has gone too far. It's not rational."

"Fixated?" She shot the word out of her mouth like a knife thrower aiming for his heart. "What if I'm right?"

"Then I'll apologize."

"Have you looked into the list of bogus addresses yet?"

His gaze veered to the side.

"If you haven't, then how can I prove that I'm right?"

He was silent.

She gulped a breath. "*Conspiracy bullshit* is absolutely right. And why is that? Because no one, not you, Sylvia, Dave or Hawk, will pay any attention to what I've been saying. Or to the fact that I took the time and trouble to uncover a few things that are pertinent to the issue." She stepped closer. "I'm asking you again. *Why?*"

He took a step backward, his face suffused with color.

"You know what I think, Al?" Her voice shook. "That I'm on to something that no one wants to face. It's easier to blame me."

Their eyes locked, neither giving ground. Al was the first to look away.

"And do you want to know why none of you will take a stand?" she asked, pressing her point. "Because all of you are only concerned about your own position, about not jeopardizing your job. You're terrified of having any connection to a person you perceive as a whistle-blower."

"And you, Liza?" He had regained his sense of outrage. "You're willing to sacrifice your position with the company based on bizarre suppositions? You've conjured up an insane scenario because you bought into the gossip of disgruntled employees."

"Former employees," she said, correcting him. A pause. "And I haven't *conjured up* anything."

He blew out a long sigh. "Precisely the point, Liza. You can't see that you're freewheeling into a brick wall."

"What *precisely* does that mean?"

"You're losing it, Liza."

"What?"

"You're losing it," he repeated, his tone lower, regretful, as though he hated to say the words.

"How dare you say that to me!"

"I dare because someone has to." He shook his head. "I know you've been under tremendous stress this past year . . . since Martin disappeared." He hesitated. "And although I'm not the practicing therapist here, we both understand about transferring feelings to a place where we can deal with them. In your case it's clients' complaints about the company."

She stared at him, incredulous. "This has nothing to do with Martin, and you know it."

He spread his hands in supplication, as though to say she was a hopeless case. "Do I? A cursory call to Sylvia Kempton and another to Dave Farrar told me all I needed to know. There is no big conspiracy going on here at International Air. No one is hiding anything."

"I guess I'm not surprised," she said, coldly. "I've always known that you'd never believe me about this."

"Because I won't buy into your paranoia?"

"No, Al. You don't believe me and let's leave it at that."

She watched him control his anger. "Look, I want to help you, Liza. I know you're on overload, that your personal life is in limbo." His voice gained volume. "The first consideration should be some time off, maybe a leave of absence. And I have the names of excellent grief counselors here in the city and—"

"Don't bother," she retorted. "I'm not paranoid, disturbed or in need of magnification glasses to see what's going on!" She yanked her door open.

"Liza, c'mon—"

"C'mon, nothing. Just get the hell out of my office. I've had enough insults for one day."

He frowned, alarmed by her response. "Now Liza—"

"Don't say anything else, Al. Just bear in mind that after I figure everything out, I'll remember this conversation, that you didn't take any of my concerns seriously. It'll all be in *my* report to the company."

"Are you threatening me, Liza?"

"Of course not, just explaining my position."

She tried to slam the door behind him, but it shut with a soft sucking sound, held back by its vacuum arm.

Liza collapsed into her chair, then slumped over the desk, her head resting in the cradle of her arms. She fought tears, and tried to swallow away the tightness in her throat. No one at International Air took her concerns seriously. And now she was in jeopardy of losing her job—because everyone would rather believe she was going crazy than face the truth.

Damn them all! she thought, jerking herself into an upright position. She *was not* going to let them take her down. She was right, whether they wanted to believe her or not. And she could not walk away from the mess now.

There was only one thing to do. Prove the allegations.

She would, or die trying.

*   *   *

Too wound-up to settle down, Liza moved mindlessly through her apartment, from kitchen to dining room and living room, then down the hall to her office and bedroom, waiting for the phone to ring.

Outside, the interminable rain slashed against her windows, and the wind whistled into the protected curve of her deck, whipping the branches of her potted evergreen shrubs.

Where was everyone? Why hadn't Dave or Erik returned her calls? Dave had not checked in all day, and when she returned home this evening he had not left a message either. She suspected that Hawk had reported to him as well as to Al. But she was disappointed that Dave would be influenced by anything Hawk would say about her.

Unless he had reason to be alarmed, reasons that had less to do with her and more to do with what she had uncovered.

Don't think that way, she instructed herself. Second-guessing would be buying into Al's assumption that she was losing it.

Liza had hoped Erik would call back; she needed a friend tonight. At the moment he felt like the only one she had. After hanging up she realized that her brief message to him about Al's attack and her job being in jeopardy may have sounded a little hysterical.

By eight she had not heard from anyone: Dave, Erik, or Detective Barnes—she'd hoped for early reports on Alice's water bottle and the envelope.

Her worries churning in her mind, tormenting her with questions that had no answers, Liza poured herself a glass of Chardonnay. She had to slow down her nervous system, allow herself to regain some perspective. She couldn't sleep and hadn't been able to eat since arriving home at six. On top of everything else, knowing she would probably be terminated at International Air frustrated and angered her.

She took a chair by the window, and considered calling Jean, then decided against it. Her sister would know something was wrong and get upset. Telling Jean her problems would not accomplish a thing. She probably had a performance tonight anyway, just as Erik could be teaching a class.

Shit! she thought, putting down the wine she no longer wanted. It was an untenable situation. There was no one to talk to about her concerns, her fears for her job, her credibility, her life.

She grabbed her portable phone and punched in Detective Barnes's number. Liza was not surprised when his voice mail picked up.

"Hey, I've been hoping to hear from you about the lab reports," she said onto the recording. "Things are getting pretty dicey at work. My boss thinks I need a leave of absence; he believes I'm losing it and won't pursue the issue of my concerns any further." Her voice sounded high-pitched, upset. Okay, she thought. Go for it.

"Since you haven't checked back, and since everyone seems to think I'm the nut, let me reiterate my position. Something is going on at IA, someone thinks I know more than I do, and that person intends to kill me. Please call me, Detective Owen Barnes. I'm very upset and I need a progress report." She hung up.

She dumped the wine down the drain in the kitchen sink. It had not helped ease the hollow sensation of dread in the pit of her stomach, and she wondered if anything could. Her stress level was in the stratosphere; she figured her blood pressure was probably up there as well. Her mind whirled and she made an effort to rein in her thoughts. They were eating her up.

About to pick up the phone again and call Dave, explain about John Ellis and Hawk, Liza pulled back her hand, suddenly hesitant. She no longer trusted Dave. She didn't even know if he was on her side. His first priority was the One Thousand Series jet, his own career. She couldn't think of a time when he had placed anything ahead of his position with the company.

You could be wrong, she told herself.

Regardless, she would not call him.

Restless, Liza took a bath, put on her nightgown and then went back to the living room and sat down at the piano. Absentmindedly, she played the mysterious sheet of music's run of notes from memory. They were in B-sharp: b, a, d, g, e. Her fingers stilled on the keys.

Could B-sharp mean: *Be sharp?* A warning?

And the letters together spelled *badge.*

Why hadn't she noticed that before? she wondered. Probably because she was trying to make sense of the music itself. Could the letters in badge be a code word to access Nate's computer at IA? If so, he had passed the very information that killed him on to her.

A frightening thought. And a long shot.

She leaned back, staring into the night sky, thinking. How would she ever be able to check out Nate's computer? John Ellis would never agree to such a thing, even if Hawk would ever allow her into the lab again.

Tonight. I could go now, she thought, exhilarated and terrified at the same time.

Why not? No one would expect her to crash the lab. Now that the software had been written for the new jet and was about in place but for the final testing, the night shifts had been eliminated for the programmers. If her company identification got her past the door guard she would be home free. Her goal would be to get in, access

Nate's computer, and then leave, no damage done. And no one the wiser.

The idea grew. She was already in trouble because of her meddling. A little more couldn't hurt. She could only be fired once.

She needed answers, just as Barnes needed proof. Tonight might be her last chance to get them. Who knew what would happen tomorrow. Her job could be terminated.

Her decision was made. Liza hurried to the bedroom, pulling off her nightgown as she went. She put on Levis and a black turtleneck sweater, clipped her hair into a ponytail and was ready to go within five minutes.

Whoa, she told herself, about to pull a jacket from the hall closet. Remember what happened the last time you rushed headlong to investigate without telling anyone. You almost became a homicide statistic.

She would call Erik again, leave a message if he wasn't there. His recorded voice sounded in her ear. Quickly she explained what she had discovered and where she was going. And then she set the alarm and left her apartment, pepper spray in her hand, a security whistle in her pocket, and the cell phone in her purse.

As she waited for the elevator she kept reminding herself why she had to go. A murderer was free, and no one had yet been able to stop him. It was up to her, even if she did not feel very brave.

Brave is as brave does, she thought. She had no choice. She was the next person on his hit list.

Surprise was on her side. No one would ever expect her to do what she was about to do. She hoped she was right.

Chapter Thirty-Two

LIZA DIDN'T RUN INTO ANYONE IN THE GARAGE, NOR WAS she followed through the city. But fifteen minutes later, as she parked in the company lot, she had an attack of nerves. Her hand on the door lever, she hesitated.

You do not have authorization to be in the lab, she reminded herself. You could lose your job, or worse—be prosecuted. Because you work for the company does not give you license to access high-security computers.

But it was now or never. She may never have another opportunity.

Her mental argument swung to and fro, even as her apprehension grew: the reasons she should get out of the Miata and go inside to verify if she had cracked Nate's code, as opposed to her accountability if she were caught. One thing she knew for sure: she was already a company pariah as far as Hawk and Al were concerned. And most likely Cooper, even Dave, doubted her credibility. What did she have to lose?

Her freedom if she were prosecuted and sent to prison.

The thought was intimidating. But if she didn't come up with some proof soon, she would become the next *accidental* murder victim.

Prison was preferable to being dead.

Someone out there knew she only needed to put her information into focus and then she would *know* what was going on at International Air. And who was responsible. Snakeoil would try to stop her, before the evidence led to him.

She had no choice, even if she resigned her job tomorrow. She knew too much. The murderer would not allow her to live.

But still she lingered. The lot was isolated, and there were only a few parked cars. She felt vulnerable; there would be no one to help her if she got into trouble.

There was the door guard, she reminded herself. He would know of anyone who went in or out of the building. No one would dare try anything with him on duty.

With a burst of bravado, Liza got out of the car and locked it. Then, her hand on the pepper spray in her jacket pocket, she headed toward the computer lab. Although the rain had stopped, she could smell it, knew another shower was imminent. A true Seattlite, she thought, inanely under the circumstances.

Gary, the guard, stood up as she approached, smiling when he recognized her. Recently, she had given him a positive evaluation, citing a happy marriage, good kids, and a strong religious background, which had helped give him the clearance for his current position.

"What brings you out on such a cold night?" he asked, opening the door and allowing her into the warmth of the hall.

"A file I need for a report on one of my clients," she said. "Would you believe I forgot it when I was here?" She shook her head, improvising. "I hadn't even realized that I'd left it until I sat down at my home computer tonight to type up my notes."

"A bummer."

She shrugged, contriving annoyance with herself. "Now, I'll have to be up for hours to get it done. Hawk Bohlman needs it in the morning."

"So where did you leave it?" Gary looked concerned.

"In the computer lab."

There was a silence.

"I don't have authorization to let anyone without proper credentials into that part of the building," he said.

"I'll just need a few minutes to find my file." She paused. "And I do have credentials to do work evaluations on lab employees."

"Well, I don't know," he said, still hesitating.

"You could go with me, make sure I don't touch anything," she offered, knowing he could not leave his post.

"It's not that I don't trust you, Mrs. MacDonough. It's just policy."

"Oh, I realize that." She wrinkled her brow. "I just don't know what I'll do if I can't get my file. I won't have my evaluation done—and you know how Hawk is when someone lets him down."

"Yeah, I know," he said, dryly.

She waited, seeing that his resolve was weakening. The comment about Hawk had tipped the balance. Almost everyone had experienced the man's short fuse when things didn't go his way.

"Okay." He wiped a hand over his chin, still uncertain but wanting to be helpful. "But it has to be our secret."

"I promise," she said, pleased. She could not have planned a better scenario. "And I'll hurry. Shouldn't take more than five minutes, ten on the outside." She repressed feelings of guilt. He trusted her word and she vowed not to get him into trouble over her lies.

"Get going, then. Before someone sees you."

She thanked him and took off. She might need every second of the ten minutes to check Nate's computer.

The guard watched her go, and hoped he had not made a bad decision. His job instructions were implicit: "Do not allow any unauthorized person into the computer lab, especially now when there is no longer a night shift."

But the counselor was not a stranger. As she had explained, she was the person who evaluated the programmers. Still, he would be relieved when she found her file and left the building.

The phone on his desk rang and he went to answer it. Outside the rain had started again and he wondered if Seattle had ever had such a wet winter—or the mountains such a record snowfall.

"Yeah?" he said into the mouthpiece.

"Is this Gary?"

"It is." He switched the receiver to his other ear, so he could watch Liza MacDonough to the end of the long hall, verify that she had turned into the lab.

"This is Mr. Farrar," the man's voice continued in his ear. "I need you to do me a favor."

He frowned. "*Dave* Farrar?" It did not quite sound like him.

"Uh-huh. Can you hear me? I'm talking from a cell phone and the reception isn't very good."

"I can hear you." Oh shit, Gary thought. He hoped the big boss wasn't on his way to the lab. Of all times to bend the rules. The counselor needed to get her damn file and get the hell out of there. "What can I do for you, Mr. Farrar?"

"We had a report that someone had tried to get in the building through the supply doors at the north end."

"I'm here at the south entrance, but those doors should all be locked up at this time of night."

"That's what I need you to verify, and then wait there until more security people arrive. I've already called for a backup."

"But I can't leave my post," Gary said, annoyed that Farrar would even ask. "I need to be here to check out authorized personnel."

"I know that, but it should only take ten or fifteen minutes until you can return to your station. Just make sure that the main entrance door is locked."

"But—"

"No buts, Gary. Anyone who needs to get in while you're gone can use their electronic card key to unlock the door." A pause. "That's the reason authorized employees have the card, so they can get inside in a situation like this."

"Yeah, I know. It's just that nothing like this has ever happened on my shift. And—"

"Gary, get going. Time is of the essence here."

"Okay, I guess it's all right."

"It won't be all right if you don't do what I say."

"I'm on my way, Mr. Farrar."

"Good."

They hung up, Gary set the door system for automatic keying, then headed for the other side of the building. He tapped his holstered pistol as he went, hoping he would not have to use it. He never had before, and he admitted to himself that carrying a gun was the only part of his job that bothered him.

He glanced at his watch. The counselor would be gone before he returned. She would know how to get out of the building. What a night, he thought, and quickened his step.

Liza stepped into the dark lab; all the ceiling lights had been turned off. But the glowing computer monitors were spots of illumination, little fishes and bubbles flickering on their screen savers. It was like being in a giant aquarium of tiny lighted water tanks in an otherwise black cavernous chamber.

She hesitated, uncertain. She was looking at dozens of computers, each one with a hard drive that stored bits and pieces of the programs for the One Thousand Series jet. And God only knew what else.

What if I erase something vital by accident? she asked herself. What if the computers have alarm systems that will notify Security that an intruder has accessed them?

Her thoughts spun with unbidden fears. But one was uppermost, and it sent her rushing across the room to Nate's former work station. She only had a few minutes and the guard would come looking for her.

She sat down in front of the screen, her hands resting on the keyboard. The room was absolutely silent but for the combined, low hum of the computers, a sound that was almost like a living thing.

A monster? she wondered. A bogeyman who could suddenly jump out of another dimension and trap her?

Her imagination at work again. Maybe that was her problem, she thought. It was possible that half of what she believed to be true was simply her way of processing facts.

No! she told herself.

She was just scared, picking up on bad vibes. If only it were just her imagination. Then she could forget Nate's computer and go home, have a dreamless sleep, go back to work in the morning and conform to Al's policy of never rocking the boat.

She hit the bar key to eliminate the screen saver. Instantly, the fish and bubbles were replaced by a request to enter a code word.

Oh shit. Maybe she was stopped before she even started. She should have known it would not be easy. She had no idea what Nate's access code had been, or John's. She typed BADGE and nothing happened. The cursor just kept blinking.

There was no way that she could bring up the programs for the One Thousand Series jet on the screen, and maybe she needed to do that before BADGE would work. But somehow she didn't believe that the company projects had anything to do with the discordant notes on the music sheet. If her suspicion was correct, Nate's composition represented a code that would access a secret program separate from any airplane software.

Liza sat back, thinking. It was amazing how her thoughts had gone from wondering, to suspecting, to being positive that Nate had been the composer of the strange piece. Faulty mental processing? she wondered again. Maybe she had missed her calling. She should have been a writer of fantasy novels.

She leaned forward over the keyboard once more. She was assuming that she couldn't accidentally destroy strategic software programs by typing various runs of letters into the computer. But what if she could?

Not possible, she reminded herself. There would be built-in safety backups. The programmers were experts who would never let that happen. She must stop thinking thoughts that paralyzed her ability to act. If not, she may as well leave the lab right now.

And lose her only chance to discover the truth.

She opened her purse and pulled out the sheet of music she had reconstructed from memory. What if the whole score was the BADGE? Then, in the box marked 'enter code', she typed the letters corresponding with the notes of the whole discordant piece. For a second she hesitated. Then she hit the return key.

The screen suddenly came to life, surprising her. Her talent for playing a tune by ear had come through for her again. She stared, at first uncertain about what she was seeing: names and numbers. Then something Alice had once said about the layoff printout popped into Liza's mind.

"All the systems from all the departments are connected to one main computer bank."

Liza clapped a hand over her mouth, stifling a hysterical laugh. Big Brother really *was* watching.

Alice's words hadn't meant anything to her, until now. She had just accessed the company payroll records, not the confidential programs for International Air's new state-of-the-art jet.

Oh God, Nate. What were you involved in? she asked him silently, suddenly grasping the implications of what he had done. He had been a computer genius, and for some reason he had prostituted that genius. What would have motivated the sensitive, high-strung man she had evaluated to do something so illegal?

But she knew. It was an extravagant lifestyle way beyond his means and his desperate need for more money to maintain it.

Poor Nate hadn't been able to live with what he had created—a secret program to hire bogus employees for their paychecks. So he'd made a fatal mistake by wanting out, perhaps even wanting to call a halt to the thievery.

And Snakeoil, who was probably the perpetrator behind the scam, could not allow that, and lose thousands of dollars each month. Too late Nate must have realized his partner was capable of murder. That was when he had called her.

Leaning back again, Liza stared at the names, addresses and tax deductions. Nate was clearly not a criminal without a conscience and he could not have coped with the ramifications of what he'd done. The fake employees, whose checks were sent out to various box numbers around the city, had taken real jobs from real people. And someone, a person Nate had known, was still collecting those salaries.

She scrolled down the list, recognizing several of the names from her printout. Liza assumed that even the seniority status of the fake people, who had been hired or fired by Snakeoil via a hacker's secret access, had also been altered, insuring that real workers would be laid off first. Protecting his illegal income, she thought. The turnover of the phony employees had been done on a timely basis, so they didn't attract attention.

Was that why her flow of terminated clients had slowed recently? Because Snakeoil was running scared? The hollow feeling was back in her stomach. If she were gone he could accelerate the process again.

Nate had probably decided to confess everything to her on that fatal Sunday, to give her the music printout along with his confession. But he must have seen the person who meant to stop him, and was forced to leave the envelope before she arrived at the mission.

Liza took a shaky breath. This was serious—life-and-death serious. Alice must have suspected what was happening and was about to tell her before she died. Was Alice also murdered by Snakeoil? And was Snakeoil the man she'd been seeing in secret? The Snake somebody that Alice's secretary Pat had told her about? Her PI had been tracking Martin—not even looking into IA employee complaints—and he had died, too. Did that mean that Martin's disappearance was connected to what was happening now? If it did, then Martin might also have been involved with Snakeoil—and murdered.

She sighed, trying to assimilate everything. One thing was for sure. She had been targeted, and she wondered if John Ellis would also be eliminated at some point. She had no doubt that John had either accidentally stumbled into the mess or had been drawn into the conspiracy by a promise to keep his job.

Quickly, Liza closed the computer file, knowing that Snakeoil could not delete the incriminating evidence fast enough to prevent her from presenting her documentation to the company. Cross referencing payroll records and hard copy files would prove that checks had been written to people who did not exist. Her mental processing brought her to another conclusion: Snakeoil had an accomplice in Payroll Records who had made sure that no one became suspicious of those files. She wondered how long the scam had been in place, how Martin fit into the scheme. Whoever was involved, Al, Hawk, Dave, even Sylvia Kempton—who had been seen at the parachute center—someone had to stop them.

What if Snakeoil was Martin?

The sudden thought released an avalanche of fears. Oh God, don't let it be Martin. That would mean he was still alive—*and trying to kill her.*

She could not think about that now. She needed to get out of there.

The screen went back to bubbles and fish.

And then the door across the room opened. Several seconds passed before it closed again. Someone was in the lab with her.

Someone who was absolutely silent.

The guard? Her gaze flew to where he should have been standing.

There was no one there.

Chapter Thirty-Three

LIZA SAT ROOTED TO THE CHAIR. INSTANTLY HER HEARTBEAT accelerated and she began to hyperventilate. She forced deep breaths, struggled to do so quietly; she could not lose her control now. Straining her ears, she tried to pick up on any altered nuance of sound. But nothing seemed to interfere with the low steady rhythm of the computers. And she sensed no movement in the room.

But she knew someone was there.

Someone who stood beyond the glow of fishes and bubbles. Someone who was also frozen in place, listening, eyes searching for her.

Slowly, trying not to draw attention to her movement, she took her purse from the desk next to the keyboard, then slipped off the chair to crouch under the computer table.

Seconds passed, stretching time as if they were minutes. Still there was no sound. Had she only thought that some-one had come into the lab? Maybe it was the guard who had opened the door to check on her, then gone back to his post. Maybe she was imagining things . . . again.

Suddenly she caught the fleeting scent of something odd. She sniffed the air, trying to identify it. Acrid perspiration. She had smelled the odor before—on the walkway between the houseboats.

Terror took her breath. Her ears roared and reality faded. By reflex, her body jerked, jumpstarting her heart.

Was it Snakeoil? She wasn't sure. But it *was* the man who was after her. Were they one and the same?

She sniffed again. The odor was gone. But she knew what it meant.

He was in the room and very close to her.

And he would know where to look for her: John Ellis's work station. She needed to get away from his desk.

A glance into the aisle between the rows of computers told her no one was within a few feet in either direction that she could see from her hiding place. She hesitated. To leave the darkness meant moving into the reflected light from the screens.

The oxygen she was breathing suddenly felt heavy, as though someone else was taking her share. She fought panic, reaching into her jacket for the pepper spray and her whistle, her only weapons.

Then she felt a new sensation. Movement behind her.

A hand reached between the back table legs for her, glancing off her back as she sprang forward, scuttling on all fours before she was able to get to her feet. The canister of pepper spray fell out of her hand and rolled away. Grabbing for it she dropped the whistle, too. She didn't dare go after them. There were no seconds to spare.

Panting for breath, she darted in the direction of the door. She could hear him in the next aisle, trying to head her off.

"Guard! Guard! Gary!" she cried, hoping he would hear her through the walls of the room, and down the long hall to his station. "Help me! I need help!" She kept running as she called to him.

Twenty feet in front of her the dark figure of a man loomed up in the half-light, blocking her escape. It was surrealistic, a specter from the black places of the room.

A murderer who would kill again, she thought, skidding to a stop. His menacing posture left no doubt. He meant to silence her. If she didn't get away she would die.

For a moment they both hesitated, staring at each other, he from behind a black ski mask that was tucked into the collar of his long, flowing coat. Again, as the other times, she couldn't distinguish his features or his size behind the disguise. But she knew he was between her and the only way out of the lab other than through Hawk's private office, which would be locked.

She turned and ran toward the edge of the flickering light from the fake aquarium scenes, hoping to melt into the shadows where he couldn't see her. Once there, she intended to fool him, move away from the door rather than toward it, then circle back and escape.

It might work if she could stay in the dark places.

He no longer took pains to conceal his movement. She could hear him bumping into tables, and his labored breathing as he sought her out. Somehow she had to get out of there. He was intent on finding her and—killing her? A tremor went through her. He was desperate. He did not mean for her to leave the computer lab alive.

No time for melodrama. The guard knew she was in the lab. He also knew about anyone else in the building, including the man in black. Snakeoil, if that's who he was, could not get away with murdering her here.

Not unless the exterior door to Hawk's office was off the guard's surveillance screen. Was that how he'd gained entrance from the parking lot without being seen?

Another scream for the guard welled up in her throat. Liza forced it back. Gary had not heard her cry before. To make a sound would only give away her location.

She slipped deeper into the darkness, careful not to make a sound as she followed her plan to move away from the door. Her mind kept pace with each step she took. Don't panic. Keep it together.

Glancing behind her, the air went out of her chest. He had disappeared. There was no sound. She had no idea where he had gone.

She shrank back into a nearby corner and then heard a faint sound.

Too late she realized he had already spotted her, his black form materializing out of the charcoal background. He had anticipated her strategy to escape.

She bolted but he grabbed her, his leather gloved hand pushing her scream back into her throat. She bit his finger and he jerked his hand from her mouth.

"Shit!" he whispered hoarsely.

The respite allowed Liza a gulp of air. Before she could run, he slapped her face so hard that her teeth came down on her lower lip and she tasted blood. Then his arm was around her neck and his hand back over her mouth, cutting off her breath. She was yanked backward against his body. The odor from his perspiration brought bile up into her throat.

She'd been a damn fool. Tears of frustration blurred her eyes. She should have kept screaming, not tried to out-smart this man who so obviously knew the room like the back of his hand.

She struggled against his hold, twisting her head from side to side. The pressure against her mouth was so tight that she could not move her lips. Her scream was a muf-fled moan, trapped by his tightening hold on her.

He meant to kill her right now. He was not squeamish about using his own hands, choke her as he had done before at the houseboats in Paradise Lost. She had miscalculated, again.

That knowledge sent a jolt of adrenaline surging through her veins. There would be no help from the guard or he would have been there by now. She had to get away herself.

Or die.

Liza socked at him with her purse and its clasp gashed his cheek. He yelped, and his hold on her lessened momentarily. She squirmed free, her body catapulting forward so fast that she slid on her knees away from him. Before he could grab her again, Liza was on her feet running.

"Fucking bitch!" He growled the words and she did not recognize his voice. "You won't get away this time."

She ran but he was right behind her, his hands coming down on her shoulders before slamming her to the floor. Instantly, he was on top of her, pressing her arms against her sides by the pressure of his legs. His eyes glittered in the darkness as his hands closed around her throat. He began to squeeze, grunting from the exertion. Liza could not escape his tightening fingers.

She grew faint. The artificial light blurred, then burst into fragments of color as the tension increased on her neck. The darkness edging the room rushed inward, extinguishing the life in the room, and her own. She was seconds from passing out, from dying. Her eyes fluttered shut, her struggles ceased and her body felt as though it was floating away from where she lay on the floor.

He felt her go limp, and took the opportunity to shift position, momentarily relaxing his hold. Sucking air, Liza knew that she had been given one last chance to get away.

Mustering all of her strength, she brought her knee up into his groin.

"Fuckin' cunt! Piece of shit!"

He loosened his grip even more. She kneed him again, Involuntarily, he rolled to the side, trying to protect himself. Liza was able to pull free, squirming out from under his hands. He cursed and she knew her freedom was temporary, a brief moment of opportunity that would not present itself again. In mere seconds she was on her feet, running, stumbling and gulping deep breaths, trying to make it to the door, her purse dangling from her arm.

She tried to scream but only a hoarse whisper emerged from her throat, her vocal cords too traumatized to utter a sound.

Where was Gary? Why hadn't he heard something and tried to help?

Yanking the door open, she hurtled herself into the hallway, moving as fast as her trembling body would function, headed for Gary's station.

He was not at his post.

Frantically, she looked around. He was nowhere in sight. He hadn't helped her because he was gone.

Liza ran to the door but it was locked and she could not see how to open it. Then she remembered. The guard's desk had a button that buzzed the door, opening the lock. She glanced down the hallway toward the lab. No one was in sight.

The madman had not followed her.

She darted behind the guard's station, found the button and pushed it. The buzzing told her the door was unlocked, if only for a few timed seconds. She rushed to it, pushed it open and plunged into the parking lot. The heavy glass door closed with a click behind her.

And then she had second thoughts.

She could not get back into the building without the guard. What if he—*Snakeoil?*—had also anticipated that and had used Hawk's exterior door?

What if he was waiting for her out here?

She ran for the Miata, wishing she still had the pepper spray. About to open the car door she heard Dave's voice.

"Liza! What in God's name are you doing here?"

She whirled around, her back against the fender, so shaky that she needed the support. He was just getting out of his Mercedes, too far from the computer lab to have been her assailant. She glanced at Hawk's exterior door. Dave had parked close to it, and because he had, may have aborted her attacker's exit route.

Liza tried to answer but her words came out in a strained whisper. She pointed to her neck and shook her head. She was unable to stop the flow of tears. Shock, she decided, and knew she had to get a grip on herself.

He left his car door open, and strode across the open space to her, his expression concerned. "Jeez, Liza! You're bloody. What in hell happened?"

"Someone tried to kill me," she managed, her voice a scratchy croak, her eyes glued to the door of the building. Through the glass doors she could see that Gary was still not at his post.

"What? Where?"

"In the computer lab."

"Why were you in the lab?"

She could only shake her head again.

"You can explain later. You're hurt, Liza. You need a doctor."

"No," she said, faintly. "I think I'm okay."

"We'll see. But first you're going to sit down."

He put an arm around her shoulders, bracing her against him as he walked her to his car. She was too upset to resist, too thankful that he was there. He helped her onto the leather seat, then closed the door and went around to the other side and climbed behind the wheel. Then he faced her, pulling a handkerchief out of his pocket to dab at her tears, and her mouth. It came away smeared with blood from her cut lip.

"Who did this to you?"

She shook her head.

"Didn't you recognize him?"

"He wore a ski mask." Her voice was a whispery croak. "And I couldn't see very well. He stayed in the dark."

Her breathing slowed and gradually her shakiness ebbed but it was still difficult to talk. She realized that her neck was badly bruised, that she might have to see a doctor later, just to make sure the damage was not permanent. She guessed that no small bones had been broken. She was lucky.

"When he was choking me I–"

"Son of a bitch! The bastard choked you?" Dave reached to gently pull down her turtleneck. "Shit!" The word was a hiss. Very carefully, he pulled her closer. "Where the hell was Gary all this time?"

"I don't know. He wasn't at the door when I ran out."

"Then the bastard who did this could still be in the building."

She nodded, her eyes darting back to the entrance.

"We'll get him. He's not getting away with this."

Dave grabbed his cell phone and punched in some numbers. There was a pause. Then, "Hey, Gary. Where the hell are you?"

Another pause as Dave listened.

"I didn't call you, Gary. Get Security down there." A hesitation. "Right fucking now!"

Dave rattled off instructions about the intruder, told

Gary that Liza had been accosted in the lab, and that he could be reached on either his cell phone or at his house.

"And watch it, Gary. The guy might still be in the building." He disconnected, then faced her. "I'm taking you to the doctor."

"No, please, Dave. I'm better. I don't think there is much a doctor could do, except give me a tranquilizer."

He considered her words. "Okay, then I'm taking you to my house. We'll see how you are after I give you a drink to calm your nerves." He hesitated. "And we can talk there, about what happened and why you were there in the first place."

"I accessed Nate's computer."

"What?" He had started the engine and was about to pull out of the parking place when his head jerked back to her.

"There is something going on at IA, Dave. It has to do with the payroll system and the layoffs and . . ." Her voice faltered.

He turned back to his driving. "We'll talk when we get to the house. We can share what we know after you've calmed down some. I've found out a few things, too."

They rode in silence until after he had turned onto the Magnolia Bridge. "What is it that you've found out?" she asked, too curious for details to wait.

He glanced. "I did take your concerns seriously, Liza. I talked separately to each one of the computer programmers."

"And?"

"There was a consensus among the men that someone had written a secret code into IA's computer system that would allow that person to access certain company files." A pause. "Seems Nate had hinted that to several people just before he died."

She expelled a long breath. "It had to have been Nate, and he felt guilty."

Dave turned up the road that paralleled Discovery Park. They were only a few blocks from his house. "Possibly," he said, finally. "I haven't determined if the mysterious code—if it even exists—has to do the One Thousand Series software or something else. So far all of the computers controlling the several million parts have checked out perfectly."

"It's not the new jet," she said, still straining to get the words out. "I told you, I've discovered which company program is accessed by this illegal code."

"How? You don't have the code to get into our software even if you were on Nate's computer."

"Of course I don't. It wasn't your stuff that came up on the screen. It was the payroll files. And the code for it was the sheet music that was left for me at the Mission Church."

"I thought someone stole that."

"I recreated it from memory. And it worked."

A long silence went by.

"It doesn't make sense, Liza. Why would Nate put a code in his computer so he could access employee payroll files?"

"It has to do with what I've been saying all along, about the layoffs and the employees who weren't real. Someone has caused people to lose their jobs, and that person—or persons—then collects thousands of dollars in payroll checks for people who've never worked for IA."

He considered her words. "Whatever is going on, your discovery will give us the chance to find out who and what is involved." He hesitated. "More important, to find out if the conspiracy goes beyond payroll files to sabotage."

Another silence dropped between them.

"Have you requested a proper investigation, Dave?"

"Not yet." He swung onto his street, then into the drive-way, waiting for the automatic garage door to open. "For the moment I'm handling this internally until I can deter-mine what's going on. The project needs to be protected. Not to mention my job," he added.

"What do you mean?" She tried to hide her sudden annoyance, remembering that he had dismissed her earlier allegations about the fake employees and the possible con-nection to Nate and the computer lab. Surely he wasn't implying that they shouldn't take this new information to company officials.

"Only that some things are a question of timing. I need to be sure about my facts before I stir up trouble that could stop FAA certification and cost the company mil-lions. The very least that would happen is that I would be released from the project."

"So you may not report the discovery of the secret code?"

"Might not be necessary. My intention is to identify the problem, take care of it, and then forget it."

She stared at the rising door, chilled by his analogy, feel-ing as expendable as the employees who had been termi-nated.

"What about the murders, Dave?" Her tone was decep-tively low.

"What murders?"

"Nate's, Alice's, the jumper at the parachute center, Steve Wendall's—maybe Martin's."

"For God's sake, Liza. As coincidental as it seems, those deaths were all accidental. And none of us know what happened to Martin."

"Someone tried to kill me tonight, Dave. That wasn't an accident."

"And that person will be prosecuted if we catch him. That's a separate incident, Liza," he said quietly. "I see no connection to the accidental deaths."

Because you don't want to see anything that might jeopardize your career, she told him silently. Her growing doubts about Dave had been correct. His sense of right and wrong had been compromised somewhere along the way. He was placing his position above personal integrity.

He drove into the garage and the automatic door slowly closed behind them. Liza suddenly felt trapped. When Dave came around the car she had no option but to grab her purse and get out. As they went into the house her apprehension grew. How did she know that he had even talked to Gary about her assailant? She had only heard his side of the conversation.

"I'll fix the drinks," he said, moving on to the bar in the living room. "You sit down. Relax. And when you're up to it, I want to hear all about the phony payroll scam." He shot her a disbelieving grin. "And about the person you think is killing people to cover it up."

Liza hesitated in the doorway, wondering how she could cut short her time with him. She decided not to tell him everything she knew, to wait and tell the proper authorities, like Detective Barnes.

The sudden shrill ring of the cell phone in her purse startled both of them. "I forgot I had my phone on," she said, trying to sound normal. "I have to answer. It could be Jean and she worries if I don't."

He nodded, and she heard ice cubes tinkle into the glasses.

"Hello?" she said.

"Liza, that you?"

"This is Liza," she said, recognizing Erik's voice.

"Where are you?" There was an urgency to his tone.

"I'm at Dave's."

"Dave's?"

"Uh-huh." She forced a laugh. "He rescued me from an attack by some phantom in the computer lab."

"What? You think it was Snakeoil?"

The words shot across the wire with a shrill force that hurt her ear. She resisted an urge to remove the receiver, pressing it tighter to her ear instead, fearful that Erik's voice would carry to Dave. *She no longer trusted Dave.*

"Yes, but I didn't see who—"

"Forget my questions and just listen. When I heard the message you left me I called Barnes who was about to call you with an update." She could hear his upset. "You've got to be careful, Liza. Nate's fingerprints *were* on the envelope and Maggie substantiated his handwriting. And Alice *was* poisoned. Martin was probably killed, too—most likely by the person behind the Snakeoil tag. Barnes hasn't identified that person yet, but all the bits and pieces of evidence you've collected point to him being connected to Nate and to the computer lab."

"Yes, it was nice of Dave," she said into the mouthpiece, smiling at Dave who was watching from across the room.

"I get it. You're right, Dave might be involved." A pause. "Barnes and I are on the way. Watch yourself, Liza. And get out of there at the first sign of trouble. You could be in immediate danger."

"Thanks, Jean. I agree. And I'll do as you say."

She put the phone back in her purse, marveling at her own control when she was so terrified. Another glance at Dave told her it was too late.

She was already in trouble.

Chapter Thirty-Four

"WHAT'S GOING ON, LIZA?"

Dave had put down the glasses and faced her from across the room. He sounded stilted. "That wasn't Jean. Who was it?"

She licked her lips, tasting blood. "Of course it was," she said, avoiding his eyes. "She tried to reach me at home, and when I wasn't there, she called my cell phone."

"Why are you lying?"

"Are you calling me a liar?" she retorted, asking a question to defray his.

"I'm saying that your sister *is* concerned for your safety." He took a step closer. "She wouldn't be talking niceties after hearing that you'd been attacked."

"Jean knew I was safe, that I'd explain later," she said, but the shakiness had begun again, deep in her stomach. "I really need that drink, but first I'd like to wash my face. It must be a bloody mess from my lip."

"I'll help you. You'll need an antiseptic on your cut."

"No," she said, nervously. "It's okay. A little water should take care of it."

There was a silence—a stalemate.

He nodded, his expression closed.

Liza started for the bathroom off the back hall, its door right next to the garage. She walked in a controlled manner, conscious of his eyes following her. Feeling vulnerable, she glanced over her shoulder.

A jolt of fear almost immobilized her. He was moving up behind her, his footsteps silent on the living room carpet.

For a second her eyes were caught by his. He wore a strange expression, one she had not seen before. Resolute was the word that came to her mind.

She had to get out of there.

She ran past the bathroom, paused to yank open the door to the garage and her purse strap caught on the knob, pulling it off her shoulder to fall on the floor. Without hesitation, she left it, stepped over the threshold and slammed and bolted the door from the garage side. Then she punched the automatic door button, and before the twenty-foot panel had risen three feet, she had scooted under it and darted into the driveway.

Dave's voice followed her outside. "Liza! What's going on?" He rattled the door. "For God's sake, get back in here where it's safe. I'm not your enemy!"

His plea gave her pause. He sounded concerned, sincere. But did she believe him? She no longer knew who to trust. He had always helped her when she was in trouble. But why had he always been so conveniently on the scene? Coincidence?

Or because he was Snakeoil?

She did not answer him.

There was silence and she guessed that he was circling

to the front door. She needed to get out of there, apologize later if she was wrong about him.

She started to run toward the street, reached the corner and hesitated, her gaze assessing her options. The road led back to a populated area but it was bordered by the woods of Discovery Park. A glance reminded her of how black and foreboding they were on a rainy, winter night.

On the other hand, there were houses and lights farther down the lane past Dave's house. That direction was her best option, she decided. She would seek help from a neighbor, then wait in safety for Erik and Detective Barnes to arrive. If the residents were leery of a stranger so late at night, she would have them call Erik's cell phone or the detective's number.

Retracing her steps, Liza headed back the way she had come, keeping to the shadows, aware that she had given Dave extra seconds to come after her. She had only gone a few steps when a dark shape separated from the laurel hedge that lined Dave's yard. Liza stopped in her tracks. He was already outside. More time had passed than she realized.

He was between her and the neighbors.

She strained her eyes into the inky night. It was her assailant from the computer lab: ski mask, dark clothing and a menacing posture.

Was it really Dave? She couldn't tell for sure.

He sprang forward.

Instant terror stopped her breath. Her spontaneous scream jolted it again, propelling her to action.

Liza whirled around and ran, heading for the park. She had no other option. Her one hope was to hide in the underbrush.

He was right behind her.

She raced for the path that veered down the slope

toward the bluffs, where she had thought she would find a cluster of underbrush—where she could hide. Wrong again. The foliage had lost its cover last fall.

Stupid, stupid, stupid. She could die from falling off a cliff even if Snakeoil didn't catch her.

She tore over the rough terrain, praying she wouldn't trip. Snakeoil would be on top of her before she could get back onto her feet. She could hear him running behind her.

At the bottom of the long incline the path veered north along the edge of the sand bluffs. Liza didn't hesitate. Her only chance was to outrun him. Far below the water of Puget Sound lapped against the rocky shoreline.

Don't think about it, she told herself. You're not going to fall over the cliff.

But it was hard not to think about it in such a spooky place. It was a perfect spot for another "accident." Only inches on the other side of the single chain barrier the unstable terrain fell away from the trail to the cliffs. She forced her mind away from the danger; the chain was only a token fence to keep people on the path. She had to make it to the houses on the other side of the park.

Where were Erik and Detective Barnes? she wondered. How far away were they when Erik called? Were they together? Or coming separately?

She thought about their conversation. They were probably ten or fifteen minutes away at least.

Another chilling thought struck her like a physical blow. What if Erik and Barnes weren't on their way? What if Erik had been calling on his cell phone from Dave's front yard? What if Erik, not Dave, was Snakeoil?

Irrational. She needed to stay focused. Or she would find out who Snakeoil was before ever reaching safety.

She was tiring, each panting breath burned in her chest. But she had to keep on. There was no other choice.

He sounded closer. She did not dare slow her pace to glance behind her. Instead she pushed herself to run faster, but each step was hampered by the deep sand that sucked at her shoes.

His hand on her arm was unexpected, violently swinging her around to collide against him. Her breath went out of her chest in a long sigh. Her knees buckled, and she folded at his feet like one of Jean's puppets.

"Slut! You're gonna pay for all the trouble you've caused me." His voice was muffled behind the ski mask. A fleeting smell of perspiration assaulted her nose, as it had in the computer lab. "I'm getting you out of my hair once and for all."

His words brought her back to life. She would not let him kill her. Not now. *Not without a fight.*

"Let me go!"

She clawed and punched at him, and struggled to stand. Once upright she began kicking, pummeling him with her fists, scratching and pinching him, moving her arms so fast that he couldn't grab her hands. First to his face, then to his stomach, then to his groin. As he protected himself in one place, she hit another. He winced, and his hold loosened as he positioned himself to deflect her blows.

Instantly, she twisted away but was unable to completely free herself. Panting and grunting, he quickly regained his control over her, his hands moving to her throat, pressing her back to her knees in front of him. Once on the ground, Liza knew she was doomed unless she could somehow immobilize him. A bite on his leg did it. She felt the skin give way under his pants.

He yelped.

But she was not able to free herself. He dropped onto his knees, forcing her backward onto the wet sand.

Straddling her, his body poised above hers, the man she believed was Snakeoil was trying to strangle her. He was totally focused on killing her.

And then rolling her body over the cliff?

Liza's arms were pinned to her sides by his legs, he sat on her stomach, and his hands were fastened around her neck, squeezing her breath from her lungs. She could not move her upper body. She only had seconds before she passed out. But he had not anticipated the one defensive move left to her. He didn't have enough arms and legs to stop her final hope to free herself.

Her knee to his groin connected with soft flesh.

He doubled up, clutching his crotch. His hold on her went slack. "You cunt!" he said, moaning.

In a flash, Liza scrambled out from under him, crawled several feet, and got up, running. She was free for several yards. He tackled her, slamming her down again.

"You won't have the chance to kick me again." His body lay across her legs as he gulped air.

Her heart beat furiously. Her body trembled from exertion. She was exhausted. Fight, she told herself. Fight or you'll die.

She yanked and pulled and twisted, trying to free her legs. He was stronger. As he recovered, he moved his body up hers, imprisoning it once more.

Don't give up. Don't give up. Her mantra.

The struggle continued. He punched out at her, the blow glancing off her cheek. They rolled under the chain barrier that separated the path from the dangerous area, sliding down the unstable slope toward the cliff.

Suddenly, they were gaining speed.

"The cliff!" she cried. "We're going over the cliff!"

"Fuck!" He tried to grab onto something.

Liza's hand caught hold of a cluster of weeds, stopping

their descent and allowing him to grab other vegetation to secure his own position. Immediately, he began to beat at her arms, trying to loosen her hold.

"My gratitude, counselor." He kept hitting at her. "But no mercy."

"I should have let you die! You have no conscience!"

His laugh was harsh. "Too late for regrets. Don't kid yourself. You would have let me go over the cliff if I hadn't been able to take you with me."

"I do have a conscience. I don't murder people."

She dug her feet into the sand to steady herself. Then able to free her right hand, she clawed at him. He arched away and her fingers scraped down his clothing, fastening on a ring of keys that was attached to his belt by a braided cord. He pushed her, and it broke free as she lost her balance.

The ground gave way under her feet.

She flayed her arms, searching for something to hang on to, grasping at the knitted ski mask that hid his face. It slid off his head by the pull of gravity as her body plunged toward the cliff and the sheer drop to Puget Sound.

Frantically, she tried to stop her descent. A tangled bush of Scotch broom snagged her jacket, and temporarily kept her from going over the precipice. She clutched it with both hands. It was her last hope. Certain death awaited her on the rocks below.

"Shit!" he said from above her. "Bitch! Why won't you die?"

"Because I intend to expose you, and all you've done to innocent people!" she screamed back, her feet frantically seeking toeholds, a solid footing so that she could climb to a safer place. But she knew it was only a matter of time before she fell all the way. She needed help and there was none.

"Like hell you will." His laugh was demonic. "Dead people can't tell secrets."

"You're Snakeoil, aren't you?" she cried, trying to place his voice now that he no longer wore the mask. His face was obscured by the darkness and the distance between them. "You killed Alice and Nate and all the others! Because you were afraid they'd expose you and your thievery!"

"You know, Liza, that's your problem. You're like all the rest of the women I've ever known. You believe you're special, that your shit doesn't stink! Trouble is, you outsmarted yourself this time." Another laugh. "Yeah, I'm Snakeoil."

"And you murdered them, admit it!"

"That's right, Liza: Nate, Alice, the skydiver, even your stupid PI. What are you going to do about it in these final seconds before I shove your fuckin' ass over the cliff?"

Then she realized that she still had his ring of keys. She managed to stuff them into her jacket pocket and zip it. If she died, the keys could be traced to him. But something about the feel of the keys and cord nagged at her mind.

God help me, she thought, suddenly knowing why they felt familiar. They had belonged to Martin. Unless Snakeoil had added keys of his own to the ring, the police would assume that they were hers because they'd fit her locks.

Was the man above her Martin? No. She immediately dismissed the thought. The feel of his body had been wrong, as was his voice.

Don't think of that now. Don't think about Martin.

She forced herself to disregard the flutters of fear in her stomach that threatened to incapacitate her completely. But reality would not be denied. Snakeoil had used those very keys to get in her car and condominium.

In that moment she *knew* Martin was dead, killed by the man above her, for reasons she might never know.

"And Martin?" She couldn't stop the question. "Did you kill him, too?"

He didn't answer.

Liza kept her eyes on Snakeoil's dark shape, wondering what he would do next. Wait it out until she finally went over the edge into oblivion?

Again he did the unexpected.

He started down the unstable slope, carefully placing one foot before committing the other. He was taking his time, aware of the danger, certain that no one knew about the life and death struggle being played out in Discovery Park. If he reached her she was dead. He had the advantage of being above her, of not having to cling precariously to a small bush.

She must not let him get away with it.

Somehow she had to save herself. Shifting position, she found a toehold a little north of the shrub. But even that small movement affected the roots and she felt them give a little under her hands.

Startled, she screamed.

Fearful that the plant could go at any moment, she screamed again, unable to stop herself. The sound echoed down the face of the bluff.

His body jerked involuntarily from the suddenness of the sound.

Abruptly, the ground gave way under his feet. It quickly became an avalanche of sand that swept him onto his side, catapulting him down the slope toward her.

"Christ Almighty!" he cried. "Help me!"

His voice had lost its low, flat tone. For the first time she recognized it. He made a grab for her as he slid past. Instinctively, she stretched a hand, trying to reach him.

Even though he had killed, she was unable to watch him plunge to his death and do nothing.

"Fucking cunt!" he hollered. "You're letting me die!"

"I can't reach you!"

Their eyes met briefly, and she saw his terror, a feeling they shared. He clutched a cluster of grass and it slowed his plunge. The next moment it uprooted.

He was again moving downward, slower this time as he grabbed at vegetation and struggled for footholds in the sliding earth. His fate would be hers if the Scotch broom did not adhere to the bluff. Fortunately, it was not in the path of his slide.

He clung to the edge for several seconds, his eyes with their accusing expression fastened on her face.

"You didn't win, bitch!"

His words followed him into the abyss. His scream echoed all the way down the cliff to the bottom. She was left with absolute silence, and the identity of Snakeoil. It had not been Dave or Hawk or Erik.

It had been Cooper Delmonte all along.

The faces of his wife Abbey, and Brandon, their sick little boy, flashed into Liza's mind. What had happened? How could the father of that precious little boy be a killer?

And Alice, and the others. No, she could not think of that now either. But Liza could not stop the deep wrenching sobs that tore through her body, and with each shudder, the Scotch broom seemed to give up more ground. Liza struggled for control. She had been wrong about Dave, Hawk, even Erik. Whatever their involvement, they were not killers. But she would deal with the meaning of it all when she was back on solid ground. *If* she survived.

Little streams of sand continued to ripple over the edge after Cooper. She dared not move. They had disturbed the stability of the slope and at any moment she could hurtle over the bluff after him. Her life depended on the roots of a wild shrub. She wondered how much longer they would withstand the strain of her weight.

From the feel of it she knew. Not long.

Time seemed suspended. It began to rain, adding to her misery. Her mind was numb from all that had happened and her body felt cold to the bone. When she became aware of the voices she did not react at first. But as they came closer she began to scream for help. The flashlight beam that swept over the slope passed her, then came back to focus on her.

"For God's sake, don't move, Liza!" Erik cried. "We have ropes on the way. I'll climb down to you." A pause. "Can you hold on for just a few more minutes?"

"I'll try." She didn't tell him that the shrub could let go at any moment. Or that her fingers were numb from the cold.

"Are you hurt?" Detective Barnes's voice this time.

"I'm okay. Cold and bruised, that's all." She hesitated. "Cooper Delmonte tried to kill me. He's Snakeoil."

"Where is he?" Barnes asked, alarmed.

"He . . . he went over the cliff and—"

"Don't talk," Erik interrupted. "Stay calm."

You can make it, Liza told herself. Do as Erik says, *do not move*. Then she became aware of more activity above her, other voices. And of Erik being lowered on a rope.

He came down slowly to the north of her, avoiding Cooper's route, careful not to disturb the sand. She was suddenly so glad that he was an expert skydiver and mountain climber, too skilled to climb down on top of her. Instead, once level with her, he crossed the few feet to where she clung to the Scotch broom.

"I've got you," he whispered against her ear as one arm circled her waist. Then he looped a second rope around her upper chest, securing it under her arms. "Now they're going to pull us up. You ready, Liza?"

She nodded, feeling his beard on her cheek.

"Let go of the shrub," he instructed gently, understanding her fear. "Remember, I've got you."

It was an act of faith. Without something connected to the ground Liza felt as if she was about to fly out over the black abyss. Erik talked her up the slope as the ropes were slowly raised. Once at the top, her legs would not hold her, and she would have fallen but for Erik's supporting arm around her waist.

"She needs to be carried." It was Dave's voice. "We can take her to my house."

Her eyes popped open, noticing him and two uniformed policemen for the first time. "No, I want to go home."

"Come on, Brown Eyes. My house is only five minutes away," Dave said, trying to console her, taking her cold hands in his. "You might need a doctor."

Liza pulled away, shaking her head. She no longer knew how she felt about Dave. Tonight had been an eye-opener when he'd talked about how he intended to handle the problems in the lab. He lacked personal integrity. He always would.

"I'll take you home," Erik said, his tone emphatic.

Barnes had been talking on his handheld police radio and now he turned to Dave. "I'll need you to accompany me down to headquarters."

"What?" Surprise edged Dave's voice.

"Answer some questions, fill in a few blanks." Detective Barnes's words brooked no refusal. Dave had no choice.

"And," he went on. "I've just been told that two officers reached Cooper Delmonte. He's still alive, barely. He's being transported to Harborview's trauma unit."

Feeling stronger, Liza briefly explained what had happened that night, ending with her flight that ended on the sand bluff. "Cooper admitted that he was Snakeoil, that he had killed Nate, Alice, my PI and the skydiver." Then she managed to walk out of the park unaided and get into Erik's Cherokee. She rolled down the window to talk to Detective Barnes before he drove off, to be followed by a solemn Dave in his car.

"Will you stop by my place when you finish downtown?" she asked. "I'd like to hear about what you found out, and fill you in on the details of what happened tonight."

"It'll be late. Won't you be asleep?"

She shook her head. "I'll sleep tomorrow. Right now I just want to get home, but I'll never rest until I know."

"Okay. I'll give a call first."

A minute later she was on her way home, relishing the warmth inside the Cherokee. Erik drove in silence, knowing she needed the time to fill her emotional well. For the moment she would not think about what had happened. Or about Dave. She was just so damned grateful that she had not gone over the cliff.

Erik waited with her for Barnes, who did not stay long after all. The detective filled her in on what he had found out from the crime lab, basically what Erik had already told her earlier on her cell phone. Alice had been poisoned and Nate's fingerprints were on the envelope—Nate was Bojangles.

"After Nate's case was closed and Alice was cremated, it became obvious that something was wrong, that someone would go to any length, even murder, to protect themselves," Barnes said. "And any clues in your PI's death burned up with him and his car."

Liza was thoughtful. "You know Wendall always carried a water bottle. He believed tap water was bad for his health. I just wonder—"

"Yeah, I thought of that, too. He might have slipped the same poison into Wendall's bottle that he put in Alice's." A pause. "Because of the fire we'll never know, unless Cooper tells us."

"But we do know what his scam was," Liza said. "He wrote the performance evaluations for his bogus employees, hired and fired them as needed, and manipulated information on the payroll manifest through his hidden computer access. All the while he collected the salary checks."

"It's kind of sad," Erik said. "The guy was brilliant. Too bad he didn't use his intelligence in a positive way."

"Yeah, he was bright." Barnes shook his head. "He also went back into the records of dead children, using their names and Social Security numbers to establish identification for his fake employees. He needed that for payroll tax deductions."

"You were checking on things all along," Liza said, smiling. "Forgive me for doubting you."

"We homicide detectives don't just sit on our thumbs, Ms. Liza," he retorted, half joking. He stood to go. "I'm headed to the hospital, to check on Cooper."

"What about Martin?" Erik asked. "Did he have a role in all of this? I know Cooper had Martin's keys and Liza believes Cooper killed him."

"He didn't admit that," Liza added, feeling sad about Martin. "Although he did admit killing the others."

"That's one of the things I hope Cooper will tell us. The docs wouldn't let me question him earlier. Told me to come back. Maybe he can talk now, if he's still alive."

The detective and Erik left at the same time and Liza

went to bed. The next morning she took a sick day and then Barnes dropped by shortly before noon.

"Cooper died about an hour ago," he told her. "But he talked, not because his conscience bothered him—he didn't have one. He wanted me to know he would have won but for you."

Cooper had substantiated that a desperate Nate, on the verge of bankruptcy, was the genius who had set up the whole illegal operation for him. Later, because he felt guilty and wanted out, Nate had been killed. John Ellis's role was to get Nate's music back in exchange for keeping his job; he was the person who stole the music from Liza's purse.

Detective Barnes continued. "Cooper was the man who attacked you, Liza. John Ellis may have been involved in the break-ins, but we'll never know that unless he confesses. The crime lab is checking the sheet music for his fingerprints."

"Did Cooper tell you anything about Martin?" Liza asked.

Barnes nodded. "Cooper was on that Christmas cruise and he pushed Martin overboard. Apparently Martin had caught on to what Cooper was doing and threatened to expose him. Martin had accepted money—the money he later sewed into the puppet—from Cooper, who'd believed he was paying Martin off. Martin had never intended to be shut up and meant to use the money as evidence when he went to the authorities with his accusation. He'd believed mistakenly that the money would add credence to his allegations. Cooper killed him instead, and then tried to get the money back by breaking into Liza's apartment right after Martin's disappearance. He didn't find it at that time, but then when you mentioned that Martin had helped create the puppets you gave Cooper an idea. He stole the puppets, looking for the money.

"Poor Martin," Liza said softly. "He was always an honest person."

Barnes went on to say Cooper did poison her PI because Wendall had started to connect Martin to what was going on at International Air. The first-jump parachuter's death was a mix-up; he had meant to kill Erik who had seen him with Sylvia and feared that Erik and Wendall would put two and two together if they talked. Liza had already guessed that it was Sylvia who had covered for Cooper in the records division. Sylvia and Alice had both been used by Cooper. Cooper had been Alice's mystery man. Sylvia and John Ellis would have become expendable in time.

As Barnes was leaving he hesitated. "I did a check on Cooper's background earlier, and this morning I spoke to his mother, a woman in her early seventies. She was shocked that her son could be a killer, said he was always a good boy, not as outgoing as his older brother or as popular as his younger sister, but he had never been a problem—except that he was a bedwetter." Barnes shrugged. "Guess we'll never know what went haywire in his head."

Liza was thoughtful for a long time after Barnes had gone. Poor Abbey Delmonte. She must have known who Cooper was beneath his mask of a caring, honest man. But Liza didn't blame her; she had a desperately sick child to consider.

Cooper could not have cared for anyone, even his little boy. He had allowed his wife to worry about medical insurance when he had thousands of dollars stashed in safe-deposit boxes at five Seattle banks according to Barnes. Subterfuge was part of Cooper's facade.

Once Liza was back on the job, Al made amends and apologized for not backing her up. She realized he was still covering his ass. Hawk was exonerated. Dave's position was never in question because the payroll conspiracy had nothing to do with the 1000 Series jet project. She listened when he tried to rationalize his reasoning, but she was no longer interested in pursuing a relationship with him. John Ellis and Sylvia Kempton were both fired and faced criminal charges. She felt sorry for Sylvia; she had believed that Cooper loved her.

Spring brought more puppet shows for Jean and two proud announcements: she and Bill would become parents in late October, and the puppets had all been restored.

While she went through her healing process, Liza considered Erik's offer of a professional partnership. She decided to stay at International Air. Her clients needed an advocate, a buffer between them and a boss like Hawk. There was another partnership she and Erik might consider in the future.

Most important, Liza finally knew that Martin was dead. He was not the shadowy figure who had always been behind her. Now, at last, she could go on with her life.

Also available from

DONNA
ANDERS

§ **ANOTHER LIFE**

§ **THE FLOWER MAN**

3024